THAT DAY BY THE POOL

THAT DAY BY THE POOL

Giles Fraser

Copyright © 2026 Giles Fraser

The moral right of the author has been asserted.

Apart from any fair dealing for the purposes of research or private study, or criticism or review, as permitted under the Copyright, Designs and Patents Act 1988, this publication may only be reproduced, stored or transmitted, in any form or by any means, with the prior permission in writing of the publishers, or in the case of reprographic reproduction in accordance with the terms of licences issued by the Copyright Licensing Agency. Enquiries concerning reproduction outside those terms should be sent to the publishers.

The manufacturer's authorised representative in the EU
for product safety is Authorised Rep Compliance Ltd,
71 Lower Baggot Street, Dublin D02 P593 Ireland (www.arccompliance.com)

This is a work of fiction. Names, characters, businesses, places, events and incidents are either the products of the author's imagination or used in a fictitious manner. Any resemblance to actual persons, living or dead, or actual events is purely coincidental.

Troubador Publishing Ltd
Unit E2 Airfield Business Park,
Harrison Road, Market Harborough,
Leicestershire. LE16 7UL
Tel: 0116 2792299
Email: books@troubador.co.uk
Web: www.troubador.co.uk

ISBN 978 1836286 097

British Library Cataloguing in Publication Data.
A catalogue record for this book is available from the British Library.

Printed and bound by CPI Group (UK) Ltd, Croydon, CR0 4YY
Typeset in 11pt Garamond Pro by Troubador Publishing Ltd, Leicester, UK

By the same author

LET'S FLY

For Diana

PROLOGUE

OCTOBER 1940

The boy was crouched in the iron hayrack on the stable wall five feet up, cowering and shivering: legs up by his chin, arms tight around them. The horse never slept so neither could he. He had never been so scared in his life.

He was locked in a small stable about twenty feet square. The horse was about eight-foot long and, according to one of his friends who knew about these things, seventeen hands high, so there wasn't room for both of them. The horse knew it as well as he did.

Twice the horse had kicked out its hooves to gain more space. The crunch as they hit his arms made him want to scream. At least most hit his arms, however painful it was. The pain on impact was as if he was being hit by an iron bar. His teeth and jawbones screeched as they slammed together.

He tried talking to the horse. He craved sleep but he didn't dare succumb in case the horse came back at him. Everyone knew it was a little mad; that's why no-one rode it. A gunshot close to its ears when it was a colt had shocked it and it had never been the same. It belonged to the owner's son, and he was away at the Front; otherwise, it would have been killed and turned into dogmeat, maybe even slipped into the boys' supper. The origins of some of the food they were served at the school was never that clear.

The full moon was bright and shone through the small skylight above him. He thought it was about three o'clock. He had been in there for seven hours at least. The smell of the horse's excrement in his nose filled his nostrils. The yard was silent bar the occasional baaing of the sheep in the field behind. The main house was in the middle of nowhere and everyone would be asleep. He couldn't hope to be saved until morning. No-one would be up until seven. If he cried out, there was a danger the wrong person might hear him.

He was dressed in his pyjamas and dressing gown. The boys had pulled him from his bed, and he had only been able to grab his dressing gown under duress. They had dragged him down the stairs and out through the back door. The gravel on the path behind the house had scratched and cut his feet. Laughing, the boys had thrown him into the stable and bolted the door and window.

It was late November in the Lake District, and he couldn't feel his hands or feet. The temperature must have been near zero. He had wet his pyjama trousers and made himself even colder.

He had known this day would come. It was inevitable after what he had done. Retribution was always going to be fast and savage. He just had to hope he could survive until morning. There was no point telling anyone if he got out.

There was nobody in charge and no-one would listen. The boys who had put him in the stable were the masters.

Two kicks from the horse had persuaded him he needed to get out of its way fast. He couldn't wait for another one. He could reach the iron hayrack if he placed his hands and feet in the gaps between the stones. Just as the horse kicked out again, he clambered into it. For now, he was safe.

When – if – he was freed, he would plan his escape. It didn't matter how long or arduous the journey might be. Nothing could be worse than what he was experiencing.

The skylight in the roof was about five foot above. He could just about reach it if he stood up and raised his arms, but he was afraid the hayrack would collapse under his weight.

The horse moved towards him again, nuzzling him, bearing its yellow teeth. He had no option. He couldn't wait until dawn.

He turned around, stood up and reached up to push the wooden window frame. It was rotten and opened with ease, so with both hands, and all his strength, he pulled himself up through the window. With one hand he reached forward and put his fingers underneath it to give himself traction. He hauled his body onto the roof and lay there panting.

The farmyard in front of him was bathed in the moonlight. He turned himself so he was feet first and dropped to the ground. His knees hit the stone first, causing him to scream out in pain. Exhausted and freezing, he curled himself up in a ball against the wall and slept.

1

JANUARY 2019

They had gone away for the weekend, the end of the third week of January, the first time since Dan had got his new job, and they had both taken the Friday afternoon off to ensure a swift getaway. Just as well as Dan usually kept within the speed limits, unless he was stressed or angry, and it was a five-hour journey up to the Lake District. On reflection Nicole would have happily settled for somewhere in Oxfordshire or Gloucestershire, but this wasn't just a weekend away.

"Dad's so pleased one of the family's going back to Blair Gowan. He wants us to send pictures as soon as we arrive."

"I doubt he'll want pictures of what we have in mind."

Nicole had done her research and reckoned she knew more about Blair Gowan than Dan or his father, Charlie. It had been built as a workhouse in the 1840s under the aegis of a local mill owner, Sir Ernest Mackleburgh, and, since 2005, had become a boutique hotel offering 'the perfect chill experience nestled in the undulating magnificence of the Lake District'. In between, it had been a private house and, pertinent to their current journey, a temporary home for Rothbury Preparatory School during the Second World War.

Germany, bombing in 1940 had driven the school to decamp from its South-East London base to the Lake District, and Charlie's father, Michael, aged ten, was evacuated alongside fifty other pupils. The headmaster, Roger De La Hay, was serving in North Africa so the school was run by his seventy-five-year-old father, Clive, a redoubtable nurse and two local women.

"Why hasn't your father ever visited it himself?" Nicole inspected her nails to amplify the spontaneity of her question. Dan gave her one of the glances he usually reserved for the wing mirror and said he didn't know. Nicole remarked that it was odd given what an important role Rothbury had played in his family's life. Three generations – and cousins – had attended the school. As far as she could see, no family gathering was complete without a thorough dissection of the latest De La Hay news. Roger De La Hay's grandson, Martin, was now the headmaster and was investing heavily to make Rothbury a leader in science and technology as well as a champion of diversity and inclusion.

"Can you check the satnav again? We can't be far now?" Dan scanned the horizon as if a welcoming committee was about to appear. Nicole covered her mouth to yawn before she prodded her phone. The afternoon off had meant working until midnight on the StudentCars' new business pitch. The creative ideas still hadn't been up to much, so she prayed Chandra, her boss, had had a brainwave since lunchtime.

"Do you think your grandfather enjoyed his time up here? I mean it's pretty odd sending your child the other end of the country then not even seeing them in the holidays. Michael was barely out of nappies. He must have been traumatised."

Dan didn't reply for a while, concentrating instead on pulling the phone to face him so he could read the route guidance.

"Got it." He leant back and guided the wheel with his right hand only. "I know. He always said it was the making of him. Camping, trekking, horse-riding. He missed home cooking and sweets etcetera, but everyone did in the war, I think. Some of the houses in their road at home were bombed, people killed, so it was the best place for them to be."

Nicole viewed the frosty moonlit hillscapes on either side of them as they wended their way down the narrow lanes. Did Dan really think it was such a paradisical experience, or was he conditioned by the family three-line whip that such a good thing didn't merit further investigation? She had to admit it looked pretty romantic, and it was good to get out of London. When she had told her mother about the trip, she had lit another fag and observed that most evacuees came back more traumatised than if they had stayed put in the Anderson shelters in their back gardens.

Dan said, "He said to me once he missed his teddy. His parents wouldn't let him take that. Told him he wasn't a baby anymore. Ten years old. Away from his parents all year. Imagine."

*

Nicole Weymouth could remember family arguments over wrong turns on car journeys back when she was small and her father was still around. Thankfully, nowadays, there was technology, and it hadn't let them down. The stone-columned entrance to Blair Gowan Hotel presented itself at the exact time the satnav had promised when they had set it in London. It was dark but there was a full moon so they could see almost as if it was daylight. The wheels of the car crunched on the gravel as they passed a series of rhododendron bushes on either side.

Nicole didn't like institutions, and a shiver passed through her. She might only be 27, but she had had enough of them fifteen years ago. Soon the hotel, three storeys with turrets, grey, damp stone, appeared before them. Behind the building, the Lake District fells rose up as high as the eye could see, with the moon resplendent and unclouded above them.

Before they got out of the car, Dan said, "Hard to believe this was a school in the war, isn't it?"

Nicole tried to share her fiancé's excitement. Whenever she had a phone signal, emails from work were coming through with questions about the presentation. She squeezed his hand and smiled at him before they opened the car doors.

"Let's hope we're not put in detention if we're late for breakfast."

As she stepped out of Dan's new Audi, a button of her new navy-blue coat caught on the seatbelt and fell off. After she had picked up the button, she shook her freshly cut blonde bob and brushed it back with both hands. Then, as she did pretty much every five minutes, she checked that her engagement ring was still on her finger.

Her wheeled suitcase bumped along the gravel as they came to the door. Dan glanced at her and leant over to kiss her on the cheek.

She thought she was looking quite good given the time of year: she had been stuck inside all the time and hadn't renewed her gym membership yet. She was lucky enough to have a strong, aquiline nose, high cheekbones, full lips and, best of all, flashing powder-blue eyes. She was a little above medium height and, most of the time though not enough in her opinion, pretty slim. Stress and long hours at work helped with that. When she looked in the mirror, and needed a boost, she would repeat her mother's words to herself: "You're a good package, Nicole Weymouth."

Standing on the doorstep, she kissed him on the lips, and, for a moment, pure joy suffused her. It was a long time since they'd taken a break together.

The eight-foot-high oak door was open, so they stepped straight into a huge hall with a fireplace as large as Nicole's bedroom at one end. Modern art, all primary colours, had been hung around the walls to lighten the mood. At the end nearest to Dan and Nicole a pert, black-haired girl who was playing with a pencil with one hand whilst jabbing at a computer keyboard with the other.

She stood up. "Hello. I'm Shona. Welcome to Blair Gowan Hotel."

They went inside and Nicole looked around. It wasn't hard to imagine this hall being the place where assemblies took place. In her mind the scene was more like a prison. Lines of small boys incanting the day's prayers in unison with adults watching them like guards in each corner. Would people who didn't know this had been a school get the same vibe? She wondered. Her own boarding school, at least for the short time she had been there, had been much more relaxed. The teachers called everyone by their Christian names and uniforms weren't worn after the age of eleven.

Based on their conversations Dan had a different view of school. He could put up with the rules as he liked the comradery. As he put it, the structure freed one's mind up to focus on the education itself. He had ended up with a First in Law from Durham so maybe he had a point. Nicole had had a place at Newcastle but, when her mother had her first cancer scare, she had had to defer it. Nine years on she was still deferring it. Over time she had grown to be suspicious of those who boasted about their academic achievements. No-one ever asked her what her A-levels were – pretty good, seeing as you're asking – because they assumed she hadn't been smart enough to get in anywhere.

Shona looked Dan up and down, and Nicole looked across at her boyfriend. Dan didn't know how handsome he was. Tall and wiry, curly black hair, eyes the colour of dark chocolate. She could excuse him the occasional admirer.

Shona explained that she was new and that they were her first ever check-in, so they found a couple of high-backed chairs near the reception desk and wrestled to activate the Wi-Fi code. The new creative ideas for the pitch hadn't materialised. It sounded as if Friday drinks had been delivered into the meeting room which, in Nicole's experience, was either a very good or, more likely, a very bad omen. Luckily Chandra didn't drink.

Dan said, "It's going to be fascinating to look around, isn't it? See if there's anything left of the school." He grinned at Nicole and said, "Shona, did you know this was a school in the war?"

"I heard. And it was a workhouse before that. If walls could talk."

*

A spotty teenager in white shirt and black tie took their suitcases up two flights of stairs to their room. The smell of floor polish hung in the air and the stairs were slippery from the wax.

The room was magnificent, about the size of a squash court with a four-poster bed, a bay window with its own seat and a sofa and chairs around a fireplace at one end. The teenager showed them how to use the TV and safe and left them to it. They both looked around the room and smiled at each other.

Dan threw himself down on the bed and encouraged Nicole to follow. She needed no encouragement – their work and social schedules meant they hadn't managed to have sex for over two weeks. Nicole straddled Dan, kissed him hard, undid his belt and worked his trousers down to his ankles. He kicked off his shoes, then his trousers and boxer shorts while Nicole moved to one side and caressed him. When she returned to her position above him, he helped her remove her cotton skirt and knickers. She lowered herself down and guided him into her. They moved as one.

Nicole found all the stresses of the week floating away as excitement coursed through her veins and took over every limb. Throughout they were all tongues and lips. A few minutes later they came together, breathing hard and laughing. There was nowhere Nicole would rather be. Three cheers for Rothbury! She flopped back alongside Dan. They lay there in silence. This was when she loved Dan most. When all their friends and family were far away and it was just them together, caressing and stroking, detached from the world, watching and laughing at it through one pair of eyes.

"Bet there wasn't much of that at Blair Gowan in the war."

Dan kissed her. "Oh, matron, you're gorgeous. Come here…"

"I say, headmaster…"

*

After a few minutes lying together, Nicole decided she needed a bath. She was still in her work clothes – at least half of them. She'd spied a basket full of oils she thought she could work her way through. Dan had found the remote and was searching for something to watch.

She filled the bath as high as she could without activating the overflow and stepped in. Water washed over the back, confirming her suspicion that she had miscalculated. An aroma of strawberry-flavoured steam filled the room as she laid her head on the back of the bath.

She wasn't very religious, but she wanted a church wedding. It had played out in her imagination since she was a child. As she relaxed, she imagined herself walking up the aisle with an ivory-white dress flowing out behind her. People, strangers mainly, turned to smile at her. She could smell the fresh roses in her bouquet. Ahead of her she could see Dan standing at the altar, smiling as if he had just heard the funniest joke. She looked alongside her and there was Patrick. Patrick, her brother, her long-dead brother, was walking her up the aisle. How could that be? Weren't fathers meant to do that? Not that she wanted her father to be anywhere near her wedding. Not after what he had done. She squeezed Patrick's hand and luxuriated in her daydream. He was much taller than her now. He had been six inches shorter than her when he died. It was rare he came into her thoughts and dreams without the trauma and agony that had accompanied his death. Her mother was turning to her, face alive and beaming this once. Nicole was so happy. At the back of her mind, even in her reverie, she knew Patrick wouldn't be there come the day. As ever her dreams didn't last long without absence and death invading them.

She must have fallen asleep in the bath again as images of small boys, sitting at desks, crash-landed into her consciousness. All the decorations the hotel had added to make it less like a school had been removed, and tall, forbidding dark walls surrounded her as she walked through the school. The smell of strawberry changed to that of Dettol and sweat. Cries of happiness and anguish filled her head. Then she was underwater, struggling for breath.

"Nicole, Nicole, wake up, wake up." A hand gripped her arm tight and was pulling her upwards. Bright light hit her as she opened her eyes. Dan was kneeling in front of her. "What are you doing, you idiot? You could have drowned."

Nicole sat up in the bath and looked at a blurry Dan. "I only dozed off for a moment."

*

Downstairs they went into the drawing room for a pre-dinner drink. The books lining all the walls suggested it was once a library. Nicole had on a dark blue velvet mid-length L.K. Bennett dress that she had bought on her Amex card to complement the sapphire earrings Dan had given her for Christmas. Her hair was swept back to give the earrings maximum exposure. Dan looked dashing in a white dinner shirt with open neck.

There were young couples in each of the far corners of the drawing room who looked up as they entered. Each of the couples lounged back on their chairs as if they wanted to look as if they owned the house. There was a lot of whispering going on.

The spotty boy who had taken their cases was now dressed in a creased black shirt and skinny tie. He sidled up and asked them what they wanted to drink. They sat back in high-wing-backed, tartan-covered chairs either side of the fireplace and grinned at each other.

Nicole said, "A bottle of the house champagne please. We're celebrating." The boy looked embarrassed, nodded and scurried away.

Dan said, "Doesn't get much better than this, does it?"

"Good old Blair Gowan, eh? Bet there wasn't much fizz being downed in here in the war."

Ten minutes later the boy came back with a bottle of champagne in an ice bucket and two frosted glasses on a tray. He looked nervous as he wrapped the top of the bottle in a towel and wrestled the cork off. Nicole's thoughts drifted back to Patrick again. Any young boy or teenager tended to trigger thoughts of what he might have grown up like. She would have given anything to have him with her today.

To kill time, as he struggled through this routine, the boy said, "Many of these books were part of the library when this place was a school in the war. Some of them are really old." When he poured the champagne, it flowed over the edge of the glasses. Dan told him it didn't matter. They were in a rush to make a toast.

When the boy had gone, Nicole stood up and surveyed the books. There were lines of classics in all different faded colours with gold lettering. Mark Twain, Charles Dickens, Jane Austen. Only the classics for the boys of Rothbury. She pulled down a copy of *Treasure Island* and sat down, leafing her way through the damp, yellow pages. Every twentieth page there was a simple black-and-white illustration with an unnecessary, long description. Some dust flew up in her face and she sneezed.

Dan looked up at her and laughed. "Bless you."

She got up and put it back, scanning the shelves. "Indiana Jones, that's me. Oh, look, *Black Beauty*!"

She reached up higher to get the book down. For a moment her heart almost stopped. It was the book, never finished, never even picked up again, she was reading the day Patrick died.

She had to stand on tiptoe and pull it down with her fingers. Dust filled the air as it dropped, and she coughed a little when she caught it. A musty smell filled her nostrils. She mouthed 'sorry' at the would-be country-house owners watching on. Then she sat back down on her chair with the book on her knee. It was a hardback, maybe even a first edition, not the drenched paperback she remembered lying beside the pool that day. Dan was halfway through his drink now and watched her with interest.

"I loved this book when I was young." It had full page, colour illustrations, not the hazy black and cream ones in her childhood copy. She flicked through the pages. "I wonder if I could take this back up to my room?"

When she got to the back cover of the book, she stopped. There was the edge of an envelope sticking out of the binding. With care she pulled it out. It was yellowed and brittle.

"Dan, what's this?" She looked around to see if anyone had noticed. They hadn't. They were too engrossed in their food now.

The envelope, much smaller than today's, was addressed to Mr and Mrs A. Slaithwaite, The Orchard, Tetbury, Gloucestershire in childish, capital letters and had a faded unfranked red stamp featuring Victoria and George VI.

"Shall I open it?" She didn't wait for his answer.

Nicole broke open the seal and took the letter out of the envelope. First, she read it then she shook herself, looked up at Dan and read it out loud. It was dated the fourth of November 1940, and the address was Blair Gowan. The handwriting was spidery and hard to read in places.

Dear Mother and Father,

I hope you are well. It has been a very long time since I saw you and I miss you both very much.

I know that you have sent me up here for my own safety, but I would like you to come and bring me home. No amount of Hitler's bombs can be as bad as what I am experiencing here. It is not like the school I went to before war broke out. There are no rules, and the elder boys can do whatever they like. They treat me no better than the animals in the yard behind us. The headmaster is never around. Last week something truly terrible happened here and nothing has been done about it.

I have to come home. I am so sorry. I know you want me to be tough and brave, but I don't think I can. Please come and fetch me. I promise to get a job and pay for the petrol vouchers if you do.

Your loving son
Peter

Nicole looked up at Dan. She said, "So, he never posted it, did he? What do you think happened? Did he lose his nerve? Did someone take the letter away from him? Did things get better? It's horrible to think of this little boy so far from home and having such a terrible time."

Dan said, "Wow! I wonder what happened to him. It sounds really terrible. And the letter's been sitting here at the back of that book for eighty years, presumably unread. Peter's probably dead. Those parents definitely are. What are we going to do with it?"

"I'm going to keep it." She looked around to check no-one was watching.

"Shouldn't you give it in to the front desk?"

Nicole thought of Shona. It would be a day-one hassle she wouldn't fancy.

"No. I want to keep it."

"Leave it in the book then?"

"No."

For some irrational reason Nicole found herself disliking this suggestion a great deal. She wanted to know what had happened to him. The words of the letter resonated around and around her head. The five-year-old face of Patrick, her long-dead younger brother, filled her consciousness. Peter wouldn't have been much older. She could picture the boy writing the letter, sobbing, somewhere quiet and private where no-one could see him. The letter never reached his parents.

But it had reached her.

"I've made up my mind. It was meant to be sent to somebody and that somebody's turned out to be me. I want to know what happened and what happened to Peter. Aren't you curious too?"

Dan had turned his attention to the menu. "Of course I am. Shall we order?"

She hadn't been able to save Patrick, and she couldn't save Peter Slaithwaite but, this time, she could do something about it, and, in Patrick's memory, she would do exactly that.

2

They had been gifted the weekend a few weeks before at Christmas by Dan's parents after they had played a game of charades post-lunch. It was an impromptu engagement present.

Games at Christmas mark a fork in the road. For some people they signal the time when the fun truly begins. For others, the time when it totally stops. This was a moment when Nicole realised, despite her best intentions, she was falling into the latter camp.

Charlie, Dan's father, said, "Go on, Nicole, you can do it. It's ours to win!"

Dan said, "Give her some space, Dad. We're ready when you are!"

It was Boxing Day afternoon at the Newhouses'. Dan and Charlie were on her charades team and neither liked losing. Charlie by nature; Dan, she liked to think, by nurture. So far, they had each scored at least four with their turns and Nicole had scored half that. Dan's mother, Jo, and sister, Bee, were the opposition and neither of them had scored as low as Nicole. Mind you, it didn't seem fair to her that the family seemed to have a store of clues all of them had seen before. No goodwill at the inn here.

Nicole said to Jo, "God, you guys really know your names, don't you? I'm going to need a lie-down after this!"

Jo said, "Don't be intimidated, Nicole. They have their old favourites. Wait until they get one they haven't done before."

It was her turn. Nicole adjusted her festive hat to stop it from falling off and picked up one of the remaining pieces of paper from the bowl. With care she stepped over Caesar, their golden retriever, who was stretched out, asleep, in front of the fire. She wanted to make a good impression. She always wanted to make a good impression with families. She wanted to be welcomed into this family. People who had proper families didn't know how important they were to one's general happiness. You had to be without one to know. Nicole knew that.

There were about seven clues left. If they were going to win with her turn, she would need to do better than anyone so far. Frowning, she examined the paper.

Bee shouted, "We need to put the clock on you, Nicole." So, no unity in sisterhood either then.

Harry Potter and the Deathly Hallows Pt 1. How the fuck was she going to do that? She signalled to Dan to ask whether she could put it back and he shook his head. Different rules at the death then. They'd let Charlie do that. Dan put his thumb up in encouragement. Nicole wished she hadn't had the port on top of the red wine. Dan had warned her that they loved playing games after lunch.

At the time she thought how nice; she and her mother never played games. After all there weren't many games that were actually fun for two to play. Nicole disliked most of them. Playing that is, not watching – she loved watching tennis, rugby and, especially, football, especially Chelsea. With parlour games everyone else always seemed much quicker witted than her, even though, most of the time, it would turn out she knew the answers. Invariably she ended up thinking that she had let everybody down.

Nicole made the movie camera motion and then, with a resigned slump of the shoulders, held up eight fingers. "This is more like it!" said Charlie and he leant forward in eager anticipation like a dog waiting for its dinner. Nicole held up three fingers, resisting the urge to lose two of them, and made the sign for a very short word. In two guesses they landed on 'and'.

She couldn't think where to go next. Both Charlie and Dan were nodding encouragement. In a moment of inspiration Nicole decided to mime making a pot. She bent down into a semi-squat and caressed an imaginary vase with both hands. In her mind she was channelling Demi Moore making pottery in *Ghost*. She also thought this would be quite funny and would alleviate the stress when it became clear to all that she was the reason they weren't going to win.

"Driving a car? Rearing a lamb?" Dan, smiling with encouragement, and his father let forth a series of guesses, all, in Nicole's view, more obscure than the word she was miming. Anyone would think they were trying to make her fail. The others were laughing hard. Bee held up the clock.

The invisible pot had collapsed. Nicole decided to change tack. She held up six fingers and cupped her ear for 'sounds like'. Then she waved her hand as if welcoming someone off a train. This didn't seem to work either. The harder she waved, the harder they seemed to find it. Jo gave Nicole an encouraging smile.

"Can I have a bit more time?"

Charlie said, "Wouldn't be fair on everyone else, Nicole." *What?*

Dan said, "C'mon, Dad. Nicole's a guest!"

In one last bid to help them, Nicole held up one finger, repeated the cupping motion and started picking at her arm. Why would they not get 'hairy'? Both boasted their fair share especially now Dan hadn't shaved all Christmas. Charlie was now visibly unamused by their lack of progress whilst Dan just grinned at her. Their guesses had descended into an embarrassed silence. It was alright for him getting clues like *King Lear* and *Love Island*. Anybody could get those.

Bee was now doubled up laughing, shouting 'don't stop, don't stop". Nicole thought her constant slapping of the sofa, some sort of theatrical attempt to put a lid on her hysteria, was unnecessary.

They weren't going to win. Nicole wished for Dan's sake that they would, but she wasn't that bothered. She doubted Dan really cared much other than a desire to please his father. Charlie Newhouse, when off his guard and lubricated, referred to himself as a 'winner'. A career in banking had afforded him an opulent lifestyle with a big house – expensive hobbies, the ability to take holidays whenever and wherever he pleased and the opportunity to help his kids with money if he felt like it.

Bee shouted, "Time up!" Nicole crumpled up the piece of paper and apologised, first to Charlie, then to Dan.

Charlie said, without much trace of a smile, "That was bloody hard, Nicole. Nice try."

Dan budged up and made space for Nicole on the sofa. He put his arm around her and kissed her on the cheek. Could a kiss be patronising? Nicole bit her lip and waited for her anger to wash through.

"I'm sorry, guys. Eight-word clues aren't really my forte." Bee had now started her turn and was motoring through the last clues.

Charlie whispered, "You can say that again." Nicole looked across at Charlie. He feigned ignorance but didn't appear to be joking. Dan was impassive now, staring straight ahead, but hugged her tighter. Christ, it was only a game.

Nicole got up. "Charlie, shall I make everyone a nice cup of tea to cheer you both up?"

*

She was getting the mugs down from the cupboard when Dan came into the kitchen and gave her a cuddle. She could see he struggled when his innate loyalty to his father put him into conflict with his girlfriend's happiness. He adored his father, often mirrored his behaviour when he was in his presence. When someone said something at the dinner table, Dan always looked to his father to respond first. Didn't matter that Dan knew more and was more articulate on most topics. But this was a time when he needed to show loyalty to her, support her.

Dan said, "Can we go out on the terrace for a moment? Get some fresh air?"

"It's freezing."

Dan took her hand. "A minute. No more."

Dan opened the door at the back of the kitchen, and they

stepped into the dusk. The terrace glistened from the recent shower. Nicole wrapped her arms around herself and shivered.

"Can we go in now?"

"Hold on." Dan fumbled with something in his pocket and got down on one knee.

"Nicole Weymouth, will you marry me?" Wobbling a little, he opened a small jewellery box. A diamond glittered in the terrace light.

Joy spread through her veins. If she had ever taken one, she would have said it was like an amphetamine rush. For a moment dumbness struck her. He knelt there looking up at her, peering for a clue as to her response.

"I'll understand if you're not sure. I know, compared to me, your life hasn't been easy. Patrick's death, your father's absence, your mother's illnesses. You've had to manage on your own for most of it. Any kind of commitment worries you because you've been let down so much before. I get it. I know I can never make everything right, but I promise I will do everything in my power to make your life better. I'm not perfect, I know that, I need to be tougher with people especially with my dad. You can help me fix that and, if you say yes, I'm yours for ever, at least as long as you'll have me. I will support you in everything you do, and I will never let you down. I'm rambling now, aren't I?."

Nicole took both his hands and squeezed them tight.

"So?"

"Wow! Yes, yes, I mean yes, of course! Oh Dan!" He got up and they embraced and kissed.

Dan said, "I didn't know what you would say."

"You don't know me very well then do you?" She kissed him again and grabbed his hand. "Let's go and tell everyone."

*

It was the first time they had been down for a while. Dan and his father had argued about his new firm's viability when they had last visited two months ago. Charlie didn't think it was a serious enough job. Why he'd gone off on one was a mystery to Nicole when he knew it was Dan's dream job. She guessed Charlie was just jealous of his son having his career in front of him instead of behind.

Wives with husbands on oil rigs saw their partners more often than Nicole had seen Dan of late. He had taken a job at a firm specialising in environmentally friendly investments. He'd spent months applying for jobs as he grew ever more exasperated at the gap between his US bank's public statements around climate change and their actions. Nicole had seen him shrink into himself as his frustration threatened to boil over. When he had, at last, found a role, he had thrown himself into it and he was in the office from dawn to late. The battle to save the planet was the other woman in his life now.

Dan said, "Sorry about Dad by the way. He's just a bit pissed. Has been all holidays. The bank has given him a new job, sideways move, looking after all their innovation. They're getting very worried about all these new finance apps and online banks. This news will cheer him up."

They went into the living room hand-in-hand. Conversation went quiet so Nicole guessed there had been a post-mortem on her performance.

Jo gave her a bright, breezy smile. "Sorry about that, Nicole. The boys start to get ultra-competitive after being cooped up here for days."

Dan said, "Doesn't matter. We've got some news!"

There was a mass of whoops and hugs. Caesar looked up for a puzzled moment. The tea plan was dumped in favour of champagne.

"Can I be a bridesmaid?" asked Bee.

Dan said, "If you agree to wear a pink marshmallow dress, Bee."

Nicole put her arm around Bee. "Yes, of course."

They all sat down. Bee said, "Well, that saved the day. I was thinking that Nicole wouldn't come back here in a hurry. Not after driving across England in the freezing cold to be humiliated at charades."

*

Nicole thought back to the previous day which she had spent with her mother in her bungalow on the hill above Bradford-on-Avon. For reasons Nicole had managed to bury in the farthest most attic of her sub-consciousness, Christmas Day was a day to be endured. The memory of a happy one was as faded and blurred as a movie from the Second World War. Before her father, Hugh, had walked out when Nicole was eleven, they had lived in a beautiful three storey, double-fronted Georgian house in the centre of the village.

Now her mother lived on her own in a 1960s bungalow that had moss on the outside walls and damp on the back wall of the kitchen. She was tall and very skinny with a strong nose and hollowed cheeks. A diet of tea and cigarettes gave her skin a leathery, yellowed texture. There wasn't much trace left of the beautiful woman in her wedding photo. Not that that photo had seen the light of day since it had been placed in a drawer fifteen years ago.

By three o'clock they had cooked and eaten their lunch and exchanged presents. Her mother claimed she didn't drink anymore – one of the legacies of her father's departure was a descent into alcoholism. So, by silent agreement, and reinforced by her latest, most serious, cancer scare two years previously, they stayed off the booze. When her mother was sleeping Nicole had done a sweep around the house to find and remove the vodka bottle her mother had hidden in the airing cupboard. She poured it down the sink. If her mother noticed – and Nicole knew she had – then she didn't say anything.

It hadn't always been that way. When Patrick had been alive, before her parents had split, they had had some wonderful Christmases, at least until the alcohol had got the better of her parents. Her grandmother, her mother's mother, Betty, and her sister, Flo, would come and stay. They had had that big house in the town then with lots of bedrooms. The hall had been spacious enough to accommodate a huge Christmas tree with all the presents underneath. She and Patrick would play with their toys in front of the fire in the sitting room. Their five years' age difference didn't matter. She would surrender to whatever fantasy world he had entered that year and join in. Then after lunch, they would all collapse into the chairs and watch a Christmas film. She would sit on the sofa with her mother and grandmother, and Patrick would fall asleep across her knees. Tinsel hung across the top of all the pictures. The smell of firewood – and cigarettes, always cigarettes – permeated her consciousness. Her father would crack jokes, and her mother would laugh. It was all a very long time ago.

*

Starting with a rerun of *Carols from King's* in the morning, it had been a long day, it always was, and Nicole had been only too grateful, if also guilt-laden, to have the excuse to leave for Dan's that night. But, as she sat on the sofa, the object of the Newhouse family's amusement, she found herself wishing she was back there. She had been an only child most of her life, a state amplified by the absence of her father. The secret, silent language of families was something she both remembered with warmth and yet had grown to fear.

There had been one conversation with her mother that stood out. When they were peeling potatoes and preparing sprouts, her mother had sucked deep on her cigarette and said, "What's the plan then?"

"What do you mean? The plan?"

"You know. For the year, for your life. All that best life baloney." She threw her hands up above her head to indicate her own relative predicament. Her mother hadn't asked her a big question like that for a long time.

"I'm just saying that one day soon you'll need to decide what you want from life."

Nicole had a flat with friends in Tooting, spent half the week with Dan at his flat in Clapham and worked in an agency promoting all kinds of consumer brands. One day soon she guessed she would settle down. She had just about enough money to pay her rent and bills, take a holiday once a year and see friends once or twice a week. She didn't need a plan, not yet.

"Oh Mum, don't say that. It wasn't your fault, wasn't my fault, wasn't anyone's fault. To be honest I'm pretty happy right now. When I need a plan, I'll get one." She put her hand on her mother's and stroked it. "And you'll be the first to know."

Nicole had been putting off decisions for as long as she could remember. She just had to work out how to make the best of each day; either go down with the ship or swim to shore.

*

Dan and Nicole were sitting on the sofa together now and he gave her a hug. Bee was teasing them about their entry into suburban, married bliss.

"Fuck off, Bee," said Dan with a smile.

Charlie arose from his stupor. "Actually, Dan, your mother and I have a surprise for you two, haven't we?"

Jo raised her eyes for a moment, causing Nicole to surmise that the jury might still be out as to whether it was a nicer surprise for Dan than her. Charlie lifted his bottom and pulled a battered envelope from out of the back pocket of his corduroys. He held it out to Dan, who got up and took it before sitting back on the sofa.

Dan opened the envelope and showed the card inside to Nicole. The writing said Blair Gowan. Nicole couldn't read the rest.

Charlie looked pleased with himself. "You two have worked so hard this year. We thought you deserved a break, so we've bought you a weekend at Blair Gowan in the Lake District."

Jo said, "Call it an engagement present."

Dan said, "Wow, Dad, Mum. 've wondered about that place."

Nicole looked askance at Dan and couldn't stop herself. "Have you?" It was a hell of a long way to go for a weekend.

"It's where Grandad went to school in the war."

Nicole couldn't work out if Dan's enthusiasm was genuine or not. If he loved the Lake District or had a long-held desire to visit his grandfather's wartime school, he had kept it pretty quiet. More likely, knowing him, he had disliked the bad feeling generated by his father's reaction to her inept charades performance and wanted to lift the mood again. Sometimes his determination to ensure everyone was happy grated, but, this time, buoyed by her desire for some seasonal cheeriness, she loved him for it.

Dan said, "Blair Gowan was where all the Rothbury boys went when London and the South-East were getting bombed. They were up there for five years. Didn't even come home in the holidays."

Charlie added, "Dad said it was the making of him. Learnt self-reliance up in those hills. Dog eat dog and all that. It's a boutique hotel now. Got a Michelin star."

Nicole, not one hundred per cent sure how much of this was tongue-in-cheek, chanced her arm, "Is there anything left of the school do you know? Do we get to sleep in a dormitory? Wear a uniform?"

Bee said, "Yeah, you'll have the all the same spa treatments as Grandad. Those little boys loved their Cowshed beauty products. Nicole, it's like being invited to visit Buckingham Palace or the Vatican. You've got the Newhouse seal of approval. I've never got the 'I' to Blair Gowan –"

Dan said, "Oh, give it a bloody rest, Bee." OK, it wasn't tongue-in-cheek.

Nicole said, "It's a really generous present, thank you so, so much. Dan and I haven't had a weekend away for months, what with his new job and me being so busy."

Jo gave her a hug. "If you're going to become part of this family, you need to know about Rothbury. Warts and all. Blair Gowan is a good place to start."

"What do you mean warts and all?"

Charlie said, "Ignore her, Nicole. Jo always likes a dig at the old place when the topic comes up, don't you?" Jo smiled and shook her head the way people do when they hear an insult they've heard before.

Charlie was looking very pleased with himself and seemed relieved that, for a moment, everyone in the room, bar Bee, always a higher bar as far as Nicole could see, was smiling.

Bee had other ideas, saying, "I'm sure Mum and Dad will give you a voucher for somewhere nearer if you don't fancy such a long drive."

Nicole gave Bee her 1000-watt smile. "It'll be part of the break, Bee. Dan and I will love the chance to chat properly, won't we?"

Bee flounced out of the room, clutching her rollies. "Rather you than me. Just the idea of it gives me the creeps."

3

The tablelights in the dining room failed to flatter the reddening faces of the diners as they worked their way through the four-course meal and accompanying wines. Whenever someone took a sip, a waiter or waitress stepped in and filled up their glass.

Dan and Nicole talked about their wedding plans. Or at least making plans to have a plan: they had both been too busy. The letter preyed on Nicole's mind. She wanted to talk about it more. In the end, when they had been served their main course, she put her hand over her glass, simpered at the waitress and asked her to leave them alone for the moment.

"I really want to know what happened to Peter, don't you? No-one would write a letter like that unless there was something seriously wrong. Let's have a walk around tomorrow and see if we can find anyone in the village who was alive then. What do you think?"

Dan skewered a slice of a giant prawn with his fork before replying. "I really think we should put it back. It's not ours for a start. This is a private letter from a son to his parents. How would you like it if someone intercepted a letter from you to your mum?"

I wouldn't mind that much at all, thought Nicole. She wasn't ashamed how much she loved her mother. Anyone was welcome to read about it.

She said, "Let's call up the Rothbury headmaster when we're back home and see what he knows about our Peter Slaithwaite. You're still good mates with him, aren't you?"

"I don't think that's a good idea. The school won't thank us for dredging up stuff like this. Rothbury is one of the most respected prep schools in the country now."

"Spoilsport. If you'd found it, you'd be on the phone to him right now."

Nicole took a gulp of her white wine. She knew all about having a shit time at school. No, she decided in a flash, you don't need to know. I'll make my own enquiries.

"What are you going to have for pudding?" she said.

*

They slept in the next morning and only just made breakfast. Nicole liked the look of it – masses of berries, fresh orange juice and multiple choice of granola. They had had quite a lot to drink, and she fancied the avocado on toast as well. Around them the staff were, with some ostentation, preparing the tables for lunch.

Dan was back at the buffet searching through the mini cereal boxes. Nicole beckoned Shona over.

"Is there anyone around here who was alive when this was a school?"

Shona gave her a nervous grin and, buying time, sucked on her pencil.

"I think one of the chefs has a mother who played here as a child. She wouldn't have been more than six or seven. Barbara, or Babs, as she's known. I haven't seen her for a while. She lives in the top cottage up the lane below Black Tree Farm."

Dan was coming back so Nicole nodded a thank you, looking towards him, to usher Shona away. When Dan asked what she was talking about, Nicole said she wanted to know where the wallpaper came from. Zero interest in home decoration ensured this killed Dan's curiosity stone dead.

When they were back up in their room and Dan was in the bathroom, Nicole googled Black Tree Farm. It was about a mile away, perfect for their Saturday morning walk.

Fifteen minutes later, coated, and scarfed, they were striding out down the still misty drive. "Where are we going?" said Dan. Nicole grasped his hand and swung it. Above them clouds hung low, shrouding the peaks.

"You'll see."

*

After a short walk up a lane they saw a sign for Black Tree Farm and, just after, a row of tiny cottages. A woman was sweeping the terrace with toddlers swarming around her feet.

Nicole shouted, "Is that Barbara's house at the end?" The women said yes but added that she didn't always answer the door.

Dan looked away from the woman and, with his face

close to Nicole's, laughed, "What the fuck, Nicole? Who's Barbara?" Nicole could smell the smoked bacon from Dan's full English breakfast on his breath.

"She used to play at the school as a child. I thought she might know about Peter Slaithwaite."

"You said you wouldn't do anything about the letter. We said we would put it back where we found it."

Nicole stepped back. "No, you said that. I didn't. I want to know what happened." As she said it, she was a hundred per cent sure she was doing the right thing.

"Nicole, please, don't! It's a waste of time."

"C'mon, it's only a bloody letter, not the Ark of the Covenant. Humour me." Nicole walked away from Dan and up the path to Barbara's cottage. Dan stayed put, generating considerable interest from the mother and young children who had moved to the front of their garden to hear the argument better.

Nicole knocked on the front door with its chipped blue paint. There was no sign of life. She knocked again. The mother shouted over, "Give her a minute. She'll be watching *Saturday Kitchen*."

Sure enough, after another minute, the door was opened by a wizened, bespectacled old woman, under five foot, dressed in a nightie with a shiny Barbour over it, with fluffy slippers, brand new by Nicole's estimation. Her white hair was thinning on top.

"Hello, Barbara, I hope you don't mind me bothering you. I'm Nicole Weymouth. I'm staying at the hotel. I gather you used to play at the school in the war."

The woman looked her up and down. "I'm watching my programme. Is it urgent?"

Nicole debated her next move. The lady didn't look like she wanted to do anyone any favours. She had her life, and no-one was going to disturb it. Nicole had nothing to lose.

"It's about Peter Slaithwaite. He was a boy at the school. Did you know…"

Before Nicole had a chance to finish her sentence, with surprising force and speed, Babs had slammed the door on her. She looked around at Dan, who pulled his 'told-you-so' face, one that Nicole disliked even more than usual at that moment.

As they walked down the lane, the mother shouted over to ask what they wanted from her and, despite some attempts by Dan to pull her away, Nicole went over and explained.

"Babs doesn't like talking about the school. Her aunt was the nurse. Everyone, and I mean everyone, had a very tough time with that lot. It was the war – no-one wanted to be there."

Nicole tried to ask some more questions, but the mother clammed up. "If Babs doesn't want to talk, then I won't either. Me and my big mouth."

Nicole thanked her and walked back over to Dan. She could almost see the steam emanating from him. He shrank away as she tried to take his hand.

"Dan! Don't be like that. It's fascinating." If anything, the woman's description of wartime Rothbury had whetted her appetite even more.

"It's not fucking fascinating; it's someone else's secret. We have no business digging up stuff like this. It's… it's… just… weird."

He stormed off ahead of her. She thought about running to catch him, but she was too absorbed in her discovery. The letter had presented itself to her; Peter had presented himself to her. It wasn't weird: weird would have been putting it back and never knowing.

*

On the walk back to the hotel Nicole's resolution hardened. It was a pretty harmless quest as quests go. She wasn't looking for Excalibur. Not that she had had many in her life. When she was a little girl, she had often set herself the task of finding birds' eggs in nests in the woods behind their house. Once she found a perfect dunnock egg, a beautiful light blue, nestled off one of the paths. It was empty but unbroken, as light as paper. She stayed in the woods, sitting against a tree, cradling it and passing it from hand to hand as darkness fell. Soon it was pitch-black in the wood, and she had become scared when her father arrived to find her. He had been shouting her name in desperation before he reached her, and he took out his frustration by telling her that she had to leave the egg in the woods where she found it. When she had asked why, he had just told her to do as she was told. Her arm was sore for days where he had gripped her to pull her up.

She didn't mention the letter for the rest of the weekend. When Dan brought it up, she changed the subject. She played along with Dan's game and imagined what the school might have been like. They drove to Keswick and wandered around the town in the rain. They read the papers and their books, ate early and went to bed. Nicole had never been happier.

*

Nicole threw her suitcase into the back of the car and pulled on her seatbelt. "Now, that was a fantastic minibreak."

"So, did you put the letter back?"

Nicole gazed up at the hills. She was coming back one day soon. "Yup, *Black Beauty* as it was in 1940." Dan appeared satisfied with this response.

"I'm so relieved. I can't tell you how important Blair Gowan is to my dad and his father. I don't get it myself, but I wouldn't want to do anything that upset them."

Dan set the satnav and, as soon as they were onto the road, put his foot down. They hit 60 on a 40 mile an hour limit within minutes. At least he had cheered up even if he was now endangering their lives. And, to think, he had got in a stink about a letter from the last century.

Nicole put her hand over her eyes to minimise her terror and half-listened to Radio 5. It was a lunchtime match, always the dullest in her experience, not Chelsea which would have commanded her attention. Soon they were on the motorway. Dan stayed in the fast lane, averaging about 85 miles per hour.

Nicole decided to cheer Dan up to calm – and slow – him down. "Jennifer Lawrence or Dakota Johnson?"

"Dakota, of course."

"Rosie Huntington-Whiteley or Bella Hadid?"

"Easy. Bella."

"Queen Elizabeth II or Margaret Thatcher?"

"Pass." Dan laughed. Progress.

"You have to choose."

"Alright, Maggie."

"Terrible choice. The Iron Lady. Scourge of the miners. Now, my turn."

Dan didn't say anything, but he put his hand on her knee and reduced his speed to just over seventy.

Pleased with her progress, Nicole decided it was a good time to fess up. She reached down and pulled the letter out from her bag. "I hope you don't mind but I didn't put it back."

"You sneaky cow. Give it to me."

"No!" Nicole moved it away from him towards her window.

"C'mon, let me have it. I'm going to throw it out of the window." He tried to reach across her whilst keeping his other hand on the wheel. The cars around them pulled away as if sensing a madman in their presence.

"Careful, Dan!! I'll give it to you later." Dan couldn't stop laughing, almost hysterical, and reached over again. The car swerved and skidded. His foot seemed to have pushed down again on the accelerator, and the car jerked and shook as he tried to steer it with one hand. Nicole was trying to hand it over to him, but he seemed to like this game where he had to grab it.

"Give it to me and I'll slow down again." His body was almost lying on her. This plan had been flawed from the start. Journey-long grumpiness would have been preferable.

"Don't be an idiot, Dan. Look out!"

As Dan tried again to reach the letter, a grey car in the middle lane, a Peugeot Nicole remembered later, pulled over without signalling. Dan, nowhere to escape, slammed on the brakes, but it was too late. The Audi skidded to one side then the other, then piled into the back of the car. There was a massive crunch of metal and shattering of glass. Nicole was thrown forward with a lurch that cut into her chest, then an airbag filled her face and pinned her back.

For a moment there was silence followed by skids as the cars behind swerved to avoid the two cars. The high-pitched slamming of brakes and the smell of burnt rubber filled Nicole's senses. It seemed like they had avoided involving any other cars and were still in the middle of the motorway.

Nicole heard Dan moaning beside her. She pushed her airbag out of the way to see Dan slumped against the steering wheel. He was motionless. His airbag hadn't fully inflated.

"Dan, Dan, my love, are you OK?" She reached over and touched his face. She couldn't breathe. As she felt his breath on her hand, she found herself looking up and thanking God. His forehead was covered in blood, and he seemed to be in great pain.

"I'm so sorry, so sorry. It's all my fault." What a fool she was. All over a stupid letter. She didn't deserve anyone's pity. She had lost her brother; her father had left her life: she wouldn't be able to carry on if she lost her fiancé too. She could just about cope with her past if she had a future. This was just too much to bear.

She sat holding him, warm tears streaming down her face, murmuring 'Dan, Dan, Dan' until she sensed an ambulance man pulling her out. They put her in a blanket on the side of the motorway while they worked on the more delicate task of extracting Dan from the car. A quick inspection by the female medical technician confirmed that she hadn't had incurred any major injuries. Watching the scene on the road, tears and her shaking blurring her vision, she wished it had been her airbag that hadn't worked. She would never forgive herself if Dan had sustained any permanent damage.

Somebody escorted her away from the car to a chair on the hard shoulder. "Will he be alright?" The woman wrapped her more tightly in the blanket and told her not to worry. It was a cold January day, zero degrees, the wind chill factor high on the exposed hard shoulder. Over her shoulder she could see the police erecting barriers, the cars lining up to form a long traffic jam and Dan being stretchered into the ambulance.

4

It was Sunday afternoon and A&E was packed. She was given some painkillers and told to wait. So, wait she did – for four hours. They could have chosen a better day to crash. She hadn't seen Dan since they had taken him off the motorway. She hoped he'd had quicker treatment.

Two smiley nurses checked Nicole over, tidied up her head wound and took her over to a ward in a wheelchair. The twelve-bed ward was full of patients and visitors. There was a strong smell of sweat and cleaning fluid.

As they took off her clothes and put her into a starched white nightie, she found, whilst light-headed, that she needed to talk. "It was my fault, all my fault." She repeated this mantra-like again and again.

The nurses tied her up at the back and put her under the bedclothes. One of them produced a couple of pills with a glass of water.

"Here, this will help, Nicole. Drink it all down." Nicole didn't ask what was but just did what she was told. After that, even though it was now early evening, oblivion came fast.

The doctor who saw Nicole when she awoke told her that she was suffering from shock and that she needed to stay in overnight. When she asked about Dan, they wouldn't answer other than to say he was fine.

The mobile started to rotate on the bedside table, so she reached over to pick it up.

"Nicole, it's Charlie. Are you alright? We've just heard." Then Dan's parents were both on the phone, talking over each other. Jo was struggling to get her words out whilst Charlie sounded like a military general on speed. She told them a sanitised version of what had happened.

"What's going on with Dan? They won't tell me."

Charlie said, "They're fixing him up now. He's got some broken ribs and a broken ankle. Quite lucky really. We're off to see him."

Nicole was about to say that it was all her fault, but Charlie had put the phone down. She lay back on the bed and stared at the beige ceiling. The sound of trolleys carrying evening meals and drugs skating along the corridors filled her ears. She closed her eyes, and the vision of the cars smashing together reared into her consciousness. Again and again, whenever she tried to eject them from her mind, an enormous cacophony of bangs exploded in her head. Somehow, even though she hadn't seen it, the image of Dan hitting the steering wheel like a crash-test dummy wouldn't leave her.

She tried to summon up her happy dreams of her wedding to take her mind off things, but they kept disappearing. When they did, Patrick's image didn't appear.

*

The next morning, Sunday, Nicole wanted to get up and leave, but the nurses wouldn't let her. They gave her a cup of weak tea, a little box of cornflakes with milk and told her to stay in bed.

Around ten o'clock Charlie and Jo strode into the ward. Both were wearing matted brown Barbours, and, in Charlie's case, a deerstalker hat. When they spied her Jo threw her hands up as if to say how clever they all were that they had located each other. Nicole could tell they were both nervous. They sat each side of the bed and asked about twenty different questions as to how she was. Apart from an ache on one side, caused by hitting the door handle, she rated her condition as better than most Sunday mornings following a good night out.

When they had run out of questions, she asked, "How's Dan?"

Charlie said, "We've seen him and he's still very groggy. He was very worried about you. His ankle is in plaster. All in all, a very lucky man. That was quite a collision."

Nicole started crying with relief. "It was my fault, you know. We were messing about."

Charlie said, "He muttered something about a letter."

Jo said, "No, Charlie, not now. Nicole, will you please come and stay with us while you recover. I'm sure Dan will want to be with us when he gets out."

Nicole just kept shaking her head. After a minute one of her nurses walked past and suggested they let her go back to sleep. Nicole mouthed thank you to Charlie and Jo then turned over and laid her head on the pillow as if she craved sleep. They sat on her bed until Jo whispered something about going back to a hotel.

*

Around two in the afternoon the doctor checked her over and she said she was free to go. He recommended she took a week off work and gave her a two-week prescription of Tramadol painkilling tablets.

Her body ached all over and it took her a lot longer than normal to put her clothes back on. When she pulled on her coat, she took out the letter and hid it at the bottom of her suitcase. During the night she had thought more about it. The crash wasn't a sign that she should forget about it – they had both survived. It was a sign that she needed to find out the truth.

Charlie and Jo were waiting for her in reception. They discarded worn and creased copies of *Hello* and *OK* respectively as they got up. Nicole gave them the most radiant smile she could summon.

"So how was Blair Gowan?"

"I could imagine it as a school if I closed my eyes. The rooms were massive with four-poster beds."

"I don't think my dad had a four-poster bed."

Jo hugged her and shushed Charlie.

When she got back to London she would try and find out what happened to Peter Slaithwaite. It shouldn't be hard. If he turned out to have had a perfect life with a nice family and steady job, she would be very happy. Then she could put the whole thing to bed.

Dan was in a ward on the fourth floor of the hospital, so they took the lift. It was full of orderlies and visitors, which meant Nicole stood close enough to Charlie and Jo that she could smell his stale breath and her jaunty perfume.

Dan was sitting up in bed with his ankle in plaster. He took his oxygen mask away from his face as Nicole approached and gave her a warm but weary smile. With trepidation she sat on the bed, put her arms around him and kissed him on the mouth.

He whispered, "It was all my fault."

Nicole had to suppress joy as it leapt up her throat and prevented her talking. "No, it was mine."

She thought Dan looked very young and vulnerable lying in his blue tunic. So different from the brash life-and-soul of the party character she had witnessed the night she met him. Just arrived in London, a friend from school had suggested she tag along to a Friday-night birthday drinks above a pub in Shoreditch. They had a meal beforehand, so the party was in full swing when they arrived. The music was turned up and people were shouting in each other's ears. To Nicole's mind everyone seemed to be dressed in the sort of shabby chic that *The Sunday Times Style* magazine had been fawning over that summer. You had to have money to look that bedraggled.

Dan was in the centre of the room in a huddle of tall men, all on the verge of hysterics with each other's wit, who gave the impression they owned it. A smaller number of women, all near six foot in their heels, flashing perfect teeth, swaying long blonde hair, laughed along.

As Nicole and her friend, Andrea, tried to squeeze past them to get to the bar, Dan stepped back on to her foot. It was a total accident, but it was agonising, nevertheless. Nicole's scream pierced the music and the braying.

Dan turned, "My God, I'm so, so sorry. I had no idea you were behind me. Are you OK?"

Nicole looked up at him. He was a few years older than her. He had dark brown eyes, a strong, aquiline nose and black curly hair. A few freckles dotted his cheeks. You can stand on my feet as much as you like as long as you stay by me tonight, she thought.

"I'm fine, honestly. I never feel like I've been to a party unless I have had my foot pinned into the floor at least once." She said this hopping on one leg.

Dan and Andrea helped her over to the side of the room where there was a line of chairs. Dan got her a glass of water.

He said, "I was hoping I would get to talk to you and was trying to work out how to engineer it. Foot-stamping wasn't on high on my list though."

"Nor mine." Her foot was throbbing. She sipped her glass of water and tried to regain some degree of composure.

As he talked, he kept his gaze on her. It didn't leave her eyes as he plied her with questions about her life, her work, her likes and dislikes. She couldn't remember the last time anyone had shown so much interest in her. Every time she thought it was time for her to ask a question, he asked another one. The conversation flowed with none of those awkward first date gear changes.

After 15 minutes Andrea had grown bored watching Nicole and Dan engrossed in one another and had been beckoned over to talk to Dan's friends. Nicole squeezed her hand as she got up to indicate it wasn't personal and wouldn't be long.

Andrea was half-Spanish with long black hair and flashing brown eyes and perfect teeth. Sure enough, she was soon in the thick of the group; the men flirting with her, the women appraising her with wary eyes. Nicole turned back to Dan.

The next thing she knew there were some raised voices. She could see Andrea against a wall and one of Dan's friends leaning over her. The joint body language suggested his proposal had been refuted.

Dan sprang up and propelled himself across to where his friend was standing and he pulled him away by his collar. The guy jerked back, tottered and, being let go by Dan, fell onto the floor with his backside. Everyone stepped back as he did so. Andrea, released, ran over to Nicole.

The guy, Tom, as she later learnt he was called, shouted, "What the fuck, mate! Mind your own business!"

As he was getting to his feet, Dan grabbed his jacket. "She said no, Tom. No. Get that? Leave her be!"

"How could you tell?"

"I know you. I can tell."

Tom was sweating and red in the face now. "I was only joshing with her. Lighten up."

"You weren't. You were doing what you always do. It's not cool. C'mon, let's get some air."

Dan put his arm around Tom's shoulder and led him through the melee to the door. Dan's group of friends stood in a circle open-mouthed. About ten minutes later Dan came back but Tom didn't. Soon after, Andrea declared she had decided to get an early night. All the time Dan sat alongside Nicole, only leaving to order more drinks at the bar. When one of his friends came up to talk, he waved them away with a smile.

After that evening Dan became her constant companion and her guide to London.

It was two years since that night. They spent every weekend and most weeknights together. They spent more time with Dan's family and friends than Nicole's, but that was simply because there were more of them. Although there had been that break before Christmas following the job argument. Charlie hadn't liked Dan moving from his big-shot banking job to the green investment company. But generally, it was easier: more fun, more laughs, more space.

Dan looked out for her. If she was ill, he nursed her; if she was hungover, he brought her remedies; if she was celebrating, he was first with the champagne. Most of the parties they went to were held by his friends, but he made her feel included and he never allowed any of his old female friends to crowd her space. She couldn't have asked for anyone better.

He had changed since they had been together. He was less patient with his friends' relentless appetite for parties, holidays and money. He spent more of his free time reading books about and attending talks on climate change. He had embarked on an online course about ESG economics at Imperial College. Any proposed holidays that included flights generated massive guilt-filled debates. Nicole wasn't quite there yet and still liked the odd easyJet minibreak. He was still the Dan of old, but he was more serious. He had, as people like to say, purpose.

She wondered what he would say about her. Prone to mood swings? Insecurity that manifested itself in last-minute changes in decisions whether it be clothes to wear, where to go out or weekend plans. A dislike of social events where everyone thought they were better than everyone else. And what about the plus side? What did she have to offer? She was always there for him, never had better plans (apart from last-minute work crises). A willingness to cook as long as she had all the ingredients and a recipe book at hand. Enthusiastic and adventurous in bed even if not all the routines she suggested led either of them to the orgasmic heights she had planned. Dan was pretty much on the way to becoming the finished article. She was, at best, a work in progress. Purpose and Nicole were never mentioned in the same sentence. At least not yet.

They held hands. Dan said, "They say I will be here for a couple of nights. You should go back to London."

"I can't leave you until you're better. I don't care what anyone says – it was my fault. You could have died." She put her head on his chest and lay there, listening to his heart beating.

"You should go. Mum and Dad can drive you back. You've got that big pitch tomorrow. You don't want to miss that. Not after all the work you've put into it." Nicole went a little red thinking of Chandra all alone in the office that weekend.

*

It had been late Thursday afternoon in the third week of January, the week before her trip to the Lake District, and people were trudging the streets of Soho with their heads down and their hands in their pockets. Everyone was skint and the pubs were empty. Bright orange sales placards festooned the shop windows. High up in a building on Broadwick Street, Nicole and Chandra were wrestling with creative ideas for their forthcoming presentation to their new client, StudentCars. Chandra had been her boss since she had joined YellowRazor, and they had been promoted in step. In many ways Chandra was Yellow Razor in Nicole's mind. They had been at it for three days and had worked their way through four freelance creatives already.

StudentCars was a motor insurance product for people under 25. It used sophisticated monitoring and algorithms to enable students to get cheap insurance if they drove with care, away from motorways. Nicole couldn't see how they would make any money, but a who's who of Europe's venture capitalists had put money in so what did she know, and Po Olsen, the founder, had been almost frothing at the mouth when he gave them his pitch.

During one of the frequent lulls in brainstorming, Nicole had been telling Chandra about her Boxing Day. She was delighted by the engagement news and plied her with questions about their plans. Nicole also told her about the charades argument. Ever since Dan's father had mocked her in front of his family, Nicole had been wondering whether she should have stood up for herself more.

"Dan should have said something. It's pathetic." Chandra smoothed down her electric blue satin blouse and, crossing her stick-thin legs, brushed biscuit crumbs off her black leather skirt. "Shit, where are these damned ideas?"

"He stuck up for me. It was just family fun. I don't think any of them meant to be nasty. They're just quite competitive when they all get together. Look, what about a campus safari? We get some influencers to drive around every single campus in the UK and offer them some sort of early-bird discount. Anyone who signs up would be allowed to join the convoy. Like one of those John O'Groats to Land's End walks."

They both agreed that this was the best idea they had come up with yet, but it would require ten times the budget allocated for the launch. Nicole WhatsApped Dan to see who was buying the food and he sent back the link to some complicated Ottolenghi vegan salad recipe. Now he had entered the renewables world, he was very serious about all his eco New Year's resolutions. She put her phone face-down and sighed.

Nicole told Chandra about her forthcoming Lake District boutique hotel visit. When she had been given the voucher by Charlie and Jo on Boxing Day, her first thought had been that the petrol there and back would cost nearly as much as the weekend. Even she was ashamed of that one. Dan was all for it. Rothbury was, as he put it, part of his DNA.

Chandra said, "I know I shouldn't say this, but do you ever wonder if you're settling for too little, too early? You're so bright, funny, young – you could do anything. And you shouldn't have to put up with that kind of shit from your boyfriend's family."

Nicole looked out of the window. The sky had grown dark, and the lights were being turned on in the office opposite. She couldn't believe her luck when Dan called for a date two days after their first meeting. He was her rock. Isn't that what people liked to say about perfect boyfriends? He was six years older than her so was, perhaps, readier to settle down. He loved his new work. And she loved the fact he loved it. With his new job he said he had found his destiny. He was doing good as well as making money. Nicole wasn't a hundred per cent sold – she could smell spin. She did it for a living. The website had all those blac-and-white photos of middle-aged men and young women in power suits the banks loved so much. But she was more than happy to give Dan the benefit of the doubt.

"What do you mean? I'm really happy. And I love working with you."

"Well, look at me: I got married at twenty-four. I've been at this agency all my working life, nearly ten years. I would have loved, would love to be honest, to have some different experiences before I have kids. If they ever come. Wouldn't have minded going out with some other men first as well. Not that I don't love Raj; I love him to bits – I just wish I'd met him a couple of years later. You? It's not too late."

"Dan's really special you know? He listens, really listens. Not many men do that do they? Early on in our relationship I told him that I had always found the anniversary of Patrick's death really hard. 25th July. I wondered if he had registered it. Certainly, I didn't mention it again. It upsets me just thinking about it. But when the anniversary came around – it was a Saturday – he organised a full day for me. Lunch out with a couple of friends, a walk in Kew Gardens then a trip to the theatre, Mamma Mia, in the evening. It was just lovely. It meant, for the first time on the day, I was looking forward not back. That's when I truly decided: he was the one."

Nicole looked at Chandra. There were few people she respected more. "Sorry, I had to say that. I think you're amazing. You are brilliant at your job, and you have a wonderful marriage. Kids will come."

Chandra looked out of the window. "I hope you're right. I've had three miscarriages now. IVF next, but that's so expensive."

"I didn't know. I'm so sorry." She had guessed but hadn't wanted to say anything. Chandra was very private. They were both silent.

Nicole said, "You can talk to me, you know. I'm your friend. I'm a good listener."

Chandra wiped her eye. "Thank you. We better get back to this."

Nicole took in the bright fluorescent-lit meeting room and the Banksy prints on the wall. She'd considered herself pretty lucky to get this job. Her first agency had been a husband-and-wife team in Bath, one where she did everything from buying the coffees to preparing the client presentations and budgets. The two owners were divorcing and came in on separate days. Getting this job, coming to London, meeting Dan had transformed her life. She didn't have to worry about her mother every day. Absence made the heart less guilty.

One of the things that she loved about Dan, unlike his father or some of his friends, was that he wasn't obsessed by money. Charlie, his father, was at an age when new jobs came less easily, so Nicole could see why he might have been nervy. No excuse for being a wanker, though.

Nicole said, "Let's kick my road-trip idea around a little more. If it doesn't work, we'll go back to floating a car down the Thames." At the thought of this PR trope, Nicole and Chandra covered their faces in unison. It was going to be a long night.

*

Nicole couldn't think of anything she wanted to do less than spend five hours in a car with Charlie and Jo, but the Audi was a write-off and, it being the end of January, she didn't have the money for the train. She spent an hour with Dan as he drifted in and out of sleep then, around four, with a promise to come up again midweek, they set off to London. *Gardeners' Question Time* was on iPlayer and Jo requested silence while Bob Flowerdew and his friends joshed and joked. Nicole was starting to ache, so she popped a Tramadol and swigged some water to wash it down.

Her phone lit up as she got in the car. Chandra's WhatsApps said she had stumbled across a brilliant idea around the time Nicole had had her crash. *PRAISE THE LORD!!* she had written.

Nicole called her and, whispering, asked her about the idea. Chandra was flying, high on the relief that a good creative idea, arriving just in time, brings. She wouldn't stop talking about it – The Virtual History of Student Road Trips. Nicole didn't know if it was brilliant or terrible. She was just glad Chandra was happy. Eventually Chandra asked her about the weekend and Nicole told her what had happened.

"OMG! Why didn't you tell me before I went off on one? Why are you even talking to me?"

"I was worried about you. The pitch." Chandra drew a heavy breath. "I'm fine, honestly."

Chandra said, "I will call you later. Look after yourself. And don't come into the office!"

Charlie turned the radio off while the sign-off music was still going. "I'm really interested to hear about your weekend, Nicole. Tell me more about Blair Gowan? And tell me all about this intriguing letter."

"I threw the letter away." Nicole's head started to throb. She hoped the pills would kick in soon.

Charlie said, "That was sensible. Wartime was tough at Rothbury."

Jo said, "I'm so pleased Dan has got this new job. He's always been so passionate about the environment. Climate change is the biggest challenge for all of us, isn't it? Wonderful that he's investing in all these companies that want to make a difference. Charlie, we should look and see if we can move any of our investments into his funds. Even when he was a small boy, he made us recycle everything. I remember him collecting up all the plastics in our dustbins once and putting them on the kitchen table. He gave me such a telling off. I just hope that he comes through this intact. Such a beautiful boy…" Her emotion forced her to peter to a halt. Charlie turned the radio back on and Nicole dozed off.

*

They dropped Nicole outside her flat in Tooting with the request that, anytime she wanted, she should come and stay with them. They also agreed that they would all drive up to Preston later in the week to collect Dan. By now Dan was texting Nicole so she knew he was on the mend.

It was ten o'clock and Nicole's flatmate, Martha, was still away for the weekend. Still drowsy, Nicole trudged up the stairs with her case. When she had set off down these stairs four days ago, she had been in a very different mood. The heating was off; an icy draught shot through the gap in the kitchen window and the fridge was near empty. A solitary can of beans in the larder and the dregs of an open bottle of red wine by the stove looked likely to be her supper.

The doorbell pinged and Nicole staggered over to the intercom. "Yes, who is it?"

"Bee. Can I come up?"

"What do you want?"

"Please let me in." Nicole pressed the button to open the door downstairs. A moment later the door swung back on its hinges and Bee appeared carrying two large carrier bags with a rucksack on her back. She charged over, her bags driving her momentum, and kissed Nicole, neck outstretched, on both cheeks.

"Awful. Awful. Awful. Are you alright, sweetheart?" Nicole pulled her face away from the embrace to say she was. "And poor Dan? Will he be OK?"

She dropped the bags onto the centre of the sitting room floor and pulled her rucksack off, placing it on top of them. Nicole didn't like the look of this.

"They think so. They need to keep him in for a few nights. It's some ribs and a single break of the ankle. Could have been worse."

Bee threw herself down on the sofa and started rolling a cigarette. "Would you mind not smoking? It's forbidden in our lease." Bee threw her smoking equipment down on the table in front of her as if it were an invasion of her own civil liberties.

"I'm here to look after you."

"That's sweet but I don't need looking after."

"Anyway, what a weekend for our family. Disaster after disaster."

"How do you mean?"

Bee snorted and said, "Didn't you hear? I got thrown out of my flat."

"Why?"

"They said I hadn't paid the rent."

"Had you?"

"Well, I had, but not often or recently enough. Do you have any wine?" Nicole thought about the half-drunk bottle by the cooker. It might be foul enough to scare Bee away. She went over to the kitchen area to fetch it.

While she was away, Bee had summoned up some tears. "Do you mind if I stay for a couple of days? I need to be close to someone who understands."

Nicole said that it might be difficult as there were only two rooms, and Martha and she had a tacit agreement not to allow friends to stay for more than a single night. She passed Bee the half-empty bottle and a glass. Bee swigged direct from the bottle and coughed.

"Christ, I thought you PR types knew your wine. Look, it's fine. I can sleep on the sofa when you are here and, in your bed when you're with Dan."

It wasn't fine but Nicole was more tired than she could ever remember, and she had to be in at Yellow Razor early for the pitch.

"Stay here tonight and we'll talk tomorrow." Bee blew her a series of kisses as she left the room.

Exhausted, Nicole slumped on her bed in the dark and texted Martha to warn her and apologise. Then she looked up Rothbury School on her phone. The website boasted that it had won more awards than any other school in the South-East. Best School Food? Most Innovative Mental Wellbeing programme?

Peter Slaithwaite might have had something to say about that one.

5

"You shouldn't be in, Nicole. Go home!! The receptionist at Yellow Razor was the first of many people to express surprise at Nicole's presence the next morning as she stumbled in. She had been woken by her flatmate coming in around midnight and hadn't been able to get back to sleep afterwards. No matter how hard she tried, the images and noises of car crashes wouldn't leave her. She was far, far away from her normal Monday morning world when the alarm punched her awake at seven o'clock.

Chandra talked her through the presentation. She was going do the insights and strategy; Nicole would do the big campaign; and Spencer, the new Account Executive, was going to cover the Press Office. With the client, Po Olsen, and his comms manager, Jaz, scheduled to come in at 10.30 they didn't have much time for rehearsal, so they agreed to focus on getting Spencer comfortable with his slides.

"I want you to go home as soon as we've done the presentation. OK?" Nicole could see two Chandras and was wondering if she needed to be sick. Her head throbbed as it never had done before. She shouldn't be here – her place was with Dan alongside his hospital bed in Preston.

Spencer had John Lennon spectacles framed with long greasy blond hair and a goatee beard. As he talked about the suggestions for rapid response and opinion pieces, Nicole studied her slides. The idea Chandra had come up with – The Virtual History of Student Road Trips – would work really well online if they got the content right. She wasn't sure why the nationals would go for it. It was too late for that now and it would be very ungrateful to raise any problems.

Jaz arrived a few minutes early and spent the time asking about Nicole's wellbeing. Like everyone else, she thought Nicole shouldn't be there. The more people consoled her, the worse she felt.

Fifteen minutes after the meeting was meant to start, Po arrived. He was wearing a floral shirt with three buttons undone and lovebeads showing, black jeans and red Converses with mud on the soles. There was a large Selfridges bag under his arm. He kissed everyone, including Spencer, picked a chair, pushed it back, put his feet on the table and said, "OK, Yellow Razor, impress me!"

Both he and Jaz loved the insights and the strategy. Nicole admired the smooth way Chandra held their hands as she set up the creative. Thank God for that. The last thing Nicole needed was an argument.

Chandra handed the clicker to Nicole so she could control the presentation when her slides appeared. Nicole loved doing a grabber to get clients fired up and she knew, despite her state, despite seeing double of everyone in the room, she was about to deliver a good one.

"Thanks, Chandra. We need something very big indeed to launch this campaign. This is a crowded market, so we need to cut through. Your audience is notoriously hard to reach, so we've got something they will share on socials especially Instagram, Snapchat and TikTok. The Virtual History of Student Road Trips will do just that. All of us at some time in our lives have been on an unforgettable car ride with friends, whether we're eighteen or eighty. We're going to celebrate the great road trips in movies and TV and ask our audience to submit their own stories as well. At the end of it the StudentCars brand will be on everyone's lips…"

"Is this your big idea?" said Po.

Nicole looked at Chandra for a moment. "Yes, it's one we think is just right for you."

"Jaz, have they run this past you?" Jaz looked sheepish and shook her head.

He pulled his feet off the table – some crumbs of mud stayed on it – and leant forward.

"I don't like this idea. It doesn't sell. You need to talk to Run Don't Walk, our new creative agency. They came up with a superb creative on Friday around value for money. You should build something on that."

Jaz said, "They haven't seen that, Po." Po leant back on his chair again, sighed, playing with his love beads, and said, "We're a fast-paced business."

All the warmth had drained out of the room. Chandra was puce with rage and unable to speak. Spencer started cleaning his spectacles. Nicole looked at Chandra, willing her to speak. She was the most senior agency person in the room, and it was her job to respond. This was one of those instances where a client was taking advantage of his authority to tie the agency in knots. If he had wanted them to use the ad agency concept, he could have asked them to delay their presentation until they had had a chance to be briefed and brainstorm around it.

Nicole said, "This is a brilliant idea."

Po said, "I don't think so. It will do nothing for our brand. Did you go on any road trips as a student?"

Nicole said, "I didn't go to university."

"I rest my case." *Don't take the bait, Nicole, don't take the bait.* "How about you, Chandra?"

Chandra said that she had twice done midnight runs in the summer down to Torquay to surf. Spencer, improvising at a speed that suggested to Nicole he would go far, said he had done them every weekend for three years. But Po didn't hear that as he had started talking again. Nicole slipped a painkiller out of her bag and, hand over her mouth, popped it in.

Po said, "Well, I never did them. Too busy coding. Jaz, have you got that deck from Friday?"

Nicole was dizzy. Her head was throbbing more than ever. Every time she moved piercing pain shot through her body. She shouldn't have come back to London, she shouldn't have come in, she shouldn't be presenting to this idiot. It was too much.

"We're not mindreaders you know. We've spent every waking hour pulling these ideas together since you briefed us before Christmas. Chandra was here all weekend. I rushed back from Preston when I should be in hospital. This has been a total waste of your money and our time."

Po stood up. "I'm sorry you feel like that, Nicole. And I know you're not well, so I thank you for coming in and presenting. And you know how much sto I place on honesty, but I think this borders on rudeness."

"Well, I don't. I'm just telling you what you need to hear. You think you're some hotshot digital genius, but you're just arrogant and rude. You should learn some manners before you pull this sub-Steve Jobs macho shtick."

Nicole slumped back down in her chair. The room was now very quiet. Who was that just shouting at the client? She looked around and couldn't see who it was. No-one did that at Yellow Razor. Fuck. The room started to move around, and her chair became unstable. Then she started to fall sideways so that she could see the underneath of the table better than the top of it. Her head cracked on a hard surface as she fell. Her lips hit the carpet and dust filled her mouth. Then everything went black.

*

She was lying on a sofa with a neon strip flicking above her head. There was a damp cloth on her forehead. Someone was about to hold a Formula One race inside her head and the revving was becoming intolerable. She'd had a nightmare that she had been incredibly rude to a client.

Chandra's face appeared in front of her. She was grinning. "Jeepers creepers, Nicole Weymouth, that was the funniest thing I have ever seen. Po's face as he stormed out."

"I should have kept my mouth shut, shouldn't I? Have they fired us?"

"Who cares. They never pay their bills. I wish I'd had the balls to say what you said. I should have – I'm sorry."

Chandra left the room and Nicole lay, shielding her eyes

from the light. She knew there would be consequences for her action. The agency didn't have so many clients that it could afford mid-level staff to incite them.

Then a tall figure dressed in a cream trouser suit enhanced with multiple gold necklaces and bangles hove in front of her. A pair of Cartier spectacles rested on a powdered nose, all surrounded by thick brown tresses, set themselves down alongside her. Judgement had arrived. The boss. Ellie Sharp.

She said, "Po is very pissed off with us. You told him he was arrogant and rude."

"Sorry." *Doesn't mean I was wrong though.*

"Yes, sorry. Indeed. He is. But that isn't the point. You shouldn't have come in. You should be at home or, better still, back with your boyfriend up north. People can't come into work forty-eight hours after being in a major car accident."

Nicole looked into Ellie's eyes. This was the closest she had come to her in two years of working at Yellow Razor. She didn't think Ellie liked her very much. She had never given her a pay rise and never talked to her at company events. Other people at her level were always being whisked off to some macrobiotic, gluten-free lunch joint. Ellie was now stroking her arm. It was all very weird, as if she was an exhibit in a museum.

"Chandra is going to get a cab home with you and then you're taking a week's sick leave. I don't want to see or hear from you until Tuesday week. Got it?"

Nicole nodded. If that was the extent of her punishment, then she had got off lightly. Po had been right. It wasn't a very good idea. Her loyalty to the pitch was based on the fact that Chandra had spent all weekend coming up with it. A text bleeped in her pocket. It was Jaz. *Hope you're OK. You're my hero.*

Ellie left and Chandra came back into the room. She had her caramel raincoat on.

"Shall we go?"

Nicole said, "Can we go and have a quiet drink?" She didn't want alcohol. It was lunchtime, but she just didn't want to go home yet.

They went across the street to a bar called Sparky's. The foot-thick oak door looked like a cast-off from a medieval castle. It was aiming for a Soho House vibe but fell short because they hadn't spent any money on the décor, so it looked more like a condemned AllBarOne. The heating was off, and it looked deserted apart from a waitress cleaning glasses. Sparky's served wine in massive goblets that could house half a bottle. The handwritten blackboard above the bar declared it was Happy Hour. All drinks half price. Chandra was behaving in an awkward manner, like a waitress who is about to take your order but knows the chef has just had a nervous breakdown. She walked Nicole down to a table away from other tables at the far end of the room and went back to the bar.

Nicole sat in the cold and composed a WhatsApp to Dan – *Missing you – think I'm about to get fired.* A reply came back by return – *I miss you so much XXX. Please come up and see me in my prison. I don't care about the job – a brilliant PR person like you can easily get a new one.* Not sure about that, thought Nicole, any reference that asked about her client relations would be a pretty effective career torpedo.

Chandra put the drinks down – a small glass of Pino Grigio for Nicole and a Diet Coke for her. Chandra remarked that Sparky's looked a lot more fun when it was full, and that Nicole could use her week to find out about that letter she had found.

Nicole took a swig of her wine and smiled. "What's up?"

Chandra spent a moment clearing her throat "Ellie's been thinking about this for some time, but it seems even more sensible in light of current circumstances." *In light of current circumstances?*

"She thinks you would benefit from a change of scene. Something to help you get back on your feet while you get better. You've got massive potential in this agency, but, well, your temper often gets the better of you at the wrong times…" She hesitated. "Please understand this isn't my decision, it's Ellie's. I want you to stay here with me."

Nicole said she couldn't think what she meant. "That time last Christmas when you had that massive argument about Brexit with that marketing manager from Sunderland."

Nicole said, "We agreed to disagree, didn't we? We've still got the account. Won an award."

"Only after she spent thirty minutes crying in the ladies. Anyway, Ellie has something in mind for you. Came up before all this but it's good timing. At least I think so. There's this fintech start-up in Canary Wharf, called Zaxxo, really hot, got loads of funding, working towards IPO, needs a PR Director for six months. The founder is amazing, apparently, incredibly bright, very tough, super ambitious. He needs someone who will stand up to him. Ellie thinks you would be perfect. I must admit it sounds OK to me too. I would grab it with both hands if it was offered to me."

Nicole didn't want to leave Yellow Razor. She didn't

want to go and work for a start-up. She didn't want to have to stand up to any more incredibly bright, super-ambitious, tough tech founders.

"If I say no?"

Chandra took another sip of her Coke and pulled a face like she'd downed a pint of vinegar.

"It's win-win. You must see that."

"You're kidding me?" Chandra shook her head, so Nicole swigged her drink down, pushed the table away and headed out of the bar.

"Anyway, I'm meant to take you home."

Nicole pulled the big oak door open and let it slam shut as her feet hit the pavement. Her head was starting to spin again. She turned down a side street to the sound of Chandra calling her name.

6

Nicole spent all Wednesday lying on the sofa in her flat doing some research on Peter Slaithwaite and Rothbury. Google had nothing on Rothbury wartime old boys. Hardly surprising for those born before the Second World War. Plenty of more recent ones though. They all looked very bright, attractive and ready for world domination. She got the letter out of her pocket and read it again. What on earth had been happening to him that was so awful that he had had enough? She hoped she would find him to be a happy pensioner in a pretty thatched cottage somewhere in the Cotswolds, ideally with a loving wife, children, grandchildren, pets. If he had been subjected to dreadful things, then she didn't want to know.

Until they had run out of money, when she was about fourteen, she had been at a girl's boarding school. It was a dilapidated 19th century manor house near Cheltenham – not THE Cheltenham, always a bone of sour contention for the teachers. A couple of times she had got on the wrong side of the school bullies. Once, they had pushed her down a bank fully clothed, three days in a row, into an icy river on the way to chapel. As she sat in the pew shivering and dripping, her house mistress accused her of attention-seeking. She hadn't been sad when she had been pulled out of class three weeks into the summer term to be told that, with her fees unpaid, her mother had been invited to come and collect her. None of the smirking and laughing of her fellow pupils as she cleared her desk had touched her, but her mother had hidden her face in a scarf as they dragged Nicole's enormous cases and bags out of her house towards their car. Her mother had held her tight as they both cried, stroking her hair, in the car for about thirty minutes before they headed out.

With some reluctance she put Zaxxo into Google. If she wanted to keep working, she needed to pass the interview with the CEO, Gal Bezman, on Thursday. A recommendation from Ellie wouldn't be enough on its own – she knew she needed to be knowledgeable and enthusiastic about the business and its markets.

Zaxxo was a new kind of bank, one that existed only on one's phone in the form of an app. It looked a little like Monzo or Revolut, which she and Dan used when they wanted to share expenses or get cheap currency on holiday. It claimed to be particularly useful for people who travelled a lot as their rates for currency were lower than anyone's. Over 100,000 customers acquired in six months was impressive. Gal said they wanted a UK banking licence as soon as possible, but, in the meantime, he had plenty to keep himself busy.

There were several newspaper profiles of Gal. Short, bearded, balding a little – he looked much older than his age. He wore loose-fitting chinos and a polo shirt with chest hair showing. All the articles commented on how little small talk he offered and how terse his replies were. He had come over to the UK from Turkey as a child, the son of a metal trader and his beautician wife. When he was sixteen his parents went back to Turkey, but he stayed put and he paid for his food and lodgings by building websites for local traders. He studied his A-levels in the evenings and got a place at LSE to do computer science. Nicole looked at his picture. Would this man take her seriously? Would he even listen to her? Did she want to work for him? One thing in his favour – he kept talking about how fat and complacent the old banks, including Charlie's, were. That might be fun.

By mid-afternoon she was bored of researching Zaxxo. She had come to the conclusion that, if she passed the interview, she would take the job. After all what else was she going to do? But all those articles about interest rates were pretty snooze-inducing from where she stood. Mind you, it would do her good to get involved in something serious like finance. She wanted to work for a company with a vision, something she could get passionate about.

Her brother had been five when he died. Every day she wondered what he would be like and what he would be doing. Patrick had been very intelligent, always top of his class, whatever top meant in Year One. She'd loved showing him her homework and teaching him maths and English and he had grasped most of it way quicker than she had. Nicole had always put his needs first. Sometimes she wondered where all that love and care had gone. Her thoughts wandered back to Peter Slaithwaite. Funny how she was worrying about him more than Dan.

Why was she thinking about dead people when she should be focused on Dan, who was very much alive? She didn't want to dig too much into the implications of that question. She needed to know what had happened to Peter as soon as she could and move on. But Dan mustn't know. It wouldn't take long. She would have sorted it by the time he was back in London.

Rothbury School's phone number was easy to find on Google, so she pressed Call.

A clipped woman's voice answered, "Hello, Rothbury School, how can I help you?"

"Could I speak to Martin De La Hay, please?"

"Who's speaking, please?"

"I'm Arabella Worthington and I'm thinking of sending my son to Rothbury."

The woman asked her to hold. Nicole hadn't thought through what she was going to say. If she said she wanted to know about someone who went to the school in the middle of the last century, he would think she was mad. That was pretty much ancient history. And, if Peter Slaithwaite was bad news, the school certainly wouldn't be interested.

"Martin De Lay Hay speaking." His voice was deep and his pronunciation crisp. One of the ruling classes. A mixture of fear and spite coursed through Nicole's veins.

"Oh hello, my name's Arabella Worthington. My son, Finn, is five and I would like him to come to your school. I wondered if I could come down and see it?"

There was a grunt then: "I'd be delighted. How about Friday morning? I have a free at 11.15?"

How would he react if he found out she was visiting under false pretences? Dan and Charlie wouldn't be very pleased either. Nicole blocked the thought out of her mind, lay back on the sofa and flicked on to Netflix. *Gossip Girl* would keep her amused for three hours until her flatmate came home.

*

No-one said much in the car on the way up to Preston. Dan's parents listened to Radio 4, and Nicole and Bee kept their headphones on. Nicole worked her way through episodes of The High-Low podcast. Dolly Alderton and Pandora Sykes were more interesting and articulate versions of her own friends and, what's more, they were always there when she needed them.

Bee took her headphones off. "Can we stop for a Maccy D's?"

Jo turned to her. "We don't have time. We need to make visiting hours. Maybe on the way back?"

"It'll only take five minutes. Please!"

The argument went on for several minutes with Bee pulling out a succession of increasingly childish pleas. As Dan often said to Nicole, in the end Bee always got her own way. Sure enough, at the next motorway services they pulled off into a drive-through McDonald's. The car stank of uneaten chips for the rest of the journey.

Nicole said, "How's Stu?" Stu was the boyfriend Bee kept mentioning at Christmas.

Bee said, "Binned. Don't want to talk about it." She munched on a McNugget.

"OK." Nicole took a deep breath. Under-sharing wasn't in Bee's wheelhouse.

"He's a massive tool. Spends his whole time trying to

make out he is some kind of mega-disciple of #MeToo then expects me to do everything for him. Why can't he be more like Dan? He's at your beck and call for everything?"

Is he? wondered Nicole.

"I quite liked him."

"Yeah, well, you like everybody. And everybody likes you. If I didn't like you so much, your goodness would make me throw up."

Bee leant over and planted a ketchup-smeared kiss on Nicole's cheek.

*

They now knew their way to Dan's ward, and they all trooped at speed along the corridors. Lunch had just finished and there were piles of plates and trays on trolleys in the corridors.

It didn't take long for conversation to peter out. It was only three days since they had last visited, and Dan was short on news. Nicole took it upon herself to amuse them with her encounter with Po. It wasn't really an episode of which she was particularly proud, but she could see it had comic potential.

"And then, having told him what I thought of him, I just fainted on the spot. Bang. God, that carpet tasted disgusting."

When she had exhausted the story, Charlie looked at her. "Dan tells us you're going to interview at Zaxxo. Are you sure about that? He's got a hell of a reputation."

Charlie told her about how Gal Bezman had sat on stage at a banking conference with one of his colleagues at the bank, called him 'a total conman', then refused to apologise. He was also rumoured to have sacked a team of coders on the spot because they wouldn't work the weekend to correct some errors he had found.

"Sounds like my kind of boss," said Dan.

Charlie, Jo and Bee said they would go and get some coffees on the basis that Dan and Nicole would want some time alone.

Nicole leant over and put her head on Dan's chest. "Have you forgiven me?"

Dan stroked her hair, "We can talk when I'm home. Even plan another weekend away for when I'm better."

"That would be lovely." Nicole couldn't think far beyond her interview and her trip to Rothbury. Guilt coursed throughout her. She didn't trust herself to speak.

*

Nicole's interview with Gal was at ten o'clock at their offices in Canary Wharf. Zaxxo was housed alongside a bunch of other fintech businesses high up in one of the massive skyscrapers that dominate the East London skyline. Smokers, shivering in shirts and blouses, lined the pavement outside. The reception desk was as long as a bowling alley and manned by ten suited women with sculpted hair and caked make-up awaiting visitors. Nobody looked like they wanted to be there. It was very different from the run-down, seedy ambience around Yellow Razor's office in Soho. For a moment Nicole wished she was back there with Chandra and her team swapping banter. This was a much more grown-up workplace – one where you traded fun for money.

When she reached the 40th floor there was no-one there to meet her and zero indication of where Zaxxo was located. Each company looked the same, boxed in with glass walls. There were company names on all the doors and young people crammed together at small desks, many with headphones jammed on their heads.

Nicole set off to follow the walkway that covered the building in a rectangle. As she walked, she noted companies with every sort of name but Zaxxo. A text popped up – *u ok? Gal.* She was about to reply when she saw Zaxxo on one of the glass doors. Inside she could see about thirty people working at computers.

A thin young girl with a powder-white, elfin face dressed in blue jean dungarees opened the door for her when she knocked.

"Yes?"

Nicole asked for Gal, and with a dismissive wave the girl gestured towards an office. "Corner."

Everyone turned and looked at her as she crossed the office. With her bright red Zara suit and navy-blue leather Emma Hope shoes, she looked out of place among the T-shirts and trainers.

Gal was sitting on the desk as she entered. He wore a thick dark brown cardigan with a hood, baggy blue jeans with holes at the knees and black suede Chelsea boots. The wide, muscular bulk of his shoulders was the first thing that struck her as he put out his hand to shake hers.

"Nicole, welcome. Ellie has told me a lot about you." He indicated a chair next to a small round table where she should sit. "Has anyone offered you coffee?"

"No."

He walked over to the door and made a drinking motion to the dungaree girl. "Black, OK? We're out of milk, I'm afraid."

He moved the other chair away from the table and sat down. A bleep caused him to glance for a split second at his Apple Watch. "Excuse me…" He lifted the watch. "Hey Siri, text Jacob *absolutely not.*" He pressed Send on the watch. He looked at Nicole. "Fucking developers and their shortcuts. Thanks for coming. What do you know about Zaxxo?"

His eyes, almost black, lasered onto her.

Nicole said, "What I have gleaned from your website, social media and the news. It's really impressive, Mr Bezman."

He waved his arm as if swatting a wasp. "Call me Gal. Take no notice of that. Everything written is six months out of date. One day soon we're going to be the most important bank in the world. Banks have been failing consumers for years and years, ripping them off, giving them the worst deals they can get away with. I founded Zaxxo because I knew that, with the latest technologies – cloud, mobile, AI, blockchain – I could build a bank ten times as good as any that exist today. Right now, we're just a card for sharing meal costs and saving on exchange rates, but we're going to be so much more very soon."

Nicole hoped he didn't ask her to explain AI or blockchain to him. "Your press coverage is amazing. Everyone talks of Zaxxo as the most exciting tech business in Europe."

"Do you think it could be better? I mean, that's why you're here."

Nicole said, "There are two areas I would look at. Firstly, you need to get your message out to people who aren't so switched on to the latest tech innovations. You need to move on from the early adopters, those wealthy, super-mobile London types, and get the message out to all the young people around Europe. Secondly, I think you could be a bit better at articulating your vision. It's brilliant, but you make it sound a little negative. You come across as a bit surly in interviews…"

Gal put his elbows on the table and started stroking his forehead with both hands. "I am scared of saying the wrong thing. My English isn't that good."

"Seems pretty good to me."

"Yes, because I'm relaxed. It only takes one bad sentence or a misunderstood statement and the FCA will be down on us like a ton of bricks But, yes, you are right about both those things. The other challenge is to take our story international as we expand into other markets. We're fine in London – everybody knows us – but we're nothing in New York, Berlin or Hong Kong."

Gal was very different from the person Nicole had expected. Weakness was the last thing she had thought she would hear from him. He also looked very tired. One of the articles had said he often stayed up all night checking the code his team had done during the day. He looked at least five years older than his twenty-nine years.

"So, Nicole, tell me about yourself. You know all about me. I know nothing about you."

Nicole told him about her work at Yellow Razor, her clients and awards. For some time, he grilled her about how she handled bad news and hostile media.

"And what about your life before work?"

"Where do I start? I was born in Somerset. My father

left when I was about thirteen. My mother didn't handle the divorce very well, so, after a year, partly because my father ran out of money, I left my boarding school and went back to live at home and go to the local state school. I did quite well in my A-levels and got a place to read Biochemistry at Newcastle, but my mother was ill, so I deferred. I had no idea what I wanted to do but knew I needed to start making a living. I got a job in a PR company near Bath. Loved the work but the owners ran it really badly, so, after a couple of years, I applied for the job at Yellow Razor and got it. It's been great."

"So, if it's all so good, why have they sent you to me?"

Nicole hesitated. What could she say? The truth wasn't going to fill Gal with enthusiasm for her. Then again, what did she have to lose? New start and all that. At least it would tell him that she wasn't all Home Counties gentility.

She explained about the argument with Po. When Gal laughed at her behaviour, she also told him about the letter and the car crash. His eyes never left her as she talked. She swallowed hard to keep her tears at bay.

"It doesn't sound like you should have been at work. I'm not sure you should be here now either. Why did you come?"

"I need the money. I have living expenses here and I need to send some to my mother." She hesitated. "And I want to be involved in something that makes a difference."

"You will certainly do that here. That's our mission, what gets me up every morning and keeps me up every night. Sorry, our coffee never came. We're always running out. No-one has time to go out and buy any."

Nicole said it didn't matter, and then silence settled between them. Gal grinned at her. "I'll tell you what. Can you stay here for another hour? I've got an interview with The Financial Post in 30 mins. Why don't you sit in and babysit me? OK?"

Nicole said she would be happy to do so. She couldn't see what value she might contribute, but she guessed she might be able to deflect any nasty questions. What did she have to lose? If she screwed up, she wouldn't see him again anyway. Gal told her to go and sit with the dungaree girl while he did some emails. Did she have the job? Was this a trial run?

There was a spare chair at the desk down from the girl's, so she sat down and looked at her phone. Dan had sent her several messages, all riffing on his general boredom and desire to get back to work as soon as possible.

The dungaree girl thrust out her hand. "I'm Anya." She had a strong Polish accent and a very beautiful, delicate face, porcelain-white smooth skin, a pert nose and azure-blue eyes. "So, are you going to work here?"

Nicole said she didn't know. "I think you'd be ideal for him. He really needs help with all the, how do you say, niceties of business life. He thinks it's all bullshit, but all the people he needs to influence think all that's very important. But it's hard work – the last PR left after a week complaining she never got home. I don't know why that was such a big deal for her; none of us ever do."

"Isn't this a nice place to work then?" No-one seemed to have spoken to anyone since she had arrived.

"I hate it. It's like #MeToo never happened. All these boys want to do is code, drink beer and eat pizza. Except Gal. He's different." Nicole noticed a blush.

"So why do you stay here?"

Anya fiddled with a silver crucifix that had dropped out of her blouse and said, "It's like a disaster movie. This is the banks." She put one arm out to her side. "And this is us." She put the other arm out. "They come together. BOOM!" She brought both her fists together then opened her fingers and exploded them out. She cackled. "That's why. I'm looking forward to the explosion."

Gal came out of his office as she made the gesture with her hands. He laughed – Nicole guessed he had seen it before – and asked her to go and get the *Financial Post* journalist who was now hovering by the door. Anya trudged off as if reluctant to undertake another menial task.

Gal beckoned to Nicole to go back into his office and pointed for her to sit down at the round table. He gathered up a pile of papers to clear it and threw them behind his desk.

"This guy's a junior banking correspondent. Hopefully, he won't have been brainwashed by his boss and the big banks yet. I'm going to push him to do a profile on us. He's been promising me one for ages."

"What's the hook?" Gal looked puzzled. "What's the reason for him to write the story now? He'll need a hook to hang the story on."

Gal looked amused and brushed his hand over his head. "America. I'm going to launch in America."

"Really?"

"Really."

Anya brought the journalist to the door. He wore an oversized greatcoat with his briefcase hanging from his neck in front of him like a schoolboy on his first day. His hair was thick, ginger and parted at the side as if with a steel comb. Gal caused him to fluster by asking him to sit down. Nicole wondered how he had managed to find his way to their offices without his mother.

Gal set off at 100 miles an hour. As the journalist, Anthony Ansell, raced to keep up with his sketchy shorthand, Gal explained why Zaxxo had been invented – because highly mobile people like him couldn't get the services he needed, at the price he wanted, from existing banks. He unveiled a series of financial frustrations – each of which had prompted some innovation once he had started Zaxxo. Gal grew more and more agitated, reeling off lots of computer acronyms that Nicole – and, she suspected, the journalist – didn't recognise. Every so often Gal returned to his central theme about the stupidity of the banks. Dinosaurs, elephants, mammoths – every kind of animal was summoned up as Gal strove to find the right analogy for his competition.

Anthony interrupted, "Surely you also need to be friends with these creatures? You might need some of their services as you expand?"

"We'd rather die. They're idiots, every one of them." Gal was a little flushed from his rant; beads of sweat appeared on his brow.

"Idiots?" Nicole could see Anthony writing 'idiots' down in capital letters with an exclamation mark.

"Yes, idiots. Greedy idiots."

"Gal is speaking offt he record here, Anthony. Consumer choice is what he really wants to talk about. The option for people to use amazing-value banking services on the move, wherever they are – Bradford, Berlin or, even, Boston. Zaxxo is going to be the mobile bank for everyone all around the world."

Gal looked askance at Nicole and raised his eyebrows as if to say 'shut up'. Nicole didn't know where her speech had come from, but it seemed to have done the trick. Anthony didn't notice as he was scribbling at 100 miles an hour as well until, after thirty seconds, he looked up.

"Boston?"

Gal said, "She isn't an authorised spokesperson for Zaxxo."

"I'll keep it off-the-record if you tell me about Boston. Are you launching in America? That's been a graveyard for European banks in the past."

Nicole said, "Gal?"

Gal looked away. "We're not ready to say that yet."

"Well, I can print the 'idiots' part if you want?" Anthony looked up like an old lady offering a child a sweet. Gal bit his lip and looked over at Nicole.

Nicole didn't think she would be coming back, so what the hell? "Zaxxo will take a softly-softly approach as its first steps into the US. It's unlikely to get a banking licence, in the first instance, so it is probable that we'll look to license some of our technologies to like-minded tech players for the first year."

Anthony whistled. "Good luck with that. Coals to Newcastle. That's a recipe for disaster if ever I heard one. Although, if anyone can do it, maybe you can, Gal." He flipped his notebook shut. "That's been really interesting. Not quite the interview I was expecting."

Now it was Nicole's turn to blush. "Better if you don't quote me."

"I'll just refer to a company spokesperson."

Gal said, "I'd prefer if you didn't write that US story yet."

"Too late. Sorry. You know how these things work."

Gal got up and showed Anthony to the door then turned to face Nicole. There was sweat running down his cheeks. "What did you do that for? We're not ready to tell that story."

Nicole knew it had already been written about in some fintech blogs, but she didn't see what use arguing about it now would be. She'd played what she thought was an ace. She walked out of his office and turned to face him.

"I know, but it's already out there. The idiots story would have been worse." She held out her hand. She wouldn't be seeing him again. "It was lovely to meet you. Good luck with Zaxxo."

Gal didn't move. As she walked through the office, out of the corner of her eye she could see Anya typing away, smirking.

7

Waterloo was rammed with commuters when Nicole arrived around eight o'clock the next morning. People parted as she meandered her way through them. Sleep had been hard to come by the previous night. She needed coffee.

Memories of the disastrous interview kept entering her consciousness with the frequency of cars circling the Arc de Triomphe. She had dressed to cheer herself up. She didn't know what had come over her in that interview. In her long black velvet coat, knee-length black skirt, and stack-heeled black leather calf-length boots, she knew she looked good. For once her outfit wasn't raising her spirits. Today could be the day when she found out what happened to Peter Slaithwaite, and maybe that would make her forget her third car crash, one actual, two metaphorical, in one week.

Her mobile rang. "It's Gal."

"Oh hello. I'm so sorry about yesterday. I was trying to impress you, and I overstepped the mark."

"I want you to come and work for me. You're a warrior. Zaxxo needs warriors and we don't have enough of them." The concourse noise made him hard to hear. Maybe he was thinking of someone else. "So, how about it?"

She would be on secondment from Yellow Razor. If it worked out, she could come on board permanently with a better salary. Nicole told him she needed to give it some thought.

"I want you here as soon as possible. We have lots to do."

She called Dan to tell him the news.

"It sounds amazing. But how do you know he won't fire you in a matter of weeks? Everything I read about them makes them sound like the Wild West. Dad says they are the bane of his life, always announcing stupid deals that cause his customers to call up and complain about theirs. And didn't you read about all those people he fired without compensation last autumn?"

Nicole said she hadn't but that wasn't entirely true. She had skipped that bit in the article when she came to it. "It's a very fast-paced business. Not everyone can keep up."

Dan sighed. "Yeah right, tell that to the employment tribunal." The announcer went on a long run of bulletins and Nicole couldn't hear Dan for a moment.

"Look, you've got do it. You need an adventure. Look at how much I'm loving my job. If the shit hits the fan, we'll all know we went into it with our eyes open. When am I going to see you?"

This was her chance to slip the news of her trip to Rothbury in, but she ducked it. Dan wouldn't approve and, anyway, he didn't need anything more to worry about. She turned 'Find My Friends' off.

"Saturday. We can toast my new job." She texted Gal her acceptance and he replied with a smiley face.

On the train she put on a podcast about the rise of cryptocurrencies. She knew Gal was very excited about them as a way of helping the 'unbanked'. The commentator on the podcast was more sceptical, suggesting the reasons some people didn't want to be 'banked' weren't always entirely legal. After about ten minutes her thoughts drifted as she struggled to keep up with the river of tech acronyms and legalese that dominated the conversation.

Opposite her, a young couple were unpeeling plasters to show each other their new tattoos on their arms. They looked very raw and painful. She looked out of the window at the back gardens of the suburban houses flying past. Zaxxo would definitely take her out of her comfort zone. She'd seen how invigorated Dan had been with his new job. It was her turn now. What did she have to lose? She was twenty-seven. There couldn't be a better time to take a chance. At the back of her mind there nagged the thought that Dan might be super-enthusiastic about the job now, but how would he be when she had to work all night for the tenth night on the trot? He was quite traditional. How many events would he go to on his own before he succumbed to one of the tall, single women who were bound to empathise with his tales of his absent girlfriend? Oh well, some people would kill for a job like this, and she'd regret it forever if she didn't give it a go.

*

Rothbury School was a three-storey, red-brick Victorian Gothic fortress of a building, the kind that – too big to be a hotel or country house – could only be a British boarding school or, possibly, a care home. Dark and imposing, it looked like something The Munsters might live in. Nicole reckoned she had knocked up an additional £10 in cab fare just being driven down the drive. The grounds looked landscaped and well kept, quite different from the scarred fields of her own boarding school.

The cabbie, fishing around for a receipt in case Nicole needed one, looked back at her before she paid and got out. "Your kids go here then? Expensive, I bet."

The hall was as big as a tennis court, with a ceiling just as high. Two forty-foot-high windows at the far end of the hall looked out on to the sports fields. There was a strong smell of carbolic soup and roasting meat. Small boys dressed all in grey scootered around in front of her. She picked on one, who had made the mistake of slowing down to look at her, to ask where she could find the headmaster. He pirouetted on the waxed wooden floor to change direction and said, "I'll take you."

The boy knocked on the door twice, and a booming voice said, "Enter." With two hands the boy pushed the thick door open, gave Nicole a shy nod and ushered her in.

The room was panelled with dark oak. School photos decorated every wall, and discarded sports equipment – golf clubs, tennis rackets, cricket bats – lined the walls. Two deep leather armchairs and a long sofa, all worn with patches on the arms, dominated the centre with an old, overweight Labrador sleeping on one of the chairs. In front of the wrought-iron fireplace there was a small table with a coffee pot and cups. Over in the far corner she could see a head of salt-and-pepper hair nestling above the largest Apple screen she had ever seen.

"Take a seat. I'll be with you in one minute." Nicole sat down at the end of the sofa furthest away from him. As she took in all the smiling faces of boys, mostly black and white, some faded colour, her subterfuge started to sink in. This was Martin De La Hay's command centre, and the house was his kingdom. He alone controlled Rothbury School. He and his family's influence, through some of the school's most distinguished old boys, had permeated every institution instrumental in the governance of the United Kingdom for over a hundred years.

What were the chances that he would welcome her enquiry about Peter Slaithwaite? She pushed her hair behind her ears and checked her phone. There were several missed texts from Dan wondering what she was up to. He never checked in with her when he was working.

A round, florid face revealed itself as the salt-and-pepper man got up. He was wearing a white shirt and a yellow and orange club tie of some description under a thick tweed jacket. The buttons of his shirt strained a little: the band of his trousers folded in on itself under the pressure of his belly, and his flies were half undone.

He gave her a buck-toothed smile as she stood up to shake his hand. He took a moment to let go of her hand. She noticed he had a chunky gold signet ring with some form of eye logo on his little finger.

He didn't take a step back, just stood in her space and stared at her. When she sat down, he was towering over her like Mr Rochester in Jane Eyre.

She looked up at him. "Our son Finn is five. I've heard so many good things about Rothbury, I wanted to come and see for myself."

Martin De La Hay quizzed her about where she lived, where Finn currently went to school and what her husband did for a living. He seemed satisfied that she met the social and financial criteria for becoming a Rothbury parent.

"We better get going then."

Martin showed her around the school. They took in the hall, the dining room, some classrooms, the art room and the science labs. When they entered a room with a teacher and children in, everyone froze and was silent. As they left Martin waved a hand and said, "Carry on."

Then they ascended the highly polished wood staircase that led up to two floors of dormitories. On the first landing they turned left into a room with ten beds. Each bed had a soft toy on it and a bedside table with personal effects such as a book or a photo frame.

Nicole was pleased to see teddies were now permitted. "Don't they get homesick?"

Martin kicked the leg of one of the beds to straighten it. "Did you go to boarding school?"

"For a while. Then my parents took me away." As she stood in the dormitory the warm relief she experienced when her mother had come to take away from her boarding school flooded back.

"We like to think we make a child. There is a very well-honed assimilation process for all new children based on the very latest academic research. My wife supervises it herself. For the first few weeks they all miss their parents and siblings, but, very quickly, they immerse themselves in their studies, the games and the activities. And they make lifelong friends."

Nicole said, "Has that always been the case? Even back in the war?"

Martin turned to the door. "Would you like to see the sports fields?" Without waiting for an answer, he walked outside the dormitory and waited for her.

They went down the stairs, weaved their way through corridors walled with pictures of old boys. Nicole couldn't see any girls even though the school now took them. They walked through a series of changing rooms and out onto a large, rather sad-looking lawn. Flowerbeds of frozen, turned soil and dormant rosebushes were dotted around the lawn borders.

Martin put his arm, uninvited, around Nicole's shoulder and pointed to the horizon. "This is an amazing sight in the summer, Arabella. Flowers in bloom. Shouts and screams of laughter. Boys and girls running around playing games, cricket, tennis, golf and rounders. It's simply heart-warming. I can never get enough of it."

Nicole shrugged his hand off. She wondered if he took as much trouble with other, older, male potential parents. "I can imagine."

At some point, without any consultation, Martin had decided Nicole also needed to see the indoor Olympic-sized swimming pool. As they walked on the hard soil path across the playing fields, Nicole thought they were getting on well enough for her to ask him about Peter Slaithwaite. She was struggling to keep up as Martin De La Hay charged on, arms swinging to propel himself faster, so she had to shout a little.

"My grandfather had a childhood friend who went to Rothbury in the war. He asked me to ask you if you knew what happened to him. They lost touch afterwards."

"What was his name?"

"Peter. Peter Slaithwaite."

Martin stared in silence at the door of the pool house for a moment as if he didn't know where he was.

"Let's have a look when we get back to my study." Martin didn't look at Nicole as he said this. He pushed open the door with both arms, and it flung open hitting the inside wall with a bang. Nicole was relieved there were no children on the other side.

The sharp smell of chlorine hit her nostrils. The pool was a warm fog of steam, full of small girls playing water polo. Screams and shouts echoed off the walls. They stood alongside each other at one end, water splashing on their shoes. Martin said, "We're looking for some investment so we can upgrade the main building and the sports facilities. Competition is relentless in our sector nowadays." He kicked a stray ball back in the pool. "Slaithwaite, you say. Our records aren't so good before about 1965. And data privacy means I can't divulge as much as I used to be able to."

Nicole smiled at him. "Anything would be appreciated. They were best friends, I gather."

They went back into the house via a walled garden. A boy, looking very pale and scared, was waiting outside the study.

"What do you want, McGuire?"

"I've been sent to you, sir. I've been rude to Miss Crabshaw."

Martin De La Hay told the boy he needed to wait outside for five minutes. When they were inside the study, he gestured for Nicole to sit down on the sofa. The Labrador opened one eye and fell back to sleep.

Martin went over to his desk and started bashing keys on his computer. Nicole looked around the study walls. The school was a world within a world. There were the rules of life and then there were school rules. The boys in the photos stared out grim-faced as impassive and erect as soldiers in the war or mineworkers in the Gold Rush. Martin and his predecessors were the kings, the lawmakers. They could change the rules without consultation and punish those who transgressed with impunity. Schools like this produced people who were determined to succeed because they had learnt that, in life, you either make the rules or you are bound by them. They had learnt from personal experience that they didn't want to be the latter. Charlie was obsessed by being in control. Everything he said or did was designed to achieve and/or exercise that power. She wondered if Dan would start to demonstrate the same traits. So far, he showed no sign of it, but his passion for all things renewable and green was palpable and, once he had settled into his new job, the moral high ground would be his for the taking. She just hoped he stayed humble and curious.

"Slaithwaite, you say?" Nicole nodded.

"He left in 1942 and died in 1963."

Nicole started. "That's very young. Do you know how he died?"

Martin got up and walked towards her. "That's all I have, I'm afraid. Our records are pretty sketchy from that period."

"Would there be a photo of him somewhere in the school, do you think?"

"I don't think they go that far back. We might have one in storage. I can look and let you know. Our records from the war aren't very comprehensive, I'm afraid."

"Thank you so much." Nicole decided to push a little further. "Do you think the boys were happy up at Blair

Gowan in the war? It must have been so hard for them all away from their parents for so long."

He pointed down the corridor to show Nicole the way out. McGuire looked at Nicole as if she might be his saviour. She whispered to him, "I was always rude to teachers at school. Never did me any harm."

Martin, possibly a little deaf as he hadn't registered her aside, said, "I have no idea. I've told you all I know. It is a very different school, today as you can see for yourself. You should go if you want to get your train." She hadn't told him anything about train times.

Nicole had forgotten to ask the best number for a local taxi, but Martin had disappeared with the forlorn boy traipsing after him. She looked around the main hall. All these children coming and going for nearly a hundred years. Someone would know. He died so young. Was it connected to what happened at the school? She could tell Martin De Lay Hay had read things about Peter Slaithwaite he hadn't wanted to reveal. He had been reading for too long just to find the year of his death. He was so cocksure. But if he thought he would be able to stop her, he was wrong.

8

On Saturday morning around 10am Nicole got a train from Waterloo down to Pulborough. She could have driven but she still didn't fancy it after the accident. And she still kept getting dizzy.

At the other end Charlie picked her up in his Range Rover. He asked her how she was and then said, "So you got the job? Good luck." Then he was silent for the rest of the journey.

When they drove up outside the house Dan hopped out, wincing a little in pain, on his crutches. Jo came out behind him wiping her hands with a dishcloth. Nicole noticed Charlie catch Jo's gaze then flash Nicole a dismissive look. If Jo disapproved of her visit, then she had made a mistake.

Nicole ran over to embrace Dan. He dropped one crutch against his side so he could get closer to her. They hugged until he signalled, with a cry of pain, that his ribs weren't ready for too much contact.

She followed him into the sitting room. He dropped down, crutches falling to the floor on either side, into one of the deep, soft armchairs and Nicole sat on the arm stroking his head. He looked five years older than a week ago. The skin around his eyes looked lined, his skin was dry and scaly, his hair greasy.

He said, "Congratulations on the job. I'm so proud of you. Not many people could come back from a car crash to impress such a feisty guy."

"I don't think he's that tough. He wants people to take control of situations. It's only when they don't do that, he gets difficult. I took an outrageous liberty with that *Financial Post* interview that backfired big time, but he seemed to forgive me. Look, shall I get us some coffee?"

*

Nicole found Jo sitting at the huge oak kitchen table peeling potatoes and carrots. Radio 4 was on in the background, some moronic panel game with no point or winners. She sat down opposite her.

"Can I help?"

"You can talk to me."

Nicole sat and wondered what they could talk about. The men tended to dominate the conversation in the Newhouse family. No wonder Bee constrained herself to flying visits. Dan obviously got his gentleness and emotional intelligence from Jo. Often, she saw her watching the verbal pyrotechnics at the dinner table with amused eyes.

Jo said, "How's your mother?"

"Same as ever."

"Bradford-on-Avon is lovely. I was brought up not that far from there: Melksham. My father was the vicar."

"I didn't know that."

"My mother, Felicity, loved it. She's buried there."

There was more silence. Then Jo seemed to raise her shoulders a little as if giving herself strength to say what she wanted to say.

Nicole said, "What did you do before you married Charlie?"

Jo turned and leant her back against the sink with her hands on the draining board. "Not as much as I planned, to be honest. As you know, I'm about ten years younger than him. I had just gone to university in Exeter, veterinary science. I was up to London for the weekend about halfway through my second term. A friend suggested we went along to an England match at Twickenham as her parents had some tickets. Against France, I think. Anyway, you probably know everyone has picnics out the back of their cars in the car park. Charlie was in the car next door with some of his City mates, shouting and messing around. Half of me thought they were very cool, and the other half thought they were complete idiots. But I must have kept looking at them as, after about ten minutes, Charlie came over to talk to me. He was really sweet, asking all about me, my course etcetera."

"Did he ask you out?"

"After the match, he did. We went out that evening. Julia, my friend, was very understanding given we had plans. He took me to an Italian by the cinema on Kensington High Street. Lots of limoncello as I remember. After that I came up to London most weekends to see him. I was a bit awestruck, to be honest, being a provincial girl from the West Country. Charlie and his friends were always having fun. It was just crazy. I got caught up in it. Then, that summer, I found out I was pregnant with Dan. Charlie wanted us to have the baby and get married. I was torn. I was still set on becoming a vet, but I knew I had been neglecting my studies and had to get serious if I was going to get a decent degree. But I really loved Charlie, and I knew I wanted children. Just not quite so early."

"You work at the vets, don't you? That must scratch that itch to some extent."

"Yes, but it's just admin work really. I'd like to do more. Maybe even get finish my degree and get qualified. I just need to sort Bee out and get Dan back on his feet."

Jo turned back and restarted on the potatoes. For a while neither of them said anything.

"Will you do anything about that letter? Who can resist a mystery like that?"

Nicole wasn't 100% sure she could trust Jo. She reckoned on balance she could.

"If you were me, would you go up there and do some digging around? If you had the time, I mean? I told Dan and Charlie I wouldn't."

Jo got up with the peels and, putting them down the InSinkErator, looked out into the garden. She still had a very slim figure for someone her age. Nicole hoped she had similar good fortune. David Mitchell's voice boomed out of the radio, invading the silence.

She stayed looking out, away from Nicole. "Between you and me? Yes, I would."

"Why do you say that?"

"I don't think you will forgive yourself if you don't. You'll always wonder what happened to him. After all, you are the one who found it after eighty years. No-one else did."

Nicole noticed that she wiped her eye before she turned back to her. "You should get our patient that coffee. You know how to use the Nespresso machine, don't you?"

A few minutes later Nicole carried two mugs back into the sitting room. Dan was still sitting in the chair staring into space.

He looked up as he took a mug, cradling it in case it was hot. "Thanks, hun." Nicole sat opposite him on the sofa.

Dan said, "Look, I've been thinking. When I'm a little better, how about you move in with me? I would love to be able to wake up every day and see you. We're engaged. It's stupid to be apart now. What do you think?"

Nicole looked him in the eyes, smiled and said nothing. She just needed some breathing space. Everything was already happening too fast.

"I know what you're thinking. He wants a nurse. It's not that, honestly. We shouldn't do it until I'm better. But it would be fun to cook and eat together every night, make a home together. Save money for the wedding too."

Her misgivings all came back to her. A new life was about to start, one that would require her time 24/7. She was determined to do well. She had waited for so long. Dan would do more than his share, but did she want to be beholden to someone else for cooking, shopping and household tasks? Right now, if she didn't want to clean the bathroom at the weekend, she didn't. If she wanted to stay in bed all Saturday watching *Friends*, she could. When she did something with Dan it was because she wanted to, not because doing it would require her to break away from the status quo. She knew marriage would require a full commitment to the Newhouses, but she wanteds some space first

She went over and knelt on the carpet in front of him. Kneeling wasn't a good look, but she figured it might make up for the hesitation. She took his hands.

"It's a lovely idea. Can I think about it? It's more about timing than anything else? We've both got a lot on."

"Of course." Dan bit his lip and looked upwards to avoid her gaze. She knew he had got everything he wanted since he was a little boy. The photos of him as a schoolboy with various teams and cups on the upstairs landing gave testimony to that. A part of her wished she could just say 'yes' just to please him, but there was only one of her and the more she thought about Zaxxo, Peter's letter, the next few months, the more the excitement built inside her.

"You're that much older than me. You've done more. I feel like I'm only just getting going. I want to be with you so much. Right now, everything's a little crazy and I just need a little time."

Dan's eyes were watery. "I know. It's not much fun looking after an invalid, is it?"

Nicole held his hand and looked into his eyes. He knew her. His eyes were wide open on that front.

Dan said, "I love you, Nicole." His words hung there for the moment. She thought about the letter. Not the greatest future-wife behaviour.

She tried to say the same words back but, for some reason, they wouldn't come.

*

Dan hobbled into the kitchen and complained his legs were aching, so Jo fussed around him with cushions. Bee had turned up a few moments before and was irritating her father by playing with her phone. Her hair stuck up like a cockatoo and there were traces of white powder around her nose. Nicole guessed she hadn't been to bed for very long, if at all.

Charlie opened two bottles of Bordeaux – say one thing for him, thought Nicole, he never stints on the booze – and sniffed the corks with an air of ostentation. He said, "2010 – what a majestic year." Then he proceeded to carve the roast chicken while Jo served the potatoes and vegetables. In the kitchen Dan leant against the Aga and stirred the gravy.

Charlie said, "Any chance you can put your phone away, Bee?" Bee turned her phone over and looked at it with longing.

They all had food in front of them. Charlie plunged his knife and fork into the chicken on his plate. "You've got quite a task on your hands with that Gal character, haven't you? I suppose you heard my new role includes overseeing our card business. We'll be in competition. You, David; me, Goliath."

Nicole swallowed hard. We all know how that one ended. You didn't have to be a financial analyst to know that Zaxxo was set on taking as much business as it could from banks like his.

She said, "I've fallen on my feet. Yellow Razor didn't want me, so it was this or get fired."

Charlie said, "You had no choice? No choice at all?"

Dan said, "C'mon, Dad. Be nice. You know how tough the job market is right now. Nicole's had a real stroke of luck with this. Zaxxo is one of the most dynamic and fast-growing businesses in the world."

Charlie said, "All I'm saying is that you need to be careful. That guy doesn't play by the rules. He doesn't care about people. Look at all those unfair dismissal and employment tribunal stories that keep appearing in the press. All he does is slag banks like us off. It is really unhelpful to the whole industry at large. Consumer confidence in all of us is very fragile. My CEO, Ralph, was on a conference panel with him the other day and Gal told him he didn't know what he was doing. Forty years Ralph has been in the industry, forty years. You'll need to rein him in."

Everyone looked at Nicole. She speared a baton of carrot and chewed on it.

Dan said, "Dad, change only happens if people speak up and act. Look at all the progress with climate change for all those car and oil companies to go green. Everyone has to work together and see the big picture. There isn't a right or wrong here. You and Zaxxo are on the same side."

Nicole said, "You know me well enough to know I won't be taken for a ride. But, at the same time, I'm joining Zaxxo because Gal has a vision, and I want to help him achieve it. Everyone expects choice these days. People our age want banks to serve us the way we live our lives – easy-to-use, easy-to-understand, no rip-offs–"

Charlie puffed, "No-one's ripping anybody off. Proper banking costs money to provide – not least because there's so much fraud. Ask your friend what his fraud provisions are. Skeletal I'll bet!! Don't come running to me when they all go tits up."

Dan said, "You need to back off Nicole right now. She's a guest and you're bullying her."

Jo, reddening, said, "Dan's right, darling." Charlie started to cut his meat up with exaggerated care.

Nicole had zero idea what Zaxxo's fraud provisions were. She took a sip of wine. She wasn't prepared to be defeated. She was about to speak out when Bee interrupted.

"I think it's great. Fuck the banks, that's what I say! Where do I get a Zaxxo card?" Bee had woken up.

Jo said, "Bee, please!"

"Fuck. Fuck. Fuck the banks."

Charlie said, "They paid for your school fees."

"Rather had the money."

Charlie said, "And your rent now."

"Moved out."

Jo said, "But where are you living?"

Bee grinned at Nicole. "With Nicole." Nicole didn't need that. But she didn't need Bee as an enemy either.

Nicole said, "It's temporary."

There was silence around the table. Everyone focussed on eating and drinking. The kitchen clock ticked. Bee turned her phone over and started scrolling through it. Nicole didn't want Charlie to have the final word on her new job.

"There's nothing wrong with a bit of competition, is there? Room for everyone. That's what ensures we consumers keep getting a good deal. Monopolies or cartels — is that what you call them? — always get busted one way or another. Anyway, Zaxxo is tiny. I don't think any of the big banks have much to worry about for a long while yet."

That seemed to placate Charlie, and the subject changed to the problems the political leaders were experiencing with their respective parties. It was Dan's turn to take the heat as he saw himself as a liberal whilst his parents were dyed-in-the-wool Tories and reluctant supporters of the current beleaguered Prime Minister.

*

After they had cleared up lunch, Nicole took Caesar for a walk with Jo in the woods and Charlie and Dan watched the football. It was Spurs versus Liverpool. As a Chelsea fan, Nicole had taken a vow at birth to hate Spurs and always told people she wouldn't watch them on principle unless they were playing Cruella. Bee had left the table claiming a migraine. No-one objected.

They walked to the bottom of the garden, through a gate, and out on to a path alongside a ploughed field. Jo was complaining about Bee and thanking Nicole for her support. Caesar bounded off into the woods in search of a squirrel. Bee had confided in Nicole that her contract at the charity was ending and sworn her to secrecy. Prospects of any contribution to Nicole's rent were zero. Jo didn't need to have that worry on top of everything else.

They entered some woods and headed upwards to a clearing at the top of the hill. Jo said, "I'm sorry about Charlie going on about your new employer. He is terrified of being put on the scrapheap. One mistake and he's toast. All men his age are these days. He sees businesses like yours as a huge threat."

They reached the top and admired the view. The clouds had cleared revealing hills, fields and dense woods as far as they could see. Caesar stood behind them panting from his exertions.

"I hope you find out what happened to that poor boy

in the letter. I hated boarding school. Never wanted Dan to go but Charlie insisted. I cried so much when he went and missed him so badly. By the time I got him back he was an adult ready to leave home. What a waste. It must have been a hundred times worse in the war – so far from home, never able to go back, hardly ever seeing one's parents."

Nicole took her hand. "I promise I will do everything I can. Just please keep it to yourself."

Jo kissed her on the cheek. "I promise."

*

Nicole went back into the sitting room where Charlie was snoring, and Dan was watching a war movie – '*Where Eagles Dare*'. One of those films where a small bunch of monosyllabic men go into the heart of enemy territory and kill hundreds of Germans so they can take over a power station or a castle. Nicole's father had loved them. She reckoned she knew her way around films like '*The Dambusters*', '*The Heroes of Telemark*', and '*633 Squadron*' better than any boy. Clint Eastwood was busy machine-gunning a succession of Germans who had made the mistake of poking their heads out into a corridor.

Dan looked up as she came and sat on the arm of his chair. "Good walk?"

Nicole relayed Jo's comments about boarding schools. It was the first time Jo had opened up in any way to her and it made her determined to keep going no matter what discouragement Charlie gave her.

She decided to go upstairs and read the book she had brought with her – *Steve Jobs* by Walter Isaacson. If she was going to work with a crazy genius, she needed to be prepared. The afternoon light was fading fast and the Newhouse's reluctance to turn the heating on meant she had to climb under the covers. As soon as she lay in the bed, the book dropped on to the floor and she fell asleep.

It was half past five when she re-emerged downstairs. Charlie, now nursing a large tumbler of whisky, and Dan, a bottle of Corona, were in the sitting room in the middle of some animated conversation. As she hit the bottom of the stairs, she had heard raised voices and the words 'Martin' and 'Rothbury'.

"Oh hello, Nicole, good sleep?" Charlie, re-dosed with alcohol, was in his charming phase, the one he spent about an hour in before the second and third drinks kicked in and he got obstreperous. Nicole went and sat on the sofa opposite them. A rugby match flickered in silence on the TV.

Charlie said, "Would you mind if you dropped the whole letter thing for a little while? I'm not saying forget it completely; just park it for a few months. What do you say?"

Nicole looked at Dan. "God, this bloody letter. I have dropped it. OK? Why?"

Charlie said, "I can't say. When I can, if I can, I will." Dan had flushed a little at the neck, often a sign that he was stressed. She didn't know why he had flip-flopped since she had been out on the walk.

Dan said, "It's a bit tough on Nicole when she has given up on something that really interests her. Can't you give us a hint?"

"No."

He was treating her like that child in the fairy tale who asks why the emperor has no clothes. If it wasn't her choice of job, it was her choice of personal obsession.

"I wouldn't have time to do anything about the letter anyway. The next few months will be pretty full on. Bashing all those big banks. Full-time job." She grinned at Charlie, and he gave her a rather hopeless smile back. Even he couldn't attack her on two fronts at the same time.

9

She was back in her flat by nine o'clock that night. She had three days free before she started at Zaxxo in the last week of February. Plenty of time to sort her wardrobe, tidy her flat and read some business books about Barclays, HSBC and Santander. Her heart sank a little at the prospect, but those Chinese proverbs about warfare always stressed that the secret to success was to know your enemy better than they knew you.

Her phone rang. No caller ID. She hated that.

"Hello."

"Hello. Is that Nicole? Nicole who was with Dan Newhouse at Blair Gowan last week?"

"Yes, it is. Who's that?"

"It's Shona from the front desk. I got your number off your fiancé, Dan. Told him I had found an earring of yours. I was so sorry to hear about your accident. Thank God you're both OK."

Nicole said that she was and asked what she wanted at such a late time on Sunday night. Shona wouldn't be calling just for a chat. It must be serious.

"I hear you were asking Barbara up the hill about the school in war and that she wouldn't talk to you."

"Yes, she slammed the door on me."

"Well, I was talking to my nan about it. She used to play with the boys when she was a young girl. She wants to talk to you."

"Why?"

Shona's speech slowed. "She's not well and her memory is going. Although she's better at what happened fifty years ago than what happened last week. She's as fit as a fiddle in my view, but she's a drama queen at heart and says she needs to talk to someone before she dies. Can you come up soon?"

Nicole thought about her proposed schedule for the next few days. She hated clothes shopping. The books looked boring. Bee would only mess the flat up again. And she didn't want to do anything Charlie Newhouse said.

"Yes, I can. I'll come tomorrow. Text me your nan's address."

She could keep 'Find My Friends' off, and she'd be there and back in day. She was nervous about driving after the accident, but it would be quicker and cheaper. No-one would be any wiser. The business books stared back at her as she fired up her laptop for a bout of Netflix.

*

Bee was asleep, fully clothed on the sofa, as she tiptoed out of the flat at 6.30. Martha had pushed a note under her door – "When is she leaving?"

When she got to her car, Nicole started it, put on all the heaters and, shivering, scraped the ice off her front and back windows with a credit card. Soon, she was travelling across Battersea Bridge and heading out west. She had downloaded an eight-hour true crime podcast to keep her amused if she got bored of her fintech ones.

Even with the relative luxury of an automatic clutch, she soon grew nervous about the distance she had to travel. It wasn't long before cars were overtaking her on either side and lorries were swaying in her direction. She ached all over and her head hurt. For a moment she wished Dan was driving, but then she remembered the crash.

Shona had been pretty relaxed about when Nicole should arrive, which was lucky as, with a couple of breaks, Nicole didn't think she would make it up much before lunchtime. The arrangement was that she would come and find her at Blair Gowan. Shona had said that her granny might want a sleep after lunch, so it made sense to come about three. The twists and turns of her podcast should have engrossed her as she cruised through the misty countryside, but she had her own real-life mystery now. In a few hours she would know much more. She just had to concentrate on staying on the road and alive. Every time her curiosity spurred her to speed up, her caution and fear caused her to slow down. Out of the corner of her eye she could see Dan's name flash up on the mobile on the passenger seat. He didn't deserve such duplicity. He didn't deserve such a domineering and difficult father either. For a moment it made her glad she didn't have a father on the scene to stop her doing things anymore but, as ever, that didn't last long. She hadn't spoken to him for a year and there was no sign that might change anytime soon.

*

She was exhausted as she pulled into Troutbeck Bridge around one fifteen. Despite a ten-minute nap in a service station outside Stoke-on-Trent, her limbs were determined to stay put as she tried to lever herself out of the car at Blair Gowan. She knew already that she wasn't driving back that night. She'd have to come up with a good excuse.

Shona came out of the hotel. "Bet you're pooped. Do you want something to eat?"

There was an office behind the reception desk. There were two desks with papers piled on them and a computer on each one. The gleaming terminals were as big as a case of wine. It smelt of air-freshener.

"Everyone's at lunch. I figured you could come in and out of here without anyone knowing."

"Look, I might need to stay the night. That drive was a killer. Is that possible?"

Shona sat down at the computer, tapped at the keyboard, and, after some delay, said she could arrange something. Then she passed Nicole over a plate of tiny, thin sandwiches cut into triangles.

"No expense spared."

Nicole said, "Thanks. I'm so glad you called. I was on the verge of giving up. How did you know?"

"My aunt was outside feeding the chickens, and she heard you and your boyfriend talking about it on the lane last Saturday." Their public row, Nicole thought, she should have known better but then, every cloud... "She told me, I told my nan and – boom – it was like a lightning strike. She was determined to see you, wouldn't take no for an answer. 'I'm going to talk to that girl if it's the last thing I do…" They both laughed and Nicole had to put her hand over her mouth to stop spitting crumbs everywhere.

"Do you know what she wants to tell me?"

"No, but she hates talking to strangers, so I don't think she is going to waste your time getting to the point."

Ten minutes later they set off in Nicole's car. All around them the peaks soared up, dwarfing everything that came into their presence. Shona directed them down a series of undulating, single-track country roads until they reached a ford. Nicole stopped and Shona signalled for her to drive over. The car clattered and bumped as it traversed the water. The exhaust pipe was already a little loose, so Nicole prayed that it survived the crossing intact. Mossy trees hung over the river and blocked out the sky.

Nicole said, "Why are you helping me, Shona?"

"Nan brought me up. My mum was never around. Working all the time. She was always telling me stories of how tough it was in the war and how awful the school was. I owe her."

When they got through the ford, Shona told her to turn left up a tired, potholed, gravel drive bordered with unkempt eight-foot-high laurel hedges. A modest box-square 70s-style cottage presented itself in front of them. A thin plume of grey smoke swerved its way out of the chimney stack and up into the clouds above. Two lanky Irish wolfhounds wandered around outside the porch.

Shona said, "Oh look, a fire. Maybe she's made a cake too?" They got out of the car and went up to the front door. Shona pushed it open. "Secure as ever, I see."

The hall floor was covered with battered outdoor

clothing and boots, crates of empty bottles, cash-and-carry stacks of tins, and old pieces of broken furniture. The ceiling had fallen in at the far end.

Shona said, "It's a toss-up as to what goes first – Nan or the cottage. In here…"

They turned left into a tiny sitting room. A haze of smoke hung around at head height, but the fire in the grate wasn't giving off much heat. There was a threadbare sofa, a TV showing some property programme, and a high-backed armchair. This, Nicole thought, was the home of a woman who was on the verge of checking out.

In the armchair, next to the fire, nestled between piles of newspapers and magazines sat a frail old lady in multiple layers of warm clothin. She looked up from her doze and gave them a gummy smile. Her top layer was a dirty, hand-knitted burgundy cardigan with a tartan rug over her legs. Although her face was as lined as a walnut, her eyes sparkled. Nicole's initial reaction was that she was in the presence of someone who had always tried to be kind no matter what life threw at her. Rather like Shona, who she was starting to like very much.

Shona said, "Nan, this is Nicole. The girl who was asking about the school in the war."

Nanny Bristow nodded as Shona talked. She pointed to a dining chair set up against the wall and mimed for Nicole to bring it over and sit next to her. Shona said she would make some tea.

Nicole sat down next to Nanny Bristow and gave her the sweetest smile her exhausted body could muster.

"Shona said you spent time at Blair Gowan when it was a school, Nanny Bristow."

Nanny Bristow's eyes were closed. For a moment Nicole thought the old lady had gone to sleep again. It was already starting to get dark and the only light in the sitting room was the flicker of the television and the orange glow of the fire's embers. But then she turned her head towards Nicole and started to talk in a low voice.

"Call me Carol, dear. Like Christmas but all the year round," she chuckled. "My mother used to go to the school to cook and clean. They were so short of staff you see. Just the old man, the nurse and a couple of girls. All the men who could had gone to the war. The old man, Clive De La Hay, he was a bit damaged by the war, the first one that is, a bit twisted in the head. He shouldn't really have been put back in charge but young Mr Roger, the headmaster, had gone off to fight, you see. You saw a lot of that around that time. People thrown into jobs, not suited to them. I used to go up there and keep my mother company before and after school. My father was off at the war too, and I wasn't interested staying at home when I could be at the school playing with the boys.

"It was a nice place most of the time, but sometimes the atmosphere changed, and it wasn't anymore. The boys got to do pretty much what they liked. The old man drank whatever he could get his hands on, and the nurse liked to shut herself in her room with a book when she wasn't on duty and often when she was as well. So, the older boys ran the place. As I got to know the school, I liked it less and less; so did my mother, truth be told, but she needed the money. The younger boys were the most unhappy. Sometimes they just cried and cried. They missed their parents, who couldn't come and see them because they were busy with the war effort and, even if they had time, there was no petrol. If the older boys thought the younger boys stepped out of line or were being too pathetic, they would punish them. They were so horrible, just horrible…"

At this point Nanny Bristow took out a handkerchief and wiped her eyes. With extreme care, anxious not to break the spell, Shona handed Nicole a cup of tea.

Nicole put her hand on Nanny Bristow's. "Go on."

None of this was in the Rothbury prospectus. Usually, schools emphasised their pedigree with extensive recounting of their origins. The second world war warranted a single line on the website. As Nanny Bristow continued Nicole became more and more convinced, she had made the right decision. Nanny Bristow fumbled in a bag for a handkerchief and wiped her nose and mouth.

"They would pick on some of the smaller boys, thinking up foul punishments just for the fun of it. Some of the boys used to boast about them to me afterwards but I just ignored them. I would just put my hands over my ears. No-one stopped them so they just kept going. They used to carry boys up the field to the shepherd's hut in their pyjamas and leave them there for hours. Sometimes they threw the boy in the lake afterwards. It was disgusting and one time, I told them so. Those boys just laughed at me and carried on. I was scared of them, if I'm honest. There was no-one around to defend me if I got on the wrong side of them.

"Then very early one morning I was in the farmyard out back and I heard some whimpering. I looked in all the animal pens – pigs, chickens, dogs – but couldn't see anything. The only place left was where they kept the mad stallion, I thought to myself there can't be anyone there, that horse's crazy, deranged from having a gun fired too close to it. But there was nowhere else the cries could be coming from, you see."

She wiped her eyes again. "I can still see it, still see him. On the ground in front of the stable there was this small boy in a dressing gown all hunched up and crying."

"Who was it? Was it Peter Slaithwaite?"

"I think so. My memory's not great on names anymore."

"So, what did you do?"

"I went over and crouched down alongside him. He was almost comatose, so I helped him get up and took him through the back door and into the kitchen, where my mother was working. She put a blanket over him and fed him some hot tea and porridge. He didn't move – I think he was still in some sort of stupor."

"And then what happened?"

"After a while he started to come round. My mother asked him why he was there. He told her that some boys had taken him from the dormitory and locked him in the stable with the horse. He could have died. Thank God he worked out how to escape."

"Do you know who did it?"

"We had an idea but no proof. My mother went to complain to the headmaster, but she said he was hungover and just kept muttering something about the law of the jungle. They had a huge row. My mother was so annoyed she resigned. She gathered up her coat and bag and we walked out. That was the last time I ever went into the school."

"Peter Slaithwaite died very young. I wonder if what happened at the school was the reason?"

"Sorry, dear, I don't know who it was. But how could

any human be so cruel to another human? Especially when such atrocities were happening all over the world in the name of peace. It was the worst thing I ever saw in my life."

Nicole showed the old lady the letter. She pulled up her glasses, hanging by a string around her wrinkled neck, and squinted at it. Her lips moved as she read it in silence. Nicole thought she read it twice. As she did so, Nicole gave Shona a quiet smile and looked around the room. Faded family photos covered every surface. Nanny Bristow had come from a large family.

Lower lip wobbling, she passed the letter to Nicole. "That brings it all back. The hopelessness of it all. In the scheme of things, no-one really cared about the hardships of those boys. They were alive and protected from the bombs. There were thousands of people being killed every day all around the world. Men from this village. Young men – and women – with their lives ahead of them.

"But I always thought those De La Hays failed the boys at the school. They were in their charge, and they let them down. Sometimes I wake up at night shaking because I've had nightmares about it. All my life." She grabbed Nicole's hand. "It would mean a lot to me if you found out what happened to this boy and, if you meet him or his family, please apologise to them on my behalf. Tell them that, if I had my time again, I would have done everything in my power to stop the bullying. I know my mother felt the same, God rest her soul. Whenever she saw the schoolboys walking along, she would avert her eyes, look at me and I would do the same. Please?"

Nicole couldn't speak. Her words were stuck in her throat, so she just squeezed Nanny Bristow's hand and nodded. The school she spoke of wasn't the same 'jolly hockey sticks' school Charlie and Dan reminisced about.

After a minute, she could speak. "Thank you so much for talking to me. I promise I will try and find out everything I can. And, when I have, I'll come back and tell you."

Nicole left the room so that Shona could say her goodbyes to her grandmother. The house was dark now, and she had to negotiate the hall passage with care.

When they got into the car, Shona looked at her. "She has never told me any of that. I have never seen her speak with such passion and anger. It was as if someone else had inhabited her."

"I'm going to go to Tetbury tomorrow on the way back. See if Peter's family still live there. Whether anyone knows what happened to him."

When they got back to the hotel, the lights were on in every window. It was so welcoming, it was hard to believe the building had once been the location of so much misery. Nicole's phone beeped, in her pocket. It was Dan, the latest in a stream of texts. *Where r u?*

She ignored it. As ever, her memory of Patrick loomed large, but, this time, maybe she could make a difference. The prospect of raw, personal risk ran through her veins, energising and enervating her. Something had changed. Maybe it was the letter? Maybe the car crash? Possibly the prospect of signing up to Zaxxo's guerrilla war? At last, she had something to believe in. Now, maybe, she could believe in herself as well.

All her life, she had felt like an outsider. Always struggling to keep up with people who were more attractive, more talented, more popular. Over the last couple of years, she had begun to catch up. She could see the life she wanted ahead. But she had always played it safe, never wanting to lose what she had. This was different. She had a chance to do something to make up for the worst moment in her life. She didn't have an option.

*

Shona found Nicole the cheapest room and gave her the staff discount as well, but, even so, Nicole closed her eyes when she put her credit card in the machine. It was a box room right at the top of the house, and you had to bend down under the eaves to get into bed, but it was warm with an old-fashioned bath in the corner. She ran as deep a bath as she could risk and lay there imagining the school as it was in 1940. Random shrieks and screams rang out and footsteps clattered along the corridors.

Her phone was shaking beside her bed when she had got out. Dan again. A part of her wished she'd never started this, and they could go back to the simple 'to-and-fro' lifestyle couples, pre-habitation, pursue.

She said, "Hello, darling, how are you?"

Dan was whispering, "Where are you? I've been worried sick." It sounded like his family was hovering about.

He didn't need to know. It wasn't fair on him, what with his broken ankle. If she could accomplish this mission without him knowing, everything would be fine. Normality would be resumed. Although, excited by the prospect of finding the truth the next day, she wasn't sure the new normality would be much like the old one.

"I'm at my mother's. She's not well, so I went down at short notice."

The whisper was raised a few notches. "No, you're not. I rang her earlier when I couldn't get hold of you. She says she hasn't seen you since Christmas. She didn't sound too good, by the way."

Nicole froze. She hated lying. Plan B. What was Plan B? Caught lying to your invalid boyfriend. Not a good look. There was no Plan B. Maybe Plan A+ would suffice?

"Well, I'm not there exactly. I'm on my way. I'm having supper at an old school friend's in Shaftesbury. Una. Do you remember me talking about her? Used to live in Hong Kong."

Dan said he didn't remember Una, so Nicole described to him the complexities of Una's travel arrangements when at school as her parents embarked on their long and painful divorce proceedings.

"Nicole, I don't care where Una used to spend the Easter holidays. Why are you being so mysterious?"

Nicole stared at the ceiling and twisted a lock of her hair between her fingers. Should she tell him? It was the right thing to do.

"Listen…" A new call appeared. It was Gal. "Work's calling. I'll talk to you later."

10

Nicole set off from the hotel just as it was getting light. She'd sat at the bar the previous night, wrestling with a multi-layered club sandwich and drinking Aperol spritzes as she, and Shona, when her boss wasn't looking, trawled the internet looking for any evidence of the Slaithwaites in Gloucestershire. It took two drinks for her to drown her guilt at not calling Dan back.

She found some Slaithwaites in the parish records including a baptism for Peter in 1933, but any further births, marriages or deaths with the name Slaithwaite petered out in the 50s. The house – The Orchard – had been sold several times in the past fifty years, so there was little chance they still lived there. Her best bet was to go there and ask around: the neighbours, the local pub, the church. Just like the detectives in those cold case mysteries she loved. The female one who hesitated mid-sentence during statements of high emotion, that's who she would try to emulate.

Shona gave her a hug before she got in the car and passed

her a sandwich wrapped in paper. "Packed lunch," she said, laughing. "Don't do anything stupid."

Shona wrapped her arms around her torso and stamped her feet on the frosty ground to keep warm. As Nicole started the engine, Shona mimed a telephone to her ear.

She didn't have the appetite to continue the podcast now she was learning the full horror of life at wartime Blair Gowan. Shona had lost her happy-go-lucky air as they searched for any clues. Her grandmother's distress had infected her. Charlie and Dan might want her to stop, but now two people, as well as Nicole, wanted her to go on. She listened to classic noughties hits on the radio to try to keep her spirits up as she negotiated her way alongside the lorries on the M6.

Gal had been texting her. He wanted to launch some new services as soon as she arrived and was quizzing her on the best way to tackle the media. 'No bank has ever done this before, and it will be front page news' was the way he described it to her. Nicole wasn't so sure. Most of Nicole's best work had been generating softer news in the tabloids, so the prospect of dealing with the business and money pages was worrying her. She knew she could do it, but she just didn't know how yet. It was a test – one that she couldn't afford to fail. The sooner she solved the mystery about Peter, the better.

*

It was just after twelve thirty when she reached Tetbury, a picture-perfect Cotswold town with a handful of residents in flat caps, headscarves, and waxed jackets shuffling along the high street. An icy wind caused them to avert their faces as they walked along. The pictures Nicole had seen of the town had all been taken in the summer – blue skies, tourists in shorts and T-shirts, stalls open on the street serving ice creams and fizzy drinks to kids. There was none of that this cold February lunchtime. She wondered if any of these people in the street were a Slaithwaite or knew them. How could she find out?

The Orchard, the address on Peter's letter, was on a lane about a mile to the south of Tetbury. With one eye on the satnav, and the other on the ever-twisting lane, Nicole was glad it was easy to find. It was nestled just back from the road on a tight corner. There were no houses within about half a mile. Findings neighbours wasn't going to be easy. She parked up on the verge outside the house.

It was still damp underfoot. She pushed open the gate and walked up the tarmac drive. Unlike Nanny Bristow's house, there wasn't a plume of smoke to indicate life inside, but there was a blue BMW and, with a passenger door open, a battered grey Golf in the yard.

She tiptoed across the yard to where the cars were. The thick, black back door was open as well, so, with her arm outstretched so she didn't step inside, she knocked on the door twice.

A short, middle-aged, red-faced man came to the door: an oversized owl in fancy dress. His glasses were misted up and his plaid shirt was untucked. Damn, she thought, I've interrupted him. He won't want to speak to me now. The sweet aroma of boiling jam hit her nostrils.

"Yes?"

"I'm sorry to disturb you. I'm Nicole Weymouth. I was hoping to ask you a couple of questions."

The owl stepped back, polishing his glasses on his shirt front as he did so. "What do you want?"

He gestured for Nicole to sit at a kitchen table covered in empty jars. "Jam-making. Messy business; sit down if you can find a spot."

After searching for and failing to find an uncluttered spot for them on the sideboard, Nicole moved a pile of faded local newspapers on to the floor and sat down. The man leant against the dresser opposite. "I'm Laurence, Laurence Simmons. My wife's out I'm afraid."

Nicole looked around the kitchen. It was a proper farmhouse kitchen with Rayburn, sideboard and rocking chair in the corner. An Irish greyhound lolloped up to her and put his muzzle in her hand. She stroked him for a minute as she summoned up the courage to talk.

"This might be an odd request, but it's very important to me, so I had to visit your house. I'm trying to find out about someone called Peter Slaithwaite, who lived here in the war."

"I recognise the name. There was a box of their old photos in the outhouse when we moved in."

A dopamine rush washed through Nicole's body. She was getting nearer. "So, do you know anything about the family?"

He took his spectacles off and placed them on the table then gave an intake of breath, as if contemplating a steep climb, before he spoke.

"Not much. The photos were pre-war so all sepia and white. There were a few quite formal ones, as if the family had gathered together and were obliged to pose like some sort of football team of undertakers and governesses. Pretty depressing, if you ask me. Not something you want to look at twice.""

Nicole nodded. This was more than she had expected. "Could I see them?"

"I haven't seen them for years, to be honest. All kinds of rubbish have been thrown in there since."

"Could I try and find them?"

Laurence looked up at the ceiling as if in exasperation. "You'd be wasting your time. It's pretty dirty in there."

Nicole couldn't let it go. "Please?" She just looked at him, and Laurence stared back at her as if his brain was whirring.

"OK then."

Laurence got up, holding the small of his back as he did so, and led her back out into the yard. They crossed over and entered the red-brick outbuilding. There was a strong smell of motor oil. It was pitch dark inside until Laurence flicked an old Bakelite switch on the wall behind his shoulder.

"Over there." He manoeuvred himself around the motor mowers and mini tractors that littered the floor. "Careful." He stood with his hands on his hips. She was on her own.

At the far end of the room there were piles of boxes and carrier bags as well as several motors and an outboard motor. Nicole walked over and started rummaging through the boxes one by one. They were full of books, videos, vinyl records and old clothes. But no photos. Laurence had walked back out into the yard, presumably to stir his jam. Nicole kept working through the boxes. After about three quarters of an hour, she had worked through all the boxes and bags. She was beginning to wonder if she was wasting her time.

Laurence called out. "Any luck?"

"No."

"Try the drawer in that bedside table then."

Right at the back, partially hidden by the outboard motor, was a dilapidated brown bedside table. She hadn't noticed it at first. She brushed the dust off the top and pulled on the handle. It came away in her hands.

She cursed and looked around for something to leverage it open with. On the ground she spied a metal tent peg, so she used that. It was going to take some brute force, but she figured the table wasn't going to see the light of day again.

After three tries it opened. As Laurence had promised, there were some photos in it.

"Found them!"

Nicole sat down on the seat of one of the mini tractors and looked at the first one, turning on her phone light to see it better. It was a family shot, eleven people in all, ranging from four, she guessed, grandparents or uncles and aunts through two couples in their early thirties to children, aged between about five and ten. The men were in suits and ties, the women in high-necked dresses. The backdrop was recognisable as The Orchard. None of the participants looked particularly happy apart from the youngest child: a girl, who was looking away from the camera, playing with a doll.

There were three photos with a similar tableau of people. In one of them there were only three grandparents, and that row looked especially downcast. Nicole wondered why they had bothered if it was such an unpleasant experience. Perhaps there had been a row? Maybe they all hated the photographer? A death, more likely: that back row looked quite infirm. Either way it was hard, on the basis of these photos, to explain why Peter had been so anxious to return home.

The next photo was smaller and, unlike the others, portrait style rather than landscape. She licked her finger and pushed away the coating of thick, oil-coated dust. At the bottom of the picture mount, in a cut-out square with flowery calligraphy, it said – *Peter Slaithwaite 1941*.

Laurence had come back, "When I bought the house ten years ago, the people who sold it to us apologised for leaving the photos here. They said the people they had bought it off – not the Slaithwaites, by the way – had said they couldn't bring themselves to throw them away."

Nicole couldn't speak. She was mesmerised by the picture. Peter. Finally. He looked so innocent and fresh-faced. She looked up.

"Why?"

"Something to do with that boy. The family were a miserable old lot, I gather. They sold up and left in a rush in the early fifties."

Nicole looked at him, encouraging him to go on. Peter stared up at her. He was dressed, as far as she could tell through the dust and sepia, all in grey – shorts, pullover and shirt. Only the tie was darker. His hair was plastered down in a side parting. The most prominent feature was his eyes, out of proportion with the rest of his face, bordered by thick, long, almost feminine eyelashes. He was standing in a garden with the backdrop of an enormous hill shrouded in mist. Photos of Patrick as a toddler appeared before her eyes. Both were gone. Both should still be here.

She looked back at the other photos. A younger Peter was in the centre of the bottom row. He didn't look any happier, but he looked more confident, as if, when on home soil, he knew where he fitted in the world.

Nicole looked up. "What else do you know about them?" Laurence was hopping from foot to foot and Nicole wondered if he was worrying his jam was spoiling.

"That's it really. There have been about five families living here since them. I keep meaning to bin those photos.

"Can I keep this one?" Nicole pointed to the one of Peter solo. Laurence nodded, looked as if he was about to bite her hand off. "And do you know anyone who might have known them?" He stared at the ceiling for a moment.

"The pub in the centre of the village – the Trencherman's. The Platt family who owns that have had it for four generations. That's your best bet." He paused. "So, why are you interested in this boy? You must have better things to do."

Nicole bit her tongue. He had been helpful, hadn't he? What the hell. She explained about the letter and what Shona's grandmother had said. As she told him she wondered for a moment herself why she hadn't just gone off to Zaxxo and forgotten about it, especially as it looked like it was starting to cause a major fissure in her relationship with both the fiancé she loved and his family. To think how excited she had been when she had started being invited down to Dan's house. A family ready to welcome her. When she had finished talking, Laurence stopped hopping from foot to foot and looked at her with intent.

"Well, be careful. The village is always a little funny about that family."

Nicole, clutching Peter's photo to her breast, excused herself and headed back to the car.

*

Despite the onset of pouring rain, the Trencherman's wasn't hard to find. Nicole aimed for the thin church spire in the distance and found herself at the pub within five minutes. The photograph lay on her passenger seat: Peter's face glaring up at her, daring her to find out his fate. As she parked, she put her coat over the picture.

It was two thirty and the pub was empty. The bar staff – a young, attractive blonde with a top knot and a stout man in his forties – were listening to rap music at high volume and polishing glasses with tea towels.

The stout man shouted at Nicole, "We're closed. Sorry!"

"I don't want a drink."

"We're definitely closed then." The blonde girl turned to him and told him to shut up. Then she leaned over to turn the music down and leant on the bar.

"I like your jacket." Nicole liked it too – suede with tassels from Zara. A treat to herself in the days when she had some spare money at the end of the month. "What can I do for you?"

"I've been told that the Platt family have owned this pub for generations and might know about the Slaithwaites who used to live at The Orchard during the war."

"I'm a Platt. Zoe Platt. That moron behind me, he's my brother." The stout man stuck up a middle finger at the girl. On further analysis Nicole could see that he was about her age: he just hadn't spent much time on self-grooming. Nicole explained what she wanted to know.

Zoe turned to the man. "Wow! A proper mystery. Bro, do you reckon Alice will know about these Slaithwaites?" So, they *were* brother and sister – she looked a lot happier with her lot than her brother. The man pulled a face that implied he wasn't sure if this Alice would or not.

Zoe said, "I'll call and ask." She pushed a button and took up the theatrical pose of someone who is preparing to wait a long time. "Bit slow on her feet. Ah, here goes."

"Hello, Alice, it's Zoe." Pause. "Yes, Zoe, you know, from the pub. That Zoe." Pause.

"I've got someone here who wants to ask you about the Slaithwaites. They lived at The Orchard during the war. She wants to know about the son, Peter." Pause. "No, you'll need to ask her." Pause. "Well, I don't know." Pause. "God, Alice, she looks really nice. Why would she want to do that?"

There was another pause and then Zoe looked at the phone. "She put the phone down. She says that she knows far more than she ever wanted to know about the Slaithwaites and was hoping not to talk about them ever again."

The brother and sister stood alongside each other. The Platts had closed ranks. But Nicole had travelled a long way and didn't have much time.

Nicole said, "Well, thank you for trying. Do you think there is anyone else who would talk to me about them?"

The man said, "No. There isn't. Sorry." He frowned at Zoe. They both turned away from her; he turned the music back up and she started fiddling with the till.

*

Zoe had looked over the other side of the green before she had called Alice, so Nicole was betting, she would find her there. Harsh, winter rain sliced into her face. In the distance, across the roped-off cricket pitch, she could see a row of thatched cottages. In her bag she could see her phone lit up with WhatsApp and text messages from Dan, Gal and Anya. She could look at those later in the car. She had come too far to back out now.

She counted six cottages in all and prayed that she wouldn't have to knock on too many doors before she hit Alice's. The first one, thick with stickers about Neighbourhood Watch and No Flyers, didn't look promising. She grabbed the knocker and let it down twice with as little force as she dared.

A very old, thin man in a smart light blue cashmere cardigan opened the door. His left hand was shaking a little.

"Yes?"

"I'm looking for Alice." He pulled a face as if her request carried great import. Behind him Nicole could see a racing meeting on the television. She wondered if he had a bet on. He seemed keen to get rid of her.

He raised his thumb as if hitching a lift. "Two down." As Nicole thanked him, he closed the door.

She walked down the paved path that ran in front of the cottages. She averted her eyes in case anyone was watching her from the pub.

She had to knock twice before a sprightly woman in a purple Lycra T-shirt and skin-tight black leggings opened the door. The woman was tanned and, for someone who looked to be in her late 80s, very unlined. If she didn't chuck Nicole out, she resolved to ask her about her health regime as well.

"I'm really sorry. Can I use your loo? I'm a bit desperate."

Alice looked her up and down with a hint of suspicion. She had piercing blue, almost turquoise, eyes. "You better come in then."

Although it was an old cottage – sixteenth century, Nicole's amateur architect's eye reckoned – the interior was very modern, almost Scandinavian. Nicole stood on the mat and took in the simple, clear, white walls. There was a painting of a large female nude in charcoal at the far end. Alice wasn't what she expected at all. She would be no pushover.

The lavatory was behind the kitchen and Nicole had to bend down under a beam to reach it. She sat on the loo and fiddled with the woollen cover of the loo roll. She thought about what Laurence Simmons had said. Would this woman tell her anything or chuck her out? She was here under false pretences. It wasn't like her at all. She deserved everything she got.

She walked back into the sitting room. It was now or never. Nicole said, "I was in the pub just now. Some girl was asking to talk to you."

Alice leant on the back of the sofa. She really was very well preserved. Nicole wondered if she had ever had any work. "I really didn't want to talk about the family she was interested in."

Nicole put on her best gormless face. "Do you mind me asking why? She seemed very persistent."

"It's none of your business, young lady." Alice looked her up and down. "I'd like you to leave now please."

Nicole started towards the door and, looking back, said, "I was just intrigued. That's all."

"Get out!" Alice opened the door and all but pushed her out.

The door slammed behind her. The outside light went off. Nicole staggered out into the dark and the sheet rain. She started to run, but her foot got caught on a broken paving stone. She fell, her elbow hitting the hard, wet stone as she tried to put her hands out to support herself. It throbbed with a deep pain that blocked out everything else. She lay there on the wet stone, water seeping through her tights.

This woman could help her, but for some reason wouldn't. She was so close to finding out what happened to Peter. Why was it all going so wrong? She was deceiving her fiancé and his family. Taking time off from a new job she could ill afford. If only she could find the truth, she could move on. Rain seeped down behind her ears. She should end it now. Simple as that. Get up, get out of Tetbury and grow up. Patrick wouldn't have wanted his elder sister to screw up her life because of him. He would want her to make the most of hers, to live out his dreams as well. It was all too much. Her tears joined the water in the puddle underneath her.

She felt a hand on her shoulder. It was Alice. Nicole pulled herself up: her elbow ached. Alice put her arm around her. "Come inside."

*

Alice gave her a blanket and gestured for her to sit down on the sofa. Nicole checked her messages while Alice busied herself in the kitchen. Gal wanted her to start inviting the press for the product launch. Dan wanted her to come and see him so they could make peace. There was also a missed call from a number she didn't recognise. Alice returne with the tea and sat down opposite her.

Nicole said, "Look. I'm sorry I deceived you. I found a letter in a book up at Blair Gowan. A letter Peter wrote but never sent to his parents about how badly he had been treated, and I made myself a promise that I would find out what happened to him. I've had a really strange time these past two weeks. I've been in a car crash, got fired from my job, upset my boyfriend and his parents. Don't talk to me if you don't want to. I deserve it."

Alice sipped her tea and took a deep breath. The room was growing cold. She asked Nicole all about the book and the letter. She didn't seem surprised by the letter's contents.

"We were family friends with them after the war. My brother and sister used to go and play with Clara and Peter. I was about five years younger than them. My mother would spend hours chatting with Mrs Slaithwaite, and I would hang around the house trying to amuse myself and not annoy the older kids. It was lovely actually, idyllic. Some of the happiest times of my life were running through those rooms. Those worn carpets and wooden floors looked so beautiful with the sun shining on them. Sometimes Peter would invite me to play with them. He liked me better than even my own siblings. But it wouldn't last long as I would annoy one of them and be thrown out of the room.

"Peter was very delicate, very gentle for a teenage boy, certainly for one around here; they're all inbred idiots in my view. He'd been sent away to boarding school up in the Lake District and hated it. Some horrible things had happened to him, so he had run away. Well, you know that from the letter. Hitched all the way across England: ten years old, would you believe it?" She paused. "I don't know why I am telling you this.

"I really liked that family. They were generous and funny. It was as if we were their own children. That went on for years. Then, on 20th June 1951 – I always remember that day – without telling anyone, the family just left The Orchard overnight and that was that. No-one knew where they went. Most of their furniture was given away. I never saw them again."

Teardrops rolled down Nicole's cheek. Alice's distress was even greater. She covered her face with her brown, veiny hands. For a moment, it was as if she had left the room and disappeared deep inside herself into some room in her memory she kept under lock and key. All the superficial glamour of her appearance now looked more like a disguise than a show of strength.

Nicole said, "Did you ever hear what happened to them?"

Alice stared straight ahead and said in a monotone voice. "Peter committed suicide about ten years later. I've never known why. I just wish I'd been able to help him. I remember once sitting with him in the barn when it was raining, and he told me all about his time at school. He was shaking as he told me, squeezing the memories out like pus from a boil. The other boys treated him so monstrously. If I ever met one of them now – hopefully they are all dead – I would kill them. How that school still keeps going I don't know. If anyone knew how Peter had been treated, they wouldn't send their children there. I can tell you that."

Nicole gambled she could risk a couple more questions. "I was told by a woman who spent time at the school that some of the boys were bullied very badly, kept out on the hills or in the stables at night. Was Peter one of them?"

Alice nodded. "He told me about one night when he was put in a stable with this crazy horse that kept kicking him. Never seen anyone so traumatised remembering." She shook her head and wiped her eye. "Awful."

"And you know nothing about what made them leave here?"

"I have told you all I know." Alice looked away from her. "Never saw them or him again."

"That's such a sad story. Do you know where he was when he died?"

"You better go. I've said much more than I intended. You're a very naughty girl sneaking in to see me like this."

"I know. I'm sorry. But you can see why I want to know, can't you?"

Alice showed her to the door. "If you find anything out, come back and tell me." Alice gave her a hug before she walked out of the door.

Her phone rang. No caller ID. A voice she recognised but didn't expect boomed out.

"Nicole. It's Daddy. You need to come home. Mummy's dead."

11

There were lights in the front room of her mother's bungalow as Nicole drove up. If she could have chosen a time to reconcile with her father after fifteen years, it wasn't this. They had seen each other on five brief occasions during that time, punctuated by terse, transactional emails and the odd phone call. He had wrapped himself into the cocoon of his new life with his young wife and only contacted her when his picture-postcard life with his former PA wasn't quite measuring up to his expectations. His high-paying job had gone south when the business was taken over and some heads had to roll. Not helped by the fact the PA had a well-liked ex-husband working in the business already. A salesman's life, reliant on long hours, luck and bonuses wasn't what she had signed up for, and Nicole had gathered that she wasn't backward in expressing her dissatisfaction from time to time. Her father had confided in her once or twice over the past ten years that they had been trying for a baby. Not much had gone right for Hugh Weymouth.

She sat in the car unable to move. Just the sight of

the bungalow – and the thought that her mother was no longer inside – ignited the feeling of helplessness she had experienced since she had heard the news. Everything in her world meant nothing because her mother dominated her thoughts, and every time she thought of her, and how their lives might intertwine in the future, there was nothing. She was at a dead end. Everything was meaningless compared to the one thing she couldn't reverse.

She had never known anything like it. Her grief was like a wall ahead of her so high that no matter how high she looked, there was no top, nowhere she could go to become normal again. She thought again about the conversation they'd had at Christmas. Had her mother been trying to gain some reassurance that Nicole had mapped out a path forward? All Nicole had been able to think about was how soon she could leave and go to Dan's. That listless exchange had been their last time together. How selfish she was. She put her head against the car wheel and wept. Her father must have been watching her from the window. Before she had got out, he had opened the front door. In the dark all she could see was his shining bald pate with a few wisps of hair flying in the wind. He came up to her and hugged her tight before she could say or do anything. For a moment she relaxed and allowed him – and herself – the moment. He was her father. She had no other. Her childhood had been shaped by first his presence and then his absence. The harsh smell of his French cigarettes filled her nostrils and reminded her of the agonising years when the marriage was falling apart in a sea of booze and arguments in front of her eyes.

He grabbed her case and dragged it along with difficulty. "Come inside. I've heated up some soup."

They stood together either side of the kitchen table in silence; a low-watt bulb flickering in a straw lampshade above the table. He stared at her, twisting his fingers together.

"My darling, my darling…" He burst into tears and covered his face as if he was ashamed.

Nicole moved around the table, took one of his hands and held it. "Is Mum still here?" Her father explained that she was at the mortuary on St Margaret's Street and that they could see her as soon as the post-mortem had been completed.

Nicole collapsed onto one of the kitchen chairs. Her mother's ashtray was still full of cigarette butts and one half-smoked one. Was that what she was smoking before she fell? A half-empty bottle of red wine stood alongside it. Was that her father's or had her mother fallen off the wagon? It had never been a house to gladden the soul. It was a waiting room in all but name.

Her father pulled up a chair opposite her like a therapist about to counsel one of his trickiest patients. He had more lines around his eyes, many of them the sharp lines of a smoker, since she had last seen him.

"She wouldn't have suffered. The doctor reckoned her arteries were completely furred up. Quite a wake-up call for me as well. He said she would have gone in seconds."

Nicole held a handkerchief bound tight around her fist to her mouth. Weakness would allow him back in. But it was an impossible task given how tired and broken she was. She thought of the days when she was a little girl, holding her mother's hand in the high street, helping her choose the fruit and vegetables from the grocer's stall. She had looked so beautiful then, tall and angular. Men had looked her up and down as she approached and turned back to get more as she passed. When they had been out this Christmas, people had stepped back on the street as if she was an invalid who needed to be allowed extra space. Life had not served her mother well. Nicole put her head on the table and wept. When her father leant over to comfort her, she touched his hand again, as if in appreciation of the gesture, and pushed him away. He lit a cigarette and watched her.

"How come you're here, Dad? You never come here?"

"I got a call from Mrs Hislop next door. Mum hadn't appeared the previous day, so she was worried. She saw her body on the kitchen floor. She tried to call you first, but she couldn't get through, so she called me. I tried your mobile then your work. The woman at your agency who answered said you had left. Luckily, I'm here. Means I can help with everything."

Help? Now? "It's a little too late for help, Dad. It was just me and Mum after you left."

"Don't be silly, sweetheart. We both need all the support we can get right now. I'm here for you. Always have been. I wasn't always welcome. Please let me help." He picked up a glass vase decorated with Chinese graphics off the sideboard. "Do you think this is an original?"

Nicole was about to say that it was fifteen fucking years too late for that, but somehow swearing felt disrespectful in the circumstances, so she said nothing, just sobbed and choked. His presence, however unwelcome, was a reassuring sign of normality. She couldn't handle any of it right now.

"This is too much. I'm going to go and rest for half an hour in my room."

"What about the soup?"

Nicole said she thought a heated-up can of oxtail would keep. Even as she said it, she knew that the comment was beneath her.

Her room was pitch-black, but she didn't turn the light on. It was a box-like room: all the possessions she valued were in London. Her childhood ones had gone to the charity shop years ago. A solitary stuffed elephant lay on the bed. She picked it up and cuddled it tight, shivering; her mother avoided putting the heating on except when she had guests. And she never had those. The thought wouldn't go away. Why hadn't they tried harder at Christmas to inject some joie de vivre into their day? It wouldn't have taken much on her part. What a last memory, the final image of a life in remorseless decline.

She knew her father was grieving too, but she had a nagging suspicion he was up to no good as well. She couldn't remember a single thing he had done for her in the past fifteen years. Not a single present, not even a birthday card. He hadn't even taken a step into the bungalow since he left. Mind you, he hadn't exactly been welcome. How he had even found that soup in the larder was beyond her. She vowed to give herself a moratorium on negative feelings.

He wanted money. He always wanted money. She would give him some on condition he took it and stayed away. The house was her mother's only asset. It would need to be sold. He could have something from that. She thought of the day when her mother had moved out of their big Georgian house, forced to sell as many possessions as possible to the local antique dealer. The new bungalow was too small for most of them, and, in addition, they had needed the cash.

Assuaged by her sudden surge of unexpected benevolence towards her father, Nicole fell into a deep sleep.

*

The fire in the grate was hissing from the wet wood. She was teaching Patrick to play Twister in front of the fire. He looked about two, so she must have been seven. Even with her help to turn his body in the right way, he kept falling over. Every time he got up, laughing and laughing. Out of the corner of her eye she could see the Christmas tree sparkling and, beneath it, tumbler in hand, her father shouting encouragement to them. Then her mother joined them so that, soon, the three of them were joined together, almost as one, laughing, falling and getting up again. Her mother's perfume filled her nostrils, masking the fumes of the fire.

Then her mother got up and sat on the arm of her father's chair. She leant over and kissed him on the cheek. They sat there, embracing and watching their children, who, in turn, stopped their game and watched them. Her life hadn't often reached perfection, but it had at that moment. No wonder other Christmases had seemed so grey. Nicole didn't want the moment to end. She wanted to be seven forever.

She was awoken by a car pulling up outside the house. Its headlights threw a bright, thin line across the back wall of her room. The voice that responded to her father as he opened the door was very familiar. It was Dan.

Shaking, she brushed her hair, threw on some old lipstick she'd left in a drawer at Christmas and went down the corridor towards the front door. She barged in front of her father and hugged Dan. She had never been so pleased to see him. Thank God for him; thank God for his family.

"I'm sorry. I'm so sorry."

"I didn't expect you at all. How did you get down here?"

Dan lifted a leg and pointed a crutch back towards a BMW saloon parked behind Nicole's car. "Annabel drove me."

"Who?"

"You know, Annabel. Our neighbour who went to Australia." Nicole had a vague memory of meeting Annabel when Dan and she had started going out. Possibly at the party where they had met. She had that annoying habit very tall women have of standing alongside tall men and looking down at other women as if they were an inferior species. Had she been wearing a cowboy hat at an angle? That rang a bell.

"That's nice of her. Is she going to come in?"

Dan beckoned for Annabel to get out of the car. A tall woman, even taller than Nicole remembered, with poster girl blonde hair sashayed towards them. She bent down a little with a theatrical flourish to hug Nicole.

"I am so sorry for your loss. I can't imagine what you are going through. But many congratulations on your engagement. Dan is a very lucky guy."

Hugh leant forwards to kiss Annabel, but she stepped back and proffered a handshake.

Nicole said, "It's so kind of you to bring Dan down. He didn't have to come."

"I wanted to be with you. Annabel wouldn't take no for an answer." Nicole thought back to her secret trip to the Lake District. Tit-for-tat.

Annabel said, "I should leave, but, before I go, is there

anything I can do? Errands? Shopping? Chauffeuring? Have you eaten?"

Nicole shooshed her with a smile and suggested they all went inside. She made a pot of tea while her father sat at the kitchen table and recounted how he had come to be the first to the scene. Somehow, he managed to make himself sound like a recalcitrant hero and Nicole the negligent daughter. Dan knew the backstory and kept quiet while Annabel, oblivious to the situation, encouraged him with exclamations of amazement. Nicole just wanted him out of the house. She wanted Annabel out of the house too. The milk was off, but she found some powdered stuff in the dark recess of the kitchen cupboard. She blew the dust off the top before she turned around. The powder made the tea a vibrant, unappealing caramel colour.

Nicole handed out the mugs of tea and asked Dan if she could talk to him alone in the sitting room. She was so glad he had made the effort to come.

She shut the door as soon as Dan had hobbled his way down the hall and into the sitting room. There were droplets of sweat on his brow.

"I can't cope with this. I want him out of here as soon as possible. Will you help me?"

She also wanted to ask Dan, even though she was delighted to see him, how come Annabel had emerged out of the blue as a cross-country cab driver, but she couldn't do that *and* recruit him to help with her father's ejection. Nicole flicked on a sidelight so they could see each other better in the gloom.

Dan said, "He's your father. He's just lost his wife. You're his only daughter. Are you really sure?"

"You know why. He walked out on us on my 12th birthday. Just as I was about to open my presents. My mother was sick and had only just got up, so she was there when I opened them. My little brother had been dead for two years. None of us had got over the shock. We all should have been making a special effort to love each other and stay together. In front of me he told her that he was in love with some girl from work and he wanted to marry her. That was my birthday treat."

Nicole walked over to the sofa and flopped down on it, head between her knees. It was starting to throb. She hadn't eaten anything since that biscuit with Alice. She was running on empty. Someone had taken over the plot of her life and wasn't letting go. Why hadn't she been there? She might have saved her.

Her words came out in small chunks. "Please, Dan. Get him to leave. I can't handle him now. Tell him I will talk to him. But not right now."

*

They went back into the kitchen. Annabel muttered something about needing to get back, and hugged Dan, a little too long in Nicole's opinion. She strode out of the kitchen saying she could see herself out. Nicole's heart was beating fast, as if she had just come up from holding her breath under water.

It was the three of them in the cramped, yellow-ceilinged kitchen. They sat down. Hugh looked up at Nicole.

"Have you had any thoughts about a funeral? Your mother wasn't much for fuss. I would imagine she would want something simple, wouldn't you?"

Nicole said, "I need to think about it. There might be something in her letter of wishes. Can you give me a little time?"

"These things get booked up, you know. I know she wouldn't want us to wallow in grief when we could be getting on with things."

Nicole slammed her hand on the table. "Get on with things! Mum's dead!" Her father gulped.

Dan said, "Hugh, I'm sorry but it might be better if you leave now. We can talk more in the morning."

"I'm not going anywhere. There's the funeral to sort, probate to organise, the house to sell—"

Nicole interrupted him, "None of which is anything to do with you! Dad, you can come back for the funeral, but I want you to go now. This isn't your house, and it isn't your business. I'm sorry."

Hugh said, "You can't tell me what to do. I'm your father."

"You were my father! You gave up when you walked out on us."

Dan said, "I'll get you a taxi, Mr Weymouth. Where do you want to go? The station? A hotel?"

Hugh stood up, face reddening. "I'm not going anywhere."

Nicole walked over to him and grabbed both his arms. "Dad, please, this is hard enough for both of us. Just go. Do it for me. You've done nothing for me for years. Do this one thing now. Give me some space."

"I said I'm not going anywhere." As he struggled to free himself, he pushed Nicole and she fell backwards, hitting a chair, losing her footing and dropping to the floor with a bang. Her head bounced and her headache got three times as bad.

From her position on the floor, she saw Dan stride up and hit Hugh in the face with one of his crutches.

Dan said, "That's enough. Go before we call the police."

Hugh was not a fit man and his attempt to retaliate was in slow motion. Dan moved behind him and grabbed his arm. "C'mon, Hugh. You're not thinking straight."

Nicole looked down. This was what she had wanted, but, now it was happening, she was doubly ashamed. Her mother dead, and her father, attempting to build a bridge, struck and cast out. There was some blood on the floor where she had hit her head.

"I've got a car. I'll go. I was only trying to do something good for once." Nicole sidestepped his kiss as he stormed out of the kitchen but put a consoling hand out to brush his shoulder.

Dan said to her, "Shall I take you to hospital?"

"No. It's only a cut."

Dan and Nicole sat at the table in silence until Dan went to get a plaster for Nicole's head. She reached for her bag on the sideboard and swallowed two Nurofen with the remnants of her tea.

She sat staring into space. The clock above the kitchen door ticked on. Her head hurt and her heart hurt more. In this kitchen her mother had tried to reach out to her and ask her about her plans. She had failed her. In her mind she looked at the road ahead, the one that would take her out of grief, and, as far as she looked, it stretched out way beyond the horizon.

12

Nicole didn't remember much about the next two days. She missed her mother so much. There wasn't a single thought in her head that didn't conjure up an image of her mother. Every item, every smell, every sound in the house triggered a memory. There was no escape. Happiness at each memory was chased away by guilt and sadness. If she had stayed, if she had visited more often, if she had been a better daughter, would her mother still be alive?

The next morning, in the bottom of the cupboard in her mother's room, she found the box full of faded colour photos in wooden frames. She knew them well and had often looked at them when her mother was out of the house. They had disappeared from the sitting room years ago, the day after Patrick's funeral. There were photos of her playing with Patrick in a paddling pool; one of Patrick on his first bicycle with stabilisers; and one where he looked uncomfortable in his new uniform on his first day of school, aged four.

Nicole sat on her mother's bed and looked at them one by one. Patrick would have been twenty-two by now. He had been too young to know what he wanted to do in life, but he loved making things, whether it was model aeroplanes or dens in the woods. How things worked was his greatest obsession, one that his father indulged as often as possible even if he didn't know all the answers. Maybe he would have been an architect or an engineer? She would have done anything to see him as a grown man. He had so much more energy and intelligence than her.

Wiping her eyes, she went back to her mother's wardrobe. Each item of her mother's clothing, tired, worn in places, faded as well, brought back a particular event or moment. Everything took much longer than she expected as the past flooded back into the present like a spectre in a nightmare.

A used tissue with a lipstick mark and a half-drunk cup of tea decorated the bedside table. Inside the drawer, bottles of pills and prescriptions were piled up on one another. Under the crumpled duvet an Anne Tyler paperback was splayed open.

They slept in Nicole's single bed. They could have slept in her mother's, but it seemed wrong somehow. They used two duvets and Dan had trouble keeping his around him because of his cast. Nicole laid her head on Dan's chest.

"I'm so grateful you came. I don't know what I would have done without you."

Dan stroked her hair. It didn't take long for tears to come again. "Once I had figured out my lift it was a no brainer. I knew I couldn't ask Dad or Mum, but Annabel was there and, bless her, she volunteered."

Nicole couldn't hold herself. "She still has the hots for you, doesn't she?"

Dan kissed her on the cheek. "There's only you. You know that. She's lost, always has been. Her swagger is just a façade. You need to cut her some slack. She's come back from Australia obsessed with fighting climate change. Always talking about this group Extinction Rebellion. They're the radical wing of the green revolution. She heard that I've got this job, and she thinks I can help her find a slot somewhere. Not sure how I can. She's never held down a job for more than about three months. Always shooting her mouth off."

Women liked Dan. It wasn't just how he looked; he listened to them, gave their views his total attention. It was one of the reasons Nicole had been drawn to him. Most of his friends thought they were part of some master race and were dismissive of anyone who fell short. Dan didn't. But, because of this, she often thought he invested more time in lost souls than he perhaps should. Sometimes she thought that's why he liked her. And, whilst she was delighted that he now had his dream job, he was a sucker for anyone who mirrored his passion for the battle to save the planet. Annabel couldn't have chosen a better pitch when she had her sights set on him.

She closed her eyes and resolved to go to sleep. She scolded herself for looking for problems where none existed. She wasn't looking forward to tomorrow so distracted herself by wondering what happened to Peter Slaithwaite. But, as she calmed and fell asleep, Peter slipped away, and memories of Patrick filled her subconsciousness. He was in the garden, in a blue plastic swimming pool, laughing and splashing Nicole as she watched him from the side.

*

The post-mortem had happened first thing, so she was phoned just after ten and invited in. She drove in on her own and left Dan to the dishes. He seemed very happy in his apron with his crutches leaning against the sink, and she loved him for it.

The mortuary was in a one-storey building next to the hospital. It wasn't how she had imagined. All beige and brown fixtures and fittings; low, dim lamps; and discreet notices all over the doors and walls. The receptionist took a few details and pointed her down a long corridor. A short woman in a white coat with a bun and thick glasses stood by the door, holding a clipboard. She asked Nicole the same details as the receptionist had asked.

Interview completed, the woman opened the door and led Nicole into a chapel. There were rows of pews.

Her mother's body lay on a raised bed next to the altar covered in a sheet. She was as still as an Egyptian mummy with the skin of her face and arms as taut and smooth as linen stretched on a canvas. Her hair was had been brushed and put into her usual side parting. Somehow, she almost looked younger than when she had last seen her.

"I'll leave you with her." The woman exited backwards like a servant in a Shakespeare play.

Now it was just Nicole and her mother. The contrast with her mother's cramped kitchen at Christmas couldn't have been sharper. So much had happened since she had asked Nicole what her plans were. The question had deserved a better answer then and it deserved one now. But Nicole couldn't find the words.

A memory came back to her. When Nicole had been taken out of her private school, her mother had taken her on a week's holiday. It was the middle of the term, but her mother was confident, for some reason, that Nicole's new school wouldn't be bothered which week she joined them. They drove to Portsmouth and took a half-empty ferry to the Isle of Wight, the sea choppy with white horses, the sky grey as porridge. It was mid-May. The holidaymakers hadn't arrived, and the streets of Ryde were empty. They bought ice creams, put on their anoraks, and sat on newspapers on the vast, windswept beach. Portsmouth, across the Solent, was obscured by mist. For a few minutes Nicole forgot the shock of leaving her friends at her old school and the terror ahead.

Her mother had turned to her; she had a dab of ice cream on her nose. "We both must make the best of this now. There's nothing else we can do. You're young. You can do anything. Just remember that. Even I might be able to find some new purpose. The future is unwritten. That's what Joe Strummer used to say." Who's Joe Strummer? thought Nicole. A long honk of the horn from some ferry punctuated her musings.

Her mother had tried so hard to make up for the absence of her father and brother. She hadn't been that well-equipped for the role, but, for many years, she had given it everything. Nicole had been too lost to even notice. But she could see it now.

Nicole took her mother's marble-cold hand and, shivering, caressed it.

"You asked at Christmas whether I had a plan. I didn't then but I think I do now. It's all sort of fallen into my lap and now I've really got my hands full. Once I've given you a proper send-off I'm going to go into battle. Firstly, on behalf of a boy who was mistreated and forgotten during the war. People don't want me to investigate it, but I really want to, and I believe Patrick is on my shoulder urging me on. You get that, don't you? I have to get to the bottom of it, for his sake. And, secondly, I've got a new job with a sort of bank, a brand new one. It's going to be super-demanding. My only worry is whether I end up leaving Dan behind in the process. We're meant to be getting married. He's not very keen on all this and his family even so less so. If I didn't feel so strongly about it, I'd stop. I love him, I know it's mad, but I can't. I can't stop now."

"Your mother would be behind you every step of the way…"

Nicole turned. Her father, red-faced and moist-eyed, unshaven, shirt half undone, hair sticking out all over the place, was standing behind her, swaying a little.

"I arrived just after you. I've been in the car park. Begging her for forgiveness…"

Nicole stepped forward and hugged him. The smell of cigarettes filled her nostrils again, but she persevered. When she was a small girl, she'd loved hugging him. In those days she had to jump up. Now they were nose to nose.

"I slept in the car last night, in a lane round the corner. I couldn't bring myself to leave her twice. When I walked out on her I wasn't thinking straight. Everything was going wrong, and I couldn't fix it. Your mother was an amazing woman. If she told you she never amounted to much, she was lying. Do you know she turned down the chance to work with Richard Curtis when she was your age? He wanted her in that *Four Weddings* film, but she had just learnt she was pregnant with you. She wouldn't tell him why she wouldn't do it. She really wanted to do it too, but we'd been trying so hard to have you she just didn't want to risk it. It killed her to pass it up. All those years doing pointless auditions where directors either treated her like shit or tried to shag her or both. Then suddenly all her dreams come true and…"

He couldn't continue; he hung his head, covering his eyes. The swaying got worse. Nicole held his arm to steady him.

"I never knew that. She just told me she worked in a solicitor's office."

Hugh's eyes were even more red now. He looked at her as if he was imploring time to turn backwards. "She did. We needed money so we figured that was a safe option until she had you. From jostling in the coffee queue with Hugh Grant to wrestling with Microsoft Word in a dull, provincial typing job. God, an angel earthbound. She would have loved what you're doing. She would have just said go for it."

"You heard me?"

"Yes, sorry. I wouldn't have missed it for the world. It moved me beyond words. Who would have thought – in a mortuary too. She would have been so proud of you, hearing you state your ambitions like that. We didn't talk much, but, when we did, she always said she hoped you wouldn't falter, that you'd grab life's opportunities with both hands."

"Dad, that was meant to be private…" Nicole was touched, but it didn't alter the fact that she had envisaged this final moment with her mother as a solitary one.

"I know. I'll go. I'll go home. Leave you to it."

Nicole closed her eyes and tried to summon up the strength for what she needed to say.

"I wish we could have a relationship again. Believe it or not, I need it. But you have done so much damage. I don't know if I have the strength to fix it. You understand?"

Her father brushed his eyes with an off-white handkerchief and nodded. But he didn't walk off. He stood there, still unsteady, eyes moving from side to side as if he was debating his next move. His mouth was opening and closing like a goldfish. He gave a sort of nod.

"I can do it. I can fix it."

Nicole smiled at him. "I wish. You'll get some money when I sell the house. Just don't pressure me. OK?"

This time he almost fell into her arms, and Nicole had to bear his weight. He stayed there sobbing as Nicole looked over his shoulder at the pristine body of her dead mother. So, she wasn't just doing it for Patrick now; she was doing it for her mother as well. She wouldn't let her down. She fished a twenty pound note out of her handbag and gave it to her father. The parental tables were turned. She was on her own.

"Why don't you go and get yourself some lunch? Something hearty and wholesome."

Her father took the money with the speed a seagull pinches a chip out of a bag and shuffled off out of the cavernous room.

She took her mother's hand again and kissed it.

"I'll tell you all about it. You can tell me what to do next."

13

Two days later Nicole was back in London and heading over, as dawn was breaking, to meet Gal at Canary Wharf. Part of her didn't know why she was still working. No-one was saying she should. She just knew she had to keep doing things or she would collapse and never get back up on her feet. And she owed it to Gal. He had made a bet on her.

One side benefit of the early start was that both her flatmate, Martha, and her unwanted lodger, Bee, were still asleep. She was avoiding their company whenever possible. In fact, she avoided everyone's company. The slightest hint of sympathy set her off back into her own world of uncontrollable grief. Just when she thought she had it under control, an image or phrase reminded her of her mother, and she lost it. She had no idea how she was going to survive the funeral.

She'd braved late-night shopping in Westfield and bought a new black wool coat from H&M and some medium-heel black pumps from Russell & Bromley. Her work handbag looked a bit battered with her laptop and briefing papers spilling out. Replacing that would have to wait for the end of another month.

They had had to work through her mother's desk. Nicole had taken a quick look and seen there was a pile of unopened letters. She didn't like the look of them. When the time came, she asked Dan to let her make a start by herself.

The first ten letters she opened were all from credit card companies. She counted six. Lots of writing, much of it in capital letters and in red. She ripped them open faster and faster hoping it was a mistake and that there would be other letters conveying that message. Her mother owed thousands of pounds. But why? She found some bank statements. All the money was owed to gambling companies. She couldn't believe it. She didn't even know her mother gambled.

"Dan! Dan! Come here!"

Dan lumbered into the room as fast as he could. "What?"

Nicole fanned the letters and credit card statements in his face.

"Shit. Let's see."

They laid all the envelopes on to the floor and put them in piles. Bank letters, credit card company letters, statements from gambling companies. It took them an hour to open them all up. Nicole slumped back against the sofa. Dan put his hands on his face as if he could cleanse away the experience.

Dan said, "It's a fortune. Spread betting. Football. And she's used equity release to pay some of them off. I doubt there's much value left in this house. I can't believe it."

I can't either, thought Nicole. Just when she thought things couldn't get any worse. She hadn't been counting on the money, but she knew someone who had, even if he had no legal right to any of it, and she knew he wouldn't be at all understanding. His new wife would make sure of that. Her mother's life had always seemed so dull. So, this was how she had kept herself entertained.

Nicole said, "It's a disaster. I had no idea. I can't remember her ever showing any interest in betting or football for that matter. What if there is a massive shortfall? I just don't have any money. What will they do to me?"

"I'll get it all to the solicitor. They will sort it out. I'm sure it won't be as bad as we think."

She looked at the mountain of threatening letters in front of them. "This can't be happening."

Dan, waving a letter, said, "It also looks like she borrowed £20,000 from this antiques dealer. We'll need to talk to him." Nicole recognised the name: they'd sold all their antiques to him when they had moved out of the big house all those years ago.

When they had finished sorting the letters into piles, Nicole collapsed across the arm of a chair and on to Dan's lap, lying, exhausted, breathing in his musky odour. She needed a drink.

He whispered, "You, OK?"

"No. I wish you and I could go away for a week. Somewhere hot with no crowds. Can we do that when all this is over?" Dan nodded.

"That would be lovely." If I can find the time – and the money, she thought.

Dan said, "I am sure Dad would help you out if you needed cash. I can ask him."

Nicole stroked his hair. "I'll think about it. Thank you."

She needed to change the subject. She didn't want to be in Charlie's debt for a single penny.

They were both silent for a minute, but Nicole's mind was still whirring.

"By the way, why is he so protective of that bloody school?"

Dan shifted away from her a little, at least as much as his broken ankle would allow. "I don't know. He won't tell me."

Nicole lifted herself up and kissed him on the cheek. "If I came to live with you, your first loyalty needs to be with me, doesn't it?"

"Of course, goes without saying. But I need to understand why he's so het up about it. Anyway, I thought you'd dropped all that."

Nicole looked straight ahead. "I have."

His perspective looks like a classic case of 'let bygones be bygones', she thought. A boy's life was ruined by a school's negligence. Possibly a family destroyed as well. Yet again, guilt invaded Nicole's consciousness. Her boyfriend had come all the way down to see her, braving considerable pain, and had enabled her to process all kinds of tasks she had never had to do before. Granted, he had brought a leggy, six-foot, blonde ex-girlfriend with him as a chauffeur, but no-one was perfect.

"I shouldn't let Annabel drive you back. It only encourages her."

"I don't want her to, but there's no alternative. Your car's too small with my leg." So that, mused Nicole, was that then.

*

When she got to the flat, Martha and Bee were in the sitting room not talking to each other. Martha hated smoking, so Bee was attempting to lean out of the window in an unsuccessful bid to keep the room free of fumes. A half-empty bottle of Echo Falls red wine sat in front of the chair Bee had been sitting in.

Martha ran over to and hugged Nicole. After a couple of minutes, she pulled Nicole into her bedroom and asked Nicole to kick Bee out. Nicole promised to try.

Back in the sitting room Bee was sitting up straight. She watched Nicole cross the sitting room and patted the sofa for her to sit next to her.

"You poor girl. Was that cow Annabel with him? Miss Hartley Witney 2012. Here have the last of the wine." She held out the bottle to Nicole, who shook her head.

"Bee, I'm really sorry but you need to leave. Martha's had enough."

Bee's eyes looked watery, and she brushed them with the sleeve of her pink mohair sweater. "I can't go. I need to be here for you. Martha can leave if she's so fucking concerned. Christ, your mother's just died. I don't know how you live with her. She just follows me around tidying things away. I found my toothbrush in the bathroom yesterday."

"Yes, well that's where we keep them."

"Well, I don't. I want it in my bag by the sofa where I sleep. People have rights, you know."

Nicole tried to explain to Bee that she had no rights. That she had allowed her to sleep on the sofa for one night as an act of kindness, but that the rental agreement allowed for two people only to live in the flat. It was Martha's lease, and she could throw Nicole out if she wanted.

Bee glugged on the wine bottle. "You need to watch that Annabel. Dan was only away at university a day before she jumped on his best friend. He doesn't know that, so keep it to yourself. Then, a week later, she chucked him for his sister. Only a fling but do keep your wits about you when she's around. He doesn't know that either, so zip-zip. I don't know why you let her drive him down?"

"I didn't have much say in the matter. He would have had to put his leg out of the window in my car."

"I'll bet. St Annabel. All hail St Annabel. What did you find out on your trip? Anything juicy you can share?"

"I don't know what you're talking about." Bee was the last person in the world she fancied sharing anything with. It would be on Facebook before she'd finished talking. "Look, Bee, I want you out of here in twenty-four hours. I'm tired. I have a massive day tomorrow and I just don't need the hassle." She put her hand out onto Bee's knee. "Understand? I'm really sorry."

Bee took her hand. "I'm here for you, Nicole, whatever it takes."

Nicole tried to summon up some sympathy and failed. "What it takes, Bee, is you moving out."

*

Nicole had beaten most of the commuters to Canary Wharf and had spent half an hour in a coffee ship downstairs giving herself a pep talk and pulling a croissant apart.

Gal was sitting at his desk bathed in the early morning sun as she entered the office. Otherwise, it was deserted. She had managed to line up five interviews. All her hit list had said yes – *The Financial Times*, *The Times*, *The Telegraph*, *Reuters*, *Bloomberg*. Anya was going to send out the press release to the wider list once they had done *The Gazette* at nine o'clock. They'd agreed to hold off for two hours so *The Gazette* could post something exclusively.

Gal looked up and said, "I got you a flat white. You shouldn't be here."

Nicole put her pen between her teeth and pulled her hair back. "It's fine. I'll need a couple of days around the funeral, but I have to stay busy. Let's practise some difficult questions."

The journalists had given her plenty of ammunition. The regulator was worried about Zaxxo's money laundering and customer security provisions – the internet was, as Dan had said, full of complaints about Gal's management style. A former director was suing for unfair dismissal and industry analysts said the company would never be profitable.

Whatever Nicole threw at Gal, he answered as accurately as he could. Nicole explained that this was a recipe for disaster that would result in the interview going down a rabbit hole from which they would never be able to recover. The key was to dismiss the question and move on to what they wanted to talk about. Do it enough and the journalist would resign him or herself to listening to – and, maybe, writing about – the story they wanted to pitch.

The trouble was, as hard as Gal tried, the new card for business sounded dull. It was the same as the consumer one just a different colour, a bigger credit limit and embellished with a dedicated customer helpline number.

"Haven't you got anything else? We're going to get fried alive."

The sun was shining direct into Gal's eyes, and he looked tired and frustrated. Beads of sweat rolled down his forehead. In an ideal world they would have spent all yesterday war-gaming these questions. It was her fault that it was all so rushed.

"No. In a couple of weeks we'll be able to announce the Series B funding. Biggest in Europe this year. It needs to be the business card story. I'll make it interesting. Don't worry."

*

They got a taxi over to *The Gazette's* offices off Tower Hill. The morning traffic was building up and the car lurched forward, stirring Nicole's stomach. Gal stared out of the window in silence.

Then he said, "How are you?"

"I'm fine. Best to work."

Tony Childs from *The Gazette* met them in reception and took them through to a stark, cold canteen area where a couple of security men were reading *The Sun* and discussing why Arsenal's new winger cost so much and did so little. Tony's tie was half-mast and there was a button missing on his shirt.

He flipped his notepad open. "We've been told the regulator wants to investigate you for misrepresenting your card fees."

Gal looked at Nicole and then at Tony. "What?"

"Your campaign says the card is the cheapest in the market, but that's not true."

Nicole said, "Have the authority made an official announcement on this?"

"No. But it's coming, we gather." Tony looked sheepish when he said this. He had a gold front tooth.

Gal said, "Well, your intel is better than ours as they haven't told us. We'll give you a comment if they make an announcement. Now, can we talk about the business card launch?"

Tony had been a journalist for over thirty years and looked too tired to humour people. "I'm going to run a story on this whether you comment or not."

Gal said, "You can't do that. You wouldn't do that to HSBC or Santander."

"You'd do better to give me a quote."

Gal jumped up. The security men looked up from their papers. "I'll give you a quote. Get out of the pockets of the fucking banks and start doing some proper reporting on behalf of the British people. They deserve a better deal from their banks and we're here to do that."

Tony said, "Alright, Robin Hood, calm down." Gal sat down again, pushed his chair back and stretched his arms back in exasperation. If Gal's fuse was this short, they would never get through the day.

Nicole said, "Look, Tony. You know as well as I do that everyone's out to get Zaxxo. Disrupting the industry – it comes with the territory. What if we gave you a better story? Would you shelve this advertising rumour?"

Tony gave her a creepy smile. Gal looked at Nicole and shook his head. Tony opened his notebook again. "Can we talk about your lawsuit with your former CFO then?"

Nicole said, "No, we're not here for that. You accepted this interview to talk about the new card. It's the best on the market for SMEs. They can operate all around the world using one card for all their transactions. The typical small business could save £5,000 a year. Go on, tell him, Gal."

Tony looked at Gal. "That's not the kind of story we run, I'm afraid."

This interview was about to end up as a car crash. Gal was a sitting duck. She shouldn't have agreed to do them. If she hadn't been so distracted by her mother's death and so determined to prove to everyone that she could cope she would have delayed these until they were ready. She took a deep breath.

"Alright, have it your way. Off the record, Zaxxo is within days of announcing the biggest funding round of any fintech in Europe this year. It will give it the firepower to launch in America and take on the UK retail travel insurance business as well. That's why all the banks are feeding you all this dirt. They're shit-scared of Zaxxo and, you know what, they've got good reason."

Tony was scribbling away. Nicole was impressed that he still did shorthand. He smiled. "Tell me who's investing."

Gal, casting an acidic glance at Nicole, said, "We can't. When we can, we will."

Nicole interrupted, "Find a way to mention the business card one day soon and we'll give you an early heads-up on the funding. How about that?"

"I don't do deals." Nicole could feel her neck reddening. She had never gone on the offensive in a press interview like this. She thought of her mother's body in the mortuary and her father's words.

"It's not a deal. It's a two-for-one offer. Just like the ones that advertising authority gets so het up about."

Tony looked at Gal. "Where did you get her?"

Nicole said, "So?"

Tony flicked through his pad. Nicole didn't think he was reading anything. He was just buying time and salvaging his pride. The security men had left, and the canteen was silent apart from a kettle boiling somewhere.

"Go on then. No promises."

*

The rest of the interview went off without incident except Gal didn't look at Nicole once. When they got outside on to the pavement, Gal walked two paces down the street on his own then turned around to face Nicole.

"My investors are going to go nuts. They've told me again and again – don't talk funding until the ink is dry. It might fall through. Last week you launched us two months early into the US and now you've compromised our Series B story with this stupid promise. Two-for-one! We're not Tesco."

Her life seemed to comprise of older men shouting at her. If it wasn't Gal, it was her father or Charlie Newhouse. The last time she'd screwed up in her job she'd had Po Olsen screaming at her. Was it really an occupational hazard of being Nicole Weymouth? It bloody shouldn't be. They all needed to learn – not her. She just needed to learn how to navigate through their crassness without resorting to going nuclear. Gal had put on weight since she'd last seen him, and it looked like he might have attempted to cut his own hair.

"Calm down. He was going to trash you. We got out of it, didn't we?" She took a swig of water.

"But we've promised him the funding story." Gal had his arms out as if he was pleading. "The investors have already promised it to the FT."

Nicole frowned. "You didn't tell me that." Gal muttered something about forgetting to tell her. "If we're going to work together, I need to know everything. Otherwise, I'm useless to you. You don't want that and nor do I."

Gal lit a cigarette and inhaled down to his boots. He held the cigarette between his thumb and index finger, the way schoolboys do who don't want to be spotted smoking. A series of texts pinged through from her father asking her about the funeral plans. She ignored them.

Gal said, "Sorry. Thank you for doing this. I'm a little out of my depth when they go on the attack."

"That's why we're going to do the same. You've got an amazing vision and a phenomenal business. Tell them about that and they'll forget all the gossip and innuendo those banks have been dripping in their ears."

There was another text. Nicole looked at her phone. It was another journalist flying a kite. "Oh, God, just fuck off. Let's get going or we'll be late for *The Telegraph*."

The other interviews went much better. Gal blasted the journalists with growth statistics and, whenever he faltered, Nicole chipped in with some too. In most interviews there was a 'What Gal means to say…' When he hit his stride, he was impressive. He was in total command of his story. Passion and ambition. There was none of the fake bonhomie Nicole saw in other clients or in Charlie Newhouse, for that matter. Judge me by what I do not what I say, that was Gal's pitch. By the end of the day there were a bunch of new stories on Google all praising the UK's most exciting fintech. The adjective most used to describe Gal was uncompromising.

*

"I'll take that," said Gal as they sat at the bar of a dingy pub behind Borough Market discussing the articles the next day. It was dark, cold, and smelt of damp. Nicole had a glass of Pinot Grigio the size of a pint and Gal nursed a Becks. "I need to introduce you to the investors. I want them to buy into you as part of my leadership team. After the funeral, of course."

"But I'm only a contractor."

Gal took a swig of his beer and signalled to the barmaid for another. "For now."

She was happier than she had been all year. For a brief moment, she had forgotten about her mother. The interviews had gone well. Her boss was happy. Moreover, he respected her, treated her as an equal. She had found there was that easy rapport two people with the same outlook on life shared. Maybe it was because they both had had setbacks in their teens and had had to fight. Not that she could compare her experiences to his teenage life on his own in London. She didn't fancy him, but she was very comfortable in his company. *Overthinking again, Nicole, enjoy the moment.*

"What's happened with that letter thing?" Nicole explained about her trip, what she'd found out and that there were still plenty of missing jigsaw pieces.

"I really want to keep going but I'm not sure I should, given everything else that's happened. I hate lying to Dan."

"You should. You would always regret it if you didn't.

So, you need to find if any boys from the school are still alive, don't you? Does the school have a database?"

Nicole had no idea what the school had, but she doubted Martin De La Hay would let her near it even if it had. Dan wouldn't help her. Charlie definitely wouldn't.

"There'll be one somewhere at the school. You just need to find it."

Her phone rang and she headed out into the street to answer it. A bearded man at a table by the door had jammed his phone into his jacket pocket and had flicked his eyes at her as she went through the door. It was the solicitors. The late middle-aged woman with the half-moon glasses.

"Ms Weymouth. It's Margo Ravenscroft. I thought you should know that we have reconciled all your mother's outgoings. Do you want a summary?"

Nicole took a deep breath and said yes. "I'm sorry to say that there won't be any value in the house after the equity release is paid off."

Nicole exhaled in shock and put her hand over her mouth. "Fuck! What do I do? There's also a £20,000 debt to a local antique dealer we've just found."

"Just send it to me and do the same with him if he calls you. It'll get paid out of the estate if there's anything left." Nicole muttered a thank you. Her father wasn't the only one who didn't like this situation. Everything was going wrong. She went back to Gal. Alcohol might not help, but it would buy her time. Her mood was back to rock bottom.

Nicole said nothing until her wine arrived then she downed the first third in one go. "There's no money. I'm screwed."

Gal put his hand on her arm. "Hey, hey, talk me through

it. I'm a money man remember?" With as much grace as she could manage, she moved Gal's arm away.

Half a bottle of Pinot Grigio wasn't helping her diction. "Dan's dad, Charlie, the banker, says he will give me a loan if I need it. I don't want to be in his father's debt. Would you want that? I mean, would you?" Gal hung his head, shaking it.

"If he gives you money, there'll be a price to pay. No such thing as a free lunch."

"I don't think I can do it. I just can't. I would have to stop the Peter thing if I did." People were looking around at them as Nicole's voice raised. Gal put a finger to his lips.

"Shall I give him a job? Buy him off?" Nicole laid her head on the bar. It was her turn to shake her head, but she struggled without knocking any of the beer bottles.

Nicole said, "You don't know anyone who could knock him off, do you?" She aimed for a sip of her wine and missed. "No, ignore that. Joke." She stared into space, admiring the array of garish bottles behind the bar. Then she turned back to face him.

"No, no, no. I'm sorry I let you down today. My anger always trips me up. I get wound up, get more and more annoyed, tell myself not to say anything. Then bang, off I go again. That's why I ended up with you."

Gal passed her a paper napkin as she raised herself up. "Your anger, as you term it, is why I hired you. We just need to get on the same page first."

Nicole said, "I wish I was like you. You don't seem to worry what people think of you at all. I'm the opposite. Whenever I meet anyone new, I automatically think they are judging me, looking for the faults. And the worst of it is,

I'm almost always the one who points out those faults and makes it easy for them. It's like a cancer that gets into your bones and starts to infect everything you say, think and do.

"I had a best friend at school. Maddie. We'd play tennis together all the time in the evenings after lessons. Really competitive matches. 7-6, tie breaks, sudden death. Nothing could split us. I would often joke how unreliable my second serve was under pressure. Not true but sometimes I did have a serious wobble. There was one place available in the school doubles team. So, it was between us two. The teacher knows we're good friends, so she gets us together to tell us that's it's a really hard decision and that the one who isn't chosen shouldn't feel bad. Really thoughtful – not always the way at that place I can tell you. Maddie pipes up, 'Nicole won't mind as she says she always screws up her serve under pressure.' Next thing you know Maddie is in the team. She's used the joke I used against myself to get ahead of me. I was so annoyed. We didn't talk for the rest of the term. It's always the way. I make a joke of my shortcomings, the things I really want to work on, and then everyone makes those jokes back to me. They become a fact of life. And it's all my stupid fault. I can't help myself. Sorry, I really am droning on, aren't I?"

She was leaning on the bar, pushing her empty glass around with her finger. "Shall we have one more?" Her head was already starting to spin, but at least, all her worries had got lost in the fug.

"It's a bit of British disease, isn't it? Self-deprecation." Gal looked puzzled. "Putting oneself down. It's not cool to be seen to want to be good at things. Better to be good at them without being seen to try. Effortless. Swan-like.

Trouble is, it's different now as London becomes so much more, what's the word, cosmopolitan. Everyone is so much more brash and in more of a hurry. They just want to be the best, be the most popular, make the most money. Push, push, push. Hustle, hustle, hustle. English modesty is out of fashion and unlikely to come back in.

"I promised myself at Christmas I would try and change. We were playing a game after lunch at Dan's house, and I was doing so badly. As ever. Dan and his family are so competitive. They just wouldn't get off my back. I hated it. And I hated myself. That day I decided I was going to stop being push over Nicole and start working on what I wanted. Get serious and achieve something. Before I settled down with Dan. The argument I got into with Po was me trying to be more assertive. Rather backfired. Then again, I wouldn't be here if I hadn't. Oh, thanks. I should get the next one."

Nicole looked at Gal. He hadn't moved all the time she'd been talking. He just kept his soft brown eyes on her. He hadn't smiled or grinned or laughed. It was very rare that she made speeches of such length.

"I think that's what this stupid letter is all about. You know?"

Gal said, "That's why I started Zaxxo. No-one else was going to put me in charge of a bank. I'm not like your Charles Newhouse. No-one is asking me on shooting weekends or inviting me to lunch at their club. I had to start my own bank. Luckily, it's much easier now we all have smartphones. When you do that, if you do it right, you upset people and break things. Your problem is that you were born on the inside even though you may not think it. It's pretty comfortable there because you know everybody, and they'll look out for you if you fall. Now you will be on the outside – with me."

Nicole said, "I really don't think that's true. I've been on the outside, just like you, most of my life."

"Maybe. It's all relative. It's a very tempting place to stay. But it's the death of ambition unless you're top of the class. You don't get anything done because everyone's keeping an eye on you, making sure you don't rock the boat. If you join me, you're going to rock some boats, perhaps even capsize a few. Your friends, your friends' parents, are going to be very suspicious of you. They'll never treat you in the same way again."

Gal tapped his bottle against Nicole's glass of wine. "I like the letter thing. Shows you're ready to do some rocking."

Nicole said, "It's about time, isn't it? God knows I've waited long enough. One more? A small one?" Gal pulled a face but signalled to the bartender. Maybe it was the wine, but, after the past few weeks, Nicole needed to talk to someone who didn't know everyone she knew, although none of the business books she had read advised on doing this with your boss. They were both quiet for the moment and watched their drinks being prepared.

Gal said, "Did something happen?"

"What do you mean?"

"Did something happen? You're smart, attractive, good with people, even me, and you had all the right beginnings. It doesn't add up."

"I don't talk about it." Nicole's mind was all over the place. The wine, her mother, her memories from all those years ago.

No-one asked her about it anymore and hadn't done for

years. Those who knew knew not to do so. Those who didn't had no reason to know. She had learnt over the years to keep the memory hidden and avoided any potential catalyst for its release. Young children, swimming pools, Portugal – she gave them all as wide a berth as possible whenever she could. Even so Patrick's face reared up all the time. Even more so as they were clearing her mother's house. Her drink arrived and she took a large swig. Was she going to talk about it? She glanced across at Gal. Her father was absent, her mother was gone, Patrick was gone. His memory, his story, her story, deserved to live.

"My brother drowned when I was ten. Patrick. He was five. We were on holiday in a villa in Portugal. First time we had ever been abroad as a family. It was lovely. White walls, red tile floors, massive open windows that let in the sun all day. I was so happy to spend time with my father as, because of his work, we didn't see him much. My mother was happy too. All the family together, sunshine, fresh food, fizzy drinks from the fridge whenever we wanted. And there was a swimming pool…"

The words got stuck. Nicole's hand trembled as she reached for her wine glass. Gal said something about not needing to talk about it. It was too late. The door had been thrown open. It was time.

"We'd had lunch outside on the terrace. Chicken with salad. Mum said it was Chicken Piri Piri, but we didn't have the Piri Piri bit. Patrick didn't like it and wanted to get back in the pool. My parents had drunk a bottle of wine and were starting to argue as usual. My mother went upstairs to have a sleep and told my father to keep an eye on us children.

"I remember that because she never told my father what

to do. So, Patrick and I played in the pool and my father sat on a chair reading a paperback. After a while I got out to play with my dolls. Patrick just got rough and started biting if he was losing a game. The sun was so hot, and I had to shield my eyes. Then my father stood up, stumbled a little, said he was going for a walk and that I should watch Patrick. So, I walked over to Patrick; he seemed fine, and I went back to my dolls. I would get so immersed. It was all very quiet apart from the plane noises and the shouts from the people in the villa next door. I remember thinking how nice and peaceful it was. No-one disturbing my game for a change.

"It must have only been a few minutes later when my father came running back from behind the house shouting. He never ran. 'Nicole, Nicole, what have you done?' He brushed past me and dived into the pool. I went over and he was pulling Patrick up from the bottom. His shirt had billowed up like a lily. Then he lifted his body up and put him on the side of the pool. My father leapt out of the pool – he never did that as he was quite fat, and started pummelling my brother's chest. My mother came out too, screaming louder than I had ever heard someone before. She was shouting, 'Save him, Hugh, save him.' My father looked up and said, and I have never forgotten this, 'You were meant to watch him, Nicole.'

"They were both shouting at each other while my father tried to breathe into Patrick's mouth. My mother ran off to phone for an ambulance. My father looked up at me in between breaths and said, 'Why, Nicole, why?' I was ten, ten years old."

Gal's eyes were moist, and his face had whitened. As Nicole spoke, the words seemed to come from someone else, someone in a film. It was a trauma that had never seemed to belong in real life.

"I didn't know what to say. It was so unfair. After a while he gave up. Patrick just lay there like one of my dolls. My mother just clung to his body, wailing. I remember my father lit a cigarette with both hands on his lighter and then stared at the sky with his hands in his pockets. I just sat on the edge of the pool sobbing. None of us said anything until the ambulance came. They put him on a stretcher and wrapped him in a sheet. He looked so tiny. Two days later we flew home with his body."

The pub was emptying, and Nicole's words hung in the air. Gal had his head down, staring at a beer mat.

"My father never mentioned it to me again. But whenever Patrick's name came up or something was mentioned that would prompt his memory, he would cast me a dark glance. I think he really believed it was my fault. For a long time, I believed it was too."

"What did your mother think?" Gal didn't look at Nicole as he said this.

"Once, about three months later, she was putting me to bed, and she saw I had one of Patrick's books under my pillow. She picked it up and flicked through it. As she put it back, she said, 'Daddy wasn't thinking.' That was it. The only time. I knew what she was trying to say, but that was the best she could come up with. Divided loyalties, I suppose. So, after that, nothing was the same. The cancer invaded every part of my family. My father left, I went off to boarding school, my mother started drinking. Like me now."

They both stood leaning on the bar. Nicole wiped her eyes with her sleeve. Gal finished his drink.

He said, "It's what made you who you are."

"You think so?" The words got stuck in her throat. Recalling Patrick's death, on top of her mother's, had finished her off. She had nothing left to give or say. Should she have told Gal, her boss? Was it fair on him? He appeared to understand. She couldn't say that of the few people she had told this story to. She had drunk too much. She shouldn't have shared so much.

Gal touched her arm, pursed his lips and nodded. She suspected he was struggling to talk too.

Nicole rallied herself and said, "Well, sorry you had to hear all that. I certainly feel pretty woozy after that lake of Pinot Grigio. I need to get home before I throw up."

14

"The UK has made massive strides in its use of renewable energy over the past ten years. Last year in one out of four days we only used renewables as a source. Your generation will only use renewable energy. That's why I believe so passionately in the mission of my firm. We're working for your future."

Dan was sitting on a chair in the middle of the hall at Rothbury with over a hundred boys and girls sitting cross-legged in a circle around him. Martin De La Hay stood behind Dan's right shoulder. He had given Nicole a couple of puzzled glances but otherwise ignored her.

Nicole sat on a chair to the back of the hall alongside Martin's wife, Brooke, who was picking at her nails and looking from side to side with a nervous twitch as if she wanted the talk to end as soon as possible. The children looked like they fell into the same camp as Brooke.

Nicole had come down to Dan's house the night before. She was in a better mood. The media coverage was broadly positive, a few snippy comments about Gal's management style notwithstanding, and, contrary to Nicole's expectations, he had been happy for her to take the day off. She needed to talk to Dan about her mother's finances and thank Charlie for his loan offer.

She had never talked to anyone about Patrick's death with the level of candour she had shown with Gal, and she couldn't work out why. He had listened and hadn't judged. Plenty of people fell into that category. The letter might have something to do with it. Every time she thought about it, the road ahead looked a little less constricting. It didn't make sense.

So, the prospect of ending her search niggled. And there was another factor to consider regarding her resolve to back off her search for the truth. She had had a call from Shona over the weekend asking her if she had made any progress. Her grandmother, fading fast, had been badgering her for news. Nicole had remembered about Dan's talk at Rothbury and, spurred by Gal's suggestions about the database, thought this might be her chance to find someone who actually knew Peter at school. One conversation with the right person could put the whole thing to bed once and for all.

She was having dinner with Charlie, Jo and Dan. Bee was up in London, presumably still staking claim to Nicole's sofa judging by Martha's irate texts. That was next on her list. Jo had cooked a very rubbery chicken pie with broccoli, so the thorough chewing required made for quite a number of silences.

Nicole said, "Dan, could I come to your talk at Rothbury tomorrow? I'd love to hear it."

Charlie said, "Are you sure? Don't you need to be back at work?"

Jo said, "Nicole can do whatever she wants, Charlie. She's only just lost her mother, for God's sake."

Charlie said, "I know. Dan says there might be a problem with a debt. I would be glad to help if you'd let me."

Nicole said, "Thank you, Charlie, thank you very much. Can I think about it?" She paused.

Dan said, "Of course you can come."

"You can do no wrong there, can you?" Dan grimaced then broke into a grin.

She waited until they were lying in bed. Dan was reading through the notes for his talk.

"I have a confession to make. I went down to Rothbury a few weeks ago to ask about Peter. I used a fake name."

"You what!?" Nicole repeated what she had said. It didn't look like it would go down any better the second time.

"I meant to tell you but what with my mother and everything." Dan threw his notes down and turned to her. He had gone a bit puce.

"So, you haven't given up after all?" She was an outsider now. Outsiders played by their own rules.

"I have now. I hadn't then. I meant to tell you. Life just got in the way. This year has just been horrendous, hasn't it?"

Dan tried to respond, but she kissed him on the lips and put her hand under the covers. "C'mon, Hopalong, put those notes away."

*

The talk had finished, and Dan was fielding questions about fatbergs as big as houses, the fate of polar bears and how plastic bags could suffocate dolphins. Nicole was full of admiration for the intensity with which he handled every question. At least one of them had found their vocation.

They had been invited for tea in the museum Martin De Lay Hay referred to as his study. Nicole had wondered if any more small boys would be waiting outside to be punished. She had hoped not and there weren't. The smell of some brown meat concoction permeated her nostrils and made her retch a little.

Dan introduced Nicole, and Martin De La Hay said, "You're not Nicole Weymouth. You're Arabella Worthington, aren't you?"

Nicole just grinned at him. Dan said, "Nicole didn't want me to know she was checking out my old school. She wanted to make her own mind up incognito."

"Bloody odd way to go about it if you ask me. All those questions about old boys."

Nicole said, "I'm just a curious person, Martin. Charlie and Dan have told me so many great stories about the school."

*

Once they had all sat down on the sofa and Brooke had played mother, a long, interminable conversation about the whereabouts of Dan's contemporaries was initiated. Nicole hadn't heard of any of the people mentioned. Brooke De La Hay fiddled with her teacup and forced a smile. She avoided Nicole's glances, so there was no opportunity to launch a parallel conversation.

Nicole said, "I feel a little sick. Where's the nearest lavatory please?"

Martin said, "Maybe go with her, darling?" Brooke got

up, offering to take her, but Nicole protested hard, and the danger was averted.

No-one noticed or said anything when she excused herself. Somewhere there would be a school secretary who knew everything and everyone. She just had to find her. A long, white-tiled passage with faded pictures of football and cricket teams lining the walls stretched ahead of her. There were plenty of open doors to explore.

The first room was some kind of music room. An intermittent scraping sound filled the air. A girl of about ten years old with light blue bottle-bottom glasses and pigtails was holding a violin nearly as large as herself and was frowning at a sheet of music on a stand. She looked up as Nicole entered.

"Can you read music?" The room was painted white and was empty bar the girl, a chair, and the music stand.

"No," Nicole said.

The small girl sighed. "Nor can I. What's worse, my mother told my teacher I can. There's going to be a reckoning."

Nicole leant against the door frame and looked backwards to check no-one was coming along the passageway. Her canary yellow blazer made her very conspicuous.

"I'm sure she'll understand. Say you need a new glasses prescription. Can you tell me where I find the school secretary?"

The girl gave her a gap-toothed smile. "Good idea. Second on the right. Miss Forshaw. Very grumpy today, I fear."

Nicole left the girl contemplating her sheet music. The coast was still clear. There were plenty of old boys to distract Dan and his headmaster for a good half hour.

*

Nicole found the room she searched for with relative ease. There was a late middle-aged woman sitting in front of an old, dirty cream monitor at a worn wooden desk in the corner. It looked like only Martin De La Hay got the flash computer. Classical music was playing at low volume on a battered Roberts radio. The smell of cooked meat from the kitchen down the hall had grown stronger and filled Nicole's nostrils.

"Yes?" Miss Forshaw glanced up and gave Nicole a measured look. The corners of her mouth turned downwards with disapproval. She looked as if she was very busy, on a deadline and had zero interest in Nicole. This wasn't going to be easy.

"I'm here while my fiancé is giving a presentation to the children. I wonder if you can help. My grandfather was at school here in the war, up at Blair Gowan, and I wondered if one of his friends, Christopher Carruthers, was, by any chance, still alive?"

There was an uncomfortable silence. Miss Forshaw looked back at her computer as if she was being dragged away from a meeting with a lover an hour before the arranged time.

"Let me see," she sighed. "There are only a handful of them left. Do you know anything more about him?"

"I think he lived in Cheltenham."

Miss Forshaw started clicking away. "Smith, Tempest, Charlesworth, Hutchinson... no Carruthers as far as I can see..." She pulled back from the computer as if her brief spate of detective work was done.

Nicole didn't care if she upset her. She needed a name

then she was on the home straight. She stepped forward into Miss Forshaw's space. "Maybe I've got it wrong. It was definitely C something. Could I look? It might jog my memory."

Miss Forshaw flapped her arm in Nicole's direction as if she was a wasp. "That's not allowed. We take data privacy very seriously. Haven't you heard of GDPR?"

"GDP what? Oh, I'm so sorry. So presumptuous of me." Nicole crossed her arms and stood wondering if Miss Forshaw might relent. After twenty seconds there was no sign of her doing so. Nicole had to think fast. She wouldn't get this opportunity again.

"Gosh. Do you mind if I sit down? I suddenly feel very faint." Nicole swayed a little on her feet and lurched towards a chair opposite Miss Forshaw's desk, taking care to crash into it with as much noise as possible. Once ensconced there she leant forward, head in her hands. She sensed that Miss Forshaw was just staring at her.

"Is there any chance of a glass of water? I'm so sorry to trouble you."

Nicole peeked through her hands. Miss Forshaw now looked exasperated that the last lap of her day had been blown off course by this intruder. She pressed her hands on to the desk to give her leverage as she got up. She hobbled a little as she set off. All middle-aged people seemed to have bad knees.

"I'll pop over to the kitchen. Give me one minute." She looked at Nicole as if she was wondering whether she should check her pulse or something but seemed to think better of it and strode out of the room.

Nicole leapt up, pulling her phone out of her pocket.

She jumped into Miss Forshaw's chair with its high-spec back support and clicked on the computer. It hadn't locked. A list of names with the year they left the school, and their addresses, appeared in front of her. She took two photos of the page to be sure then scrolled down in case there were more. There weren't. It was a very long time ago. She now had the names, addresses and phone numbers of five Blair Gowan boys who were at the school in the war. Hopefully at least one of them was still of sound mind and willing to talk to her.

She heard footsteps and moved back over into the other chair. She cradled her head in her hands and awaited her glass of water.

"We wondered where you were. Do you feel any better?" It was Martin De La Hay.

"I felt sick walking back from the lavatory." Martin De La Hay frowned. Nicole reckoned he had a good radar for play-acting. She clutched her stomach.

"That's in the other direction." Now Miss Forshaw entered the room. "Ginny, you should have sent our guest back to my study. We would have looked after her. She has recently had a major bereavement, poor thing."

"She wasn't sick when she came in. She was asking about boys who were at the school in the war."

Martin De La Hay's face turned strawberry red. It looked like he couldn't decide whether to go full prep-school headmaster nuclear or keep a lid on it through his respect for Nicole as the mourning fiancée of an honoured old boy. He couldn't control himself.

"What is it about you and our old boys? Their lives are their affairs and theirs only. You have no right to try and trick Ginny here into giving you information that isn't hers to give. Does Dan know about this? You should be ashamed of yourself."

Nicole looked at him. It was hard to see how this overgrown scout troop leader commanded so much respect from Dan and Charlie. "Well, I'm feeling a little better now. Can we go back to your study?"

Nicole couldn't help wondering why an innocent question about some old boys was causing this extreme reaction. He had been quite friendly about it before, even if he hadn't got back to her. Both Charlie and Martin De La Hay were cut from the same cloth. If she wasn't sure about pursuing her investigation before, then she certainly was now.

"I only want to know what happened to one of your oldest pupils. It's no different from all those personal updates in the annual magazine. Why would you or anyone be against that?"

Martin was recovering himself, putting his hands into his pockets. With a slight stammer he said, "Let's go back to my study, shall we?"

Nicole nodded to a stone-faced Miss Forshaw and followed Martin De La Hay out of the room and along the corridor. Anyone would have thought she was a transgressing pupil herself.

In the study Dan and Brooke were sitting on the sofa looking at a photo album.

Dan looked up. "Oh, hello. Do you feel any better?" Brooke beckoned her to come and sit down.

Martin De La Hay said, "She was snooping around Miss Forshaw. Trying to get names and addresses of old boys."

Dan, not looking at Nicole, said, "Nicole wouldn't do that. She just got lost, I'm sure."

Nicole said, "Women's problems if you must know." Not that Martin and Brooke De La Hay seemed at all interested if that had been the case.

She said, "OK, fine. I want to know what happened to Peter Slaithwaite. I have promised Dan I will stop my investigations, but if you could tell me anything now, before I give up, I would really appreciate it."

Martin De La Hay said, "Tell me what you know."

Nicole told him. He listened while leaning on his desk. Nicole sensed this was one of his go-to comfort positions. He could show what an approachable laid-back guy he was whilst still showing a degree of authority. This was his kingdom after all. He was judge, jury and executioner. Nicole sat on the arm of one of the chairs and gave Martin De La Hay her sweetest smile.

"Plenty of boys were damaged by the war. No matter how good our school was, they were still away from their parents, worried about their fathers at the Front, deprived of all the staples they had known in peacetime…"

Nicole said, "He was shut in a stable all night with a crazy horse. The woman that found him said he was barely able to stand he was shaking so much with fear and cold. In his letter he said he had seen some terrible things here. He ended his life at the age of thirty-one."

Dan said, "Nicole's entitled to ask. It will go no further."

Nicole had had enough. She couldn't go forward if she didn't say what she thought and stand up for what she believed was right.

"Tell me what happened."

Martin De La Hay shuffled some coins in his trouser pocket. "Nothing happened, as you so dramatically put it. By all accounts he was a boy of exceptionally nervous disposition. Boarding school didn't suit him, but his parents had no choice. My great-grandfather and his team looked after him for as long as they could."

"And then he ran away. That's how well your great-grandfather looked after him!"

"I've got his reports somewhere. He visited Matron much more than other boys."

"I can't believe you take all this so lightly. This all happened at your school!"

"Dan, why don't you take your girlfriend home? I do appreciate it is a very challenging time for you, Nicole, but this is our family's and the school's reputation you are seeking to undermine. I would be grateful if you don't come and visit us here ever again."

Dan said, "She deserves an answer."

"Well, she just got one. And it's all she's going to get."

"It's not much to ask." Dan grabbed his crutches and stood up. "Well, you won't see me here again either then. C'mon, Nicole, let's go."

"With pleasure!" said Nicole.

Nicole headed out of the study with Dan following behind. Martin De La Hay shouted to their backs. "Ask your father, Dan. He'll explain."

In the corridor, as they passed yet another pupil waiting to face the headmaster's judgement, Nicole turned to Dan.

"Thank you. What do you think he meant by that?"

Dan said, "I've always hated that study. I'm really glad to have a reason not to go in it again."

15

They had agreed that they would go back to Dan's house for supper before Nicole returned to London. When they had chosen the train option, they had forgotten the elusiveness of rural cabs. They had to wait shivering in the dark on the drive outside the school for twenty minutes for the cab. Through the large windows, they could see boys and girls lining up to have something for tea out of large metal urns. The clatter of cooking equipment drifted out of the open windows in the dining room.

Nicole sat on a mossy, damp bench next to Dan and checked her emails. Martha was demanding to know when she would speak to Bee. She replied that she planned to talk to her tomorrow night. Her father wanted to know about progress with the funeral again.

Gal… Gal had been interviewed by the police about an allegation of physical assault against a female colleague at an office party and wanted to know what he should do.

She walked out of Dan's earshot and called Gal. "Hi. I got your email. What on earth?"

"I was in the office this morning and these two police officers turned up at reception. Man and woman. Mr Nice and Mrs Nasty. They made sure all the staff saw them and then they interviewed me in my office. This woman, a salesperson who used to work for us, is accusing me of sexual assault at the Christmas party. There were loads of witnesses, apparently."

In a low voice Nicole said, "Is it she just trying it on or is there something to it? I need to know."

"She had a massive drink problem and missed all her targets. She jumped on me in front of a bunch of people. I pushed her away. Two months ago, in January, we had to put her on performance review. We gave her loads of chances. She just wasn't up to it."

"It doesn't look good though, Gal, does it? You need to keep out of trouble."

"I never do things like that. Never. I know what an easy target I could be. And I am categorically not that sort of person." Nicole had to agree with that. "I don't get why the police would want to humiliate me? One of the investors has got wind of it. Having kittens, is that what you all say? Timing's shit."

Nicole agreed to keep an eye out for anything overnight and that they would discuss it in the office the next day. It was serious and, if she found there was any truth in it, she would be off like a shot. Gal didn't sound his usual ebullient self. She hoped he had the ability to bounce back like her first impressions of him had led her to believe.

The cab, a black Ford Mondeo, battered outside, warm and smelly, as it turned out, inside, drew up alongside them. Given the trains only ran once an hour, Nicole prayed the one they were aiming for wasn't cancelled. The station had two exposed benches and a direct line to the winds of Siberia. It was twenty minutes late and they froze.

They sat holding hands all the way back. Tired, and a little shocked, they said nothing for ten minutes until Dan broke the silence.

"My hero."

"My eco-warrior," she replied.

"That's the end of it then?"

Nicole looked out of the window and nodded. She hated herself, but she'd made a promise to Peter – and Patrick.

*

There was a fire blazing and an open bottle of Chianti on the side table in the sitting room when they arrived at Dan's house. Jo had picked them up from the station. En route they told her about Martin De La Hay's behaviour.

Jo said, "Good for you. He can be awfully overbearing. Charlie laps it up. Can't think why. So, did you find anything out?"

Dan said, "No. Nicole's going to stop investigating now."

Jo said, "Oh."

Nicole said, "I've got too much on. And I don't want to upset any of you."

Jo said, "You wouldn't be upsetting me. Terrible man."

Nicole hadn't told Dan about the information she now had on her camera. If one of the names on her list delivered the goods, then she was home and dry. With Zaxxo entering intensive care, she didn't have time to do much more, and then there were bound to be conditions associated with Charlie's loan offer.

Charlie Newhouse was seated by the fire, Caesar at his feet, still in his pinstriped suit, tie loosened, and, alternatively, chugging wine and throwing peanuts down his throat. He can't do very long hours if he's home by this time, thought Nicole. Maybe he's got nothing to do?

"Hello, you two. Pissed off any prep school headmasters recently?" It was one of those utterances that started out as a joke but lost its nerve halfway through. Did Charlie really hate everything she did, or did he just hate the world in general and she happened to be standing in front of it?

Dan stood in the middle of the sitting room leaning on his crutches. Nicole hung back.

"Dad, Martin was so rude to Nicole. She got lost on the way to the loo and felt faint. He treated her like she was a naughty pupil. It was outrageous."

Charlie took another huge slug of wine. Why were all the father figures in her life borderline alcoholics? They sat down together and sunk into the sofa.

"Martin called me straight after, said Nicole was asking about those bloody old boys again. Haven't you got the message yet? You need to lay off. I wasn't joking." The wine had loosened his tongue and his control of his manners.

Dan said, "But why? It's a letter from eighty years ago."

Charlie said, "Nicole, you should back off once and for all for all our sakes. Dan told you about my offer, I take it?"

"That's right." She flashed him a weak smile. She would prefer to sell a kidney.

Dan said, "Don't threaten her, Dad. She's going to stop."

Dan had taken Nicole through the whole story on the train. Her mother's debts – overdrafts, cards, the antique's shop loan – totalled about £75,000. The estate, basically the value of the house after the mortgage company and taxes were paid, would cover some but not all of it. There were no savings, no investments, no cash in the bank. The antiques dealer would just have to join the queue. She had no obligation to pay him off herself and she wasn't going into anyone's debt to make things better. She wasn't going to put herself in hock to Charlie Newhouse.

Nicole said, "It's only money. I'll find it. I wouldn't want it to come between us."

Dan shuffled over to the table and poured them both half a glass of wine. Charlie had already made substantial inroads into the bottle. Wobbling a little, he handed one to Nicole.

Charlie said, "Calm down. Humour the old man. It's been a long day. Sit down and tell me what's new at Zaxxo? Sounds like Gal's got some big guns lining up on his team."

Nicole looked at the fire and wondered if it would be easier to jump into it. In this house it was like she was a tennis ball that got batted to and fro between conversations about Rothbury and Zaxxo. She was almost nostalgic for the Christmas charades. At least there she could walk out of the room and her involvement was over.

"We had a day of interviews the other day to launch his business credit card. Most of the journalists wanted to talk about other stuff. Surprise, surprise. Gal seems to generate more stories about his business from competitors than he generates himself. Anyway, the coverage is looking really good. All in all, I was pleased."

Charlie said, "How about that girl who used to work for him. That doesn't sound very edifying."

Nicole took a slow swig of her wine. "What girl?"

"The one who's accusing him of assault. I would have thought you would be the first to know. All pretty public today, according to my sources."

"I don't know what you're talking about."

"You should take a good look. Not the first – or the last – according to City gossip."

"Stop this, Dad, or we'll go back to London now. Nicole's a guest in our house."

Charlie pulled himself up, tucked his shirt into his trousers, and, as he left the room, said, "Just trying to help." As he closed the door Nicole found her tears wouldn't stop. How could anyone be such a callous monster?

She hugged Dan. "Thank you."

They sat in silence as the fire spat out embers that bounced on to the hearth surrounding it. In the kitchen, Big Ben's bells sounded for the six o'clock news on Radio 4.

Dan said, "Don't take any notice of him. Mum says he's been in a foul mood all week. There's some big restructuring going on at the bank, the second this year, and he's worried his job is on the line again."

"Why does he have it in for me though? It's not like I make any difference at all to his work or his life."

"Yes, but his boss has given him this strategy job working out how to compete with the new banking entrants. Every time a business like Revolut or Monzo or Zaxxo does something new he gets an email from his CEO asking why they haven't done something similar. It's almost as if he gets an electric shock whenever you make an announcement."

"And why does he get all het up about the letter thing? He can't be that proud of his old school?"

"There's something up. No idea why Martin De La Hay seemed to think I should know though."

Nicole picked up her glass and finished it in one go. "Aren't you just a little bit curious now?" Dan sighed and muttered something about keeping promises.

She was on her own.

*

Nicole got back to the flat just before ten o'clock. She wanted to work so had left Dan at his parents'. Bee was on the sofa crying and Martha was standing behind her shouting. The TV was on full volume and the HomePod was blasting out Taylor Swift.

"Why won't you just leave? Nicole has asked you a thousand times and I've asked you nearly as many. You stink the place out with your fags and your joints. Your friends turn up all times of the night and treat it as their own flat. If you're not out by tomorrow morning, I'm calling the police."

Nicole mouthed sorry at Martha and got a dismissive look back. She could see Martha had an overnight bag in her hand. This was one situation in her life where Nicole was, without doubt, bang out of order. Bee looked up at her with eyes red from rubbing.

"I've nowhere to go. I've been fired. My dad's cut off my allowance. If I leave now, I'm on the streets. I'm on the bloody streets!"

Nicole bent down and took her hand and, in a quiet voice, said, "Don't be so melodramatic. What about all your schoolfriends you go out with so often? One of them must have a spare room. Araminta seems to have a flat the size of

Blenheim Palace, for a start. Martha and I could get thrown out if our landlord finds out about you. You have to go. Go home if need be. I've just been there. It's lovely and warm and your mum's a fabulous cook!"

"I hate home. I'd rather lie in a doorway on The Strand."

"Why?"

Martha butted in. "You two sort it out. I'm going to Jonno's. I don't want that train wreck here when I get back tomorrow night."

In private, on WhatsApp with Nicole, Martha had been more considerate in light of her bereavement. This harshness was for Bee's benefit.

When Martha walked out, Bee collapsed lengthways on the carpet as if felled by a shot.

"My dad hates me. Ever since you turned up. Nicole this, Nicole that. Anyone would think you walk on fucking water. Nicole is a career woman; Nicole is someone who really holds her own in a room; Nicole dresses for suc-fucking-cess. Don't chuck me out, Nicole; I really have nowhere to go. Nowhere."

For the next hour, when Nicole had been hoping to do some research about Gal's travails, she cuddled Bee and listened to her tales of (relative) childhood slights (or what she called misery). Nicole reflected on all the despondent evenings she and her mother had spent eating ready meals in front of the television and then compared it with Bee's childhood mansion and rowdy, bacchanalian feasts. Mind you, she thought to herself, living with Lord-of-all-he-surveys, Charlie Newhouse, and Dan, the boy-who-could-do-no-wrong, can't have been easy.

16

When Nicole got into the office the next morning at eight fifteen, there were more people in than usual. It was the first time she hadn't been excited to go in. Memories of her mother, guilt about her last days – as well as her hangover and lingering back pain – made it hard to get out of bed. Her head reverberated with worries, noise and colours, and nothing would stop them.

As ever the office was silent, but groups were huddled around laptops, muttering. Gal's door was shut. Anya had her hair in a topknot and was dressed in a black leather jacket with the collar up. When Nicole sat down next to her, she saw she had way more make-up on than usual. With her strawberry red lipstick and heavy blusher on her cheeks, she looked ready for battle.

Anya said, "How are you? Coffee?"

Nicole beamed at her. Anya's unsolicited kindness gave her a glow she hadn't experienced for a while. She hoped she didn't look as muddle-headed as she felt.

"I hear you and Gal got drunk in Borough Market."

It wasn't a statement designed to elicit any mirth from the situation. He hadn't told her anything, had he? Nicole set her laptop down, pushed the power button and ignored her for a moment.

Nicole said, "You look good. Going out later?" No-one looked more like they needed a decent party than Anya.

"Did you have a good time? Cheer you up?" Some of the boys had pricked up their ears and turned around. They clearly weren't used to such excitement.

"We went out for a drink to debrief after the media tour. I got emotional about my mum, so he listened. Just what I needed. What's everyone doing?"

Anya looked over at the gossiping boys and shrugged. "You know he wants you, don't you?"

"He so doesn't. You, more like."

Nicole looked over her shoulder at Gal's office. The blinds were down, but she could see that he was staring out of the window. It was rare he wasn't hunched over his keyboard or shouting into his phone.

She lowered her voice. "Anya, it was work. OK? It's been a crazy, few weeks. Relax."

Anya exhaled with a theatrical flourish and returned to hitting her keyboard with the venom of a concert pianist who has just been dumped by her first love.

Nicole went over to Gal's office door and pulled it open. She was conscious of being watched. No-one went into his office unless he invited them.

"Got a minute?"

Gal looked up. His eyes were watery. He gestured for her to sit down with a grimace.

"What do I do?" His voice was much thinner and reedier

than before. Did he really fancy her? It was hard to believe. And, much as she admired his chutzpah, sexual attraction didn't enter into it for her.

"You are certain there's nothing in it?" Gal made the sign of the cross across his chest and nodded.

"Good. I thought as much. I don't think you're a predator. Not for one minute. So, we're going to go on the front foot. First, you're going to tell that lot out there that you deny everything and won't hesitate to use the law if need be. Then we'll issue a statement to all the media who have covered it. Nothing fancy. You deny all allegations and will not be making any further comment while the police investigation is ongoing. Too late in most cases, but at least they know where we stand and will be on their guard. OK?"

Nicole spent half an hour working up a one-paragraph statement with Gal. She had a further paragraph for the staff stating his commitment to the company's values. If that leaked, so much the better. As Gal talked to the staff, Nicole watched everyone to see how people reacted. His voice wobbled to start with but gained strength as the words gave him confidence.

"You've all read about the allegations against me. I want to say to you now that I totally refute them, and I will co-operate fully with the police in their investigations. They are totally without foundation, and I will willingly go to court to prove my innocence if needs be.

"We are often in the news for the wrong reasons right now. Zaxxo is making waves in the world of finance and competitors will stoop to anything to trip us up. You can be sure that, in the next few months, Nicole will be working day and night to ensure the Zaxxo brand grows stronger and stronger and that we continue to thrive. You can expect more dirt being thrown at us and you can expect us to fight fire with fire."

There was a loud round of applause from the staff and then they shuffled back to their desks. Anya didn't clap. She just stared at Nicole as Gal spoke, as if she was guilty of placing him under a spell. Nicole's mental list of possible suspects gained another addition. Once he had finished, Gal had bowed and headed back into his office.

Nicole pinged the statement out to the five journalists who were covering the story, then she dug out her phone and looked at Ginny Forshaw the school secretary's list. She had a few minutes before they all started calling back. There was an empty meeting room that would avoid Anya's prying. Everyone would think she was crisis-managing and, if any more journalists called, she would be.

She soon found that finding octogenarians wasn't as easy as finding younger people. They don't use social media, and their jobs stopped before the internet really got going. In the end, she had to sign up and fork out for 192.com, which gave her phone numbers for the three names who lived in the UK.

"Hello. Can I speak to Ian Weatherall?" The female voice at the other end of the phone was abrupt in her refusal. He had died six months earlier. Nicole expressed her condolence and rang off.

She dialled the next one. Matthew Johnson. He would be over 90. The phone rang for several minutes, and she was tempted to ring off. Then a quavering male voice answered. This was it.

"Hello. This is Nicole Weymouth. Can I speak to Matthew?!" There was silence. "Hello?"

"What do you want?" The voice sounded very nervous.

"I'm the daughter of an old boy and I'm doing some research about his old school. I wondered if you could tell me about your time at Rothbury?"

There was a pause on the line.

"Oh yes. Rothbury. What a place. What do you want to know?" A little more confidence in the voice but stuttering. Nicole hoped he couldn't hear the thud of her racing heart.

"Did you know Peter Slaithwaite? He was a pupil there with you."

Silence again. "No, I didn't. Matthew would probably know about him."

"But I thought you were Matthew." Her heart sank.

"No, I'm Michael. Matthew's been dead twenty years." Nicole took a very deep breath and promised herself to be nice. "Sorry, my hearing aid battery is dead. How can I help?"

As it turned out, he couldn't. He had only been born in 1940. Nicole wondered if she was wasting her time. Had she reached a dead end? One to go. Her heart racing with fear she dialled the final number.

Bingo! Jeff Kerslake wasn't only alive, but he answered the phone. She decided to be upfront with him.

"I hope you don't mind, but I would like to come and talk to you about Peter Slaithwaite. Would that be possible?" There was a prolonged bout of coughing at the other end of the phone followed by a crackle.

"Oh, him again. Who are you?" Nicole ran through the background to her call. Coughs continued to punctuate the conversation. She should get down there as soon as she could before he collapsed or something.

"I'll ask Steve." Steve's identity wasn't clear, but it involved Jeff leaving the phone for some time. The next time someone spoke it was a much younger, less genteel voice.

"Yeah?"

Nicole ran through what she wanted and asked if she could come up at the weekend.

"He's an old man. He doesn't need hassle. Half an hour. No more. Got it?" Nicole affirmed that she got it. A time was agreed at a house in Summertown, just north of Oxford. Morse country. How appropriate.

Nicole had another call waiting. It was Anthony from *The Gazette* wanting to know if there was any more detail on the allegations. Nicole told him they had said all they intended to say on the matter.

After a grunt Anthony said, "She's good-looking. I've heard one of the tabloids is doing a deal with her. Anyway, talking of deals, where's my funding story?"

*

Dan had been brilliant, using his time off work to organise the church, the undertakers, and the catering at the wake. He had also taken responsibility for working with the solicitor to buy some time with the creditors and keep Nicole's father off her back. One day soon she would have to tell her father there was no money. Despite all the pain he had caused her, she didn't relish telling him that news. She was hoping the conversation could be delayed until after the funeral.

There was a text from Dan asking how she was. *Not great* was the answer, but she didn't feel ready to tell him much more yet. As the funeral drew nearer, he had taken a more proprietary view of her whereabouts, presumably because he knew how much strain she was under, but it came across as if he wasn't convinced that she had totally given up on her search for the truth about Peter.

The fact that Annabel seemed at his side whenever Nicole wasn't also annoyed her. But she couldn't have her cake and eat it. If she wanted to have Dan to herself and end the badgering texts, she could just go and sit alongside Dan in the sitting room at his flat. She would call him when she was back in the car.

*

Jeff Kerslake's house was a big, double-fronted red-brick house off the Woodstock Road. There was a Golf and a BMW in the driveway. A tall man in a black T-shirt, a pot belly, and faded jeans with holes in the knees came out to greet her. He was frowning and had a knob of tissue on his chin. It didn't appear that her arrival would improve his mood.

"You Nicole?" He shook her hand and pumped it up and down. "I'm Steve. Jeff's my uncle and my last living relative. I promised his sister, my mum, nothing bad would happen to him. Get it?" Nicole, yet again, got it.

His hair was greased and spiky but shorn at the sides. Nicole thought he looked like a surprised hedgehog. She forced out her PR smile.

"Come with me," he said.

Nicole followed him into the house. They went through an immaculate hall with black and white tiles into a kitchen at the back. It stretched the whole rear of the house and had a massive island in the middle. There was evidence of a female touch, but there was no sign of one. No sign of Jeff Kerslake either. Steve ushered her in and shut the kitchen door behind them.

"Sit down."

He pointed to a kitchen table to the left. Nicole sat down on a chair and felt for her phone in her coat pocket. He pulled up a chair, turned it round the wrong way and sat right up in front of Nicole like an interrogator in a US cop show. A whiff of cheap aftershave filled her nostrils. "What's this all about? Some dead bloke? Eighty years ago? You a journalist or something?"

"Nothing like that. I've nothing to gain. I found a letter from the war, and I want to know what happened to the writer. Your uncle is one of the few people who might know. It won't take long." She paused to control her emotions. "I've got my mother's funeral in a few days."

Steve stroked Nicole's cheek with the back of his forefinger and continued its trajectory to move a lock of her hair from her forehead.

"I'm sorry to hear that. You're very brave coming here."

She pulled her head back and resisted the temptation to slap him.

He said, "So what's it worth?"

Nicole stood up. "I'm leaving. Please apologise to your uncle." She headed towards the door. She felt a hand grab her arm.

"Steady on. Don't be like that. I'm only joshing you. How about a drink?" Nicole shook her head and looked at the door. This could still go either way. "Be like that. I'll go and get him." Steve swept out of the kitchen. Nicole walked towards the bay window and looked out into the garden. The lawn was threadbare and the flowerbeds empty, but it looked tidy and loved. She wondered if this was how Jeff Kerslake spent his days. She doubted that Steve was green-fingered.

After about five minutes a bent old man in a tweed jacket and navy gilet appeared in the kitchen doorway. Steve walked alongside, guiding him towards the kitchen table. The hand Jeff Kerslake proffered was as smooth as a baby's.

Steve got Jeff settled in a chair and offered to make some tea. Maybe he wasn't a complete tosser, thought Nicole.

Jeff started his signature cough as he moved around to get his thin frame comfortable. Every movement he made was in slow motion and required a deep breath like bellows to power it.

"He's a good lad, Steve. I couldn't have survived without him since Cecily died." Nicole resisted the temptation to ask about the beneficiary of the will. "He won't let me go out on my own. He's like my own private bodyguard." Jeff's chuckle at his own joke turned into another spate of coughing.

"I wonder if I could ask you about Peter. You were at school together?"

Jeff smiled. "Everyone wants to know about Peter Slaithwaite. I had another woman, quite a bit older than you, come and ask me about him. Must have been ten years ago now."

"Who was she?" Nicole frowned.

"I really can't remember. Very courteous woman, middle-aged, well-dressed. Asked a few questions about what Peter was like and then left. I might have fallen asleep, of course. I tend to do that, don't I, Steve?"

Nicole told him what she knew about Peter and that

he had written a letter about some dreadful things that had happened: the bullying, the night in the stables, the running away. When she told Jeff about the letter, she thought she detected a tear in his eye.

Steve served them each tea in a cup and saucer. It had more sugar in it than Nicole had had all year. Jeff eyed them as he processed what Nicole had said.

Steve moved back and stood behind her. She could tell his movements by the varying strength of his aftershave. "He hates talking about his school days. You're lucky he said yes."

Jeff wracked a cough that reached down to the pit of his chest and took two sips of tea.

"There was a bunch of them. Monitors. Meant to look after the smaller boys. My arse! Terrorised us. The headmaster encouraged it because if they policed us all, he didn't have to. He was a useless bugger, holed up in his study drinking himself senseless. Once lessons were over, if you can call them lessons – I never learnt anything – then there was loads of free time. We did a bit of sport, but there wasn't much equipment. Endless country runs in the snow and rain, that's how they kept us out of trouble. The elder boys just loved keeping us in our place. Beatings, whippings, fisticuffs – you name it, they did it. Peter got it worse as he was quite a pretty boy, the closest anyone got to a girl in that place. Me and my mates tried to protect him, but they always found a way to separate us. They got some sort of sadistic kick about seeing what they could do to him."

Jeff took another sip of his tea and started coughing again. Steve walked over, took his cup and saucer and thumped him on the back.

"Thanks, Steve. There was a ringleader who decided

what punishments they would mete out to us. He was always crowing about the latest ingenious way to make boys suffer. We went to the headmaster, the nurse, even the local priest once, and complained but no-one took any notice. Once I had to go up to the top of the hill at three in the morning to go and find Peter in the freezing cold as he had been locked in a cowshed. It was inhumane. I wrote to my parents about it, but I don't think the letters ever reached them."

Nicole chanced her arm. "Who was the ringleader? Do you know?"

"I can't say. Mr De La Hay made me promise years ago that I would never do so. And if I did, he said he had some dirt on me he would tell my wife."

Nicole didn't have much to lose. "That doesn't matter now, does it?"

Steve said, "The De La Hays have been very good to Jeff. Paid for some of his medical care when the insurance wouldn't. Let sleeping dogs lie. That's what you say, isn't it, Jeffrey?" Nicole thought she detected Jeff shake his head when Steve said that.

"What about the night that Peter was shut in the stable?"

"That was the worst night. They had been warming up to do something terrible. Peter wouldn't say much about it to me, but he implied it wasn't an accident."

Nicole startled. "What do you mean?"

"One of the boys was found dead in the quarry. Eric McArthur. No-one knows what really happened."

Nicole's heart took yet another leap, the highest yet. She knew it. A murder. There had to have been something more. The incident in the stable was terrible, but this explained everything.

"Go on." Jeff peered at her as if to check he hadn't misjudged her. It was a cover-up. Just like when her dad blamed her that day by the pool.

"The police investigated it and said it was misadventure. I've always had my doubts. Clive De La Hay did a very good job putting them off the scent. But Peter was there. He knew something. And those boys knew he did." Jeff coughed for a few moments. It didn't seem like he wanted to dwell on Eric McArthur's death.

"What happened to Eric? Don't you know anything?" Jeff was silent. "Jeff?"

Steve said, "He doesn't know any more. That Peter wouldn't tell him."

Nicole hesitated. Peter was her priority, wasn't he? "So, what happened that night?"

"Me and Carruthers tried to stop them, but they tied us to our bedposts with our ties. Poor Peter was screaming as they took him down through the school. I couldn't believe they didn't wake one of the adults up. Mind you, there were only four of them. We didn't see him all night. Christ, it was a cold one. And we knew that bloody horse had gone a bit nuts. We all joked about it. I was worried whether we would ever see him alive again. I was so relieved when I heard that one of the cleaning ladies' daughters had found him…"

"Carol Bristow. I met her. She told me about it."

"Really? Carol? Still alive? Send her my best. And her mum, God rest her soul. I think they saved his life. He ran away as soon as he got better. Got home too. Don't know how he did it. Talk about cross-country."

"Did you ever see him again?" Nicole figured Jeff was tiring. She only had a few questions left.

"A couple of times. He was never the same. And something happened at home when he was a teenager. Whatever that was, it didn't help. Some mishap with a girl, I think. I saw him about a year before he died. I bumped into him in Regent Street. God, he looked awful. I put out my hand to stop him and say hello. He looked up, didn't stop moving, mumbled, 'I can't, Jeff, I just can't'".

"What did he mean?"

"At the time I thought he meant he couldn't talk to me about school, but, looking back on it, knowing what he did to himself, I think he meant living." Jeff was still, mouth open, stopped in his tracks. "He couldn't carry on living."

Nicole sat back. The De La Hays had much more to lose than she thought. Her time must be up. Steve was hovering. Jeff's lips were trembling now. Nicole could feel tears streaming down her face. One more question.

"Why won't you tell me who did this? I can see why you might be loyal to the De La Hays, but this is too terrible to keep secret. Your wife's dead. You have nothing to lose."

"There's lots no-one's saying about that school. Clive De La Hay wasn't a well man. No-one was in charge. I told his family all about it about ten years later at an old boys' day. It shook them so badly I even felt sorry for them. So, when Martin came back to me on it after his dad's death, I promised him the identity of those boys would go to my grave. Don't look at me like that, young lady. We needed the money. Cecily was very sick. I had to make a choice and I'm a man of my word."

Steve touched Nicole's shoulder. "He is. You better go. It's time for his pills."

Wish it was time for mine too, she thought.

Nicole was being ushered away as she said, "I still don't understand why you wouldn't say who they are given the awful things they did. It doesn't make sense."

Jeff gave his half-empty teacup a morose look. He didn't look like a man comfortable with his decision. "You will find someone to tell you. If you do, then tell the world and I will applaud you. To be honest I think that other woman knew. I don't know why she hasn't said something."

Nicole wanted to ask more about the woman, but she was propelled out of the kitchen and on to the driveway. Then Steve stepped in front of her and said, "Are you sure you won't have that drink?"

"No. You've been really kind, but I have to get back to London."

Nicole brushed past him, ran down the drive and across to her car. As she marshalled her breathing, she looked back to check Steve hadn't followed her over. As she got into the car, another bout of nausea hit her.

17

Nicole was shaking all the way home. She didn't trust herself to drive fast, so she stuck to the slow lane and contemplated what Jeff Kerslake had said. She now knew everything that had happened to Peter. She just had to find who was responsible.

She got back to the flat just before seven o'clock. She WhatsApped Martha to ask what her dinner plans were and got a series of exclamation marks in return.

When she entered the flat, she could hear why. Martha was standing in the middle of the living room floor mid-rant. Bee was curled up in a ball on the sofa.

"And you don't even buy any bloody food! You just eat half of anything I buy then try and glue the packaging back together. Not very well either. Nicole let you stay here for one night and, two weeks later, you're still here like an unwanted ghost that won't leave... Nicole, thank God for that, get rid of her, will you?"

Nicole slumped down in the armchair. She'd hoped that Bee would have taken the hint and left while she was away.

All her family had told her it was time to go. Post-it notes on every appliance had reminded her.

"Bee, it's not fair on Martha. Go home. You've got a lovely bedroom there. And you get fed properly."

Bee looked up at her, nose red and dripping. "But I need to support you."

Nicole raised her voice. "You don't. Martha, I'm so sorry. Bee, you have to leave… NOW."

Bee rolled on to the floor, grabbed her bag, sprung up and scampered into the bathroom, locking the door.

"Great," said Martha, striding off towards her room. "So, it's the pub toilets for the rest of the night."

Nicole sat staring into space. She was so close now. Why wouldn't Jeff Kerslake tell her the name? It was so long ago. Why would anyone care now? Any villain of the piece was probably dead. The woman who had been to see him before her. What was that all about? And should she go to the police? Would they care about a crime committed so long ago? She got out her phone. Google said there was no time limit on when to report a crime.

The intercom sprang into life. Usually, it was a neighbour who had forgotten their key. Not this time. A florid face filled the screen. Hair all over the place, glasses misted. It was Charlie Newhouse.

"Nicole, can I come up? I've come to get Bee. Is she there?" His speech was even more slurred than usual. Charlie's history of erratic, aggressive behaviour gave her little incentive to invite him up, but if he got Bee out of her, and especially Martha's, life, it would be worth the hassle. She pressed the buzzer.

Charlie filled the hallway with his paraphernalia:

raincoat, briefcase, hat, umbrella. Droplets of water sprayed on to Nicole as he disrobed. The smell of booze hit her nostrils like an overflowing bottle bank.

"Jo and I believe we have been negligent allowing Bee to squat in your flat when you have had so much going on in your life. Where is she?"

Covering her nose to avoid the smell, Nicole led him into the living room. "She's locked herself in the bathroom. This is Martha. Martha, meet Bee and Dan's father, Charlie." Charlie doled out a stream of 'hail-fellow-well-met' platitudes, some only partially intelligible. Nicole went down the corridor and knocked on the bathroom door as the sound of loud tears greeted her.

Charlie lumbered up alongside her, wet tweed joining the smell of stale alcohol, and knocked louder on the upper part of the door. "Bee, come out. I want to talk to you. Come out now!" He wiped his brow and grimaced at Nicole. "God, that girl." He resumed his knocking. "If you don't come out, Nicole and Martha are going to throw all your possessions on to the street, and I won't stop them." Charlie signalled a whispering sign at Nicole to play along.

"That's not true, Bee. But, please, come out."

After a moment the door opened, and Bee stood in front of them. Her arms hung down by her sides like an out-of-action string puppet. The pupils of her eyes were like pinpricks and her nose shone. For the first time since she had moved herself in, Nicole pitied her.

Charlie didn't appear as moved by her appearance. He leant forward, grabbed her by the shoulder and tried to pull her out of the bathroom.

"Fuck off, Dad, leave me alone!" Charlie tried again. Nicole looked back at Martha, who looked embarrassed but seemed reluctant to intervene. The end, presumably for her, justified the means. Something wasn't right. Bee shrunk back and tried to close the bathroom door again. "Just fuck off. Leave me alone. Nicole, stop him!" Charlie was trying to force his way into the bathroom.

Nicole said, "It's alright, Charlie, leave her be. We can sort it."

Martha shouted, "No, we can't. We haven't. Charlie, go ahead, be my guest."

Charlie retorted, "You can't just lie around on people's sofas taking drugs and blaming everyone else. You need to pull yourself together and get on with life! C'mon, darling. This is so unfair on Nicole and Martha."

He, exhaling wine breath all over Nicole, said, "I thought you wanted her out. Isn't that the point?"

"Yes, but not like this. Not by force." She hoped Dan didn't have any of this violence squirrelled away somewhere. Martha had stepped away, back into the living room.

"You don't know my daughter."

"Maybe, but I know about respect for women." This was a man who was slandering her boss and trying to cover up for the De La Hays. Dan's father or not, he deserved no sympathy from her.

Charlie's eyes, bulbous, red, and veined behind his glasses, focussed on her. "I'm trying to do you a favour, Nicole. Surely you can see that?"

"I don't want a favour from you. I can look after myself."

"This is one favour you should take, Nicole," said Martha. "For my sake."

"Yeah, but not like this. Charlie, this is our flat and I would like you to leave, please."

He slumped against the wall. "What is it about you, Nicole? Why can't you just let people help you? Instead, all you do is cause trouble. You just don't know what damage you're doing. Can't you just focus on yourself for a little while? Give your mother a decent send-off?"

Nicole saw red. How dare he use her mother like some sort of human shield.

"Get out. Now!"

"That bloody letter you're so obsessed about. Poor old Martin De La Hay is about to do the deal of his life with some blue-chip investors, and you're set on trying to expose some schoolboy's stupid fantasy from eighty years ago that will derail it. There could be Rothburys all around the world if this goes ahead. You are a fantastic, smart woman, but sometimes I think you need your head examined. I'm sorry but it's true."

Charlie hung his head, exhausted. He was pathetic. He wasn't worth it. She had her ammunition now.

She said, "OK. You've said your piece. Go."

Martha said, "And take Bee with you. For Christ's sake, Nicole. He's right. You do need your head examined."

At that moment Bee stepped out of the bathroom and stood between them. "Nicole should be allowed to do and say what she wants. She's been an incredible friend to me these last two weeks, a time when my family has basically disowned me. Those money men should know what's going on before they waste their money."

Charlie said, "Don't be so stupid. Don't say things when you don't know the full story. We all have a lot riding on this deal."

Nicole said, "I'm not messing up any deal you're doing. I'm not doing anything. I know nothing about any investment from China, and I don't care about it either. How was I to know there was a deal? No wonder Martin De La Hay was so spiky."

"Well, now you know. Keep it to yourself, please. If you don't, you can forget about that loan."

Nicole said, "Don't threaten me, Charlie."

Bee shouted, "Keep it to your fucking self! Jesus Christ! In the end it's always about you, isn't it, Dad? Always about what's best for Charlie Newhouse. Even this mercy trip was about warning Nicole off her letter. Well, as far as I'm concerned, I hope Nicole finds out everything there is to know and posts it on Twitter so the world can see what a shitty school Rothbury is."

"OK, everyone, that's enough." As if out of nowhere, Jo had appeared and was standing in between the three of them. Her eyes were glistening with anger. She must have been waiting in the car and Martha had let her in. She took Charlie by the arm and pulled him away. "Charlie and Bee, I'm taking you home. It's time to give Nicole some space."

Nicole put her arm around Bee's waist. It didn't matter what she said now. "Thank you, Jo. Your husband needs to calm down. I've stopped my investigations because Dan doesn't want me to." Jo raised an eyebrow at her.

Charlie said, "That's the right decision. That's always the problem with secrets. It's the consequences."

"I said that's enough, Charlie."

Bee said, "Yes, that's enough, Dad."

"Enough applies to you too. You've outstayed your welcome here, Bee."

Charlie had calmed down a little now. There was sweat on his brow, which he wiped off with his tweeded sleeve. He turned on his heels and headed off down the corridor. "Oh, for fuck's sake. C'mon, Bee, do as your mother says. Goodnight, Nicole Goodnight, Martha."

Nicole kissed Bee on the cheek. "I'll see you at the funeral."

18

Sometimes, Nicole convinced herself that it hadn't really happened. The grief hit her in waves like a virus, overcoming her when she least expected it. Her mother was down there in Bradford-on-Avon waiting for her next visit. In her imagination she was still bustling around the kitchen making tea and spilling fag ash.

As the funeral approached that fallacy was disintegrating. In addition, she would not, as the only surviving child, be able to avoid being the centre of attention at the funeral. At the best of times, she hated that, and this wasn't the best of times by a long shot.

And, for the rest of her life, it would be just her. No brother, no mother, and a father she didn't want to see. People with no support system couldn't afford to alienate the people who cared about them, but that's what she was doing. When the car stopped at the next traffic light, she hit her head against the steering wheel until Dan told her to stop. She wished her grief would consume her so that she could be confident that, one day, she would reach the other side and move on. But there was no other side: just a dark void she could never escape.

Most of her family and friends had given up on her mother years ago. Anyone who came to the funeral would be curious as to what had happened to her and, if they felt any guilt about their absence, would want to assuage it with a quick chat with Nicole. In an ideal world her goodbye to her mother would be solitary, maybe just with Dan, and her father if he was on best behaviour. But that wasn't going to happen and just at the time when she craved privacy.

Those concerns notwithstanding, she was very lucky to have had Dan, who still wasn't fully recovered from his injuries, as event organiser. He had organised the service at the local church, St Dunstan's, and a wake at a hotel convenient to the church with a wide, flat pavement and ramp for the elderly and plenty of parking spaces close to the front door. Nicole had chosen the hymns and readings. Her mother's only stipulation, that Nicole could recall, was that the service shouldn't feature 'The Day Thou Gavest, Lord, is Ended' as it had been an omnipresent depressant for her as a girl.

They had no idea of likely numbers. A notice had been put in *The Daily Telegraph*, the local paper, and the parish magazine. Nicole had found the phone numbers of the few surviving relatives. There were a couple of cousins in Wales Nicole had liked as a child. Their visits had stopped after Patrick's death. Her mother had often joked that the villagers loved a funeral but that her outbursts at the Parish Council would deter most of them from coming to hers. Either way Dan had ordered enough food and drink for fifty people for two hours, and when it ran out, it ran out.

She travelled to the funeral from Charlie and Jo's house.

Packing proved impossible. Dan tried to help, but she had stopped him. She had grabbed anything she could think of from her flat, but, in her daze, she had forgotten half her toiletries and make-up. Her black dress had been at the back of the cupboard for a year and could have done with a dry-clean. Jo had given it a once-over with a sponge, and they would have to stop for any other bits and pieces at the motorway services.

Dan said, "How are you feeling?"

"Weird. Weirder every day. Especially today." She was going to try very hard to hold it together for as long as possible. Her lower lip wobbled, and her throat bobbled up and down.

She was starting to feel even more odd. Her body was giving her different signals from normal, and she was nauseous when there was no reason. She was always very careful, but she was late. It couldn't be. She decided she would put it out her of her mind until after the funeral. She certainly wasn't planning to tell anyone. She looked over at Dan, loathing the person she had become as she strived to be the one she really wanted to be.

Dan, lying back in the passenger seat of the car, tried to make the case, without much belief or success, for his father's behaviour the previous evening.

"He never told me anything about this Chinese investment – HVAC, they're called. I knew he advised Rothbury on finances, but I thought that was limited to the bursary fund. I don't know why he didn't tell us the day after we found the letter. Thank God you've stopped digging."

Nicole put her guilty thoughts out of her mind. They turned on to the motorway. Nicole shivered and resolved to keep within the speed limit. She honked at a white van that was swaying across all three lanes. Dan had gone very pale.

"If he wasn't your father, I would have called the police. He treated Bee like shit. I know I want her out but not like that."

Dan was silent. "How do you feel about your dad being at the funeral? Do you think he'll behave? He doesn't know about the house issue yet, does he?"

"I don't want him to know until afterwards. I want to get through this with the minimum of fuss. That's what Mum would have wanted." She stumbled a little: the wellspring of her grief was starting to burble somewhere deep down from a place out of her control. Everything was out of control. She focussed on the driving. It was the first time since the accident they'd been in a car together. Nicole hadn't taken as much care since her driving test. Dan's grip on the door handle stayed tight.

*

The undertakers were situated not far from the Town Bridge in the centre of town. There was an impersonal information desk to their right and a strong smell of cleaning fluid and air freshener. Everyone they passed gave them a sad smile.

In the yard at the back, four grey-faced men of varying ages in worn, shiny black suits and shoes were loitering. In front of them was a gleaming hearse, and inside it, a polish-fresh coffin with a restrained bouquet of flowers on it. And, inside that, her mother.

Nicole's chest was tight. This wasn't happening. It happened to other people. It was as if she was in a movie she was being forced to watch. She covered her face and looked away. Holding it together was going to be impossible. She forced herself to conjure up a happy memory of her mother from when Patrick was alive. They were laughing in the sitting room, playing a game of snap. Patrick looked beautiful in matching blue Aertex shirt and shorts. Her mother's almost perfect profile was caught in the sunlight flooding through the window. For a moment she luxuriated in the memory. And then it was gone. The stark brick wall in front of her was her reality now. When she turned back, tears streaming, her father had materialised. He pointed to a black saloon behind the hearse.

The funeral procession travelled at a snail's pace up the hill to the church. It was hard to believe that gleaming wooden box in front of them contained her mother. Nicole sat alongside her father, and Dan sat opposite them. The smell of cleaning gel fought a brave battle with her father's tobacco in Nicole's nostrils. He took her hand as they set off and Nicole gripped it tight. Against her better instincts, as he had said, blood was thicker than water. Despite everything, she wanted to say goodbye with him. He had had a sharp haircut and the grey bristles he usually forgot under his chin were absent. Dan's family were following in their car behind. Nicole tried to think of memorable movie funeral processions but failed to get beyond the Mafia ones where everyone stands in the town square and gets machine-gunned from the back window of a car.

Her father started talking about how happy her mother was the day she was born. Nicole stared out of the window and imagined Patrick was alongside her. He would be a very tall and good-looking man by now. Through university, hopefully with a brilliant job and a girlfriend (or boyfriend) she liked.

What would her life have been like if he had lived? Would her parents have stayed together? Would both have been happier? Would she have been a different person? She knew the answer to all these questions. Yes, yes and yes. The window misted up as she stayed tight-lipped. She squeezed her father's hand tighter. His grip, smooth, thick fingers, tightened on hers. She wished she could stay in the car and drive around the town all afternoon.

*

Dan got out of the car first and held her hand as she stepped out. She'd plumped for heels and knew she would need to work to stay steady today. In front of them the pall-bearers, man-handled the coffin out of the car and onto their shoulders.

There was a row of trees either side of the path as they followed the coffin towards the church doors. She walked hand in hand with Dan, and her father followed behind. She had never appreciated Dan's presence more than today.

It was a big church, and it looked about a quarter full once everyone was in. Nicole, her father and Dan went to the front pew on the left. A place between her and her father was reserved for Patrick. Before they sat down, the vicar, a shaven-headed man in his early forties, came over and shook their hands.

"Superb turn out for a much-loved parishioner," he whispered to Nicole as the organist lengthened the chords to convey restful contemplation. Only three hours until I can get away, Nicole thought to herself.

Nicole looked back for a moment. Apart from some people who looked like much older versions of her Welsh cousins, she couldn't see any more of her relations. The Newhouses were all gathered in a group halfway back. Bee wore a bright pink shawl – an oasis in a sea of black. Annabel was in a floor-length black coat with a high fur collar, gazing into the distance as if drowning in emotion. Nicole gave herself a mental slap. Out of the corner of her eye, Nicole could see Ellie and Chandra from Yellow Razor. Their presence was a very welcome surprise.

*

Halfway through the service, after an introduction from the vicar, a shaky hymn, and a reading from her father, Nicole walked up to read out her eulogy. She hadn't wanted to do it. It was too soon. Everything she really wanted to say was too personal to share with so many strangers. She didn't know how to pay tribute to her mother without hurting her father or bringing back the horror of Patrick's death and the destruction his departure had wrought on them. But she didn't want anyone else to do it. Nobody was better qualified than her to stand up and tell them what her mother was really like before life took its toll.

Nicole caressed the folded pieces of paper in her lap as the vicar announced her impending arrival at the lectern. She looked askance at her father. He was staring straight ahead, lost in his own world. Further down the pew Dan threw her an awkward smile.

When she stood up, the first thing she noticed was that Gal and Anya were at the back of the church. Gal caught her eye, and she smiled at him as she unfolded the sheets of paper. She hadn't invited them, and she hadn't told them the location, but she was pleased they were there. Maybe her worries about alienating people were premature? Annabel, in the row behind Dan, shook her blonde hair back and tied it into a ponytail with both hands. Nicole looked up at the image of Christ in the stained-glass window at the other end of the church and resolved to think well of everyone who had made the journey that day.

"My mother, Angela Christina Wenlock Weymouth, was born in Cambridge on 14th June 1964..." Nicole's hands shook, and her voice trembled as she embarked on a brief synopsis of her mother's life. The early years were relatively easy to recount, full of promise, hope and fun. She had been an attractive, bright, funny woman who had found company and adventure arrived at her door without the need to search for them.

"In 1988 she met my father, Hugh, at a dance in Holborn and married two years later. They had two children, Patrick, who is no longer with us, and me. For nearly five years we were a very happy family unit." She halted. Her father was studying his order of service. Dan nodded at her, encouraging her to continue. At the back she could see Gal, his eyes tight shut. In the rows between, the elderly mourners looked at her in puzzlement. From here on in she was in virgin territory.

"Patrick was a wonderful little boy, full of life, love and laughter. His death was a tragic accident and when he died, something in our family did too. None of us knew how to cope and we fell apart. My parents' marriage was never the same again and my mother was only half the person. I like to think, if he lived his life again, my father wouldn't have left her. But he did. And he left me too." Nicole looked up at her father again. His eyes were as watery as oysters and his lips were pursed in contrition. "I'm not blaming you, Dad. I'm not blaming anyone. All of us, that day in Portugal, let Patrick down. But, for the rest of my mother's life, she was a shadow of her younger self. Of course, we had happy times, holidays in the West Country and the South of France, brilliant Christmases with our cousins, but the lights had gone out for her and..." She paused, as much for her emotions as for emphasis. "...they never went back on." Nicole looked up at the eaves in the church ceiling and willed herself forward. She closed off the congregation and focussed only on her mother's memory. Then she looked down at the tiled floor, gripped the lectern hard, and waited for her emotions to subside.

"She loved poetry, especially the works of Yeats and Wordsworth. She never tired of watching detective programmes, especially *Inspector Morse* and *Lewis*. She did lots around the parish, as many of you here today will know. But truthfully, I think she had given up. I don't think anyone knows what really went on in her head these last fifteen years, but I do know I loved her more than anyone in the world, and she loved her children. She gave me everything she had and much, much more besides. Now she is with Patrick, and they can have the life together they both missed. One day I will join them. And I relish the thought of that day. In the meantime, I am determined that I will live the life she wished she had had. That's the best that I can do for her. Not to allow life to grind me down, keep going no matter what, set ambitious goals and achieve them. I know that's what she would have wanted. Mum, that's my promise: I will make you proud of me. Mum, I love you and will miss you until my dying day."

Nicole bowed her head, folded the paper, and walked back to her seat. Her father got up to let her in and, as he sat down, he leant over the empty space reserved for Patrick and kissed her on the cheek. Dan touched her shoulder.

Bee leant forward and whispered. "You are so brave," into her ear. The most difficult part of the day was done. She had said what she wanted to say to her mother. The vicar announced a final hymn – 'O god, our help in ages past' – and, with effort, Nicole pulled herself back up on to her feet.

*

The crematorium – just her father, herself and Dan – was a welcome respite, a fifteen-minutes' drive to the east of the town. After he had complimented her on her eulogy, her father said very little. Her mother's coffin disappeared within a couple of minutes amidst a wash of comforting music and the drop of a burgundy curtain. The wake awaited.

Nicole and her father sat in the back, Dan in the front. Her father broke the silence in the car. "When do you think the house will be sold?" Nicole gave him an incredulous look. She didn't want to tell him anything today.

"I don't know. You know as much as me about how these things work. Three months at least. I don't think property is moving much in Bradford-on-Avon. Unless it looks like something out of a Jane Austen novel."

Her father picked at his fingernails. "Yes, our old house

must be worth about £3 million now. Well, anything I can do to help…"

Dan said, "Now's not the time, Hugh." Hugh gave him a stern look.

Nicole ignored him. She stared out of the window and wondered at how she had managed to keep herself together to the end of her eulogy. For those moments she had been someone she didn't recognise.

They didn't speak any more until they reached the hotel. It was a three-storey Victorian building near the centre of town set back from the main road with a half-circle black tarmac drive in front and trees pruned back to sharp stalks with green buds. It lacked personality, as if it had been stripped back to the bare bones so it could withstand the rowdiest of parties. Nicole thought the sheer volume of tacky award certification plaques on display on the wall next to the front door rather undermined the premium quality status it claimed on the website. Her mother had often questioned whether it was about to close down when they passed it in the car on the way to the supermarket.

The chatter that greeted them bore testimony to Dan's attention to detail on the catering strategy. The house champagne was nearly as cheap as the wine, so they had agreed it was worth the investment, and the bubbles had raised people's spirits fast. Nicole took a glass from a tray as she entered. The locals, with half an eye out on the staff entrance from which canapes might emerge, smiled at her as she moved into the room. Several of them came up to shake hand or hug her and compliment her on her eulogy. More than one shared an anecdote about her mother's generosity. It appeared that she hadn't just spent her money on gambling. Nicole was surprised by the affection in which her mother seemed to have been held. There had been no clue when they had been out and about in the town.

She saw Gal and Anya in the corner and went over to them. "Thank you for coming."

Anya, stick thin in her black two-piece, neat square kneecaps on show beneath silk tights, said, "We thought you would appreciate the support. We didn't know your mother, but your words made us feel as if we did." Nicole promised herself that, however annoying Anya might be in the future, she would always give her the benefit of the doubt.

"Well, I'm very touched that you did. Thank you." It was hard not to channel some minor royalty when everyone was on edge and wanted to talk to you. "Shall I introduce you to some people?"

At this point Nicole found herself being knocked sideways as Bee put her arms around her and smothered her. "You, absolute legend, sweetheart. I don't have any tears left to cry." Bee then disproved this statement by clinging onto Nicole and wetting both their cheeks. They swung together and Nicole tried to avoid spilling the contents of her glass. Anya took it as it swung past her. After thirty seconds, Bee stopped.

"Bee, you can help, actually. This is Gal and Anya from Zaxxo. Would you mind introducing them to anyone you know? They've very kindly come a long way and don't know anyone."

Bee kissed both Gal and Anya on each cheek. "You are total heroes to me. Nicole is so lucky to be working with you. You are the future, aren't you? You must meet Dad."

"Maybe try some of the locals first?" Nicole said.

"Just leave it to me, Nicole. I'll look after them." Bee grabbed both Gal and Anya by a hand each and dragged them off.

Nicole wasn't on her own for long. Chandra and Ellie came up to her. Both wore skirts, a little shorter and better tailored than the rest of the guests. Ellie had shades on her head for some inexplicable reason. They both gave her one of those theatrical hugs that women give each other when they don't want to spoil their make-up.

Ellie said, "Gal says you are doing brilliantly."

"I haven't really had a chance to get completely into it, but I'm enjoying it a lot. I think I can make a real difference there."

Chandra said, "Better boss than Po then?" Ellie gave her a playful nudge as if to indicate it wasn't appropriate.

Ellie said, "You can come back whenever you wish. You're part of the Yellow Razor family. You know that, don't you?"

"I didn't. I thought I was in disgrace. But it's good to know. The fact that you've come all this way shows how much you care. I'm really touched."

Nicole took a sip of her champagne and tried to dial down the cut-glass Duchess of Somewhereshire accent that took over her vocal cords whenever she was nervous. She wondered why Ellie would come all the way to Wiltshire for the funeral of someone she had never met when she had never as much as taken her over the road for lunch. Then she remembered her promise to herself about the people who had made the effort come.

"I'm set on Zaxxo for now. Turning the world of banking on its head and all that. I'm part of the senior team."

Chandra said, "Do you think we could get the account?"

Nicole shook her head. "Dan's sister seems to share your enthusiasm. She seemed dead keen on getting Gal and her father to talk."

"I know." Oh shit. Not today.

Bee was still furious after the previous night's confrontation. If the last few days of mourning had taught her one thing, it was that sometimes it was better to let things lie. But not everyone in the room agreed with that.

*

Nicole was half-listening to a tale about parking permits from one of her mother's WI friends and contemplating slowing down on the champagne, while watching Bee touching Gal and her father on the shoulders and pushing them together. There was a word for how she felt – discombobulated. Could she ever have predicted all the people she knew would be in the same room?

She thought again of her mother. She wouldn't have enjoyed being the centre of attention. She would have wanted to slip off home to get a cup of tea and read a book. Nicole wondered if she had been a little harsh on her father. Had she over shared the family story? It takes two to make and two to break a marriage, they said. But if she hadn't talked about Patrick's death and the aftermath, there wouldn't have been much left. And wasn't a church a place where you were meant to tell the truth? That day in Portugal flooded back into her memory for the umpteenth time. Sometimes she wondered if she had ever moved on at all. Her whole life since then just a mirage.

A huge man in a tweed three-piece suit barrelled in front

of her. His ginger beard was covered in crumbs from the vol-au-vents and his eyes were a little bloodshot.

"I'm Harry Pearson. I wanted to pay my condolences."

"Oh, thank you. Did you know her well?"

He leant over and lowered his voice. "Well enough to lend her £20,000."

Nicole looked around her. Dan was nowhere to be seen. Were you allowed to do this at a funeral?

"Ah."

"Yes. Sorry to bring it up here. I could really do with it back." She noticed Harry's watch, a Rolex, probably worth as much as the sum as he lent to her mother.

"You need to talk to the solicitors not me. It's all in their hands."

Harry frowned. "I lent it to her in good faith. I don't want to be fobbed off like everybody else."

Annabel arrived in front of her, moved in front of Harry Pearson, bent a little and whispered, "Came to rescue you. How're you holding up?"

"Good. Thanks for coming over. You're sweet to ask. Where's Dan?"

"He's talking to your dad about money." Harry Pearson, miffed at his relegation, nodded at Nicole, touched his nose as if to say 'later' and moved off towards the drinks.

Nicole said, "I'd better go over." This funeral was turning into a magnet for trouble. She tried to move off, but Annabel held her arm saying, "Are you sure?"

Nicole didn't need Annabel monitoring her behaviour at her own mother's funeral. Anywhere, in fact. But Annabel meant well this time. She shook it off in as slow and as appreciative a way as possible.

She had to smile and ignore a couple of well-wishers as she strode across the room towards the bay window where she could see her father, red-faced and glimmering, having a heated conversation. Dan was leaning against the window with the air of a man who wanted to be elsewhere.

"Why didn't someone tell me? That's our money she spent. It's… it's unethical. Totally unethical."

Dan said, "It's Nicole's money, actually. You would have signed away any rights with the divorce, I'm afraid. The debts too."

"Hello, you two." Nicole turned on her 'Welcome to British Airways' smile and hoped for the best.

"Did you know about this, Nicole? Did you?" Nicole moved over and leant against Dan. Across the room Annabel squinted at them with curiosity.

"Know about what?"

"The debts, of course." Nicole made a shush sign with her finger.

"I was waiting for the right time to tell you. It was a shock to me too. I'm sure something can be sorted out. Can't it, Dan?" Dan pulled a face, tried to take a swig from his empty glass and said, "Well, if you tell us how much you need, Hugh, we can keep our eyes out for any spare cash."

Under his breath, her father said, "We had an agreement. You promised."

Nicole said, "There isn't an agreement. You just keep asking me."

Dan said, "Hang on, Hugh. This is Nicole's mother's, your ex-wife's, funeral. It's not the time or the place."

Hugh signalled at a waitress for more champagne.

Nicole said, "Dad, should you be drinking?" Hugh Weymouth grunted and took a theatrical final swig.

Nicole could sense a space widen around them as the mourners kept an eye on their argument. She turned her back on them.

"That's enough, Dad." Nicole took his glass away and handed it to a waitress. "Show some respect. Show some bloody respect."

Her father looked out of the window and his lip trembled. Nicole and Dan stood in silence. It was better if they kept an eye on him in this state. Minutes seemed to pass. Her words seemed to have triggered something in him.

He turned and said, "I'm so, so sorry. I should never have blamed you. Everything was going so wrong in my life at that time, and I couldn't take another hit. I should have stayed at the pool and done my job as a father. It was my fault. I'm so sorry. I know I can never undo the damage. Never. Never."

He turned and hugged Nicole tight with his head on her shoulder. She could feel his tears seeping through her dress. After so long, why did he want to say this now? She had waited so many years to hear these words. As much as she had dreamt, longed for, his acknowledgement, it was way too late. The guilt laden on her shoulders so young had shaped her forever. It was the part of her heart that had hardened most. Other things might still break her with ease, but the entrance back for the father was bolted up and locked with the key thrown away. This man had failed her, her brother and her mother. But this was her mother's funeral. It wasn't her right to make a scene. Nor his, for that matter.

Her father stood back. "I was in such a mess. Our marriage was on the rocks; I was about to lose my job. I didn't feel worthy to be your father. Drink seemed such an easy escape."

But it wasn't just that one moment. He had kept the lie going. Never apologised. Never man enough. That was the unforgivable part. Sod the mourners.

Nicole said, "None of that's an excuse! You were an adult. My father. I was a child. People are meant to look up to, not down on, their fathers. You should have admitted your mistake. Instead, you just ran away. You preferred to run away than tell the truth! It's too late. Too bloody late!"

Nicole stood her ground. He tried to hug her again, but Nicole stepped away. Dan was standing open-mouthed. He didn't know the whole story: she had never had the courage to tell him. He held her hand as she stood shaking, trying to suppress further tears. Dan deserved better from her.

She knew she had to reverse out of this. There was silence across the room. It took everything she had to find placatory words she didn't feel. "Well, it's ancient history, Dad. We've all had to move on. Now, come on, pull yourself together."

Most people who hadn't heard the exchange would think he was grieving for his dead wife. She held him by the shoulders and pecked him on the cheek. The clink of glasses and cups became more marked. The room had become very hot. She decided to go outside for some fresh air. She shook her head when Dan mouthed whether she wanted him to come with her.

*

When she came back into the room ten minutes later, the volume had risen again, at least in one corner, and she recognised the owners of the voices.

"You have no idea the damage you're doing to people's lives. You offer them these fantastic deals without thinking of the consequences. Banks like ours are set up to handle risk, but you aren't. In this new world we get all the pain and none of the gain. It's simply wrong."

Gal grimaced as Charlie Newhouse ranted, but it didn't look very genuine. Anya looked puzzled and had her arms crossed. Bee, a fish out of water if ever there was one, seemed to be acting as referee.

She said, "You're just being rude, Dad. Gal and Anya have come all the way down here and you're just insulting him. Zaxxo is a brilliant business. You're just jealous you're not in one instead of your crusty old bank."

Gal said, "I don't mind, Bee. I just wish they wouldn't spread lies about me to the papers. That's the one thing I object to."

Charlie said, "We never spread lies about anybody. That's slander."

"I know for a fact your bank does even if you don't personally." Gal was still smiling but his eyes were dead with dislike and disgust.

"Anyway, we don't need to. The internet is awash with your wrongdoings. You're a one-man bad news factory."

Bee said, "Shut up, Dad, just shut up. I brought Gal over because I thought you would like to meet him."

"I did. I do. I've been waiting to tell him."

Nicole moved into the group. Anya whispered in Nicole's ear, "That man's an arsehole." Loyal as she wanted to be to Dan's father, she couldn't help but agree. This was meant to be an event to commemorate her mother's life, and instead she was knee-deep in angry men sounding off.

Nicole said, "Gal. I'm sorry you've had to endure this unpleasantness. It was uncalled for."

Gal said, "He's just scared. I understand." Nicole couldn't help but admire his sangfroid. He had no need to be so tolerant of Charlie's behaviour.

Charlie said, "Scared. I've never been scared of anything in my life. How dare you!" At this point Annabel appeared and pulled Charlie away by the arm.

Nicole looked at her watch and then at Dan. "Do you think it would be acceptable to start suggesting people head off home?"

Dan whispered, "Why didn't you tell me what happened when Patrick died? It's so awful."

"Would it have made a difference?"

"Of course it would."

It was going to hurt her, but Dan deserved the truth, had done for a long time. "I have never told anyone because I always thought it could have been my fault. I should have been paying more attention. I knew my father had disappeared. I might have been only ten, but I looked after Patrick more than anyone. I was horror-struck when I realised he had drowned so close to me. So, when my father accused me, a part of me thought he was right. A part of me still does. I've been stuck. I've been waiting for his apology for years, but it doesn't mean I don't feel some guilt. I think I always will. Sorry." She kissed him on the cheek as he stood dumbfounded.

*

The waiters and waitresses had been briefed to start clearing away the glasses and plates. Nicole gathered herself and toured the room thanking people for coming. It took little to persuade the townspeople that it was time to leave. She was pleased to see Harry Pearson, the antiques dealer-turned-moneylender, had disappeared.

Soon only the people Nicole knew were left. She stood with Ellie and Chandra catching up on Yellow Razor gossip. Dan, Annabel and her father were behind her, and she could hear their conversation.

Dan said to her father, "Feeling better now?"

Hugh said, "I should have apologised to Nicole years ago. So, yes. But I now need to work out where else I'm going to find the funds I need. Annabel has a few interesting ideas. Bright girl."

She excused herself and stepped out into the garden through the French windows. It was getting dark, and the lawn was damp underfoot. She found a bench nestled along the side of a sandstone path and got out her phone.

"Steve? Could I talk to Jeff for a moment, please? I'd really appreciate it." Steve muttered something about the price being a drink with him, and Nicole promised him it would happen next time she was in Oxford. *Note to self: never go to Oxford again.*

It took several moments before Jeff Kerslake made it to the phone.

"Jeff? It's Nicole here. I think you need to tell me who it was. The De La Hays are selling the school to some Chinese investors. Very soon your secret will die with the school. You've got to tell me. Please? It's the right thing to do."

"I can't. I told you. They will expose me."

Nicole looked up at the darkening sky and wondered what cards she had left to play. The De La Hays didn't deserve Jeff's loyalty. They were about to make a fortune out of their duplicity.

"Jeff. I'm at my mother's funeral. She died very suddenly, and I miss her so much. I can't remember a time when I have been so broken and empty. All I have to keep me going is the chance that I could do the right thing for Peter. Please, please tell me. I promise I won't tell anyone it was you. I will protect you."

There was silence at the other end of the phone. Jeff was breathing hard. She could almost hear his heart racing.

"Jeff, it was murder. A crime. You can't remain silent anymore."

"I'm sorry for your loss. Do you have family who can look after you?"

Nicole didn't reply. Now it was her turn to hold her breath. She had nothing left to offer him. At the other end of the line Jeff was breathing even faster.

"The boy who bullied Peter Slaithwaite was called Michael Newhouse. That's spelt N-E-W-H-O-U-S-E. He was the ringleader. He was up at the quarry when Eric McArthur died too."

Nicole held her phone tight as she trembled. "Are you sure?"

"Of course I'm sure."

"What happened up at the quarry?"

Jeff hesitated. "I don't know. I just know that's where he died."

Michael Newhouse. It couldn't be. Although she had known there was always a possibility that it would be Dan's grandfather, she had been praying that it wouldn't. A ticking timebomb had landed in her lap. She should have stopped weeks ago, then it wouldn't exist.

If she was going to build a life with Dan, this news had to stay with her. She could still find out what happened. It would satisfy her curiosity. But no-one else could ever know. Did Charlie know? Was that why he was so anxious that she didn't pursue the truth behind the letter? Or was it simply that he didn't want the Rothbury name to be sullied at the wrong time? Or maybe it was both. Either way, against her real desires, she would have to make do with the satisfaction of knowing the truth.

"And I have something else for you…"

"What?"

"The telephone number of Sally, Peter Slaithwaite's widow."

19

Nicole, sober enough now, in her view, drove back to her mother's house with Dan. She knew he would think Nicole's pensive mood was only to be expected given the occasion and, in particular, the argument with her father. He wasn't to know about the call with Jeff Kerslake. She wasn't sure if he should ever know about that. He'd been right to discourage her from pursuing the letter. Just desserts, as her mother would have said.

She thought about the possibility of being pregnant. Of course, she had always thought about that possibility. Just not now. Particularly not now. Then again, a new life emerging as an old life disappeared. A pleasing symmetry. If it was so, she wished her mother was still around to experience it with her.

The house was dark and smelt of damp. They put every light on to try and bring it back to life, but it was still more a museum than a home. Nicole resolved that this would be the last time she would stay there. Her mother's possessions – piles of books, some watercolour seascapes, a China tea service in a cabinet – could go to auction. She wanted none of it.

Dan was in the kitchen making them a cup of tea. She needed to drop the whole letter thing and concentrate on building back their relationship. The dreaded Annabel would soon disappear when she saw how close they were. Maybe they should try another weekend away? Maybe skiing if his ankle would take it. Maybe not given what she suspected was going on inside her. The miserable weather wasn't helping either of their moods.

*

Dan came into the sitting room and sat down next to her, handing her the cup of tea and a chocolate digestive. He kissed her on the cheek. She was shaking a little and felt sick. She wanted to talk and be a lovely girlfriend again, but everything was piling up. The funeral hadn't been the end; it was just the start.

"Sorry." He passed her another biscuit. "Do you feel any closure now after what your dad said? I had no idea how Patrick's death changed absolutely everything for your family."

"Can you bin Annabel?" She hadn't planned this. It just blurted out.

"She's like that with everyone. You don't need to worry."

"No, just with you. The sooner she disappears out of our lives, the better. We're engaged to be married, remember." Dan tried to defend her, saying how helpful Annabel had been to him and around the funeral. Nicole decided that she didn't need to stoke that particular fire any further. Not when she had an even larger incendiary device newly installed in her back pocket.

Dan looked at Nicole. "You still love me, don't you? Annabel means nothing. You know that."

Nicole thought about Annabel. She had inserted herself into their lives with all the dexterity of a pickpocket in Oxford Circus. Dan had needed help when he was incapacitated, so she had filled the gaps when Nicole couldn't. What was so bad about that? It might have helped if she wasn't quite so stunning.

"Yes. I do. You know I do." She put her hand on his far cheek, pulled it towards him and kissed him on the lips. They kissed for a minute then Nicole got up and, clutching Dan's arm to help him along, led him out of the room and up the stairs.

*

Two days later, on Friday, Nicole was in the office in Canary Wharf with Gal and the Zaxxo CFO. They were discussing Zaxxo's Series B fundraising. The target was $1 billion from venture capitalists, at least one in the US as they wanted to open up there as soon as possible. Nicole didn't know much about finance, but she had told Gal she wanted to be in the meeting, and he didn't object.

She had been all over the place back at the flat. She couldn't stop thinking of her mother and their sad last day together that Christmas. How she should have tried so much harder to cheer her up. And, if she had, maybe her mother would still be around to share in her good news, the news that was making her nauseous all the time right now.

The CFO had been talking through a dense spreadsheet

of numbers for an eternity and had excused himself to go and talk to their lawyers.

Gal, smart for a change, dark blue suit and open-necked white shirt, said, "You, OK? You don't have to be back yet if you're not ready."

"Can I ask your advice? I don't know who else to ask." Gal, a worried look crossing his face, nodded.

"I have pretty much got to the bottom of what went on with the letter I found. I know what happened in the war and I know what happened to Peter afterwards. Well, most of it. I also know who was responsible for bullying him…"

"So?"

"Dan's grandfather, Charlie's father, was the ringleader. I think he was party to a murder too. If I make that public, they will never forgive me. It won't do my relationship with Dan any good, especially as I have promised him to stop investigating. I can't see how I could have a place in their family. Charlie has been on at me every which way to stop – he says because the HVAC investment in the school would be jeopardised, but I bet he knows something about his dad too. Even though, for reasons I can't fathom, Jo, Dan's mum, has always seemed keen that I persevere."

Gal stroked his beard. "What's the issue then? Just stop." Nicole explained about the murder.

"You need to go to the police."

"I will if I can find out more. It's too early. I promised the people who have helped me that I would tell them what I have found and that I would expose what happened. How was I to know it was my bloody boyfriend's family at the heart of it?"

"So, what do you want to do?"

"I don't know. That's why I am asking you. I figured you would give me some sensible advice."

The CFO was about to walk back into the room, but Gal put his hand up and he retreated.

"You know it would suit me to have Charlie Newhouse disgraced in public. Taste of his own medicine." He looked up to see Nicole's nod of agreement. "But I don't think you can destroy the family you may spend your life with. This letter isn't that important in the scheme of things. Half the people involved are dead and the rest don't want to be reminded of it. But I get that you want to draw a line under it and honour this guy's memory. I would write everything down and share it confidentially with the people you promised to tell. Ask them to read it and destroy it. What do you think? Could you trust them?"

Nicole stood up and looked out of the window on to the City of London. An industry built on handshakes, promises made, promises broken. Gal deserved better than them.

"I hope so. We all get closure, and, if we play it right, no-one gets hurt. Perfect." *Risky but perfect.*

Gal stressed again that she should go to the police as soon as she was ready. "Now, sit down for a moment. I want to ask you something."

A weight had been lifted from her mind. She hoped he wasn't going to add a new one. Life at Zaxxo was always frenetic but even more so right now. In a matter of weeks, the business had gone from plucky British start-up to the name everyone mentioned when they talked about a European tech success story. The names involved got bigger and bigger and the stakes higher and higher. Much of the time she was involved in discussions she'd never been part of before. It was the only upside of all the travails she was experiencing elsewhere in her life: she hadn't had time to worry about it.

"We need to go to the US. To set up a business and get some investment. We can't replicate our business model here, but we have some amazing tech we can white-label and rent out to other software companies. I figure you could use a change of scene, and you could be a real help out there. What do you think?"

"I don't know anything about setting up businesses or fundraising. And I don't have a visa for the US. What use would I be?" *Especially pregnant.*

"Not true. You are smart and know how to tell a great story. We need to hire staff, set up suppliers, get media coverage, recruit investors. And, more importantly, I trust you."

Nicole thought about Dan and their fresh start. She thought about Annabel wallowing in the shadows like a shark contemplating its next meal.

"I would love to, but I don't think the time is right, to be honest. Can't I do regular trips and then do the rest from here?"

"You're dead on your feet. You owe it to yourself. Three months. All expenses paid. Nice apartment, hire car. Think about it?" Gal nodded to the CFO who was pacing up and down outside.

*

Nicole left the meeting and found an empty booth people used for solo calls. She dug out Sally Slaithwaite's phone number. The phone rang for nearly a minute before it was answered.

"Is that Sally Slaithwaite?" A rather shaky 'yes' came back.

"I'm Nicole Weymouth. Jeff Kerslake said I should call you. About your husband."

"Why are you so interested?" Nicole gave her a succinct explanation.

Sally was quiet for a moment. "It's still all quite painful. I really don't think I can help much."

"I am sure you can. Please. I won't take much of your time. Honestly."

"No, I don't think so."

Neither of them said anything for a moment. Nicole put her hand over her mouth to cover the sound of her breathing.

"I'm sure you would like to hear what I've found out."

There was silence for a moment longer.

"Oh, alright. Are you in London?" Nicole confirmed she was. "Come and meet me after the Sunday morning service at St Paul's. I know a nice little coffee shop."

Nicole put the phone down. This wasn't in the script. But it was only for her own interest, wasn't it? No harm would be done.

*

It was Saturday. The first of the month, March. Martha had gone home to her parents. Dan had gone to the rugby with mates. Bee had come back – 'just for a couple of days until she found her feet' – against Nicole's better judgement, and was out giving away free sample cans of energy drinks at Waterloo Station. She said it was good money even if she was subjected to unwelcome verbal harassment on a regular basis.

Nicole lay in bed thinking about what she needed to write. But first of all, she needed to know if what she suspected was true. She'd definitely missed her period. First thing was the best time, everyone said. She went straight out in the rain to Boots on Tooting Broadway and bought a pregnancy test.

Back in the flat, hands shaking, she went straight to the bathroom and took the test. As she sat on the side of the bath waiting for the result, she contemplated how she would feel if it was positive. Her head told her that the timing was terrible. She was so looking forward to working at Zaxxo and taking some trips to the US. At long last she had a job she believed in and where she could make a real difference. Her heart pointed in a different direction. Her family was gone. She had a boyfriend who wanted to build a life with her. Here could be the start of a new family, one where she could rectify all the mistakes her own had made.

The results didn't take long. A strong line appeared on the strip. It was positive. She was pregnant. A glow of happiness radiated through her body. Nicole held the strip above her head and did a little dance. She was glad no-one was in the flat. Part of her wanted to tell someone and part wanted to luxuriate in the secret.

She went back to her room and sat at the table under the window. There was an immobile, fat pigeon sitting on the window ledge to her right. She ought to tell Dan, but she wasn't ready. She wished she could tell her mother. She could only be about six weeks gone. She had a few more weeks until she needed to tell anyone. That would give her time to put Peter's story to bed and do at least one trip to the US.

*

The flat was almost as cold and damp as her mother's house, but at least she had all her stuff around her. She put some Taylor Swift on and settled in front of her computer. The story was ready to be written. For posterity. That sounded almost medieval. Nowadays, everyone put everything up on social media as soon as it happened, sometimes as it happened, for the whole world to see. The idea that she would write about something from over seventy years ago that only about four people would ever read was ridiculous.

She set to work. As a preamble she talked about her trip with Dan to Blair Gowan and how she found the letter. Then she transcribed the letter in full. She talked about why the school was up there and who was in charge. Then she ran through what had happened to the boys and who had been responsible. She alluded to Eric McArthur's 'accidental' death and the circumstances leading up to Peter being put in the stable. She spent plenty of time describing what happened to him there, not because she was a voyeur but because she believed people needed to know why this wasn't just some run-of-the-mill school bullying.

She named Michael Newhouse as the ringleader. She used Nanny Bristow's account to explain how little the school did about it. Then she moved on to tell Peter's story after the event – how he had run away; how he had made friends in Tetbury, including one special friend; and then how the family had moved away so suddenly. In one short, terse sentence she said that he was believed to have committed suicide in 1963, but she resisted the temptation to suggest it was because of what went on in the war. Finally, she recounted the resistance she had encountered when trying to find out the truth from Rothbury School and the relationship between that resistance and the possible Chinese investment.

When she had finished, she read it back to herself. It was over 2,000 words long. Her overall impression was that – the wartime backdrop and related privations notwithstanding – it was an even more horrific tale than she had first thought. It was incredible to think that the truth had been hidden for so long. It was even more incredible that she was proposing to inform just a handful of people and then bury it. Thank God she was going to the police.

She reread Peter's letter. It was a cry for help that had never been answered. The only person it had reached was her, and she was going to let him down. She slumped at her desk and put her head in her hands. She got up and walked into the kitchen. There was yet another half-finished bottle of white wine in the fridge. She took a sip, but it tasted of metal. Just as well.

*

Bee was snoring on the sofa when Nicole went out on the Sunday. She tiptoed past her, reflecting that she had had plenty of time to regret the shot of blood to the head that had prompted her to tell Charlie that Bee could stay.

She was excited and scared. Sally was the one person who had known Peter as an adult. Nicole had grown to care about Peter very much. He had suffered enough. She wanted some happiness for him now.

Sunday morning London was quiet as she exited St Paul's tube. A few tourists puzzled over phones. Cyclists in Lycra whizzed past in small peletons. A busker was massacring *Something* by The Beatles. When she walked around to the front of St Paul's Cathedral, it was much busier as the congregation flooded down the steps. As was so often the case when she was around churches, Nicole wondered if they knew something she didn't.

The café was off a narrow sidestreet. It had a dirty red and white striped awning and two wrought-iron tables outside. Sally had said she would be sitting at the table in the front to the left. Sure, enough there was an old woman sitting there as Nicole entered.

Nicole's first reaction was that Sally looked nothing like what she expected. She looked very frail and at least eighty-five years old. Her hair was sheet white and pulled back off her face. A set of AirPods sat on the table alongside her phone.

They shook hands and Nicole sat down. Sally said, "I promised myself I wouldn't talk about Peter anymore. It upsets me too much. But you must have made quite an impression. Jeff was insistent, and Peter was always fond of him. Let's order and then you can tell me what you know."

Nicole got out her phone and ran through a precis of what she had written down in her piece. She also showed Sally Peter's letter. Sally listened without interrupting, her eyes glistening. She pushed her AirPods around the table as Nicole talked.

At the end Sally said, "Well, you've got pretty much all of it. Well done."

"Thank you." Nicole took a sip of her now lukewarm coffee.

"Of course, you need to remember that Peter was a terrible fantasist. Always making up stories."

"Oh God. Which ones?"

Sally touched her hand. "Don't worry. I know that the tales about being left up on the moor at night and that awful stable story are true. He also mentioned that story about the quarry once. But it seemed too painful for him to talk about it. Peter would have nightmares almost every night. Shouting and screaming. He would wake up shaking. How those boys that bullied him didn't get expelled I will never know. Wartime or not – it was barbaric. But I think he actually enjoyed school for some of the time."

"Why did his family leave Tetbury so fast?"

Sally fiddled with her AirPods. It was starting to get a little irritating, but Nicole kept her counsel. "Peter didn't talk about it much – nor did his family. But I know he got a girl pregnant – a 16-year-old, Alice someone. The child, a girl, was given away. Peter said he had never met her, although I've never been that sure about that. The family left Tetbury as soon as the news was made public."

"That Alice wouldn't be Alice Blyth, would it?" Nicole thought about the glamorous woman who had sent her packing and then called her back.

"Yes. I only found out about her as she came to the door once after Peter died. Said she was a teenage girlfriend and wanted to pay her condolences."

"Can I ask? How did Peter die?"

Sally didn't answer for some moments. The proprietor took away their cups and wiped the table as Nicole was waiting for her to respond.

"They call it PTSD these days. Basically, the experiences up at Rothbury in the war scarred him for life. He tried to talk to the De Lay Hays about it, but they just blocked him and started to threaten him with legal action. They wouldn't acknowledge any of it. His nightmares got worse and worse. He kept losing jobs, he stopped going out. After a while he stopped talking to me. It was awful. I was a young, inexperienced wife. I thought it was me." Sally was crying now. It was Nicole's turn to take her hand. "I loved him so much, but he wouldn't let me love him. One weekend I went off to stay with my parents, just to get a break from it. When I got back, he wasn't there. The police organised a massive search. But they came up with nothing. Three months later some ramblers found his clothes washed up in near Bembridge on the Isle of Wight. His wallet was in his trousers: that's how he was identified. We never found the body. But someone local said they had seen a man striding out to sea on his own at dusk the week before, and her description sounded just like Peter. Seven years later the court declared him dead. To be honest, he's dead to me: I've had to move on. It was all so agonisingly painful. I don't think I would want to see him if he turned out to be alive."

They were both lost in their thoughts. The proprietor was about to ask if they wanted anything else but backed away when he saw their tears.

"I've never been able to mourn him. You can't imagine how terrible it is when there's no body."

Sally couldn't speak. She bit her lip and stared at the

wall. Nicole waited and then said, "What do you think Peter would want me to do?"

"He would want the De La Hay family to pay a price for their actions. Go to the police and tell them more evidence has emerged. They had a duty of care for those boys, and they failed them. I know it was the war and I know they had a skeleton staff but even so. It was wrong, just plain wrong. I don't think anything is to be gained by publishing it, but I am pleased that you decided to pursue it. Peter would have been very touched. He kept a diary. I never read it. I haven't seen it for years. I've moved about so much, you see."

"Could I see it?"

"I don't know where it is. I've tried to look for it on and off. I'll give it another go."

Nicole could tell she sensed her disappointment, and Sally changed tack. "So why are you so interested in all this?"

Nicole didn't have a clear answer. She had found the letter. Nobody else had any reason to investigate it other than her. The truth would lay buried forever unless she took action. For the first time in her life, she had been given a true purpose. One way or another she had felt a bystander in everything that had happened to her so far. The biggest single event in her life – Patrick's death – had seen her unwillingly transformed from bystander into protagonist. This was different and it had come to her at just the right time. Someone needed help and only she could provide it.

"My younger brother drowned when I was very young, and I was blamed. It drove my father away and destroyed my mother."

"Oh, you poor love. No-one should experience that."

She paused. "But I have to ask – what's that got to do with Peter?" She had stopped playing with the AirPods at last.

"I don't know. I have so much on my plate. My mother has just died. I've got a new job I really like. I've got engaged to a man I love. People keep telling me to drop it. But then, just when I decide to do that, someone else emerges from Peter's past to tell me more and persuade me to keep going. I don't even understand it myself. I guess it's because I'm the only person who can sort it out."

"It doesn't sound that stupid to me. It sounds like the one thing in your life that's straightforward. You know what needs to be done and only you can do it. Don't let them get away with it. Not many people receive a gift like that. Lucky you."

Lucky me? Nicole couldn't think of a less likely take on the situation. So far it had only caused her grief. And it didn't look like any of the possible scenarios ahead would present her with anything different. If she publicised, it the combined retribution of the Newhouses, the De Lay Hays and God knows who else would rain down on her head. Yet if she didn't, she would have a sense of guilt itching away inside her for the rest of her life. Hobson's choice as her mother would have said. All of that notwithstanding, she admired Sally Slaithwaite's positive spin on the situation.

"There's something else. No-one knows this, so please keep it to yourself. I've found out I'm pregnant."

"Ooh! Congratulations! That's wonderful. How far gone are you?"

"Not sure. Probably only about six weeks."

Sally continued, "All the more reason to move fast. If I were you, I would go down to see Martin De La Hay as soon as you can and tell him what you know. Then I would get on with your life."

Nicole wiped her nose. "That's just what I'm going to do." They stood up and hugged. "I'll let you know what happens. Wish me luck." Sally crossed her fingers and waved her goodbye, pulling on her overcoat and scarf.

As she walked out she said, "And, if you ever find the diary, I would love to see it!"

She stood outside the café in the drizzle. It was two o'clock. She could be in Hampshire by four. The next week was full of meetings about the fundraising, and she couldn't take any more days off. Gal wouldn't want anyone going to the US who wasn't fully committed. She was pretty impressed that he, a man who only stopped work to sleep four hours a night, had been so easy going about all the absences so far.

20

It was dark by the time Nicole pulled up at the top of the drive at Rothbury. The massive oak front door was shut, and a single bulb hung to the side illuminating the white, saucer-sized doorbell. She pushed it several times. Maybe a bell would be ringing deep in the recesses of the house, but, if there was, there was no evidence of it. Nicole tightened her woollen scarf around her neck and pulled her coat tight. As she waited, her nervousness grew. Should she turn back?

After about five minutes a small boy dressed head to foot in grey, carrying a large satchel, walked past her. In one of the highest male voices she had ever heard, he said, "Can I help you?"

Nicole told him and he replied, "He doesn't like to be disturbed on Sundays. It's family time, but I know where he is. He's at the squash court playing with his eldest son, Conroy. I can show you where to go if you like."

Nicole wanted to pat him on the head to say thank you but guessed there was some guideline somewhere that forbade expressions of gratitude of that sort unless you had a DBS check.

They set off down a gravel path around the back of the building. The boy walked with an exaggerated swing of the leg as he struggled with the weight of his satchel. Only the light from various windows high above showed them where to go. After about five minutes a large, nondescript boxy white building with skylights presented itself. The thud of a squash ball and occasional grunts and screams could be heard inside. The De La Hays played to win.

The little boy gestured to a door, disappeared and Nicole entered. The smell of stale sweat attacked her nostrils. It looked like only one of the three squash courts was being used. She climbed the stairs to a viewing gallery and, without declaring herself, watched Martin De La Hay and his son battle it out. Conroy must have been about fourteen, just hitting puberty. Martin seemed to be struggling a little with the pace, but he was stronger. Nicole didn't know anything about how one scored in squash, but she got the impression that it was a close match that Conroy was just about shading. It might have been the case that Conroy was playing within himself a little to avoid humiliating his father too much. All in all, not great timing for the dollop of bad news she was about to pour over Martin De La Hay's grizzled, greying head.

After about ten minutes they stopped, with Conroy emerging as the victor. Martin gave him a playful punch in the stomach as they exited the court. Nicole took the stairs two at a time so she could catch them before they left the building.

"Mr De La Hay!" They were opening the door and

about to leave. Nicole realised that her emergence from the dark was going to make the unwelcome surprise even worse.

"Who's that? Show yourself!" Martin said. Nicole did as he asked. *Arrogant sod. Enjoy your moment because you're not getting another one.*

"Mr De La Hay, can I talk to you for a moment?"

Martin told her that he hadn't expected to see her at the school again after the episode with the school secretary. It wasn't difficult to make that latter observation sound rather menacing and Martin didn't bother to sugar it.

"It's about Peter Slaithwaite. You know, when Rothbury was up in the Lake District in the Second World War."

Martin said, "Not that again. Go back to the house, Con. I'll see you in a moment. Get yourself in the shower."

Conroy said, "Can't I stay? I love stories about the war."

"Go home. Now!" Conroy scurried off with a theatrical 'tut'.

"Let me turn a light on." Martin flicked a switch and sank down onto a bench. The neon strip light flickered at one end. He wiped his face with a towel and brushed his hair back off his forehead. "Mixed emotions when the younger generation start beating you. So, what's so important that you come down here unannounced and uninvited on a Sunday? I thought you weren't coming here again."

Nicole steeled herself. She was on her own. No-one knew she was there. "I now know everything that happened to Peter Slaithwaite in the war. I know who did it, who covered it up, what happened to Peter afterwards. I know about Eric McArthur's death. So, I know why you don't want any of it made public. And I've written it all up." The only sounds were Martin's heavy breathing and the whir of the ventilation system.

"I thought you'd dropped this."

"I changed my mind." Nicole was determined to stand her ground no matter what.

"You've no evidence for any of this. We have lawyers who will destroy you."

"I think I have enough."

He paused. "Are you going to let me read it then?"

"No." It came out even firmer than she expected.

"You can't be that confident about it then."

"I am. Totally. I'm going to the police tomorrow." Checkmate beckoned.

"You haven't been talking to that demented fool Jeff Kerslake, have you? Nothing he says makes sense. You have no evidence."

"I have enough. I've a duty to report it even if it is a long time ago."

"Well, I doubt they will take it seriously. And I hope you're not planning to do anything with this story of yours. That would serve no-one any good." Martin, cheeks blazing red, glared up at her. She was pleased that she was the one standing.

"That rather depends on you. It's a terrible story. One that deserves to be told."

"You don't know what you are playing with. The future of this school is in the balance right now. We have investors in the wings who would take flight at the first sign of bad publicity…"

"I know. HVAC. Charlie Newhouse told me about them."

"Yes, the Chinese people. Good people, sound ideas. Their money could transform this school. Create a new Rothbury in China too. My family has put every penny we have into this school to keep it amongst the best in the country. But it still isn't enough. We need more technology, more learning support, more facilities. Tell the police, publish your fantasies and all of that stays a pipe dream. Do you want that on your conscience? Do you?"

Nicole looked at this podgy middle-aged man pleading with her. He wasn't the king now.

"What about your conscience? Your family's conscience. Death, torture, cruelty. Suppressing the truth. Refusing to acknowledge the wrongs committed on your watch! Blackmailing an old man who only wants to tell the truth. That's what you should be worried about."

"Put yourself in my great-grandfather's position. The German bombing is killing people all over the South-East. Parents are begging him to protect their children while they go off to fight or support the war effort. His son, the headmaster, has gone off to fight. With his mental scars and physical disabilities, he can barely look after himself, let alone anyone else. But, nevertheless, at short notice he goes off and finds somewhere safe where he can take all his pupils. When he gets there, he can't find many teachers or support staff as they are all engaged in the war effort. How well would you manage? How well would any of us manage? I am so proud of my great-grandfather for what he did. It was our family's finest hour."

"How can you call it that? Not only was there widespread bullying of the most horrible kind but your grandfather was told about it again and again and refused to do anything about it. Even after the war when Peter came to see him, he was told he was imagining things…"

"Yes, well he certainly had a vivid imagination according to what I've heard…"

"Your great-grandfather did nothing. Your grandfather did nothing. Your father did nothing. You're doing nothing. Why should I suppress the truth now it is finally ready to come out?"

Martin stood up. His odour was overpowering. He walked around her as if sizing her up. She knew this was a kamikaze mission. She thought of Peter, she thought of her mother. Carpe diem.

"I doubt Dan would like to know what you've been up to with that Gal Rezman chaps would he? Cosying up in a Borough Market pub? Planning trips to the US together?" US trips? She hadn't told anyone about that. "If you publish your findings, we'll have you all over social media as well as in court before you know it. We're a dab hand at all that here. You think you can throw dirt at us: well, we can throw twice as much back."

"Gal and I have a professional relationship. He took me to the pub to cheer me up after my mother's death. If you think that's going to discourage me, you're mad. Throw whatever dirt you want. It won't stick. Unlike you, I have plenty of reliable witnesses."

Martin was continuing to circle her. He said, "OK, what do you want from me? Everyone has their price."

What Nicole wanted was her brother Patrick back. She wanted that more than anything. Now she was carrying his niece or nephew, that emotion was even stronger. But that wasn't to be, so the least she could do would be to finish what Peter tried to do all those years ago and bring the De La Hays to account.

"You need to apologise to Sally Slaithwaite. I'm going to go to the police. I have to. But I won't publish the story. If it comes out, that's down to the police."

Martin stopped spinning the racquet. He looked from side to side as if help might be on its way. Instead, the flickering light switched itself off. It was on a timer. He threw back a fist and punched the switch.

"If you go to the police, I will make sure your life is a total misery. Rothbury has friends in all the right places, you know."

If the police didn't act on it, some dreadful wrongs could stay hidden, probably forever. Was it a price worth paying to assuage the man she loved and his family? People who had pinned their hopes on her would be disappointed and wouldn't understand. And this louse of a man was happy to make up libellous stories about her. It made her sick.

"I'll take that chance." Nicole pushed past him. He couldn't afford any more charges against him.

She ran off at pace to her car and didn't look back.

*

Nicole got back to her flat about eight o'clock. Martha was still away, thankfully, but Bee was there, as always, sprawled on the sofa, shoving pizza slices into her mouth whilst watching an ancient episode of *Friends*. The space around was littered with her possessions like a camping site at Glastonbury.

"Hi, Nicole. Good weekend?" Whatever other faults

Bee had, sociability wasn't one of them. Nicole muttered something about needing to go and lie on her bed. She wasn't lying: the events of the day had finished her off for good. And she needed to be sick.

Once out of the toilet, she lay down and called Dan. Chances of him picking up were 30/70. Judging by his Instagram feed, he wouldn't have got much sleep. If any.

"Hey, what's up?" Dan's voice had dropped two octaves and rasped like Rod Stewart, but he was awake. Nicole made up her Sunday: gym, shopping, work.

"What do you think about coming to live with me?" *What? Now? Why now?*

There was no reason why she shouldn't. She loved him. He was her fiancé. She needed somewhere to call home. She had someone who would need a home. She so wanted to tell Dan, but she didn't quite feel ready to do it over the phone when he was hungover.

"Dan, yes, I will!"

"That's amazing, just amazing. I love you!" Nicole held the phone away from her ear for a minute and frowned. Then she realised it was a moment and she needed to be in it with him.

"There is a condition though."

"Of course. Anything." Nicole knew the next bit was a little unfair, but hadn't she just taken 'one for the Newhouse team'?

"Annabel. I don't want you to see her anymore. I know she's an old friend and I know she's been a star over the last few weeks, but she's after you and I can't relax knowing she's skulking around you."

"Annabel's a family friend. She's a rock."

"Well, from now on, she can be someone else's rock. Deal?"

Long silence. Loud outtake of breath. "Of course. Deal."

"You better get some sleep. Talk tomorrow?"

"Let's get some people around for drinks as soon as you're in. We should celebrate our engagement now we have the chance."

Nicole told him she loved him, blew him a kiss, put the phone on her chest and stared at the ceiling. Would the police do anything? They didn't even pursue burglaries these days. What did John Lennon say? Life is what happens when you are busy making other plans. If they did anything, Dan would soon know she hadn't been as good as her word. She wondered whether she could square moving in with Gal's invitation to spend some time in the US. She'd never been to California.

Nicole got up to go to the loo and bumped into Bee as she came through the door. Bee staggered back into the opposite wall then sprang back.

"Oh hello. Good news. I'm going to move in with Dan."

Bee started at her as if she had just announced an alien landing. "That's great for you, but what's going to happen to me?"

Nicole could sense herself blushing. "You're well past your moving-out date, as we both know."

"Jesus. Why am I the only person St Nicole doesn't do good deeds for?"

Bee walked over and collapsed full-length on the sofa with her arms over her face.

"You're so insensitive! How could you! And you've given up on that letter. That awful family allowed such horrors to go on and then covered them up for centuries! You have to tell the world what happened. The people that give that school all those prizes and awards need to know what a disgusting organisation it is!"

Bee's breath was being pumped into her face with each angry bellow. Nicole put her hand up to divert some of it. She was going to confess to Dan pretty fast now.

"Between you and me, I didn't. I know a lot more. I've written it all down. I'm going to the police."

"They'll do jack shit. You need to let everyone know."

"It's not that simple, Bee. You know better than anyone the people it will hurt if I go public. Think about it!" Against all her sensory instincts, Nicole grabbed Bee by the shoulders and hugged her. "You think I don't want to tell everyone? I'm going to tell the police. That's the right thing to do, isn't it?"

Bee leant against the wall. "They won't do anything. There's no firm evidence and it's over seventy years ago. Let me do it. You can still keep your promise. I'll be the bad guy."

Nicole imagined Charlie Newhouse's face on hearing his daughter had dropped the family name in the proverbial shit. "Tempting but no. No-one gets to release this information but me. They are my informants. It's my story. My reputation. This new job carries a whole level of profile I haven't had before. And I value my relationship with Dan more than words can say. It's just not worth it."

"I thought you were better than that, Nicole. I've loved the way you've taken our family on. Dan is bloody lucky to have you. Surely you aren't going to go down without a fight?" That wasn't how Nicole saw it. Quite the opposite, in fact. But she would take the compliment.

She kissed Bee on the cheek. "Look, I'm really touched with how passionately you feel about this, but you're wrong. Now, I need to get some sleep. It's a big week coming up at Zaxxo."

Bee wagged her finger. "Sleep on it. You know I'm right."

That night Nicole dreamt she was in the corner of the stable up at Blair Gowan in the war. A massive horse towered over her, snorting and stamping its hooves. She awoke time and again, sweating and shaking. On the other side of the stable door Martin De La Hay was laughing at her.

21

Work was going to dominate the next week. Meeting after meeting with advisors and investors. Endless tweaking of Power-Point presentations over cold pizza. Countless calls from journalists and analysts fishing about progress and, in some cases, rumours and smears cooked up by competitors. Zaxxo was the story. The one to topple at the first opportunity. And it was Nicole's job to keep the good stuff in the papers and the bad stuff out of them. By and large she was succeeding.

Nicole could now see that Gal didn't just need her for her communications skills, which was lucky as there were many aspects of the job that she was making up as she went along. They had hired a financial PR firm, Monro Chambers, to help her, and the account director there was always available to give her advice however stupid the question, but she had other clients, and none of the team there had the stomach – or budget – for the regular 2am finishes. Gal needed her to reassure him that he was behaving and communicating like a CEO should. Even after an internal meeting he would pull her in and ask how she thought he had handled it.

*

Moving her stuff over to Dan's meant she didn't have time to go to the police until the Wednesday. She had ignored all the calls and texts from Martin De Lay Hay and Charlie Newhouse not to involve them. She was too busy to take them anyway.

The policeman at the desk greeted the reason for her visit with some amusement. He called over to his colleague, "Hey, Robbie, we've got a cold case here."

Detective Sergeant Robbie Halstead turned out to be a pleasant thirty-year-old with thick curly hair and a slight lisp. He took her down a dark corridor and into an interview room with a table, four chairs and a recording machine. It was painted the colour of cabbage and had graffiti over all four walls. He sat her down and asked her to tell him everything she knew. The recording machine was switched on.

As she ran through what she knew, she realised that the only new evidence was that a, long dead, man had been at the quarry and had told someone he didn't think it was an accident.

Robbie was very sympathetic. "It's good that you've come to see us. We'll talk to our colleagues in the Lake District and ask them to send down the files, assuming they still have them. I am sure we will want to talk to Mr De La Hay, but I must admit that we don't have much new to go on. If you find anything else out, please pass it on to us."

He stood up and gestured for her to do the same. The meeting was over.

As Nicole walked down the corridor alongside him, Robbie Halstead told her how much the police appreciated people like her coming forward. She was more downhearted than she expected. They were busy. The case was old. There was no new evidence.

In reception Robbie said, "Call us if you turn anything else up. And thanks for coming in." The bearded policeman behind the desk looked up and gave her an encouraging grin.

She was a fool to think anything would come of it. It was the right thing to do, but the truth would never see the light of day.

*

Gal and Nicole were sitting opposite each other, looking at their phones. He said, "Are you feeling better? Thought any more about going to the US? I think you could make a big difference there."

Nicole said, "I really don't think I can. I've just got engaged – not that you would know it; I haven't even had time to choose a ring – and I've just agreed to move in with Dan. I just need some normality. I can do everything with some trips from here. Sorry."

"Final answer?"

"Final answer." Nicole smiled. "Doesn't mean I won't be moving heaven and earth to get this funding round done."

"I want you to have some options at some point, probably six months' time. A nice sum, around a year's salary, if things go the way we hope."

"Fuck." That could be the deposit on a flat. Gal blushed. "Sorry, Gal. I mean. Thank you."

"You will earn it. Now, Desmond is coming here in a moment. You and I need to meet with him."

"Who's he?"

"I've been meaning to tell you. He's the guy Monro Chambers are seconding to us for the next few months. He's their best IPO guy."

So that's why Gal wanted her out in the US. He wanted to park her there while someone else did the IPO work. She couldn't believe it. Gal didn't blink. He just put his fingers together like a cut-price Bond villain.

"What's he got that I haven't?"

"It's not like that. He's got 20 IPOs under his belt. The advisers want more experience."

"Sod the advisers. You gave me the job. You haven't once said I wasn't up to it." Gal looked out of the window, face reddening for a different reason this time. She guessed he had hoped the options would sweeten the pill. Some chance.

"It's my first IPO too. There are no prizes for nearly getting this right. Too many people's futures are riding on it. You must see that."

Nicole looked at her shoes. She was so tempted to walk out. It couldn't be happening again. She had to stay calm. Stand her ground.

"You want me out of the way. You've just tried to buy me off."

They looked at each other. Gal's eyes glistened. He said, "Having you out of the way is the last thing I want. But real life isn't like that."

Out of the corner of her eye Nicole could see Anya

peering in through the broken blinds that protected Gal's office from curious staff. She never took her eyes off him.

She had to cut and run before things got out of control. She stood up, scrabbling for her bag and briefcase around her feet. Gal tried to lean forward to help her, but she gathered them together just in time. So much for standing her ground.

As she strode out of the office, she turned. "You made me think you believed in me."

*

Nicole ignored Anya as she whizzed past her desk and disregarded the puzzled looks of all the news-hungry coders and programmers bent over their computers. A lift arrived within seconds, and it was empty. She leant back against the wall and inspected herself in the mirror opposite. Her mascara was running, and her cheeks were as shiny as apples. Her hair needed cutting and dying. And was that a grey hair muscling its way into her parting?

In four hours, she needed to be on amazing form, hosting everyone at Dan's flat. She couldn't think of anything worse. Especially now she couldn't drink. She just wanted to roll up under the duvet in bed and flick a V-sign to the world. Worst of all, she'd promised Dan she would go and buy some canapes and nibbles at M&S on the way home. Clothes shopping, she loved; food shopping, she hated. She could never decide what to buy and always ended up buying the wrong things.

It was four o'clock. Midday in digital start-up land. She could see a few city traders playing with pints and phones in the bar opposite. She went in, sat down and ordered a lime and soda.

Her phone rang. "Nicole? It's Shona? Have you got a moment? I'm going to put Nanny on. She isn't at all well, but she wanted me to call you."

A very quiet, shaky voice came on the line. "So, Nicole, what did you find out for me?"

Nicole turned away so that she wasn't talking in front of anyone and told Nanny Bristow everything. As she went, Nanny Bristow murmured words of approval. By the time she had finished, fifteen minutes had passed.

"I hope you're going to make sure everyone knows about this. They can't get away with it."

Nicole explained the promise she had made to Martin De La Hay. A huge snort emanated from the other end of the line as she finished her sentence.

"Those De La Hays have turned you over – just like they do everyone."

Once again, as if a switch had been flicked, Nicole found herself at rock bottom. "I've gone to the police. They say they will look into it. That's the right thing to do. You don't understand. It's my boyfriend's family who are implicated. If I reveal all of that, I lose him, I lose everything I love. Don't you see? Please see…"

The phone went dead. Nicole held it tight on her ear in the hope that she was missing an even quieter voice. After a moment Shona came on the line.

"Nicole, I didn't think you would do this. She is so disappointed. I don't think she will recover. She was keeping herself going waiting for you to tell us the good news."

"Shona, don't you see? I just can't." Nicole could sense Dan back at the flat laying out glasses and plates, looking at his watch. "I so wanted to."

Shona said, "I have to go. She needs her meds."

Nicole just wanted to go home to bed and stay there for a week. Nanny Bristow was right. She had failed.

22

Nicole took the Jubilee Line to Waterloo and stopped off at the M&S on the station concourse before getting the train to Clapham Junction. The shop was empty and cold; the neon lights on the low ceiling flashed off the plastic food wrappings.

Downstairs a shopping assistant dressed all in black offloaded packs of food on to the shelves from a trolley in silence. Nicole couldn't have been less in the mood for a party, and she threw the packets of miniature sausage rolls, chicken satay and salmon rolls stuffed with cream cheese into her basket as if she hoped they would bounce out. She unpacked a mini pork pie and munched it as she walked around.

Despite Gal's rationale, and her commitment to Dan, the US still seemed tempting. For a start she'd never been there and had always wanted to go. And it would enable her to forget all the stress and start afresh. Maybe it would help her to manage her grief better. Dan would understand if he knew he would be getting his old Nicole back upon return.

Especially if it meant they could sell his flat and buy a bigger flat, or maybe even a house, together. There was a chance his company would let him go out there too, although she had no evidence for that. When he read *The Financial Times* on Saturdays, he was always going on about the boatloads of green investors all over the US.

But she had just agreed to move in with him after refusing for so long. How would he react if she told him that she would be disappearing for a month? It wasn't fair on him. That predator from the Pony Club, Annabel, would close in for the kill, and who could blame her? Or him? No, Nicole had to commit if she was going to get the future she wanted. Kicking herself for not bringing bags, she stuffed everything in two of them and, the bags banging against her knees, nipped upstairs to buy some tights.

When she came out of the shop a busker by the stairs was playing an old David Bowie song, the one where the singer gets lost in space. She put a fifty pence piece in his hat, saying as she passed, "I know the feeling."

*

"Hello, darling, you OK? Here let me take those."

Dan was at the door dressed in an apron covered in splashes of tomato. He leant forward like a crane to kiss her on the cheek, so he didn't get her cream-coloured coat messy. As she knew from his WhatsApp pictures and messages, he was in the middle of producing an industrial-sized quantity of chilli con carne. There were balloons tied to the ceiling of the flat all along the hallway.

Every surface of the kitchen was covered in food, and

the floor was full of bottles of champagne, wine, beer, and water. Nicole recoiled a little at the prospect.

Nicole asked, "How many people are coming?"

Dan kissed her on the lips. "About twenty, I think. Amazing how many people didn't seem to have any plans."

That meant it would be mainly Dan's family and friends. Nicole had meant to invite Martha, but the Bee episode seemed to have put their friendship on ice. There were a couple of other schoolfriends she had invited, but they hadn't confirmed even though they had been so enthusiastic about her engagement. She had texted Chandra on the off-chance and hoped she could come. Dan had hordes of friends from school, university and London who seemed able to turn up at zero notice, flick a switch and create a ceilidh in a matter of seconds.

"I'm going to have a bath." Nicole sensed that wasn't the most helpful suggestion given the time and the tasks to be done, but she knew that, unless she did something to change her mood, she was going to say the wrong thing within minutes and doom the party to failure. Dan grinned and turned back to his chopping. Maybe there was a cohabiting self-help website she could find? Even she could see there was work to be done now she had made the decision.

She ran the bath a little colder than she might have wanted so that she didn't emerge strawberry red. She lay back and forced herself to think of the positives. She had just been given the biggest sum of money she had ever had in her life. That was worth celebrating. The man she loved wanted her to move in with him and marry her. Some girls would kill for that. She was going to have a baby. She had solved the mystery that had been bugging her for weeks, told the police and had the brave decision to let bygones be bygones. And her father had finally apologised to her.

Fifteen years too late, three lives destroyed by a lie, but an apology nonetheless. There had been years when his refusal to acknowledge his duplicity had been the only thing she could think about. Exams had been failed, job interviews screwed up, relationships detonated before they reached the starting block: all because of one moment of weakness from a man who should have loved her more than anyone. Someone who should have put his daughter's future before his own. *Positive thoughts, Nicole, positive thoughts.* She shivered a little and ran the hot tap some more.

*

She had a drawer and some hanging space in Dan's bedroom, and she was relieved to find the black velvet, low-cut, mid-length party dress was still there. It seemed to have survived the pre-Christmas drinks party thrown by Dan's friend Jeremy without any noticeable stains. And she had bought a new pair of black silk tights from the upstairs section of M&S. She would have preferred shoes with higher heels than her work shoes, but they would have to do.

She sat on the bed wrapped in a towel and, as she waited to cool down, gazed up at the *Sopranos* poster on Dan's wall. That and the Megan Fox pictures in the lavatory would need to go. Would he put up a fight or was he just waiting for her to bring a feminine touch to his mancave? It wasn't as if she ever demonstrated much interest or expertise in interior decoration. When they had gone to buy paint for the kitchen at B&Q last year, she had stayed in the car and checked her emails. She would need to make more of an effort in that department. She surveyed the room and wondered how she could transform it.

"Nicole, can you come and sort out the drinks and snacks? People will be here in thirty minutes." Nicole looked at her watch and shivered again. She had been daydreaming for longer than she thought.

"Fuck. Coming!" In her bra and pants, Nicole tried to rub her hair dry with a towel. A hair dryer would be high on her Amazon list. After five minutes it was dry as it was ever going to get. Then she dressed and did her make-up at high speed. She looked herself up and down in the mirror and gave herself seven out of ten. Another half an hour in front of the mirror might have pushed her up a point, but those snacks wouldn't unwrap and put themselves on plates on their own.

When she entered the kitchen, Dan – and most of the surfaces – were still covered in the brown sludge of chili con carne. A pot the size of a space hopper was ready to boil half of China's annual rice export.

"Whenever you're ready, Nicole. Do you want a drink?" Nicole said she would wait.

"I'm sorry you don't have a ring to show off."

Nicole cleared a space on the kitchen table and started opening a can of Pringles. "It's OK. Gal said he planned to give me some options today."

Dan turned and wiped his hands on his apron. "Jesus Christ, Nicole, that's brilliant. Congratulations! Come here!" He stepped forward, lifted his apron off to avoid spillage, and gave her a massive hug. Nicole rubbed her cheek against his and inhaled his aftershave. She brushed his crotch with her hand and felt him stiffen.

"Can we cancel the party and just Netflix and chill?" Dan groaned a little with pleasure, bent down to kiss her between her breasts and muttered something about him wishing they could. They pulled apart and continued with their tasks. Soon Nicole had managed to load three large plates with all kinds of snacks and canapes. She decorated each with some celery and cherry tomatoes cut in half. Dan had put some Bob Marley on, and they swayed to the rhythms as they worked.

She said, "I'm glad I'm here. It just took some time to see sense. You know that, don't you?" Dan smiled and continued stirring his vat of chilli con carne.

*

On the dot of seven the doorbell rang, signalling the arrival of Charlie and Jo Newhouse. They looked a little awkward on the doorstep before Nicole ushered them in. Both gave Nicole two kisses on the cheek, Charlie's a little more tentative than Jo's. Nicole took their coats and laid them on Dan's bed.

When she came back, she gave them her brightest smile. The mirror in the bedroom must have recognised it owed her a favour, so she had put herself up to eight.

"No Bee tonight then?"

Jo said, "She said she had a work thing." Work? She didn't even have a work thing in the day anymore.

The furniture in the sitting room was pushed back and they stood together with their drinks while Dan joined the conversation with shouts from the kitchen. Nicole told them about the options but didn't say how much and said nothing about the US possibility. She was determined to make sure this party was a fresh start, a celebration.

Jo said, "Congratulations on your engagement. And we're so pleased you're moving in with Dan. He's at a complete loss when you're not around. I hope he realises how lucky he is to have you."

Nicole smiled and gestured that she needed to go and answer the door. As she moved away, she touched both their hands and tried to flash a diamond smile like an actress in demand at a film premiere. "I'll be back."

Soon the room started to fill up and Nicole lost herself in a frenzy of kisses and hugs and food and drink distribution. Dan had come out of the kitchen sans apron and, with the help of two of his mates from school, was serving out bowls of chili con carne to everyone.

Out of the corner of her eye, Nicole spied Chandra at the door. Realising that she wouldn't know anyone, Nicole picked up a glass of water and went over to her.

"I'm so pleased you came, Chandra. Thank you." Nicole gave a kiss on one cheek and a hug, as was the norm. It used to be a kiss on both cheeks, but US culture had decided things needed freshening up. She had ended up putting her lips on several other people's lips when confused during the transition period.

"I wanted to see how you were. I've missed you. Sounds like Zaxxo has been a madhouse."

Nicole paused and whispered, "They want me to go to the US for a month and help set up there. I haven't told anyone yet. Dan doesn't know. I told Gal I wouldn't because of this…" She threw her arm back towards the living room.

"And? You should go." Chandra spoke quite loudly, and Nicole had to shush her.

"I can't. I need to commit."

"I would go if I were in your shoes." Anything you want to tell me, thought Nicole, thinking back to the conversation at the office before she got transferred.

Nicole introduced Chandra to Charlie and Jo and continued her tour of their guests. Her schoolfriends had come, so having offloaded the drinks duties to Dan's best mate, Jeremy, she luxuriated in the warmth of reminiscences from long ago. She had been so focussed on her work and the ructions caused by Peter's letter that she had failed to reply to most of their WhatsApps and missed all their recent get-togethers. She was glad she had made the effort to cheer herself up for a party. Dan was puzzled she wasn't drinking but didn't push it. He would know soon enough. She had made Dan and his parents happy and, in doing so, had, for the first time this year as far as she could remember, done the same for herself too.

Then she heard a banging, and a space opened up in the room. Dan was thumping a wine glass on the table and beckoning her over to his side of the room. He looked flushed, possibly from the heat of the stove, more probably the result of catching up on the drinking. He put his arm around her and kissed her on the lips. Nicole allowed herself to relax and smiled at everyone. Charlie and Jo were both beaming at her.

Dan said, "Welcome. everyone, and thank you for coming at such short notice. Nicole and I wanted to take the opportunity to celebrate our engagement. I thought we should do it as quickly as possible before she changed her mind." Dan paused to allow for laughter and heckling, and Nicole blushed. "As you know, it has been quite a year for us, especially Nicole with her mother's sad passing, and we simply haven't spent enough time with any of you or, indeed, each other. I know we both hope we can rectify that in the very near future.

"I knew from the moment I met Nicole that she was the one. She's so smart, so funny and so beautiful. I am so lucky."

Dan took a swig from his wine glass. "Nicole, thank you for agreeing to marry me. I love you. Thank you."

A massive cheer drowned out Nicole's reciprocated 'I love you'. She hugged Dan's waist tight and, hiding her face in his shoulder, took a moment to block out the hubbub of the party. Her father had acknowledged the wrong he had done her. She could have stopped Patrick's death, but it wasn't just her fault that no-one had seen him in time. The pain of his death, and her father's words to her on that day, would never disappear, but maybe they would fade a little. The shadow that had blotted out the brightness of her present and her future had been lifted. She could move forward. For the first time ever, she could focus 100% on being the person she believed she could be. A happiness that seemed to turn her blood to molten gold as it flooded through her body. She hugged Dan tighter, and he hugged her back.

She went back to her schoolfriends and put her arms around them both. For the first time since she could remember, her horizon was pure blue.

22

"Jesus Christ!" Charlie's rich, slurred voice rose above the chatter. "I can't believe it!"

Before Nicole knew it, Charlie was standing in front of her holding his phone right in her face. Spittle covered his lips, and his eyes were protruding like billiard balls.

"You couldn't resist it, could you? You just couldn't help yourself."

Nicole tried to focus on the phone, but the screen was too close. Dan pushed his father away. "What's going on, Dad? Are you drunk?"

"No, I'm not drunk. Your bloody girlfriend has only gone and published a whole bunch of damned lies. And a bunch of left-wing lunatics have been retweeting it like there's no tomorrow. Martin De La Hay just called me…"

Nicole said, "I didn't do anything. I made a promise to you, and I've kept it."

Charlie was snarling now. "That's impossible. You know more than anyone. My father dragged through the dirt, and he isn't alive to defend himself. You selfish, self-centred cow!"

Dan said, "Don't you dare speak to Nicole like that. Let's see what it says. Mum, get him away from me before I hit him."

Nicole shrank back and sat on a chair arm. "I didn't do anything. I swear." She took out her phone and searched for Rothbury. Sure enough, a series of tweets led her to an online article – anonymous – headlined:

TOP PREP SCHOOL ROTHBURY WARTIME SHAME EXPOSED

Leading preparatory school Rothbury, located near Andover in Hampshire, has a terrible secret going all the way back to World War 2. A secret that the school, currently in negotiations with a leading Chinese investment group, HVAC, has tried to suppress for over seventy years.

It is a story of bullying and pupil abuse.

During the Second World War, the school relocated to the Lake District in order to protect its pupils from the German bombing of London. Run by the great-grandfather of the current Rothbury headmaster, Martin De La Hay – and resourced with a skeleton staff of local women, the school's senior boys quickly took charge of the school and introduced a reign of terror that resulted in the unexplained death of one boy and the permanent scarring of many others. Boys were beaten, left in the fields all night in freezing cold and locked in the stables with the horse. When staff complained about the boys' behaviour, the headmaster Clive De La Hay refused to do anything.

The cover-up was discovered when Nicole Weymouth, a twenty-seven-year-old public relations executive, visited Blair Gowan, the site of the school in the war and now a boutique hotel. She came across an unsent letter, dating back to the war, from eight-year-old Peter Slaithwaite, one of the boys. In the letter Peter revealed that he had seen something terrible happen, and, having been bullied by the senior boys, wanted to be taken home. Eventually he ran away and travelled the length of England on his own to be reunited with his parents.

Nicole investigated the background to the letter and interviewed former pupils and staff at the school. Her investigations revealed that Michael Newhouse, father of the top banking executive Charles Newhouse, was the ringleader in the bullying. He was also the person responsible for locking Peter Slaithwaite in the stables all night with a crazy horse. He was in the close vicinity of Eric McArthur when the boy fell to his death in the quarry on the school grounds – an event that friends of Peter Slaithwaite claim he witnessed. In his letter Peter Slaithwaite begged his parents to come and bring him home. He ran away from the school shortly afterwards and, after an unhappy life, committed suicide at the young age of 31.

Nicole has asked the current headmaster of Rothbury, Martin De La Hay, on several occasions to confirm these allegations and to go on the record, but he has refused as he claims that they would jeopardise the potential HVAC investment that he says the school badly needs.

Nicole has since reported the case to the police and requested they reopen it.

Martin De Lay Hay said, "I am so proud of my great-grandfather for what he did for all the school's pupils in the war. It was our family's finest hour."

A spokesman for HVAC refused to comment when contacted.

The story had been posted on a blog named Rothbury Rumours and simply said Anonymous where the author's name should be. It looked like it had been set up specifically to carry this story, as they weren't any others.

There was only one person who had access to all this information – Bee. Nicole covered her face as Charlie continued to bellow. This wasn't meant to happen. It was what she wanted, of course, but she had made a promise. Now it had been broken. How could Bee do this to her own family?

The tweets kept coming. A member of the shadow cabinet had retweeted it. Hundreds of people were wading in with their comments. For many it was vindication of their belief that public schools shouldn't exist. Outside this room she was becoming a news item, a whistle-blower of a corrupt establishment.

Dan started reading it over her shoulder. She could sense his breathing grow faster as he read it.

Charlie wasn't stopping. Dan was almost crying when he came around in front of her and said, "Why did you do this, Nicole? You told me you wouldn't. Why? Why? Why?"

Nicole wished she was on a flight to America, better still outer space. "I didn't. I did keep investigating it. I did write everything up. That's true. But I didn't publish this. I promise!"

"I can't believe it!" He stomped off to the other side of the room. Everyone at the party had created a space around Nicole. The noise and general hubbub had abated.

"It's true. I decided I didn't want to do anyone any harm, no matter what I found out!" She looked at everyone as she said it, starting at Charlie, pleading for allies with her eyes.

"I have told the police though." Charlie stopped shouting. Dan starred at her, eyes and mouth wide open.

Then it was Charlie who was creating the space. He had retreated away from her, clutching his chest and was making different noises. He looked blue in the face and was starting to stagger. He fell to the ground with a huge thud, his lips mouthing slow-motion requests for help. For a moment everyone stared, and no-one moved. Then Jo threw her wine glass aside, leapt to his side and shouted for someone to call an ambulance.

One of Dan's friends, Quentin, rushed over and started to administer CPR. Jo was beside him, screaming. Some guests glanced at Nicole every so often as if she herself had struck Charlie. Nicole ignored their glances. She sat, staring at her phone, unable to move. She hated him right now for his outburst, but she would never wish such suffering on anyone, least of all her potential father-in-law.

The few minutes seemed like an hour as they waited for the ambulance. Nicole's mobile was lighting up with calls from numbers she didn't recognise. Her Twitter feed had gone nuts. Her schoolfriends came over and comforted her. They knew nothing about Rothbury, Peter Slaithwaite or the letter.

The CPR seemed to have worked as Charlie had opened his eyes, breathing short and shallow breaths. Nicole walked over and kneeled beside him alongside Dan. She put her hand on his arm, but he swatted it away. Jo, tears streaming down her face, flashed her a grim look.

Everyone would think she was the villain in this. Charlie's heart attack caused by her relentless desire to see the truth revealed. How ironic that when she had, at last, decided to halt her investigations someone else had intervened to ignite the fireworks she had so denied herself. police wouldn't be impressed either. As she watched Jo suffering the unthinkable agony of a husband on the verge of death, Nicole wished it were her on the floor.

Nicole got up and went back to her chair. Chandra came over and put her arm around her shoulders. She said, "Don't take any of this to heart. It wasn't your fault."

She reached for her phone and, not expecting a reply, texted Bee. *Was this you?*

Two medics, a man and a woman, arrived. Within a minute, they had put an oxygen mask over Charlie's face, lifted him onto a stretcher and taken him out of the room. Jo left with him. No-one said anything. People took glasses and plates into the kitchen just for something to do. Some concentrated on their phones as if they had important business that wouldn't wait.

Nicole walked over to Dan, who was standing alongside the medics. "I'm so sorry, so, so sorry." She grabbed his hand and tried to hug him, but he pulled away and headed off to the kitchen. The guests started murmuring to each other. Nicole stood alone with her schoolfriends and Chandra in the middle of the room.

The exact thing she didn't want to happen had happened. She was innocent, but everyone had decided she was guilty. She had been caught red-handed having lied to her boyfriend.

Chandra leant close to her. "I'm getting you out of here."

"I need to speak to Dan."

Nicole walked over to the kitchen. Dan was leaning against the sink, ashen faced, with a couple of his friends on either side. There was evidence of some half-hearted attempts at washing-up.

"Can I talk to you, Dan? Alone?"

Dan nodded and gestured for his friends to leave. Now they were two people in a kitchen amidst the detritus of a party.

"I didn't do it. Honest."

Dan wiped his eyes. "So who did?" It wasn't the time to drop Bee in it. She didn't know for certain.

"I don't know. But you know I promised Martin De La Hay I wouldn't publish anything, and you know me well enough to know I wouldn't break my word. Don't you?"

"You promised me you would stop looking into it. You promised me that weeks ago. It was all a big lie, Nicole. What have I done to deserve this?" He threw his arms up in exasperation.

Nicole tried to grab his arms, but he pushed her away. "I wanted to stop so much but I got it in my head that I had to do it for Patrick. I so wanted to put my guilt to rest so I could focus on being with you. Don't you see that?"

Dan looked up at the ceiling, eyes misty, "All I can see is that my fiancée has been lying to me and my father has had a heart attack as a result."

All the warm feelings from earlier had disappeared. She might have found out the truth, but it had come at a very high price. No wonder he didn't believe she hadn't published it: she had lied about researching it.

Dan said nothing and just played with a tea towel in his hands. They just stood there. Nicole staring at him, Dan ignoring her gaze.

Then he spoke, "I thought this was a new chapter, but I was wrong. You haven't really committed, have you?"

"That's not true. I told you I was ready to move on. If it had just been up to me, I wouldn't have kept going. There were others I couldn't let down. And I didn't publish it. I swear. Someone else must have done that. I know I went to the police, but I had to do that." Didn't he know how hard it was for her to trust people after the way her own father had let her down?

He said, "The trouble with you is that you want it every which way. You want to do what you want when you want it, but, when it goes wrong, it's someone else's fault. If anyone challenges you on that, you tell them they don't understand and put it down to what a tough time you had growing up. I know it wasn't easy for you, but you're getting through it. Your mother's death was a massive shock, and I know it will take ages to get over it, if ever, but you will, and I want to help you. You'd found me. We've found us. And things are sorting themselves out. Even your dad has seen the light and asked for forgiveness. But you had to keep going with your stupid obsession even when you could see it was going to cause a lot of people a lot of harm. I love your energy and your determination, everything about you, in fact, but you need to start stopping to think before you do stuff. Otherwise, our lives will keep lurching from disaster to disaster."

"That's so unfair."

"I don't believe you. Why should I?" Dan's lip curled up and quivered.

"I know I should have stopped. So much happened so fast. Our engagement, the accident, the job, my mother's death." She nearly added to the list but stopped herself. "And, at the back of my mind, my determination to come to terms with what happened to my brother. I just couldn't handle everything all the time. I had to compartmentalise to get through it. Rothbury, Peter, it just made me so angry. It was as if Patrick was asking me to help Peter because no-one else had. It was my penance for not saving him that day by the pool. Even though I knew the dangers I couldn't not do it."

"I know all that, but you did it. You've lied. You've lied to me. You've lied to everyone. You just don't call it lies. For you it's self-defence. Justified because the world is out to get you."

Nicole couldn't think what to say next. If that was what her boyfriend thought of her, then there was no reason to stay. Dan had his head in his hands, leaning over the sink.

"That's so unfair! What happened at that school is just horrible. You should be proud of me, not critical. I don't know why I'm with you. You're as bad as your father!"

As she turned, somebody tapped her on the shoulder. Chandra grabbed her hand. "I'm taking you out of here, Nicole."

This wasn't how this evening was meant to be. This was meant to be the start of something new. Thank God she hadn't told him about the pregnancy. All the baggage jettisoned. I won't be back here, Nicole thought to herself. Someone else can clear up the mess…

Nicole kissed her schoolfriends as Chandra led her out of the party. Awkward smiles and weak waves from Dan's friends who lined her route down the passageway and out of the front door. They had all heard everything. It was a walk of shame when it should have been a walk of triumph.

When they stood on the pavement, Nicole wiping away her tears with her sleeve, she turned to Chandra and kissed her on the cheek.

"Thanks so much. That's decided it. I'm going to San Francisco."

*

Nicole still had a key to Martha's flat, so, in the absence of anywhere else to go, she went there. It had started to rain, and the streetlights had turned the puddles on the road orange. There was still a bed in her room even if there weren't any sheets. The new tenant wasn't moving in until the weekend, and Martha was away in Seville spending her deposit.

She opened the door to a dark flat. The only light, the light of a phone, lit up a face on the sofa. It was Bee.

"Oh? Hello, Nicole. I didn't think you'd be here." Nicole switched the main light on and Bee covered her eyes. She had been crying.

"Why did you do it?" Nicole stood with authority she didn't feel, hands on her hips in the middle of the room.

Bee looked up at her. Nicole could sense her brain whirring, calculating whether a denial had any chance of flying. Her features slumped after a moment, suggesting she didn't like the odds.

"They didn't deserve to get off scot-free. The police will take ages and bury it. All my life my dad has been going on about how wonderful the De La Hays are and how Rothbury made him the man he is. Then you discover all this shit they have been covering up for years. And my grandfather, who we virtually had to kneel in front of when we visited him, turns out to be the villain, possibly even a murderer. You really think I was going to allow all that to be buried? No way!"

"I told the police. That was enough."

Bee shrugged her shoulders. "They won't do anything."

"Your father is in hospital. He might die. And everyone thinks it was me. You need to own up."

"I'm sorry. I didn't think people would blame you. Miss Goody-two-shoes." Bee pulled her hands to her cheeks like a 1950s film starlet. "Anyway, he's OK. Dan texted me."

"Are you going to own up?" Bee turned her head into the sofa. Nicole was very tired. Her phone rang.

"Nicole? It's Martin De La Hay. I'm getting calls from all over the world. HVAC have pulled out. The police want to interview me tomorrow. Half a dozen parents have already said their children won't be coming back next term. This is curtains for Rothbury – and all because of you!"

"Listen. You are bloody lucky I agreed to that, as what your family did was a disgrace. Not many other people would. As it happens, I kept my word. Someone else released that article. It wasn't me."

"No-one else knew what you knew. If it wasn't you, it was someone you knew. Someone who had access to all your research. Very convenient indeed. That article is libellous. I will have lawyers on to it in the morning."

"It's all true and you told me so yourself."

"Charlie Newhouse is dying in hospital…"

Nicole killed the call. She was through being lectured. Maybe Martin De La Hay would suffer a heart attack as well. Now that would be proper justice.

In a voice muffled by the sofa, Bee said, "I'll fess up. Promise. Just give me a few days."

"Do what you want. I'll be gone." She told Bee about her plans. "Don't tell your family. Dan and I are finished."

Bee rushed over to hug her. "I'm so sorry. I had no idea that would happen." Nicole pulled away.

"Bit late for that. But do me a favour. Be out of the flat for good by the time Martha comes back tomorrow night. By the way, how did you find it, the article I mean?"

Bee wiped her eyes with the sleeve of her pullover. "You left a crumpled-up copy in your bin."

Nicole turned and headed off to her sparse and decluttered room for a final night. In her heart of hearts, she was grateful to Bee. She was right. It was too terrible a story to remain under wraps.

Her room was bare. A cleaner had been in in readiness for the next occupant. She found an old blanket and lay on the stained mattress. An appropriate end to a day from hell. This time tomorrow she could be in San Francisco.

All day she had been putting on a brave face. Gal's decision to replace her on the team, Charlie's tantrum and his collapse and Dan's disbelief. Through it all she had refused to crumble. Resilient but self-aware, capable of holding her own whatever life threw at her. But she had run out of juice. Tears convulsed her, choking her and filling her nose with mucus. And they wouldn't stop. After what seemed like hours, her desire for sleep proved too much.

What seemed like a few minutes later but was probably several hours, she woke up to find a warm body next to her. For a moment she thought she was with Dan. But it was Bee, snoring, her body curved in the shape of Nicole's to gain maximum warmth.

23

"I'm really pleased you decided to come with me. These US VCs are hard nuts. We might think we're hot, but they get businesses like ours pitching to them every day."

Nicole took a sip of her pint glass of Napa Chardonnay and, in a jet-lagged daze, let Gal rabbit on about the week's meetings. She had had to accept the wine, but she would leave the rest of it: Gal couldn't know for a while yet.

He seemed to be coping better than her with the time difference. They were sitting at the bar of the Hotel Zetta in the centre of San Francisco. A couple of top-knotted software developers – she presumed that's what they were, were playing pool in the corner. Otherwise, the bar, which doubled as reception, was empty. It was only ten o'clock at night. Pictures of The Beatles in their mid-sixties pomp adorned the walls.

She hadn't expected Gal to be on the trip. She thought she was going to meet with their new US office head to discuss marketing and PR. Somehow, during the call to tell him of her change in plans, he had decided he needed to go and see the venture capitalists a week earlier than planned. The next thing she knew, he was sitting in the aisle opposite her in Economy. Usually, he travelled Business if his board signed it off.

"So, do you want to talk about what happened? Why you changed your mind?"

"No. I'd prefer not to. You know…" Gal nodded with an exaggerated flourish as if he was an expert in matters of the heart. "Tell me what you're worried about."

Gal said, "We're not a bank and we're not a software company. If we're a bank, we will need a licence for the US and we won't get that for some years. If we're a software company, we need a hero product and we don't have one. So, they will be investing in potential and that comes down to whether they buy me."

"Well, that's OK then. Anyone with half a brain will do that."

Every so often well-dressed men and women hauling wheelie suitcases charged in and, with the minimum of fuss, checked in and moved over to the lifts. The girl at the bar polished glasses and stared into space. Gal kept talking and Nicole half-listened, mainly thinking about the stream of unopened texts from journalists, family, friends and, most of all, Dan.

Twenty-four hours hadn't assuaged his belief that Nicole had deliberately gone against her word and trashed his family's reputation. Martin De La Hay had gone on the offensive and had told anyone who would listen that it was a mentally unstable women called Nicole Weymouth who was responsible for this 'concoction of libellous allegations'. Some journalists had taken this as a cue to link the story to all the dirt about Zaxxo, and the story had spread to the business pages. Gal didn't seem that bothered with that, to his credit. He could just add it to the list of lies being told about him and his business.

Gal said, "Sorry, I have been going on. Can I ask you something?" Gal's eyes bored into her. Nicole jerked herself out of her jet-lagged stupor and nodded.

"Ask what?"

Gal blushed. "Do you want to stay on for the weekend? Taste some wines up in Sonoma?"

It wasn't as if she hadn't thought about it. He was kind, smart and, in a rather hirsute 70s kind of way, good-looking. But they had very little in common and, deal-breaker all round, he was her boss. She had to let him down without affecting their relationship. But she didn't have the energy to sugar-coat it. He should have worked that out.

Somehow, she managed to generate a smile she didn't feel.

"That's a lovely idea, but let's keep this business. OK?" She reached out and tapped the top of his hand. "We've got a great working relationship, and I'm totally committed to helping Zaxxo become a massive success, but I think we should leave it at that. Sorry."

Gal slunk back. That monosyllabic pitch must have been a long time coming. In an instant she regretted that she had had to be so blunt. Her boyfriend and his family had decided, without a trial, that she was a pariah. Here was a lovely man, without any baggage, and no connections to Rothbury, telling her he wanted her.

The thud of the pool balls, followed by a yelp of satisfaction, were the only sounds in the bar. They both sat back on the sofas and looked at their phones. Then the pool players left, and one of the two receptionists went off shift. After a minute Nicole, starting to feel nauseous again, hauled herself up and said, "It's going to be a long day tomorrow, isn't it? I'll sort us a cab for 7.30. People say the traffic down to Menlo in the mornings is terrible."

*

The next day was nothing like Nicole had ever experienced. By the end of it, for the first time, she could see why Po had ended up being a complete dick. They were joined by someone from their corporate finance advisors called Judge, who wore a navy-blue blazer, pressed jeans, and moccasins. He was six foot four tall and treated them as if they were naughty schoolchildren on a day out. Gal didn't seem to mind and hung on his every word.

They seemed to spend most of their time driving around enormous business parks and walking between identikit box-shaped buildings, all flanked by huge palm trees, trying to find the right address. Often the buildings had numbers like 2543. Waze sent them down so many last-minute shortcuts her head spun. Given one of Nicole's many tasks for the day was navigation, it wasn't the confidence booster she had hoped for when she was flying out. Judge made regular calls to someone called Billy-Christine in the office, who helped steer them to the right destination.

The first two meetings seemed to consist of men in hoodies and polo shirts turning up late and joshing with Gal about soccer and the royal family. Each time, after about ten minutes, Judge called them to order, and Gal ran through his PowerPoint. Gal was right that they couldn't see what the attraction was. One potential investor asked whether it could become a decacorn, which meant that it could be worth a trillion dollars. Gal said yes. What else was he going to say? thought Nicole.

At lunchtime she got a text from Bee: *Just call me, OK?* She excused herself from the third meeting: they had finished the business part and were offered huge doorstop-sized sandwiches wrapped in brown paper.

Once the receptionist had given her a pass and agreed to let her back in, she went out into the car park and called Bee. There was a cold wind, and she pulled her jacket around her tight.

"So…"

"I've told them. God, I thought Dad was going to have another heart attack. The nurse ordered me out of the room. Anyway, you're off the hook."

"Thank you. It was the right thing to do."

"Yeah, well, I don't have a career to worry about. I'm sorry. I didn't think it would be such a big deal."

During the day Nicole had seen all the emails, texts, WhatsApps and Google Alerts. She had never been so popular, albeit for all the wrong reasons. If she had had this many media opportunities for any of her clients when at Yellow Razor, she would have been over the moon. She was very glad that she was out of the country and eight hours behind.

"Dan and I were back on track. You knew what might happen. Why, Bee, why?"

"You have to have lived my life to know why. Dan always the golden boy. Bee always the stupid embarrassment. Mum getting shouted down when she stood up for me. Once I won a race at school. I was so pleased. You would have thought everyone would have wanted to say well done that evening. Not a bit of it. We had to talk about some pathetic football match going on the other side of the world. I bring a boy home for the first time, at the age of nineteen, I might add, and Dad and Dan just watch TV. We have to sit in the kitchen with Mum, so we don't disturb them. That's why I did it. To shake them out of their patriarchal complacency. To teach them a fucking lesson."

Nicole stared at the gardener running around the parking lot trying to catch windswept paper and packaging. Bee had a point. It wasn't an experience new to her. She thought about her father and Patrick. Even they had always seemed to have keys to a room she didn't have.

"Bee. I can see all that, but why did you have to make me collateral damage? You knew what a tough decision I'd made. You knew what was at stake."

Bee was crying now. "Have you seen the picture of you and Gal? There's an article in the *Mail Online* that implies you two are shagging."

"What?" Nicole put the phone on speaker and scrolled the Google Alerts. Sure enough, there was one from the *Mail Online*. She didn't think he was high profile enough for them. There was a photo of Gal and her in that pub in Borough Market. Their heads were close together as if they were intimate – a terrible photo from someone's phone. It was when she had told Gal about Patrick's death.

"It's complete crap."

"Well, Dan's seen it. Annabel too. She was over to his flat like a 999 call when it came out. I'm sorry, Nicole. My brother was always a little flaky."

"He wouldn't do that. He promised me."

"Yeah, well, I'm really sorry. I'm going to try and get them all to forgive you."

"For fuck's sake. Forgive me? Why? I didn't do anything. What planet are you on? You are such a fucking liability, Bee. I can see why you piss all your friends and family off. All you care about is yourself." The gardener had stopped working and was staring at her.

"That's so unfair. I've moved out of the flat. I've confessed. What more can I do for you?"

Nicole ended the call and put her phone into her bag, smiling at the gardener. He shrugged his shoulders and went back to chasing litter.

*

They got back to the hotel around six and stood at the lift. They hadn't talked in the car. Nicole was looking forward to room service and Netflix – she had about a week of *Ozark* to catch up on. Once she had deleted the river of messages that were still appearing on her phone. Gal had other ideas.

"Shall we meet down here at seven? I've booked a table down at The Slanted Door in the Ferry Building. It's right on the water. Best fusion food in the city. I know we're both dead on our feet, but we must eat."

She had to admit she was hungry, having ignored the loaf-sized sandwiches and flavourless lettuce she had been offered at their lunchtime meeting. If he was prepared to eat in silence, she was on.

"See you down here in an hour then." Gal grinned and held the lift door open for her.

Once Nicole was in her room, she kicked her shoes off and threw herself down backwards on the bed. Bee's words echoed around her head. "Get them to forgive you." Where did she get the nerve to even consider that would appease her? That family were so out of touch. Something terrible had happened and their relative was responsible. They should be livid regardless of their public embarrassment. It was almost as if they all wanted a fall-guy as that was the only way they could get through it. She wondered what Jo thought.

The Gal photo worried her. Any sympathy people might have had was going to be diminished by the allegation that she had been two-timing Dan. There was some guilt there as well. She remembered how close she had felt to Gal that night. Add the fact that Zaxxo was every paper's bete-de-jour, and her reputation was trashed. Somehow, given the enormity of what she had discovered, it didn't seem fair.

Anyone she knew in England would be asleep. She was on her own. Just in case, she texted Chandra. *Sorry. R u awake?*

Within a minute Chandra called back. "I couldn't sleep. I was worried about you."

"How bad is it?" Chandra was quiet as she scrolled through the stories on her phone.

"Could be worse. *The Mail* loves the photo. Martin De La Hay seems to have taken it as a green light to say what he thinks about you. I won't read it out. It's all garbage."

Nicole lay on the bed and took some deep breaths. She eyed the chocolate with longing.

"Your story is trending on Twitter. Congratulations. Our clients will be very jealous."

"Seriously, should I stay out here?" A few days away wouldn't do any harm was Chandra's verdict. "Trouble is, if I talk to any journalists right now, they just want to talk about me. I can't do my job."

"Get some sleep. I doubt it will be a story by the time you get back."

*

They took an Uber down a long street strewn with tramps either lying on the pavement or pushing supermarket trolleys. It was hard to imagine that this was one of the richest cities in the world.

The restaurant was right on the water and was full to bursting with people. It was only early by London standards, but it seemed like midnight in terms of everyone's inebriation. The waitress showed them to a table in a far, dark corner of the restaurant close to the kitchen. Nicole watched a group of women in crop-tops stand up and down shots as the waitress ran through a long list of specials. Every component of every special had to be described in terms of the region or town it came from, so it took a long time. The men at the next table cheered and applauded as the girls sat down. The list of adjectives on the menu was exhausting to read. Nicole chose the burger.

After about ten minutes the waitress brought Gal a margarita the size of cereal bowl with a salt-encrusted rim. No wonder everyone was so merry. Nicole ordered a Coke, protesting jet lag.

"You know we're a story, don't you?" Nicole sipped her drink and stared at Gal.

"It's not fair, is it? My lawyers say there isn't anything we can do. I'm still battling that sexual harassment allegation."

The men had bought shots too now, and the women were cheering them on as they sprinkled salt on their hands and squeezes of lemon in their mouths in preparation. Gal grimaced at the noise as if to apologise for the venue, and Nicole waved her hand to dismiss it.

The party mood of the restaurant permeated their corner, and soon, Nicole had forgotten about her tiredness and woes. Anxious to keep things on a professional level, she plied Gal with questions about his plans for the business. He was both serious and funny, aware that he was an outsider and unused to many of the niceties of middle-class English life but prepared to laugh at his misunderstandings and failures.

"I went to a Goldman Sachs dinner in a T-shirt and jeans. Everyone else was in suits. The former Chancellor of the Exchequer asked me if I was his cab driver."

Nicole laughed. "That sounds like Charlie Newhouse. I hope you told him to fuck off."

"I flashed him my watch. That shut him up."

They finished their meal fast. They were both yawning. Gal paid the bill and made to order another Uber.

The city stretched out ahead as they walked out of the Ferry Building door. This was the world Nicole had only seen in films. It was a shame to waste it. She said, "Let's walk a little. It's not far."

As they started to cross the road outside the Ferry Building, Nicole stumbled and Gal caught her arm. He kept hold of it after they had crossed. Nicole was wide awake to what he was doing – indeed what she was doing – but didn't stop him. When they reached the pavement on the other side, she looked about, taking in the lights of the tall buildings all around her and from across the bay behind her. Everything that had happened to her in the past weeks was now a blur. It was as if she had been cast in a movie and, ignorant of the plot, had to battle every catastrophe thrown at her. But what did it matter? She was still standing. Fate would have its own plans for her regardless.

Somewhere, thousands of miles away, Annabel would be laying siege to Dan. And, if it wasn't her, someone else would be plotting to put themselves forward for the vacancy. Dan was a good man and one who, if he could get out from under his father's shadow, could be a very good one. He deserved better. But, right now, so did she.

She turned to Gal and kissed him on the cheek, then the lips. They stayed, locked, as the late-working city commuters headed home either side of them.

*

It was a fifteen-minute walk back to the hotel and they had held hands as they walked. Along the way they chatted about tomorrow's meetings. He seemed nervous. She guessed this didn't happen to him every day.

There was a moment, in the bright light of the elevator, when she looked at both of them in the mirror, when she first wondered if she was making a mistake, but Gal stroked her cheek in the tenderest of ways, and it passed. She wasn't drunk on alcohol but a first night in a city she'd always dreamt of visiting had had the same effect. And, pretty soon, for quite some time, she wouldn't be doing this with anyone.

When they reached his room, Nicole stood in the middle

of the floor and Gal undid the buttons on her blouse one by one, kissing her neck and breasts. His hands moved up and down her back. He had a grace and gentleness she hadn't expected from him and hadn't experienced before.

Then she looked across at them in the full-length mirror. As if she had stepped out of the situation and was looking at them as a spectator. This was her boss. It didn't matter where it was happening. She had managed to win his respect. It couldn't happen.

"I can't do this. I'm sorry!" Gal looked up at her.

"But why? You started it."

"I know. I shouldn't have."

He looked very vulnerable. Like a dog that feared a blow. "Why?"

She sat on the bed and patted the space beside her to indicate for him to sit down. The whir of the air conditioning broke the silence.

"You know why. Firstly, you're my boss. We both know that's a big no-no. Secondly, although Dan and I have had our problems, he is still my boyfriend, my fiancé in fact, and I don't want to jeopardise our relationship." As she said this, she realised quite how much she meant it. "And, thirdly, and I didn't want to tell you this for a while, as it is still early days, I'm pregnant. So, for all those reasons, much as I like you, this doesn't make sense. My fault for leading you on. I'm so sorry."

Gal slumped forward, head in his hands. He looked beaten. She got up and ran out of the room, covering her undone blouse with her hands, across the corridor to hers. The corridor lights flickered.

When she reached her room, she got out her phone. She needed to speak to someone but who? There was no-one she could call at that time of night. Buried deep in the list of messages on her phone there was a WhatsApp message from Dan.

Bee has explained everything. I was wrong. I'm so, so sorry. Dad might not pull through. I need you. Please come home. XX

The message was several hours old. He would be asleep now, so there was no rush to reply. She wanted to talk to him but didn't know what to say. She lay on the bed and closed her eyes. She was so tired.

After a while, the phone fell out of her grasp onto the bed and, her dilemmas parked unresolved, she slept.

*

It was about six and still dark when she woke. Thoughts of her aborted night with Gal filled her mind. She wasn't looking forward to breakfast. She lay staring at the ceiling wondering what to say to Dan.

Lovely note. I'm sorry to hear that about your dad. I still need to think.

Within seconds he replied. *Please please come back N. My life is nothing without you. I know why you did it and I've learnt my lesson. Love you so much. XX*

And then another.

BTW there is a weird parcel for u here. Feels like a book. Salisbury postcode.

She didn't know what to reply. It was very good news he was coming around to her viewpoint. She kicked herself that she was so intrigued by the last part. She needed to see that parcel as soon as possible.

When she got downstairs to the restaurant attached to

the hotel, Gal was already there at the end table. It had a black-and-white chequered floor and burgundy red walls. He was in a fresh shirt, pressed blue jeans and loafers. A copy of the *San Francisco Chronicle* was open in front of him.

She sat down. "I'm really sorry about last night."

"Don't worry. I understand. Congratulations on your news." *He could be so sweet.* Then Gal told her about how much needed to be done in the next two days. Nicole could only think of the parcel with the Salisbury postcode.

"I need to go back to London. Charlie's not well. I can come back on Monday."

"You only just got here. I need you. You've got a job to do here."

Nicole grabbed Gal's hand. "I know – and I'll be back. I'll work on the flight. I have to put family first for the moment and I need to tell Dan about the baby."

Gal withdrew his hand. She said, "And c'mon. Be real. This isn't how business works anymore. You know that. We're an HR crisis waiting to happen. Look at the coverage our drink in Borough Market got. It will never end."

Gal looked like he was about to cry. She didn't need any more of this. She was an idiot. She had been playing with fire. There wasn't a fork in the road. Only one way out. The waiter, hovering, about to ask for their order, stepped away.

"I need 24 hours. I will come back here as soon as I can. I know there is lots to do, but I need to be with Dan." This didn't seem to cheer Gal up at all.

She said, "And Anya loves you. Remember that." All Anya's elfin-like expressions of envy played across her memory. Anya would never let Gal down. You wouldn't find her doing a runner back to London from a San Francisco hotel room after an almost night of passion.

He looked up, "Are you saying she is more my type? That you're too smart for me? I want you. Not her."

"Life isn't that simple; you've got a grand plan, one that's going really, really well. A relationship with me won't help that. Let me help you but just professionally. This was my fault. OK?"

She kissed him on the cheek. But she knew it would take more than that to get them back on track.

24

When Nicole got to Arrivals at Terminal 5 on Saturday morning, she had nowhere to go or live. It had been a bumpy flight, requiring several trips to the toilets. Sleep had been impossible.

She had moved out of Martha's flat, and virtually all her stuff was at Dan's, but she couldn't go there. Her mother's bungalow was technically an option, but she wasn't going to go all the way down to Somerset.

She sat on her suitcase amongst the chattering minicab drivers all bearing cardboard name signs. Despite her jet lag, the sight of families and friends reuniting lifted her spirits. She started to scroll her phone for someone who might give her a bed for the night. A week ago, she was queen of the hill – a successful businesswoman with serious options about to move in with her boyfriend and a job in the US on the horizon. How the mighty and all that.

A man in a black Harrington jacket and his shirt hanging out came up to her. "Are you Nicole Weymouth?" Nicole nodded.

"What do you have to say about the workplace harassment allegations concerning Gal Bezman?"

"Nothing. Go away."

The man took a step closer. He smelt like he had been out all night. "Is that because you and he are an item?"

"Fuck off." Nicole was so tired she could only think and speak in monosyllables. If she had ever had the skills of a PR, it had been in another life.

The man thrust his phone into her face. His eyeballs were reddened. "Can you repeat that? My readers would enjoy it."

Nicole looked back down at her phone. Chandra was her only option. "No. Fuck. Off."

Two of the minicab drivers standing close by came over. One asked Nicole if she was OK and she shook her head. The other shooed the man away. After all, this was their patch. The journalist tottered away backwards like a spider crab on the beach heading back to the sea.

*

On the Piccadilly Line to Chandra's house in Ealing, Nicole, as she swung between wakefulness and sleep, took stock. Dan wanted her back, but it would take more than a couple of WhatsApp messages to convince her that was a good idea. He had been far too fast to blame her. If he truly loved her, he would have given her the benefit of the doubt.

But didn't she need to forgive Dan now? His father was still on the critical list in hospital after all. And Jo didn't deserve any further hassle from her even if Bee did. She'd left Gal to fend for himself in the Sonoma vineyards. Things hadn't been the same once she had announced she was heading back to London, and, by the time she had left, she was wondering if he was going to keep her on. She was a very expensive – and reluctant – bag-carrier and had done a pretty crap job keeping a lid on the bad news.

I'm at a complete dead end she thought to herself. No boyfriend, no family, and no accommodation. And she was pregnant and hadn't told the father. Worst of all, her mother wasn't at the other end of a phone anymore. She was very lucky Chandra hadn't cut her off when Nicole had stormed out of the wine bar.

Then she remembered Dan's message. The packet from Salisbury. Sally Slaithwaite came from Salisbury. It couldn't be. Could it?

Her curiosity overcame her reluctance to see Dan. She had to tell him sometime, regardless of whether they stayed together. When the tube hit daylight, the bars reappeared on her phone. She still had Dan on 'Find My Friends' and he was at the flat. She texted Chandra; apologised, saying she would see her later. If only all her friends cut her as much slack as Chandra did. She really couldn't face seeing Dan yet, but if the package was what she thought it was, then she had to have it. At some point she was going to have to try and start again but not quite yet.

*

The Dan that opened the door to his flat looked as if he was about to go on a first date. His aftershave hit her like a tsunami. Hair neat, stubble removed, shirt ironed: she wondered who he had been expecting.

"Wow! It's you. I thought you were in the States?!" He lunged forward and, before Nicole had time to step back, kissed her on the lips and bear-hugged her. "I never thought you would come back so fast."

Nicole extracted herself from his clutches and shuffled past him into the flat. "Nor me." He followed her at a dignified distance. The trailing suitcase saw to that. No attempt at further physical proximity.

"Sit down. We have so much to talk about." He led to the faded pink George Smith sofa. Dan held on to her hand. "Have you forgiven me? We were all way out of order. I should have believed you. I will never ever forgive myself."

She had been expecting this speech. She had wanted to hear it. But it still didn't really add up when she heard it out loud. She looked him up and down and gave him a theatrical sniff.

"I've been in the hospital pretty much all the time since you left. Mum told me to go home for a bit."

"Why did you think I would lie to you?"

"I didn't want to. Of course I didn't want to. I just couldn't think who else might have done it. I was so conflicted. Dad has been so protective of everything that happened between our family and Rothbury. And at that moment he was so vulnerable. I didn't know what else to do."

Vulnerable? Unlike your girlfriend who had just lost her mother. "So, you blamed your girlfriend. In front of all your family and friends?"

Dan went red and withdrew his hand. "Well, yes. If you put it like that. I mean, it was your work. Regardless of who sent it out into the world."

"What have you done about your sister? The person your family should really be furious with?"

Dan didn't seem to have an answer. He just wiped his glistening eyes and then looked up at the ceiling like an 18th-century governess who has heard something distressing.

She said, "I need that package. Where is it?" Dan got off the sofa, went to a table at the side of the room and brought it over to her.

"It feels a book," she said. Nicole turned it over in her hands. The brown paper was tied together with string like an old-fashioned present.

"I'm going to open this later." She composed herself. "Look Dan, I have something big to tell you. I'm pregnant."

Dan's mouth dropped. "What!" His head swivelled as if he was expecting someone to pop up and say, 'April Fool'. "That's amazing!"

They both started crying and hugging awkwardly. Nicole, pulling back after a moment, explained how far gone she thought she was. That she needed to go and see the doctor and get a scan as soon as possible. Dan started talking about what they needed to think about, but Nicole shushed him. She wasn't ready for any of that.

She said, "Our relationship is up in the air. We have to separate out the baby from any decisions about that. We both know this isn't great timing."

"But you know I want you back. I was really, really stupid and I regret it so much!" He wiped his eyes. "Give me another chance. Please."

Nicole resisted the temptation to buckle. "I'm pleased you've apologised. I know it took guts. And, believe it or not, I still love you. I just don't know what that means for us right now. So, you need to give me some time. OK? And prove to me that you mean it. You know what that means."

She stood up, kissed him on the cheek, then hurried out, clutching the package, dragging her suitcase, before he had time to respond.

"Let's keep this between ourselves for now. It's early days. Send your mum my love."

*

By now it was mid-morning, and she was exhausted. She had probably ruined whatever plans Chandra and Raj had made, so she spent thirty minutes knocking her suitcase into the ankles of Saturday morning shoppers in the search for some chocolates posh enough to apologise with.

She needn't have worried. Chandra and Raj, both dressed in immaculate gym gear, were delighted to see her. Their terraced semi, knocked through into one huge room on the ground floor, was all white, spotless and minimalist. An aroma of fresh coffee and croissants filled her nostrils. If they were trying to sell their house, she was a buyer.

She dropped her bags and hugged them both. Tiredness and relief engulfed her. For the first time since she could remember, she could relax. Martha's flat, Dan's flat, her mother's bungalow, the Newhouses' house: all those places were just campsites, places where she had to perform to justify her status. Here, for a few hours, she could be herself.

It seemed like Chandra could sense all this from her face.

"Sit down. Relax. Stay as long as you need."

They put coffee and croissants in front of her, went over to the kitchen and left her alone. She looked around at the picture-perfect house with its stark white walls, huge IKEA sofas and 60s pop art prints. This was the kind of place she had dreamt of owning one day. Simple and unpretentious.

She must have dropped off, as she found Chandra picking her half-full coffee cup out of her hand the moment before it obliterated the glaring whiteness of the sofa.

"What's in your package?" Chandra sat down opposite her and nodded to the brown parcel next to Nicole on the sofa. Raj stayed in the kitchen, preparing and chopping vegetables with what sounded like military precision.

Nicole pulled hard at the knot of string. It wouldn't undo. After a moment Chandra went and fetched some scissors. It was like pass the parcel with multiple layers of brown paper. After the removal of the fifth layer, the contents revealed themselves.

There was a cloth-bound book, faded orange in colour, with scuffed corners as if it had been carried around without protection for a long time. There was also a thick brittle cream envelope with an illegible ink-pen scrawl and a stamp of some long-dead king.

A white postcard fell on to the floor. The address at the top said Sally Slaithwaite, Wayside, Penrith Lane, Salisbury SP2 8FG with a phone number and email address underneath.

Nicole,

I had a good look and found these items! So, I want you to have them. Do with them what you will.
Best wishes
Sally

Nicole opened the book. On the inside front page in type,

it said 'This is the Diary of…' Then there was a space for a name. And then there was a space for the year.

In neat, childlike writing he had written his name – Peter Slaithwaite – and the year – 1940.

She closed the book, looked up at Chandra. "Oh God!"

*

Chandra knew Nicole's moods well enough to know when she wanted to be left alone. Once Nicole had drained the remnants of her coffee and finished off two croissants without dropping the crumbs on the white carpet, Chandra led her upstairs to a spare room. Until she picked it up for fear of scratching the teak stairs, Nicole's suitcase clattered.

The room was small and tidy. There was a single bed, a desk and chair, and, under a sheet, what looked like a cot.

Chandra said, "Make yourself at home." She saw Nicole had noticed the cot. "Hope springs," she said, biting her bottom lip and turning on her heels. "Anyway…"

Nicole pulled out the chair and sat at the desk. The window looked on to a small, immaculate garden with a patio and a postage stamp-sized lawn. So, Chandra had been expecting a baby. A baby that was taking its time to arrive. Maybe even one that started but didn't make it? She thought of the creation growing in her abdomen. She wished for moment that it was Chandra's.

Everyone has a burden to carry; it's just that some people keep it from view. Of the two of them, Chandra made more effort to find out about other people's burdens and help them. It wasn't Nicole's strongest attribute. She made a mental note to be more like Chandra.

The diary was lined and covered three days to a page. Every day, Peter had filled the space available with neat flowing handwriting. The first day's entry – 2nd October – marked his arrival at Blair Gowan.

We are here. We have spent seven hours on the train from London to Windermere with a stop at Manchester and we had to make our one bully beef sandwich and tin of water last the whole journey. It was quite jolly as a platoon of soldiers sang all the way in the next carriage and one gave me a sweet. It was dark and very late when we arrived. A tiny, old woman called Mrs Barton gave us a bowl of warm soup and put us in our beds in our clothes. She said we could unpack tomorrow. I whispered a very long prayer to myself before I went to sleep.

The second day wasn't much more auspicious.

We were woken at seven and told to queue in the corridor for our turn to wash in a tin bath of lukewarm water. Blair Gowan is very cold, and we are all shivering all the time. A small boy called McArthur has been crying very loudly and two older boys – Newhouse and Pilkington – have been calling him names. Two older boys from the village carried our trunks up and put them on our beds. A bell rang and we were sent downstairs into a big hall with long tables and benches. We had scrambled eggs made from powder and stale 'ersatz' bread for breakfast. The tea was made with powdered milk. I was hoping for cow's milk. I don't mind as it is our contribution to the war effort.

Nicole read on. Peter seemed to have a very mundane existence most of the time. The headmaster – or 'beak' as he called him – Mr De La Hay, taught all the lessons. He seemed to devote most of the time to Latin, Greek and maths. Peter spent many hours copying out what Mr De La Hay wrote on the board. In the afternoons, after lunch and before afternoon lessons, they were sent out on long cross-country runs and hill walks under the supervision of an old man from the village. Rugby games were an aspiration of the headmaster that seemed hard to achieve in practice.

For the past week an old man called Mr Leadbetter has been supervising making a rugby pitch on one of the fields by the river. He has made posts from some trees in the woods and got us to dig holes for them. We also spend ages removing rocks and stones. We never seem to do a good enough job for him, and he shouts at us. Sometimes Mr De La Hay comes by and hits anyone who is slacking with his walking cane. Today the sun shone, and we took it in turns to push the old mower across the field. I don't think it didn't cut much grass and Mr Leadbetter got cross.

Ten days later, on a Saturday afternoon, the pitch was ready for use. Thirty boys were picked to play out of a hat. Each team had boys ranging between eight and thirteen. Peter, who had never played rugby before, was selected.

Today was the worst day of my time at Rothbury. The pitch was not ready, and it still had many stones on it. Newhouse and Pilkington were on the other side and spent their time tackling our team so that they fell and cut themselves on the stones. McArthur hit his head on one and I cut my knee. Mr De La Hay just clapped his hands on the touchline, and it was only when Nurse Wiseman spoke to him that he stopped the game. Fourteen boys were in the infirmary after the game and two, including McArthur, had to go to the local hospital.

As the weeks drew on it was clear that boredom, interspersed with occasional bouts of chaos, had set in for all the boys. They were under-supervised with Mr De La Hay often absent at assemblies. No-one checked if they did their homework. Food was basic and scarce, and Peter continued to complain of being cold and homesick. Although he didn't say it in so many words, it appeared to Nicole that the two oldest boys, Newhouse and Pilkington, were pretty much in charge of the school.

I spent today reading a book in the corridor close to the headmaster's study. There is always an adult walking past there so I can be sure I will not be disturbed. Many of the boys are outside watching Newhouse and Pilkington carrying out one of their 'dares'. Today Smith has been challenged to walk across the deepest part of the river on a log. If he falls in, he is made to do it again. I don't think it is fair as the wetter his clothes get the harder it is for him to balance. I have lent McArthur a book so he can read next to me and keep out of trouble.

About a week later, one Sunday, things got out of control.

On Sunday evening, when it was dark, Newhouse and Pilkington took McArthur up to the quarry for his 'dare'. McArthur didn't want to go and was crying in one of the cubicles in the washrooms. I told him I would follow him up there. They found him and marched him up the field to the quarry. They wouldn't let anyone else come with them. I followed behind them and watched them from behind a mound. In the clearing in the middle of the quarry I could see Mr De La Hay dressed in a head-dress with devil's horns. He was waving a big stick and shouting. There were torches with flames on sticks either side of him. Newhouse and Pilkington were dragging McArthur towards him and McArthur was screaming. Mr De La Hay shouted something about baptism. When they reached Mr De La Hay they stopped. At that moment McArthur managed to wriggle out of their clutches, and he ran towards the land at the bottom of the quarry.

Peter had run out of space and had moved into the next day's entry.

Newhouse chased him and shouted at him to come back. McArthur reached the edge. There was a big drop in front of him. He tried to run back but Newhouse wouldn't let him. Then McArthur fell over the edge with a scream. There was a thump then silence. Newhouse just stood there. I turned away and ran back to school as fast as I could.

The next two days' entries were, for the first time in the diary, blank. Nicole sat back, unable to process what she had read.

McArthur's body has been found. Everyone at the school says it was an accident. That he went for a walk and got lost. I have already written to my parents to tell them what happened so they can come and collect me.

The garden grew dark outside, but Nicole read on. Peter had skipped a week.

At McArthur's funeral no-one wanted to sit next to me. Newhouse and Pilkington smirk when they see me. I hide whenever I can outside lessons. I have a bad cold, but Nurse Wiseman won't let me go to the sanatorium. My parents have not replied to my letter.

Nicole looked out at the red evening sky. She knew the ending and she didn't want to read on.

Last night, when everyone was asleep, Newhouse and Pilkington woke me up, put a gag in my mouth, took me out of my bed and dragged me out to the stables. Newhouse said to me, "Now Judas, you have to pay the price." They said they had seen the letter to my parents. The stables looked beautiful in the moonlight. They opened the door of the stable where the big horse lives and pulled me around the walls to avoid being kicked by it. Then they left me there. I have never been so cold but, if I moved, the horse kicked out at me. I managed to pull myself up onto a hayrack to escape it and then out of a skylight and onto the stable ground. I thought the night would never end and I didn't want to go back to the other boys. It was so cold. I did not sleep. I just sat crouched, silent. At last, I heard footsteps, and I cried out. It was Mrs Bristow. She took me into the kitchens where she put me by the cooker on a chair, wrapped me in a blanket and gave me some hot tea.

After this the diary reverted to Peter's usual humdrum descriptions of meals and classes. It was as if nothing had happened. The only change was that he didn't seem to have any friends anymore. Apart from the odd mention of Nurse Wiseman and Mrs Bristow, who seemed to take great interest in his welfare and often took him into the kitchen for extra food, he might as well have been alone. And there was no sign of his parents. Petrol rationing wouldn't have allowed them to visit, but there wasn't any evidence of letters from them either. It was as if Peter had been cast out of the community.

Then about a month later, just towards the end of term, two weeks before Christmas, there was this entry.

Today I am going to run away and go home. Mr De La Hay will do nothing. Mrs Bristow says she has told him what Newhouse and Pilkington did to me. They have not been punished. They are now Head Boy and Deputy Head Boy. They continue to torment me as I am the only boy who will stand up to them. They torture all boys. They lock them in shepherds' huts overnight up the mountain; they throw them into cold baths and force them to stay under water until they choke; and they shut boys on the roof all night until they are so cold, they have frostbite. I would prefer to die walking home than stay here.

Nicole shut the diary. It was the last entry. Peter must have taken it home with him but decided not to continue. He must have wondered what the point was. All these terrible things had happened, and no-one had taken a blind bit of notice except, of course, the indomitable Nanny Bristow. So, she had tried to do something after all. And Peter must have reached his home. Moreover, he had kept the diary, knowing that, one day, someone would find it and do what he had been unable to do in his lifetime.

Chandra knocked and put her head around the door. "We're going to have a drink in a moment. Do you fancy one? Thirsty work, I'd imagine?"

Nicole said, "Can you give me ten minutes? I think I've made a terrible mistake."

"Do you want to talk about it?"

"Later? OK?"

The letter lay alongside the diary. It was postmarked 11th May 1954, Tetbury. Nicole prised open the envelope and took out the letter. It was a single sheet of thick, cream writing paper. The address was printed on the top in Cyrillic type.

The Cottage, Lower Pond Lane, Tetbury

Dear Peter,
It is a very long time indeed since I last saw you. When you disappeared so suddenly, my world collapsed,

and it has never been the same again. I don't think I have ever forgiven you for what you did, and I don't think I ever will. I know we were young, but I was so in love with you, and I think I always will be.

Your letter to me was harrowing in so many ways. Firstly, the surprise of hearing from you after so long and, secondly, the state you appear to be in. I always hoped that, when you ran away, at least it would give you a fresh start, a chance to forget the past. It doesn't seem that you have been able to do that.

So, in these circumstances, the only positive thing I can do is to answer your question. Even though I know that it is not, in all probability, a good idea.

Our daughter is alive and well. She has been adopted by a very nice couple in Melksham, not far from Bath – a vicar and his wife – and, as far as I know, because, as you can imagine, I hear very little, she is doing very well indeed. They have called her Margaret. Not one of the names you and I used to joke about when we were together but one that I think suits her.

Yours
Alice

Nicole sat back in her chair as the sun started to throw long shadows on to the garden lawn. There was something nagging her about the description of Peter's daughter's adoptive parents, but she couldn't put her finger on it.

After five minutes she was no nearer the answer, and the thought of a gin and tonic was too tempting to resist.

Chandra and Raj were sitting at the kitchen table with

drinks in front of them. She reckoned Chandra's was made of that Sipsmith non-alcoholic gin and she asked for one of those. Raj leapt up to make one for Nicole.

Chandra said, "Not drinking?" Nicole told her the news.

"Wow, that's so brilliant. Raj, did you hear that, Nicole's pregnant. Congratulations."

Nicole hesitated, knowing about Chandra's spare room. "Thank you. Makes life quite complicated. Bit of a shock, to be honest."

They talked about early-stage pregnancy for a while. As Nicole suspected, Chandra knew a lot more than she did. For the first time, she could truly appreciate how lucky she was.

Then Chandra took a swig and said, "So, what did you find out?"

"I'm so ashamed. It was far, far worse than I thought. Barbaric, in fact. Devil worship by the headmaster. A boy was murdered, and they did nothing about it. The school covered it all up. Have done for over seventy years."

Nicole told them everything she had read. She didn't mention the letter from Alice. As she talked, she became more and more convinced she had been negligent. The right thing had been staring her in the face, and she had allowed herself to be talked out of it. At least she had told the police. Now she would need to go back to PC Robbie Halstead with her new information.

"I can't believe I have let myself be fobbed off. God, I just wish I hadn't found that letter."

Raj put a frosted glass down in front of her. At the back of her mind Alice's letter kept nagging at her.

Chandra said, "So what are you going to do?"

"I don't know. Drink this lovely drink for a start." Nicole took a large gulp.

"Don't you think this has caused you enough trouble already? Arguably you would still be at Yellow Razor. Still be happily partnered up with Dan. Why don't you drop it? Raj? What do you think?"

Raj grinned. "You know what I think. Anything that upsets the establishment is alright with me."

Chandra said, "Helpful. You can tell who makes a living looking after reputations in this house. Now what about food? Poached salmon with new potatoes suit you?"

Then it came to Nicole. Melksham.

"I need to make a call. Will you give me a minute?"

25

By nine thirty the next day, Nicole had picked up her car in Balham and was driving down to Hampshire. Chandra had agreed to say Nicole was ill at her house and couldn't be disturbed. Nicole's world comprised Chandra and nobody else now. Patrick was gone, her mother had gone, her father was, if not gone, then at least assuaged, and content to keep out of her way. Dan was for another time.

She drove down a series of ever tighter, more winding, leafy lanes. The early morning dew dropped on her windscreen from the hedgerows she brushed past. Billy Joel lamented his lowly status to his lover on the radio.

The Cricketers opened for coffee at eleven, and, as Nicole pushed up the latch, it was clear she was the first arrival. It was an old pub with blackened beams and a tiled floor that undulated like the sand in a desert. The barman, turning the music down, nodded at her request for a coffee, and she took a seat at a table in the far corner. Fishing pictures decorated the walls.

After about ten minutes the pub door opened.

Jo Newhouse.

Flushing in the face, an awkward smile, Jo strode over to the table. Nicole stood up and they hugged, kissing on each cheek.

Jo sat down. "Sorry," she said. She covered her face with both hands and bowed forward. Then she said, "So you know."

"I had some help. Jo, it's all so…" Nicole reached out and they held hands over the table.

Jo said, "I need a drink." She turned her head towards the bar and asked for a glass of white wine. "You might need one too."

They said nothing and waited for Jo's wine to arrive. When it did, she drank half of it with one gulp.

"Tell me what you know."

Nicole explained about Peter's diary and how the De La Hays had covered up everything that had gone on at Rothbury. She didn't attempt to sugar-coat the central role of Michael Newhouse in either Eric's death or the bullying of Peter Slaithwaite. Nor the cover-up by the De La Hays. Jo nodded and wiped her eyes with a crumpled-up tissue she kept pulling out of her open bag.

"It is the most terrible story I have ever heard. I can't believe Clive De La Hay or Michael Newhouse were capable of this."

Her eyes were watery but with a faraway look in them. It was if she was thinking back to all the times when she could have done what Nicole had done and was remonstrating with herself.

"How did you know it was me?"

"Sally also sent me a letter Alice had sent to Peter telling him about their daughter. You told me in the kitchen that time that your mother was the daughter of a vicar in Melksham. I figured there couldn't be two of those. And I could never understand why you were always encouraging me to push on with my investigation when clearly your husband wasn't."

Jo said, "I'm ashamed I didn't do more." She downed the rest of her glass. Shafts of bright sunlight lit up the table.

"It's not too late."

"My mother never knew her real parents. She had a pretty tough life. Her adoptive parents loved her, but they were old and very strict. They were so busy running the parish, they didn't have much time for her beyond checking she was fed, stayed healthy and did her homework. When she reached 18, her adoptive parents told her what they knew about her birth parents. A teenage romance that had gone wrong. A break-up that caused one of the families to leave the village. And she told me once that she knew her real father had had a troubled life and had committed suicide. I don't know how she found out about that. She never mentioned either of their names. I only found out Peter's name when my grandfather got drunk one Christmas and blurted it out. I must have been about fifteen at the time. It didn't mean much to me, of course, but I made a note of it at the back of my diary. I used to fantasise about meeting him one day.

"I met Charlie when I was eighteen – he was ten years my senior – and we had Dan and Bee very young. It was only about ten years ago when my mother had died that I decided to find out more about her real parents. She had a photo in a box that she kept locked on her dressing table. I unlocked it when I was sorting out her things. Faded, brown and white, a couple of teenagers sitting on a hay bale at a fair. On the back it said Peter and Alice. Look, will you have a drink with me? I could really do with another one."

The barman, who might have been listening to everything given his swift reaction, brought two glasses over within about a minute. Nicole wasn't sure how she felt about Jo yet. She needed to hear more. She didn't touch her drink.

"I found Alice through my mother's birth certificate. It wasn't easy as she was using her married name, but I hired a detective who knew someone at the Public Records office. She's quite something, isn't she? I don't think she liked her grandchild turning up unannounced much. Didn't believe who I was. When I proved to her who I was, she fainted. I think fifty plus years of secrets had damaged her inside. But, later on, when she had recovered, she told me all about her time with Peter and gave me enough information to follow his trail including his time at Rothbury."

"Didn't that worry you? Knowing Charlie's father was there at the time?"

"I didn't think about it. I just wanted to know about Peter. I managed to find this Rothbury School yearbook and that led me to Jeff Kerslake. Incidentally, isn't that relative of his, Steve, a piece of work? I nearly walked out. Anyway, once Jeff found out who I was, he was charm personified and told me everything he knew. Or at least I thought he had. I was on the floor when I heard about Peter's night in the stable."

"And he told you who did it?"

"No, he wouldn't. But I guessed when he started describing Michael. I couldn't believe it. I threw up in the lavatory. That's when that Steve guy got all difficult. Seemed to suggest I could make up for it by giving him some 'comfort', as he rather seedily called it. I'd spent my married life hearing how wonderful Rothbury had been for Charlie and his father and now I was learning the truth. It took everything I had to walk out of there. I couldn't go home. Told Charlie I had bumped into an old girlfriend and was going to stay the night at her house on the Iffley Road. He didn't seem to mind as he was going out drinking with the boys that night."

Jo was taking deep breaths between each sentence. Her eyes were closed half the time as if she was pulling her words up from somewhere in her consciousness that she visited only when she had to. Nicole wanted to know more but could see she would need to tiptoe.

"So, you've known for ten years? How did you feel knowing your husband's father had bullied your grandfather so badly he had run away from school? That Peter had been set on a path that ended with him taking his own life?"

"Suicide? You know they never found his body, don't you?" Nicole nodded. "Sally is convinced he took his own life, as you'll know. Anyway, I was scared. A few weeks after I had found out, I asked Charlie about his dad's time up at Rothbury in the war. He clammed up, said his father never talked about it. I asked him how come he was always going on about how brilliant it was if it was that bad. Charlie just told me I didn't understand and walked out of the room. I had a therapist in those days, and we talked about it. She recommended I let it be. That the happiness of my family was more important."

"Someone died, Jo. Occult. A black magic ceremony that went wrong."

"God. That's so terrible, terrible. I love Charlie. I love my children. I couldn't do anything to hurt them." Jo wiped her eyes until they were red. "When I met you and heard about the letter, I was so excited. I so wanted to tell you what I knew but it would have been the end for Charlie and me. I had struggled to hide my discoveries since I had been to see Jeff Kerslake and I don't think he would have been able to live with the shame. I just had to keep giving you these pathetic bits of encouragement. Oh Nicole, I'm so sorry you had to go through all this. Dan is so lucky to have you."

"Well, he doesn't. This has split us up."

"Really? I hope you can work it out. It shouldn't come between you."

Nicole debated whether to tell her the news.

"Dan is your husband's son. He is very loyal."

"Too loyal sometimes."

"So, what about Bee? Did you know she would leak my investigation?"

"I knew she was up to something. She alluded to it when she called me that day. But I didn't tell her to stop. I hoped she might do something."

Nicole said, "And now it's your turn. Will you help me finish the job with the De La Hays? Tell the world how Eric McArthur died? We can't guarantee the police will do anything about it. Your grandfather deserves that, doesn't he?"

They both sat in silence. An old man and his dog, a cocker spaniel, had sat down at one of the tables close to them. He flashed them a watery smile and patted his dog. The dog was panting with its tongue sticking out.

Jo said, "What's the point? The police saw Charlie in hospital. They didn't seem very interested. Look, Nicole, I can't do it. We've been through too much. I'm so sorry."

Nicole couldn't look at her. She had expected better. Her

words came out unedited. "You coward. I don't believe you."

"It's the truth. A proper family was everything I always wanted. I can't destroy it now." Nicole reflected that that was what she had always wanted too but it wasn't stopping her.

"It didn't seem to bother Charlie. Or Bee for that matter."

"You just don't understand. You can't."

"Jo, I can't tell you how to live your life. You have children whom you love and who love you. A husband who does as well, whatever his faults. I understand why you might hesitate."

She couldn't control herself. She slammed the table with her hand and stood up. "But Jesus Christ! If you don't help me now, I will lose all respect for you. And, I can tell you, that's a lot of respect to lose. It's an awful lot to ask, I know, but you're the only one who can do this with me."

She hesitated for a moment. There was nothing to lose now. "And there's one other thing. I'm eight weeks pregnant. You're going to be a grandmother."

Nicole grabbed her bag from beside her chair. Jo was bolt upright with her mouth moving up and down like a goldfish. Nicole got up and didn't look back. The barman averted his eyes from the drama, and the dog got up from his sprawl. Nicole walked out of the pub door and set off to her car on the damp black tarmac of the lane. It looked like the fibre broadband people had been round, digging up the road and doing their usual shitty job putting it back. She wondered why she had taunted Jo. She didn't deserve it. She had been faced with a choice and she had chosen her family. If Nicole had had a family left, she would have done the same. Not everyone had the luxury of total autonomy. If she saw Jo again, she would apologise. If she ever saw her again after what she was planning.

*

Then she heard Jo's voice. "Wait. Nicole, wait."

She was standing on the side of the road. Hands on hips. Defiant. "I'll do it."

They stepped torwards each other and embraced. A BMW driving too fast pushed them into the side of the road and sprayed water on them, causing them to fall onto the bank. They leant against each other breathless.

Jo said, "A baby. I don't know what to say. That's wonderful."

Nicole said, "It will be the end of your marriage."

"Maybe. But you're right. I want to do the right thing. If Charlie truly loves me, he will forgive me. I know my daughter will. For all her faults, when it really mattered, she knew what needed to be done."

"And Dan?"

"Dan wants everyone to love each other. He loves you. He knows he was wrong to blame you. The ball's in your court now. You should do whatever you need to do. See how everyone reacts. Then see how you feel about him."

Nicole sat on the wet grass of the verge and looked out down the road. Jo sat down beside her.

"Yes, I agree. These last few months have really changed me. I still don't really know what I want. I just know that I'm the only one that can sort it. Now I know everyone is weak as everyone else. I know I can't rely on anyone. When I met Dan, I thought he was the port in a storm. The person who could take away all the worries I had and take all the decisions required to give me a happy and carefree life. It was stupid to expect that of him, wasn't it? Stupid to expect that of anyone? I have to look after myself and do what's right for me. I'm just as good as anyone else out there and I have more choices ahead of me than I can handle. It's just taken me a little longer to find all that out than most people."

"I wouldn't beat yourself up about it. I don't think I've got there yet either."

Nicole put her arm around Jo's shoulder. "Shall we go and have another drink. Discuss plans?"

*

"In twenty-four hours, I'll be all done. I can get on with helping Gal to get ridiculously rich or go back to Yellow Razor, if he won't have me."

Nicole was walking on Ealing Common with Chandra as dusk fell. She'd told her all about her time with Jo. Chandra, ever the cautious strategist, wasn't so sure.

"You know everything now. Charlie's in hospital. That awful De La Hay man disgraced. Don't you think you should stop? Dan will have you back. If you want him, that is."

Nicole looked up through the branches of the trees where leaves were starting to form and watched the plumes of the aircraft heading towards Heathrow. Unresolved issues had been her life: Patrick's death; her father's deceit; her mother's despair.

Her phone rang. It was Gal. He sounded breathless.

"I met this fintech blogger at the airport. One of those

guys who thinks I walk on water. He told me something very interesting."

"What?"

"Your boyfriend's father is the one behind all the dirt being thrown at me. Including those rumours about us."

Nicole looked at Chandra and pulled a face. "You're joking. He wouldn't. He couldn't."

"I didn't have to ask. I couldn't stop him. Most of the national journalists have lost interest, thank God. Charlie Newhouse's people were trying to dump some on this guy."

Nicole put the phone down, having promised Gal she would be back at work in a couple of days. He hadn't mentioned their night together.

She looked at Chandra. "Sorry about that. Well, that makes my decision pretty easy."

Chandra swished her cashmere scarf over her shoulder. "I still don't think you should do it. You've got a career to think about. People won't go near you."

"Gal's options would buy me some time if and when they're vested. I could set up an agency. You could do it with me."

Chandra muttered something about being focussed on other things for now. For a moment Nicole was ashamed that all she ever talked about when she was with Chandra was herself. She took Chandra's hand and swung it a little.

"Thanks for being here for me. If you weren't, I don't know what I would do."

"Even though I don't think you should do anything more on this, I can totally understand why you might. Those poor boys up there in the middle of nowhere. It was barbaric – murder, torture. No-one stood up for them then. At least you can now."

"I don't know how to repay you. I just hope you and Raj get what you want very soon."

They walked on along the path, dodging rampant dogs and overzealous cyclists. Darkness had set in, and car headlights flashed across the path ahead of them. Whatever happened next, a new life would be waiting on the other side.

*

It was late afternoon. The cardiac ward at Chelsea and Westminster wasn't easy to find. It was way at the back, up three storeys in a lift then at the end of a maze of corridors. Nicole thought back to the last time she was in a hospital, when Dan was injured. She hadn't been a very good girlfriend then. She definitely wasn't one now.

After enquiring at the reception desk, she found that Charlie was in a private room. Of course he was. Only the best for Charlie.

She knocked on the door and was presented with the sight of Jo, Dan and Bee all sitting around the bed. Charlie looked very white, a lot thinner and had tubes coming out of his mouth and nose. But his eyes were open, and it looked like he was laughing.

"Hi." Jo leapt up, walked over and hugged her.

"What are you doing here?" asked Dan. He also got up and kissed her on one cheek with a nervousness she didn't associate with him.

Bee stayed seated. "I'm not talking to you," said Nicole with the hint of a grin. Charlie had stopped smiling and was glaring at Nicole.

She went over and held his hand. "Zaxxo's valuation

has hit $2 billion, Charlie. All publicity seems to be good publicity after all."

Dan said, "Stop it, Nicole. What are you doing here anyway?"

"I've come to pick your mum up. We're going to the Rothbury Old Boys' Drinks. Are you coming?"

"Of course I am. But I didn't think you wanted any part of it, and I don't think Martin De La Hay would want you to be either. He's been rallying everyone. A show of unity. Business as usual."

Nicole said, "I changed my mind. This school is important to you all, so I thought I would go as your guest. I could apologise for all the grief I have caused the school."

Dan didn't seem to be that excited by this proposal. He didn't think she would be very welcome. Nicole could see his point, but it wasn't going to deter her.

Dan said, "Bit late for that, isn't it?"

"Call it closure, my love. I won't stay long."

Jo said, "C'mon, Dan. You're always saying how much you want Nicole to be part of your life. The De La Hays can look after themselves."

Dan gave Nicole his serious face. She shouldn't be playing games with such a sick man in close proximity. He said, "As long as you promise. Have you decided about us? That's what I'm more worried about."

Bee put her finger down her throat as if pretending to be sick. She said, "Quit while you're ahead, Dan. She's coming on your big night out, isn't she. All your old mates will love your choice of arm candy."

Jo said, "I'll leave you with your father, Bee. Try not to start World War Three while I'm away."

Nicole thought Charlie looked perplexed that so many of them were so keen to attend the Rothbury drinks. Nicole grinned at him. A part of her pitied him so reduced, but then she reminded herself of everything his father and he had done. He didn't deserve pity.

She leant over, kissed him on the cheek and whispered, "Get well soon and, just so you know, I know everything."

Charlie's eyes seemed to pop out of his skull in surprise. Bee, having half-heard what she had said, muttered something about whether there was a competition for creating the most havoc. Nicole, performance over, ignored her and followed Dan and Jo out of the room. She knew she should have experienced some shame tormenting a sick man ,but, just at the moment when she thought it might come, there was nothing.

In the corridor Dan touched Nicole on the shoulder. "Can we talk?"

"Sure. What about?"

He leant against the wall. An orderly clutching a large folder rushed past them. "What's going on here?"

Nicole touched his lapel. "It's better you don't know."

Dan was quiet for a moment and pursed his lips. She thought to herself how lovely he was.

"I love you, Nicole. I know I've been a bastard about all this and I'm not proud of myself. I've put my family before you and that was wrong. I doubted you when I shouldn't have. From now on, whatever you do, whatever you say, I'm with you. I will never let you down again."

Nicole kissed him on the lips and gave him a long hug. At the other end of the corridor, she could see Jo tapping her foot.

"Thank you. I love you too. We should go, shouldn't we?"

*

A little before six o' clock, the three of them sat in the black cab as it stopped and started down the Fulham Road. Jo and Dan hung on to the straps above the windows and Nicole tried to balance herself in the middle. She didn't want to give Dan any encouragement by sliding into him. It was by no means certain that he would be so keen on a reconciliation in a couple of hours' time. Nicole watched Jo sitting in silence, staring out the window at the last-minute shoppers and commuters heading home. Nicole wondered what was going through her mind.

"All those Ubers. Bloody liability." The taxi driver had looked keen to talk since they had got in but must have sensed the tension in the cab. His Spurs pennant fluttered from his central mirror alongside his air freshener. The jam in front of him was the spark he needed to let rip.

Dan started to talk to him about the need to remove traffic in London because of the climate emergency. Nicole admired the way he took such high ground that rational arguments just shrank away. She was a little sorry for the cabbie, but it reminded her that Dan could be very engaging when he tried.

As they got out of the cab, Dan said to Nicole, "I still can't work out why you two want to come? Do you really care about how some old boy has progressed in his insurance broking career and whether he intends to send his son to Rothbury?"

Once inside the club, they were sent downstairs to

separate male and female cloakrooms. When she could see Dan was out of earshot, she whispered to Jo.

"Poor Dan."

Jo put her hand on Nicole's shoulder. "He'll survive. Think of Peter."

*

The drinks party was at a gentleman's club on Pall Mall in a massive room with high, stucco ceilings and giant chandeliers. Waiters and waitresses in white coats held silver trays of champagne, wine and orange juice. The sound of a party already in full swing greeted them: waves of laughter, shouts, the odd scream of delight.

Jo had recognised a fellow former parent by the door and fell into a deep conversation. Dan's height was an advantage as he surveyed the room, and he soon saw some of his friends. He grabbed Nicole's hand and pulled her along. "Come and meet this bunch." She played along. Business as usual, to quote Dan. Lots of people stared at her as she passed them.

As they crossed the room Nicole saw Martin De La Hay regaling a circle of admirers with an anecdote that seemed to demand a broad selection of hand signals. He froze for a millisecond as he saw Nicole then recovered himself.

Nicole scanned the room. This was an entitled generation. The men – and it was pretty much all men – looked prosperous with well-cut suits and shining hair. Maybe some were now parents themselves. There was an air of celebration, a coming-together of like-minded souls. They could be themselves here. I would never fit in if I stayed here a century, thought Nicole to herself.

A bearded man in a dark suit came up to her. "Mr De La Hay would like you to leave."

Dan stood in front of him. "She's not leaving. She's my guest."

"It is an order from the headmaster."

"I'm not at school now. Go away." Dan turned his back on the man and smiled at Nicole. The man sloped off.

The room was now packed. The waiters kept trying to fill up her glass with champagne and she put her hand over her glass. She couldn't see Jo. They would need to be together soon.

Then there was the sound of someone tapping a glass, and the hubbub died away. At the far end of the room, she could see Martin De La Hay standing up on a stage. She pulled away from Dan and sidled across the room to where she had last seen Jo.

Martin De La Hay started out on what seemed would be a very long speech. It was, after all, the school's centenary, and the event was the first of a series planned to mark the occasion. The achievements of his great-grandfather figured prominently in his opening salvo. It was as if all that bad news hadn't happened.

Nicole waited for Jo but couldn't see her. The speech rumbled on, provoking sporadic bouts of merriment and applause. But it was long and, as is often the case when drink is served, there were the murmurings of conversation from those at the back who couldn't hear. Nicole scanned the room frantically for Jo. There was no sign of her. This was a disaster. They had a plan. It was going to take two of them.

Martin was giving out presents: bouquets of flowers to

the women and pewter tankards to the men, presumably those who had helped the school and were still alive. She could see Dan coming towards her out of the corner of her eye. It was now or never.

She pushed up towards the stage at the far end of the room, trying to avoid knocking people's glasses as she went.

She got to the front and stepped up on to the stage. Martin De La Hay, half-rimmed spectacles halfway down his nose, looked up and glared at her. He had been enjoying his captive audience.

"Hello. I have an intruder. Do you mind returning when I have finished, Ms Weymouth? You have done enough damage to the school, don't you think?"

Nicole ignored him and turned to face the throng. She pulled her sheet of paper out of her bag. She hoped the type was large enough to read.

Martin said, "Please go, Ms Weymouth." The sound of many slightly inebriated people agreeing floated up to Nicole.

"No. I'm staying put. I have something to say, and it needs to be said now."

Martin walked towards her. "Dan, could you come and get your girlfriend? I haven't finished my speech."

"I'm not just his girlfriend. I'm his fiancée."

There was a shout from behind Nicole. "Leave her alone." It was Jo. She had come on to the stage from the side. "Everyone needs to hear this." Martin De La Hay stood back a little at her command.

Jo nudged her as a sign to start. The room, even the troublemakers at the back, fell silent.

Nicole, throat drying at speed, said, "Some of you will have read about this already, but it deserves to be repeated.

And, since that article a week ago, we have found out more through the discovery of Peter Slaithwaite's diary.

"Over seventy years ago, during the war, Rothbury moved up to the Lake District, to Blair Gowan. As we all know, it was a terrible time. The Germans were bombing London; many men had gone off to fight. The school was understaffed, but it made sense to take the boys away from danger. It was a brave move that would challenge all who went."

She paused and looked around the room. Mouths hung open. Drinks left undrunk. No-one knew where she was going next.

"Clive De La Hay was not a well man, but his son had gone to war and there was no-one else to run the school. He ran it with the help of a couple of women from the village including Carol Bristow, whose daughter I have grown to know these past few months.

"But there is no excuse for what happened. A small number of older boys were allowed to bully and torture with no comeback or punishment. And, worst of all, we now know from a direct witness at the time, Peter Slaithwaite that there was a murder. One boy, Eric McArthur was murdered by Michael Newhouse at a black mass event organised by Clive De La Hay, the headmaster…"

Alongside her, Jo now spoke, loud and strong. Nicole could see Martin De La Hay crouched on his haunches, holding his head in his hands. His wife was stroking his head.

"And, as you may all know, my grandfather, Peter Slaithwaite, witnessed this, and, to force his silence, was tortured by being left in the stables with a crazed horse overnight. An experience so traumatic that he ran away after he reported it, and nothing was done about it. Twenty years later that experience contributed to his death."

Jo paused and swallowed. Only Nicole knew that the hardest part of her speech was still to come. The room was silent, even the waiters and waitresses had stopped whispering.

"It was my husband's father, Michael Newhouse, my children's grandfather, who was the ringleader and the murderer. He has blood on his hands, God rest his soul. And I am ashamed to say that I knew some of this for many years but did nothing about it. Two weeks ago, Nicole reported all this to the police, and they have reopened the investigation."

Jo continued, "But, even more than Michael Newhouse, we must lay the blame at the feet of the De La Hays. They presided over this carnage. Clive De La Hay was in charge of the school and was the architect of all the evil. You De La Hays knew and did nothing. The family have been well aware of what went on for many years and have hidden it because of pride and a desire to maximise their profits. Even this year, when Nicole here tried to alert Martin to what had happened, he threatened her because he didn't want to jeopardise a possible investment in the school by HVAC. They have run a school claiming to espouse the virtues of decency and integrity when they, themselves, have failed to meet those high standards and have knowingly done so. They should all be ashamed of themselves."

An awkward murmur started again but this time without the laughter. The waiters and waitresses stood at the sides exchanging puzzled looks.

Then a shaky voice came from the back of the room. The

crowd parted and, right at the back, seated on a chair with the familiar Steve alongside him, was Jeff Kerslake.

"I was there. It was every bit as awful as these two fine ladies say. Clive De La Hay shouldn't have been allowed to run a school then and his family shouldn't be now. I am appalled at this story and so glad the truth is finally out. I'm ashamed that I allowed myself to be bullied into silence." His voice was faltering now. "I congratulate Nicole and Jo on their courage in standing up in front of you all."

Nicole didn't know what to do next, but Jo did.

Jo said, "Now you all know the truth, it is time to leave. If you still have children at the school, take them away. When people ask about the school, tell them what you know.

"My husband's father destroyed my grandfather's life, killed an innocent child, and ruined many other boys' lives. As many of you know, Charlie is a good man and has had no control over what his father did. But I have lived with the pain of Peter Slaithwaite's tragedy all my life and I owe it to him to act. I just hope my family will understand."

There was an embarrassed silence until the staff started collecting glasses. Still standing on the stage, Jo put her arm around Nicole. She could see Dan in the centre of the room with his head bowed. She'd done it. They'd done it.

"You fucking bitches!" Nicole felt a thump in her back as she and Jo tumbled off the stage. She managed to protect her head with her arms as it hit the burgundy patterned carpet. Out of the corner of her eye she could see Jo falling as well. She turned herself over to see Brooke De La Hay on the stage, shaking, eyes bulging and fingers pointing.

"How dare you come here and tell such lies about my family! In front of all these people who love them. People whose lives have been made by Rothbury. Slander and libel all based on the imagination of some child who died fifty years ago. You ought to be ashamed of yourselves. Look at my husband – he's broken!"

Nicole looked across at Martin De La Hay. He was slumped on a chair staring at the floor like a disused marionette.

"You need to leave. And leave now. Everything you have said is a pack of despicable lies. Lies that have destroyed Rothbury's future. We were about to get investment that would transform the school, and you've put paid to that. So just fuck off out of here now! And never, ever come back. You'll be hearing from our family's lawyers."

Jo stood up and Nicole followed her suit. Jo shook herself a little and said, "Are you calling Peter Slaithwaite a liar? Are you calling Jeff Kerslake a liar? We have written evidence of everything we have said. Boys whose safety was entrusted to your family by their parents. Do you really think I would jeopardise my marriage if I didn't think all of this was true? Do you think I would stand up in front of all these wonderful people, some of whom I have known most of my adult life, if I thought there was the slightest chance I was wrong?"

Brooke hadn't finished. "What is it about you that's so set on demolishing the reputation of my family? Why couldn't you just let the past stay in the past? What's to be gained by digging up these lies from the past. It's seventy years ago. So what! Everyone suffered in the war. No-one came out of it the same."

Nicole could see that Jo was only just holding herself together. She had never seen her so angry.

Jo said, "I'll tell you why, Brooke. Your family's actions – or lack of action – meant my grandfather couldn't cope with normal life ever again. He had a child he never knew. He couldn't work properly. He couldn't cope with human relationships. It meant my mother had to be adopted, never knowing her birth parents. It has meant that, all my life, I have had to live with this terrible mystery. And then, when I found out about my husband's family's role in all this, I had to live a lie and pretend I knew nothing about it. My life has been blighted and it's all because of you and your wretched family. So, don't try and tell me I shouldn't do this. The only thing I've done wrong is not to do anything all these years. It's only thanks to this wonderful woman here that I finally have. I'll never forgive myself for leaving it so long."

Brooke De La Hay stared at her, mouth open. To Nicole, she looked spent. It had been like two heavyweights slugging it out, neither ready to fall to the canvas. She had never thought that Jo Newhouse would have such depths of anger.

Dan stepped forward and bear-hugged his mother like a drowning man. She dropped her head on to his shoulder, and they stood there as the sound of someone clapping filled the room. It was Jeff Kerslake. Soon he was joined by others until the whole room was filled with applause.

Nicole's phone bleeped and she pulled it out of her bag. There was a text from Gal. *Can you come back? We really need you here.* He would have to wait.

She walked over to Jeff Kerslake and kissed him on the cheek. He stopped clapping and put his hand over hers.

She said, "Do you know why Peter's letter never got posted? How come it ended up in that library book?"

Jeff looked up at her. She had never noticed how piercing

his blue eyes were. He said, "I know about this because I pieced it together. Peter told me a few weeks later that the little girl, Carol Bristow, found it under his bed when her mother was cleaning. She told him that she would post the letter for him, that it was too dangerous to post it through the school system in case someone found it and opened it."

"But it was never sent?"

Jeff sighed. "I know. I don't know why, but I have an idea. Clive De La Hay didn't like it when he got complaints. He went bananas and used to punish anyone connected with the complaint. The perpetrator, the victim, anyone within throwing distance, everyone. I reckon she decided it would be more trouble than it was worth for poor old Peter. So, she just found somewhere to hide it. In case she ever needed it or changed her mind."

"I wonder if she ever regretted that? She seemed so keen to tell me everything and for me to pursue it. Maybe that's why?"

"She's not the only one, my dear. I think a lot of people were egging you on today. Dead and alive. None of them had the balls to do it themselves. Including me."

Nicole saw Dan coming over. She said to Jeff, "Well, we got there in the end."

She turned to face Dan. The room had emptied. Jo was nowhere to be seen.

He said, "I'm so proud of you. I don't know anyone who would have the courage to do that." He tried to hug her, but Nicole took a step back. She didn't know how to react. Did she still love him?

She kissed him on the cheek and touched his hand. "I'm tired. I need to go back to Chandra's. I'll call you. OK?"

*

Nicole was on the pavement of Pall Mall. It was cold and dark. She needed to get moving before anyone else found her. Out of the corner of her eye she saw Brooke De La Hay helping Martin into a cab. He looked like he had aged ten years in an hour.

She walked towards Haymarket and called Gal. She told him what had happened.

He said, "God! Well, that's the end of it? Yes?"

"Bloody well hope so."

"Good. Because I need you back here. It's going crazy. I've got more investor meetings than I can handle. Half the software companies in town want to meet. Google wants to licence some of our stuff, and they want to announce it next week at some funky bootcamp they're planning. I only brought one change of clothes."

No hard feelings then? It was Thursday night. "Send me everything. I'll look at it tonight and come over Saturday. How about that?"

"Why not tomorrow? This is a big deal, Nicole. Anya can't cope." Anya? How the hell had she ended up in San Francisco? For a millisecond a shard of jealousy pierced her consciousness, but it didn't last long enough to make a home. She was glad Anya was with him. That would make things simpler.

"I have unfinished business, if that doesn't sound too dramatic."

"It does, actually. Come back as soon as you can. We need you."

"I will. Promise." Gal said something about needing to go shopping.

Nicole laughed and rang off. She strode up Haymarket towards Piccadilly Circus tube.

26

The next morning Nicole left Chandra's house around seven o'clock and headed off to the tube. She had booked a train from Euston to Newby Bridge in the Lake District which would take her about four and a half hours. Overnight Gal had sent her all the documents about the Google deal, and she would need to turn it all into a press release, backgrounder and Q&A by the time she got back to London. She hoped the Wi-Fi worked on the train as there were a stack of acronyms she would need to get her head round.

When she had told Chandra her plans, she had told Nicole to fly straight back to San Francisco and get on with the job, that Gal didn't give out share options for fun and that he expected lots of hard work in return.

"You've done what you set out to do. Everyone who needs to suffer has. Your potential father-in-law is in hospital." "Father-in-law? She wasn't even sure if Dan was still her boyfriend. "You've done enough damage now? Haven't you?"

Nicole gave as good a defence as she could, but Chandra gripped her mug of peppermint tea and stared into the mid-distance. Nicole thought Chandra would be good at poker.

"I'm off the day after tomorrow and I'll stay there as long as he needs me. Loose ends: that's all this is."

Chandra said, "I hope that's true. You certainly know how to fight your corner these days. Now you need to start thinking about the people at the other end of your punches if you know what I mean?"

Nicole said she didn't. But she did.

"When I met you three years ago, you let everything run all over you. I couldn't understand it. This year it's like a switch has been flicked. You decide what you want to do and bugger everybody else. I love it. But you've gone to the other extreme. It must be exhausting."

Nicole had reserved a window seat, and she took in the grubby, graffitied brickwork as the train pulled out. Shona was meeting her at the station so they could go straight on. She gathered that time wasn't on their side. She settled down to read the two hundred pages of documents in her inbox.

A Twitter alert popped up. Rothbury School was closing its doors after over a hundred years owing to an unprecedented number of pupils being taken out of the school. A Labour politician had demanded a public enquiry into how the school had been allowed to remain in business. On the back of Nicole's call to Robbie Halstead, the police had announced a full investigation into the death of Eric McArthur. Martin De La Hay had disappeared and was unavailable for comment. There was a suggestion that he and his wife had left the country. Nicole looked at the dozens of missed calls and messages on her phone. Some of them might relate to Zaxxo. She had no idea how she would be able to fillet those out without calling some of the journalists who wanted to know about Rothbury.

*

Shona greeted her with a massive hug outside the ticket office. She'd had her hair cut short in a bob and dyed it ash blonde.

"I've never met a celebrity before." Nicole complimented on her hair. "Got promoted. They say I'm management material. I've put Blair Gowan on the map apparently. We better hurry. This is what I really care about."

Spring was coming and there was blossom on the trees as they hurtled down the narrow lanes. Shona kept up a non-stop diatribe on the vast array of visitors the hotel had been getting in the past weeks. Nicole let it flow over her and thought about the meeting ahead.

When they reached Nanny Bristow's cottage, it looked much the same except there was no smoke coming out of the chimney and a few more slates had fallen off the roof. There was another car in the drive. A battered Polo.

"District nurse. She comes twice a day to dole out the drugs. Lucky old biddy. Nanny refuses to move out."

The nurse, harassed and, possibly, late for her next call, was coming out of the house as they entered. Shona delayed her for a moment on the doorstep to ask after Nanny Bristow's health. As they entered the house the smell of Dettol had joined that of wood smoke.

Carol Bristow was lying on a single, iron-framed bed under a pile of blankets in the front room. An electric fire blasted out heat and, with closed windows, the room was airless. Apart from the television in the corner, all the furniture had been removed.

Shona said, "Nanny, Nicole's here. You remember? The woman who found out about Peter Slaithwaite."

Carol Bristow opened her eyes and gave out a murmur of recognition then closed them again. She was little more than a skeleton and her walnut-grained skin now looked as if she had already been embalmed.

Nicole sat on the bed and stayed still. Now she was here, she was in no hurry. In a measured pace she recounted everything she knew.

She said, "I did what you asked. Finally. I exposed them all. Everybody who did wrong was named. There is a police investigation. Rothbury is closing down."

Shona said, "Nicole was so brave, Nanny. She stood up in front of all the old boys with Peter's granddaughter and told them what the De La Hays had done. You would have been so proud of her."

Nanny flashed her gums and said something that sounded like 'well done'. Shona went over and muted the TV.

Nicole leant forward. "I want to ask you one thing, Carol. Do you know why Peter's letter didn't get sent? If it was so important to him, surely he would have made sure it got posted?"

Carol Bristow's eyes misted up then closed. Nicole wondered if she had left it too late.

"I would really like to know this. It's all I want to know from you."

For what seemed like ten minutes but was probably only one, Carol Bristow remained silent with her eyes closed.

Then she started to breathe in and out as if she was powering up a set of bellows.

"We knew each other a little and used to talk in the kitchen when I was with my mother after school. He found me when no-one was around and gave it to me to post. I knew he had been beaten when they had found his previous one, so I decided to read it before I posted it. I… I…" Her sobbing stopped her talking. Nicole and Carol looked at each other.

Then she screwed up her face and continued, "…I couldn't let that happen again, so I went to the library and hid it in one of the books. *Black Beauty*. My favourite. I thought I was doing the right thing. But I wasn't. I was only a kid."

Nicole touched where she thought Carol Bristow's hand might be under the blankets. "You were only, what, eleven? I think it's amazing that you made that decision yourself. Few people would be that brave or caring in those circumstances."

Carol's words could only just be heard through her sobs. "It's been a very long wait to see it put right."

Shona gestured for Nicole to move away. It looked like Carol Bristow was finished for the day. Maybe forever.

Nicole couldn't resist one final question. "Do you know why Eric McArthur's parents didn't come and ask how their son had died? Why wasn't there a full investigation?"

Shona tried to pull Nicole away by the sleeve of her coat, but Nicole stayed put. Carol Bristow whispered, "They came to get the body, all the way from Cornwall. I heard Mr De La Hay told them he had a fall when walking. He lied. They believed him. Accidental death. Bastard." She closed her eyes, and this time it didn't look like she planned to open them again in the near future. Before they left the room, Shona turned the volume back up on *The Repair Shop*. Very apt, thought Nicole.

As they walked out, Shona whispered, "You'll never know how much that meant to her."

*

Before she went back to the station, Nicole wanted to do one last thing, so Shona drove her over to Blair Gowan. Peter never had a chance. He had been a prisoner. What must he have thought when he realised his letter hadn't reached his parents for the second time? No wonder he had run away. It was so sad.

They parked the car outside the hotel. It was warm for March and the sky was cloudless. They walked through the hotel reception, down a corridor and out into the yard behind. The stables were still there. Nicole shivered as she walked towards them.

The stables were being converted into rooms. A builder pushing a wheelbarrow squinted at them, rollie hanging out of his mouth. A couple of crows screeched and took off from the far buildings. Breeze blocks were being put in place to create new walls within the wooden stable walls.

Shona said, "Five-star luxury, we've been told. Hard to believe, eh?"

Nicole smiled and walked over to one of the new walls in the far stable. There were holes in the breeze blocks where, she presumed, the pipes would be placed. She picked the nearest one, took Peter's letter out of her bag, now wrapped in a plastic bag to protect it from damp, and pushed it through the hole. She put a finger in to check it had dropped out of human reach.

She said, "Rest in peace, Peter."

Shona pulled her coat around her and shook back her bob to clear her hair from her eyes. "Cup of tea before you go?"

Nicole took her arm as they walked out of the stable. In front of them loomed Blair Gowan, still as grey and unwelcoming as it must have been all those years ago.

Nicole's phone rang. "Nicole. Dad. He's dead."

"What? Dan? When?"

When she had last seen Charlie Newhouse, he had looked on the mend. That was partly why she had been emboldened to leave her parting shot.

"Last night. When I told him about everything that happened at the Old Boys' event, he had a relapse, and he never recovered. It was my fault, Nicole. I shouldn't have told him."

Nicole remembered Chandra's words of advice. "You were just the messenger. So was I. So was your mother. If anyone is guilty it's your grandfather and the De La Hays."

"He didn't know the full story, Nicole. Honestly, he didn't. He was as shocked as anyone."

He didn't know the detail, thought Nicole, but he knew enough not to want it to come out. And his friends. the De La Hays, had been prepared to risk everything to stop it, including blackmailing Jeff Kerslake. She forced herself to put herself in Dan's shoes. She'd had her moment in the sun. It was time for her to build bridges and help him like he'd helped her with her mother's death.

"I know, my love, I know."

Nicole put her hand over the phone and said to Shona, "Got any rooms free tonight?" Shona nodded.

Nicole said, "I'm up at Blair Gowan and tomorrow I have to fly back to San Francisco. I'll come back down tonight."

At least he now knew she wanted to come back.

"Just before he died, I told him about our baby. He smiled. A big smile. His final one." Dan's words came out in ones and twos as he wrestled with his emotions.

He was helpless and she was the only one who could help him. So, she had to do so. And, maybe, working through their grief, they could make a fresh start.

"How's your mum? She must be distraught. The courage she showed was unbelievable."

"She's in shock. We all are." Words were hard for him. He needed her. A flush crept up her neck. As she was learning, you can have both, but you still can't be in two places at a time.

"I'll come and see you all as soon as I'm back. Send her – and Bee – my love and condolences."

Dan was trying to reply, but his sobbing got in the way.

Nicole said, "I love you. I will be with you soon."

She had no plans to visit Blair Gowan ever again. If it was up to her, it would be bulldozed to the ground. But it was the place where a flame had been ignited inside her and it deserved a proper farewell, as a mark of the catalytic role it had played in her life, before she left it behind for good.

She had given Peter's story the ending it deserved and, in doing so, had assuaged, at long last, the agony she'd suffered. Patrick's death hadn't been her fault. He wasn't her ward. She could have done something, but she had been young, very young.

Nicole had proved to herself that when someone came to her asking for her help, that she could do so, whatever the potential cost. Her guilt about Patrick's death was no more. Only her love for him, and her memories, remained. And, when the time came, his name, in one form or another, would live on with her child.

As she walked with Shona back through the remains of the stable yard to the house, she didn't shiver this time. The ghosts of 1940 had been laid to rest.

EPILOGUE – SIX MONTHS LATER

The two figures, both dressed in monochrome dark colours, stood facing each other on the doorstep as Nicole, Dan, and Bee watched them from the road in Tetbury. Caesar sat at Bee's feet. Looking at them standing together, Nicole could see their physical similarities. The pink roses around the door were still in bloom and they framed the two women as if they were in a medieval religious fresco.

For a second neither of them moved, as if frozen on the spot, then there was a moment of sudden, visible relaxation followed by a yelp of joy as they clung to each other. Nicole grabbed Dan's hand and Dan put his other arm around Bee. Caesar barked in sympathy.

The two figures stayed as one, rocking together to maintain their intimacy, then Jo released herself from Alice's clasp and, turning, beckoned for the others to join them.

*

After Charlie's death Dan and Nicole spent as much time as they could with Jo in Hampshire. Bee had moved back home, having appointed herself Jo's 'companion' (as if she needed one). Nicole had managed two trips to San Francisco before Gal – and her obstetrician – had told her to stop. Now she went into the office two days a week and worked from home the rest of the time. The US was growing fast, as was the valuation. A flotation was on the cards next year.

It was an early evening in the first week of August and the four of them were sitting in the garden in Hampshire drinking rosé (or fizzy water in Nicole's case), munching on olives, luxuriating in the heat. It had taken them some time to enjoy such gatherings without being reminded of Charlie. For all his faults, he had known how to make social events go with a swing.

"I'm ready," said Jo.

"What for?" asked Bee.

Nicole knew.

"To see my grandmother again. Talk to her about my grandfather."

Alice had contacted Nicole a few weeks after the old boys' drinks. Could she see Jo? Would she be willing? Nicole waited for the right moment and asked Jo, but she demurred. They were still sorting through Charlie's possessions, answering letters, organising probate. And she had secured a place as a mature student at the Royal Veterinary College in London starting in September. She said she didn't have the emotional bandwidth.

Nicole and Jo's relationship had deepened since Charlie's death. It was as intimate as a mother – daughter relationship.

Nicole sensed that Jo oscillated between her guilt and grief around her husband's death and the liberation she had experienced at being able to avenge her grandfather and call time on the secrets she had kept from her family. It was a very strong bond. Almost as strong as the one Nicole had had with her own mother.

Dan had struggled to come to terms with the events that had led up to his father's death. Once she was back from the first San Francisco trip, Nicole had moved into the flat with him but didn't think she was much help in that area. He spent as many hours at work as he could and talked little when he was at home. If they made love, it was at Nicole's instigation and it was over in a few minutes. He talked in his sleep and ground his teeth so hard it woke Nicole up.

His behaviour didn't overly worry her. She knew he was still processing his father's death and the prospect of fatherhood, all in such a short space of time. And, to top it all, he had to live with the knowledge that his girlfriend had been instrumental – at least in an oblique way – in his father's death. Charlie had cast a huge shadow over Dan. In time, she hoped he would free himself and emerge his own man. All in all, he had been administered a very strong cocktail, and she planned to give him as much time as he needed to digest it.

It was when Alice had prompted her five months after her initial contact to ask if she would ever see her granddaughter, before she died, that Nicole suggested to Dan that they should make a trip to see Peter's childhood home and, if she was willing, take Jo to see Alice.

Dan's willingness to do so surprised her. "I'd like that. Dad's family was always so dominant in our lives, I think we owe it to Mum to know more about hers. And Bee and I want to learn everything we can."

*

"This is wonderful, just wonderful. I never thought I would live to see this day." Alice was at her front door hand in hand with Jo. She looked thinner and more bowed since Nicole had last seen her, but her eyes still gleamed with life. Nicole, Bee, and Dan stood on the path in front of her. "I never thought I would see my great-grandchildren. I think I can even see some resemblance. What do you think, Nicole?"

They all went into Alice's sitting room. Unlike the previous time Nicole had visited, the room was flooded with natural light. Alice was still very fleet of foot for a woman of ninety. No doubt the excitement of the moment had energised her. Dan and Bee were tiptoeing around in case they broke the spell. Nicole had never seen Bee so quiet. Caesar sniffed around the skirtings and then collapsed at Jo's feet.

After Alice had made some tea and put some chocolate biscuits on a plate, they all sat down around the fireplace. Slapping her hands on her thighs, she said, "So where shall we start?"

Alice was very curious to hear all about the Newhouse family and spent the first hour asking all about their lives. Dan and Bee relaxed and soon they were laughing as they recounted the stories all families use to remind themselves of their shared history. Jo didn't join in much but watched them with a serene smile on her face. Nicole said nothing. She was just glad that this meeting was happening.

Then Dan asked Alice about Peter, and she told them about their brief teenage love affair. When she got to the pregnancy. Alice reached out, touched Jo's hand, and said, "We both wanted to keep your mother and bring her up together. But we didn't have much say in the matter as it turned out. Things were so different back then."

When Alice reached the end of her tale, Jo said, "Apart from that letter Sally passed to Nicole, did you communicate with Peter before he died?"

Alice hesitated then said, "In the years before he disappeared, we had taken to meeting about twice a year in London. We would just sit on a bench in St James's Park and feed the ducks. Go to a gallery if it was raining. We didn't even talk much. He didn't seem up to it, to be honest. When we weren't chucking bread at the ducks, we held hands. After the traumatic way we parted, that's all we really wanted. To know we were still in the world together and cared about each other. But I must admit, after a while, it started to unsettle me. I think I thought there might be more. So, I told him I wanted us to stop seeing each other. He was very upset, ran away. Again. Very much Peter's standard response to trouble, I'm afraid."

Jo said, "Was he ever happy again in his life? It seems like it was all sadness after Rothbury."

Nicole took a chance. "Martin De La Hay implied he might still be alive."

Alice's face hardened. The temperature in the room dropped. Jo looked at Nicole as if to ask whether she had gone too far.

Alice got up and walked over to the window that overlooked the green. She seemed lost in her thoughts. Nicole wondered if they had blown it. It had all been going even better than she had hoped. She had never seen Jo so radiant.

Jo said, "Has Nicole said the wrong thing? She didn't mean to cause you any pain." Alice smiled and shook her head. Her hair, thick with lacquer, didn't move as she did so.

She said, "Give me a minute." And she disappeared upstairs.

Bee looked at Nicole and pulled a WTF face. Dan took Nicole's hand and Jo stared at the floor. The clock in the corner struck the hour and a motorcycle backfired in the distance.

Five minutes later, Alice came back down. She had put some pink lipstick on and had a floral scarf around her neck.

She moved over to the front door, took a deep breath and said, "You'd better all come with me."

*

She led them out of the front door and along the paved path Nicole had taken when she had first come to meet Alice.

Alice knocked at the door Nicole had first knocked on to ask where Alice lived. For a moment nothing happened, then the old man who had answered the door that time appeared on the doorstep. His cheeks were hollowed out and his sparse white hair stood up in unruly wisps. Clumps of white stubble were dotted around his face, demonstrating how shaky his hands must have been when shaving. Eyes as blue as the August sky above flitted from side to side, scanning the group in front of him.

Alice said, "This is Peter. Peter Slaithwaite."

His mask-like face broke into a thin-lipped smile, and

he grabbed on to the door frame. Nicole, Jo, Dan and Bee all let out a spontaneous cry of surprise. They all looked at each other, and then at Alice and Peter, open-mouthed.

"Peter, I'd like you to meet your granddaughter, Jo, and your great-grandchildren, Dan and Beatrice. And, of course, Nicole, without whom none of us would be standing here together today. And, I might add, who is carrying our great-great-grandchild."

Nicole didn't know what to think. It was if she had been airlifted by rocket to another planet in a split second without her consent, brainwashed and then dumped back on to the earth's surface from outer space. It couldn't be. She looked around. Jo's mouth was moving up and down as if she wanted to speak, yet no words would come. Dan and Bee had their hands over their faces as if it was a dream. Peter and Alice just kept glancing at each other, looking embarrassed. There was too much shock around for handshakes, kisses or hugs.

After a minute Peter, brushing back his sparse hair with his hand, said, "We owe you an explanation. Why don't you come in? We can sit in the garden at the back. Don't worry about the dog. He's welcome too." His voice was hoarse and quiet, hard to hear.

The house had the same structure as Alice's, but the same level of care and love hadn't been devoted to it. In fact, it looked like it was someone else's house. They all had to duck as they went through the back door into the garden. As they walked, they all continued to wonder at Peter's surprise appearance. He led, walking at a funereal pace. He held one of his hands to his stomach as if to stop it trembling.

As they walked out, Alice turned back to Nicole. "He has Parkinson's. Good days and bad days. We won't have long."

There was a moss-covered table and six chairs on the terrace. Or maybe it was a patio. Nicole wasn't sure. Peter needed help pulling out and getting into his chair. They all looked at each other. Alice said she would go and get a jug of water and some glasses.

Before she headed off, she said, "You don't have to do this now, Peter. They can come back." Peter reached out to touch her arm and said that he did. He looked around at all of them before he spoke.

"I did a very bad thing. I faked my own death." He paused for a moment as everyone took an intake of breath. It was as if he had been practising this speech for many years.

"I was never right after that terrible time at Rothbury. The only time I was ever happy was those few months with Alice here. When our family left Tetbury so suddenly, I thought my world was ending again. The thought that there was a child of mine that I had abandoned, just as my parents had abandoned me, was too much. I had thought my time with Alice was a reward for those dreadful days at school."

Peter fell silent, wringing his hands together as if he could wash his guilt away.

Bee said, "What about Sally? She was your wife."

"Sally is a lovely woman. She didn't deserve to have me to worry about all the time. I was damaged."

Alice interrupted, "So he went and found me again, didn't you? I wasn't that pleased to start with. My young lover who had run off and left me in the club. But Peter explained how he had always wanted me and that it was his parents who made him leave, so I decided to give him a chance. I didn't need much persuading. I've always loved him."

Nicole listened to them and stroked her belly. The baby

was moving a lot now. They could be an old married couple talking about their early years.

Peter said, "But we couldn't be together. I couldn't live a double life. That wouldn't have been fair to Sally. I needed to get away. Start again. It was so hard parting from Alice again. So, Alice and I hatched a plan whereby I would get a new identity. It was easy in those days. You got the birth certificate of someone roughly your age who had died as a baby and went from there. I found someone in the churchyard just down the road in Marlborough. Dan Linklater. Better name than Slaithwaite, I've always thought.

"I got a passport in that name and flew to Boston and, as I said, started again. Took odd jobs as a teacher and, after a few years, got a visa to work. I was very happy. Never married or had children. That wouldn't have been fair on Sally, or Alice for that matter. Happily, Alice was able to come to see me sometimes when we could afford it. Those were the happiest times of my life. All in all, I've had a much better life than I could have ever expected."

Jo said, "So why have you come back?"

"I'm ill. I want to die in England. And be next to Alice until I do." He explained about the Parkinson's. Jo went over and gave Peter a hug.

He continued, "Then Alice told me about Nicole here's visit. She said she had found my letter. What a stroke of luck! And the truth might finally come out. That confirmed I was right to come. I wanted to see those De La Hay people get their just desserts."

Nicole said, "What does Sally know? Does she know you're alive? That you're here? It seems really tough on her." Peter looked sheepish. Alice fiddled with her scarf. Nicole was hoping she would like his answer. All that hard work and pain to save a bastard.

"I contacted Sally when I got back from America. Took quite a lot to convince her who I was. Then she told me she had already mourned me and didn't want to see me. I couldn't blame her for that. Indeed, I wasn't looking to start again with her. I just wanted her to know the truth."

It was as positive an answer as she was going to get. Relieved, Nicole said, "I read your diary. Sally sent it to me. So, I went to the police about Eric McArthur's death. They are investigating it again even though everyone involved is dead apart from you. They'll want to speak to you."

"My diary? I was hoping someone would read that one day. I took enough risk writing it. If someone at Rothbury had found it at the time, I would have been in the quarry with Eric."

Nicole said, "Will you talk to the police?"

"Of course."

Jo said, "It has been such a wonderful surprise to know you're alive. I only expected to meet one grandparent today. I wish we had met years ago."

Peter said, "I am so impressed with what you have done, Nicole. I never thought I would see the day when the De La Hays got their comeuppance. And, as for seeing the granddaughter I never thought I would meet – well, old age has its rewards, I guess."

Nicole said, "I still don't really know why I kept at it. I hated lying to Dan." She glanced at him, and he smiled. "Every time I resolved to stop, I found I hated myself more. And when I started again, I felt my brother Patrick's presence back sitting on my shoulder, willing me on."

Dan said, "We're going to have a boy. He's going to be called Patrick."

Nicole let Dan explain to Peter and Alice about the choice of first name. She didn't mind. The story she had never spoken about was now out in the open and it no longer caused her the same pain.

She sat back and watched them talk – the Newhouses finding their way towards an understanding of their new extended family. Charlie's death had created a huge hole in their lives and now it was about to be filled in a way none of them had expected. Her crusade to find out about the letter had ended up filling a hole in hers too. She hadn't been able to put her own family back together, but she had been able to take the first steps to creating a new one and, along the way, help Jo, Dan and Bee find theirs.

She was ready to go forward and live her life. She had learnt who she was and what she wanted. She knew how capable she really was and what she could achieve when she set her mind to it. No-one would scare her anymore. Nothing would hold her back. The choices were all hers.

She reached over and squeezed Dan's hand, and he squeezed her back with a grin. They would be alright now; she was sure of it. She loved him. He loved her. They would bring up Patrick together. Hopefully, other children would come along as well. She could put all the pain behind her. She would have a family of her own again.

But, in the future, at Christmas, every so often, she would definitely ensure she won at charades.

THE END

ABOUT THE AUTHOR

Giles Fraser studied at the Faber Academy and published his first novel, *LET'S FLY*, in 2021. He lives in Barnes with his wife, Alex, and has three daughters and one granddaughter. He co-founded and runs the market-leading tech communications agency, Brands2Life.

ACKNOWLEDGEMENTS

Many people have been very generous in their support during the writing of this book, notably: Alison Marlow, Andy Laurence, Helen Trevorrow, Lucy Crewdson, Karl Knapp, Kelly Allen, Piers Westerman, Richard Skinner, Sarah Scales, Simon Ludlam, and, especially, Alex, Charlotte, Cesca and Arabella. Many thanks to all of you and apologies to anyone I have forgotten to mention.

This book is printed on paper from sustainable sources managed under the Forest Stewardship Council (FSC) scheme.

It has been printed in the UK to reduce transportation miles and their impact upon the environment.

For every new title that Troubador publishes, we plant a tree to offset CO_2, partnering with the More Trees scheme.

For more about how Troubador offsets its environmental impact, see www.troubador.co.uk/sustainability-and-community